Give Me a Reason

A.L. JACKSON

A.L. Jackson
www.aljacksonauthor.com

ISBN: 978-1-946420-54-1

Cover Design by RBA Designs
Cover Images by Michelle Lancaster Photography
Editing by Susan Staudinger
Proofreading by Julia Griffis, The Romance Bibliophile
Formatting by Champagne Book Design

The characters and events in this book are fictitious. Names, characters, places, and plots are a product of the author's imagination. Any similarity to real persons, living or dead, is coincidental and not intended by the author.

More from

A.L. Jackson

NEW YORK TIMES BESTSELLING AUTHOR

Redemption Hills
Give Me a Reason
Say It's Forever – coming 2022
Never Look Back – coming 2022

The Falling Stars Series
Kiss the Stars
Catch Me When I Fall
Falling into You
Beneath the Stars

Confessions of the Heart
More of You
All of Me
Pieces of Us

Fight for Me
Show Me the Way
Follow Me Back
Lead Me Home
Hold on to Hope

Give Me a Reason

Chapter One

Trent

IT WAS JUST BEFORE TEN WHEN I EASED MY BIKE INTO THE packed parking lot at the front of the club.

Darkness had long descended on the small city of Redemption Hills, California. The sky above was nothing but a blanket of black. Against it, the neon lights gleamed and glowed from the two-story building like beacons of debauchery, flashing over the slew of cars and bikes lined in a row near the entrance.

I stopped at the front and planted my boots on the ground so I could roll my bike back. Killing the rumbling engine, I kicked the stand and swung off. The glow of club lights and the sound of heavy music seeped through the thick block walls.

I lit a smoke and strode for the entrance, my boots crunching on the loose gravel as I went.

"Mr. Lawson." Kult dipped his head as I approached.

Awareness rustled through the bodies standing at the door to get inside as I advanced on the crowd.

"Kult," I returned as I came up beside him.

"How are you tonight, Sir?"

"Still breathing."

He chuckled. "All we can ask for, isn't it?"

Kult was a bouncer who'd been working for me for the last four years. Intimidating as fuck. Loyal to the bone. Exactly what was required.

Stamping out my cigarette with the toe of my boot, I scanned the scene. "All quiet tonight?"

"So far, Sir," Kult responded, his burly frame forever on guard.

"Way I like it," I said, gaze sweeping the faces of those who'd turned to stare at me. Like every person there had taken note of my presence. Every eye compelled to look my direction.

My father had always said respect wasn't earned, it was taken.

You had to own it.

Possess it.

As much as I'd despised the pig, he'd at least had that one thing right.

Proof of it was in the way every person had shifted. Now on edge. A shot of self-preservation injected into their bloodstreams.

Like they'd felt the rumble of the earth vibrating beneath the approach of my bike.

Felt the shift in the sordid, stagnant air.

I always found it ironic that they all seemed desperate for the promise made by the blue neon sign hanging from the front of the building.

Absolution.

Absolution from whatever sins they were running from.

Absolution from any choices they might make that night.

Absolution from feeling anything at all except for pleasure.

Still, they gaped at me like even in the midst of their thirst for indulgence, they felt wickedness in their presence.

They wouldn't be wrong.

"At capacity?" I asked. There were at least twenty people in line, but I made it a habit to know everything going down in my club.

"Yes, Sir, since about nine."

"Good."

"Always is." He cracked a bearded grin.

I lifted my chin in parting before I wound behind him so I could slip through the double doors and into the dingy glow of the bar. Music blared through the speakers and reverberated along the floors. It set up the vibe in anticipation of the band that would be taking the stage in about an hour.

Absolution was this cross between luxe and dive.

Fuckin' kick-ass bands and the best drinks in the small, trendy mountain city that was tucked in the most northeastern corner of California.

A biker bar that had the rest of Redemption Hills flocking in droves for a chance to dip their toes into the danger they could feel seeping from the walls and still be able to walk away from it in the morning without feeling an ounce of guilt.

I edged deeper into the belly of my bar.

Place I'd built from the ground up with a little help from my brothers.

My attention swept the enormous room. The lights hanging from the cavernous ceiling were dimmed. Mood rowdy.

The bottom floor was surrounded by booths that lined the walls, tables and couches in the open space, and the stage and dance floor were to the far right.

The upper floor was home to pool tables and a second bar, and it wrapped around like a horseshoe, creating a balcony that was open in the middle to give a view of the stage.

I headed for the long matte black bar that ran the far wall on the main floor.

The floating shelves on the back wall were welded steel and glass, the rows of bottles running top to bottom cast in a glow of blue neon lights.

I wound through the couples snuggled on the couches and a few groups of college boys who were clearly out looking for a taste of the wild side.

Sage was behind the bar. He lifted his chin in welcome when he saw me coming. His dark tattoos looked like seething demons writing across his even darker skin. Dude looked about as menacing as they came except for the grin that cracked his face.

"Yo, Trent. About time you decided to show your lazy ass."

He was all cocky smiles as he poured me my regular. I slipped onto the stool in front of him, and he slid the glass my direction.

I took it with a scoff, taking a sip of the scotch and letting it soothe the disorder I couldn't keep from raging inside. Way it always did. Begging to break loose.

"You gonna write me up for being late?" I razzed, quirking a brow.

Asshole loved acting the boss.

Considering he kept this place running when I wasn't around, he might as well be.

Sage laughed a sound that was pure pity. "That would be a hard pass. Hard enough cleaning up your messes around here. You really gonna ask me to take on more?"

I tipped my glass his direction. "Only one I trust to do it."

"Guess I need to start slacking then, yeah?" he taunted with a grin.

"Hell, no. Place would be in shambles without you. How is it looking tonight, anyway?"

He dried his hands on a towel. Sage was my general manager, but the dude loved playing bartender. It put him front and center. Where he could always keep an eye and an ear open. Be in the middle of the mix. Blending in so the rest of the staff thought of him as one of their own and let down their guard.

He always knew when something shady was going down before anyone else.

Plus, he actually fuckin' liked people, so that was a thing.

"All's good. Deliveries are complete and accounted for. Safes are full. Numbers are on your desk. Band is in the back ready to roll. All staff showed except for Laila. Shocker. Speaking of, there is someone waiting on you for an interview. She refused to leave until she saw you, if you want to know what you're up against."

His brown eyes played as he cracked a smirk and gestured toward one of the booths running the left wall.

I let my attention wander there, to the blonde who was sitting tucked in the booth sipping a Coke, looking so out of place I could actually feel her discomfort all the way from where I was sitting.

Frown taking hold, I swiveled my attention back to Sage. "Are you kidding me? Who let her in?"

Fighting laughter, he shrugged. "I did."

Annoyance left me on a sigh. "Should only take a glance from you to know she doesn't belong."

Hell, she looked like raw meat set out for wolves to devour. Weak and ripe for the kill. Girl would get torn to shreds in a place like this.

Fact my dick jumped at the sight of her was evidence enough.

"Besides, interviews are by appointment only," I added like he didn't know the routine.

Sage lifted his hands to the side. "Hey, man, don't blame me. She sat there all pretty like in that booth and ordered herself a drink. Paying customer and all. Of course, she's been sitting there since *three*, refusing to leave until she got to talk to the one in charge, you know, since the *bossman* didn't show for her interview that had been scheduled for that time."

"Shit," I grumbled, scrubbing a hand over my face. "Totally let it slip."

Sage arched a sarcastic brow. "Really?"

"You could have handled it."

"Went out there, and she flashed me a winning smile and said please. What's a gentleman to do? Besides, don't want that position, remember?"

Gentleman?

I scoffed and stood. "Fine. I'll get rid of her."

I swiped my drink from the bar and started her direction.

Girl sat facing out, her attention flitting all over the place. Anxiety ripped from her and sent little shockwaves pulsating through the air.

This tingly, nervous energy that blistered and blew.

Inhaling deep, I pinned on my most indifferent expression because fuck...I could scent it like prey.

Goodness.

Vulnerability.

I should send Kult over to toss her because I had the sense that I should tuck tail and head the other direction. Stay as fucking far away from this girl as possible.

Knew better than getting twisted in something like that. When a bad idea presented itself? I usually found myself standing in front of it like I was on the goddamn welcome committee.

And there I was. Hit with an urge that had me itching to take a closer look. A feeling I hadn't felt in a long, long time.

To dip my dirty fingers into something pure. Like maybe it could offer a second's reprieve from who I was.

But did I stop?

Nah.

I was drawn.

Moving closer.

Thing was, didn't think I'd ever seen anyone so uniquely plain or indecently stunning before.

Her nose was probably a little too big and the contours of her face a little too sharp for her to fit into that perfect formula for beauty. Thick, blonde hair was parted in the middle, and it was curled in these fat waves that rolled over her shoulders, like the style hailed from another day.

Her chin was shaped like a heart and her mouth was a tiny pink bow written in an innocence so sweet I had to think there was a chance it'd never been devoured before.

Came to the quick conclusion it was the sum of them that made her striking.

This stoic sort of beauty that could bring a wicked man to his knees.

She felt me coming the way everyone else did. A frisson slaked through the air as I made my way to her. She looked up. Eyes the color of November took me in. A kaleidoscope of browns and greens, yellows and reds. Fallen leaves that sparked and shimmered beneath the muted light and sent another shiver racing for my dick.

Her stare ran down my body like she was cataloguing everything she could about me.

First and foremost, fear.

Danger.

Distrust.

Good girl.

Problem was the way something else struck in the space between us. Something palpable yet imperceptible.

I saw the evidence of it prickle across the surface of her flesh.

Chills that ran wild.

Motherfuck.

She brought her shoulders up high like she could protect herself from it, all while lifting her chin in a show of confidence that made a smirk tick up at the corner of my mouth.

Nothing but a ferocious little kitten.

I slipped into the booth opposite her. As casual as could be, I slung an arm over the back and kept my other hand wrapped around the glass that I set on the table.

Before I had a chance to say anything, she asked, "You're the owner?"

Her voice was this breathy, seductive thing, and shit…

"Yes," I gritted.

She shoved her hand out across the table. "Hello. I'm Eden Murphy. I'm really grateful for the opportunity to meet you."

Yeah, well I wasn't so keen on meeting her because I was overcome with a severe bout of insta-lust. Kind that had my fingers twitching and the tiny spec of a conscience I still possessed telling me to stay the fuck away from the sweetness that was fillin' my nostrils like a drug.

My own sixth sense.

Because to a guy like me? It was the light that was the danger. Thing that left me vulnerable. Put me at risk.

I just glared at her dainty little hand like all it had to offer was a viper bite before I cocked my head and bit out the reply, "Trent Lawson, and I'm sorry to waste your time, sweetheart, but we aren't hiring servers."

I started to get the fuck out of there when her voice hit me again. "Um…wait…what?"

Could feel her confused dejection floating around me.

Gripping on.

Talons digging into my skin and dragging me back.

Words started to flood out from behind. "It said you were hiring in the job ad, and I had an interview at three o'clock today. I'm qualified. I worked at a café all through high school and at a coffee bar during college."

"You and everyone else, sunshine," I tossed out without glancing back because looking at her had become a dangerous thing.

This chick with the autumn eyes and the thrumming heart.

"Please, I'd appreciate you at least talking to me." Agitation bound her words as I kept moving away. Then they flooded with panic. "I'm qualified and I'm fast…and…and I've danced my entire life."

I whipped my head around fast enough to witness her delicate throat tremor when she said it, like maybe she could swallow back up the words after she'd released them.

I chuckled a dark sound.

Was she serious?

I sank back into the booth, no clue where this girl thought she was going with this, but some sick part of me liked the idea entirely too much.

"So, tell me about this dancing, Kitten, that you've done your *whole* life."

She flinched, her delicate throat bobbing when she swallowed, the words hard when she pushed them out.

"I've done ballet since I was a child," she said. "Now I teach classes to children."

A rough chuckle scraped from my throat. "Ballet?"

"Yes. I can demonstrate, if you like?" A clear challenge tilted her head to the side when she said it.

Hard laughter slipped free, and I took a sip of my scotch, raked my teeth on my bottom lip as I sank back farther to take her in.

"What I want to know is how dancing has anything to do with you gettin' hired as a server here? This look like a strip club to you?"

"No. I just…I thought it might…" She trailed off, chewing at her bottom lip.

Hiking a brow, I blatantly let my gaze rake over the bits of her I could see from over the top of the table. Girl was wearing a fucking baby-blue blouse that she had buttoned to the base of her throat, a suit jacket over the top like she was applying to be a teller down at the local bank.

Hot as fuck, but not even close to fittin' in around here, though I got the sense she was trying to convince me that wasn't the case.

Nah, we might not have dancers, but it was no secret our servers weren't shy to tempt imaginations. To tease minds into desire with bits of flesh rather than showcasing everything hidden underneath.

Untouchable where they roamed like fallen angels through the raving pack.

Girl sitting across from me might be an angel, but not the kind who owned these floors.

The scrape of my laugh was like razors. "Sorry, Kitten, know exactly what you're sayin'. Think it's safe to say you don't quite fit the bill."

The offense that flashed through her expression almost overrode the desperation. "And what exactly is that supposed to mean?"

Pushing to standing, I moved over to plant my hands on the table and leaned her way.

I was slammed with another shockwave of energy.

That fear and distrust.

But this time, the other piece was unmistakable—stark, terrified attraction.

My mouth moved close to her ear. "It means you'd get eaten alive."

Most likely by me.

Shivers raced her spine.

I felt them.

Her nerves ricocheting against mine.

Had to restrain myself from leaning in and licking her jaw.

Because fuck, I wanted a taste for myself.

I edged back an inch, figuring she'd slip out in the bare space and run the hell to safety.

But no.

Not this girl.

She lifted that defiant chin again. "I'm far less fragile than you think."

I inhaled her honeyed scent. Had to force myself to be a good little boy considering I was dying to test that theory. "Believe me, sweetheart, I'm doing you a favor. Girls like you don't belong in a place like this. Now go home and lock your door behind you before you regret walking through my door."

"Are you always so condescending to the women who apply here?"

Desire and disdain.

They seeped from her skin.

This time, I let my nose run the edge of her ear as I murmured, "Only the ones who look like you."

I pushed back and started to walk, only to freeze. Struck by the bolt of lightning that speared through my body when her hand wrapped around my wrist.

She gasped like she'd felt it, too. Then she gritted, "I don't need your protection, Mr. Lawson. What I need is this job."

Chapter Two

Eden

FLAMES IGNITED IN THE SPOT WHERE I'D GRABBED HIM BY
the wrist. Heat blistered, searing up my arm and spreading
like a flashfire through my chest. It jumpstarted my heart into
mayhem. Into a confusion, chaos, and greed I couldn't fathom this
stranger could invoke.

The second I'd stepped through the doors of this club, I'd known
I was treading into dangerous territory. Dancing into a devil's den.

This guy was right.

I'd likely get eaten alive. I didn't belong here. Didn't fit in. Not
that I wanted to or was ashamed that this place had me feeling on
edge. Completely out of my element.

But I didn't have another choice.

There were times in your life when you had to suck it up and
make the sacrifice. When you'd step out of your comfort zone if it
meant it might help the ones who meant the most to you.

Even if my efforts only made the smallest bit of a difference in
my father's life, it would be worth it.

I squeezed his wrist tighter while he glared at me like I was going
to regret having the audacity to touch him.

No question, I would.

I swallowed my pride, the fear, the apprehension, and tried to put on a brave face. "Please."

His darkly beautiful brow curled in cruel disbelief. "So, the dancer needs a job."

He was mocking me. I could hear the tenor of it sliding off his tongue. Baiting me on his hook.

Why had I told him that? But that was the thing when you were desperate.

You'd say anything—do anything—to fix your situation. To help those you love.

"She does."

"And does she have…any other talents?"

He cracked a menacing grin.

It sent another rush of chills skating my flesh. Sent my belly tipping, sloshing with a sensation I didn't want to recognize. Like every nerve ending in my body had suddenly sparked to life.

"Like I said, I used to be a server for many years, and I'm a quick learner at what I don't know. I'm sure you'll teach me whatever that is."

There was no keeping the bite out of my tone. No stopping the way my hackles rose. The way he had me feeling something I couldn't pinpoint.

Like I was teetering a razor-sharp edge between disgust and desire.

And I'd met him not five minutes before.

It was a terrible sign, if I was being honest. A sign that warned I should just leave. But I remained rooted to the spot.

The man laughed again in this unholy way.

How he made stepping back a foot appear predatory, I didn't know, but I felt the threat created in the movement. In the way he hovered and writhed in the small space. A gorgeous wraith who eclipsed me in shadow.

His aura was this seething electricity. A compulsion that led the weak toward destruction.

His hair was a raven shock, shaved on the sides and longer on top, and his eyes were a sooty, smoldering gray.

Lures that drew you toward temptation.

He wasn't as thick as the bouncers. Instead, he was slender and tall, his frame rippling with fierce, sinewy muscle. Somehow, it made him appear even more intimidating.

Ink covered most of his exposed flesh. It rode out from under the sleeves of his leather jacket and onto the back of his hands and over his knuckles. More climbed from the neck of his tee and rolled up his throat where the designs disappeared behind his ears.

And there he stood, taking me in with a face that was cut into the most distinct, unforgettable lines. This daunting, terrifying beauty.

I wasn't sure I'd ever encountered a man as electrifying.

As darkly alluring.

A jumpstart to the senses.

As hard as I tried, the only soft thing I could find about him were his plush, pouty lips—that was if you could look past the sneer they seemed to be permanently curled into.

I could feel it shivering across my skin and shouting from my soul.

This boy was bad.

Bone deep.

And there I stood, the fool begging him for a chance. "I'll do whatever it takes."

Wrong thing to say because he cracked a smirk. "Ah, I see how it is, Kitten. You like to play with fire."

"I don't," I told him. Honestly. Truthfully.

I didn't want any trouble, and he clearly had plenty of it to offer. I just wanted a job.

No matter if he made my belly quiver and my fingers tremble. No matter if he stirred something inside me that had been dead for a long, long time.

His gaze raked me again.

Calculating.

Analyzing.

Then he jutted his chin. "Follow me."

Spinning on his heel, he started across the bar without further warning.

This guy gave me whiplash.

I scrambled to follow. "Where are we going?"

He didn't answer. Instead, he parted the crowd as if every person there felt him coming.

I tried to keep up as we crossed the bottom floor of the bar that was completely packed.

Anticipation high. Inhibitions freed. People letting go while salivating for the band that was setting up on stage.

I peeked to the side as if I were looking for a buoy. For a raft in the middle of a stormy, toiling sea.

My attention landed on the bartender who'd let me set up post for the entire day. He'd been kind to me, but right then, he was grinning the smuggest grin I'd ever seen.

The kind that screamed, *sucker*.

I didn't know if it was meant for me or the man who cut a path to the opposite end of the bar.

Mr. Lawson hooked a left into a narrow, dank hallway. There was a sign at the side that read *employees only*. I skated around the sharp corner, clutching my purse to my chest and rushing to keep up while my heels slid on the slick concrete floor.

Great.

Scoring all the points.

A second later, he suddenly stopped to toss open a door to the right. He held it open as he spun back to look at me.

On a gasp, I skidded to a stop, unable to keep up with the turbulence vibrating through the dense air.

Still standing in the dim shadows, he quirked a brow. "So, tell me Eden Murphy, is it the thrill or the money? Trying to piss off your *daddy?*"

Those sooty eyes gleamed and glowed with the challenge.

Wow. I wanted to tell this guy where to shove it.

The only reason I was there was because I was trying to save my daddy.

My daddy who was in dire straits.

And I would do absolutely anything to help the man who'd sacrificed so much. The one who would do anything for me. Lift me up. Support me. Hold me.

Now, it was my turn to return the favor. But this jerk didn't deserve an explanation, no matter how gorgeous he was.

I gulped down the irritation and anxiety.

"I told you I needed this job. The answer to that should be obvious."

"And I also told you that you don't belong. Plenty of other jobs in the city."

Hurt curled through my senses. Of course, a guy who was clearly rolling in it would spout it as truth.

"Are there?" I couldn't help but sneer it.

Those fierce eyes sheared through me as if I were standing there bare, dragging from my eyes and down my quivering throat to where my trembling hands were clutching my purse.

Down, down, down, along the length of my legs exposed by my pencil skirt, to my heels, before he was somehow both leisurely and voraciously dragging them back up.

Shivers raced beneath the unabashed perusal, my stomach churning with a mix of revulsion and fascination.

The man was nothing but a smolder when his gaze met with mine.

"I'd take you as the type who'd show more...caution." He said it like an insult.

"You think you scare me?" I spat the words like they could become steel around me. A hedge of protection.

He suddenly reached out and fluttered the tips of his tattooed fingers across the erratic thunder at the pulse point in my neck.

A wild, reckless pound.

Shivers raced and my knees nearly buckled.

He tilted his head. "Don't I?"

I struggled to swallow. To breathe. I gave a harsh shake of my head to break the trance. "Do you have a job for me or not, Mr. Lawson? Because I'm not here to play games."

He cracked a wry, cocky smile and widened the door. He gestured inside. "After you, Kitten."

Gritting my teeth, I strode into his office with as much confidence as I could muster. It wasn't that hard. I might appear delicate and fragile. Unworldly. Naïve. But I'd experienced enough tragedies, enough heartache in my life, to know when I needed to dig in my heels and get done what needed to be done.

He gestured at a chair set in front of a desk that sat facing out on the room.

"Have a seat." He said it like a proposition.

I had to stop my eyes from rolling when I sat down, but there was nothing I could do to keep them from jumping around the office that was much larger than I'd anticipated. Taking it in. The massive black desk and black leather chair. But it was the glass case against the side wall that stole my attention.

It was filled with relics and treasures and paraphernalia from another time. Guns. Swords. I gulped when I saw a few pieces of ancient, rusted torture devices on display like a prize behind the glass.

I shifted in discomfort.

Everything in this room screamed sadist.

My chest tightened and I itched in my seat.

He was suddenly there, leaning over me at my side, dragging a finger down my cheek while he murmured in my ear, "There's still time to run, Kitten. I promise I won't even chase you."

I swallowed the screaming reservations down, the ones that told me coming here was hunting down trouble unlike anything I'd ever experienced in my life. Self-preservation urged me to get up and go and never look back.

But I had a mission, and I wasn't backing down. "Like I said, I need this job."

He hovered there, at my side for far too long before he let go of a long sigh and rounded the desk. He folded himself into the huge leather chair. He dug into a drawer and then shoved a stack of papers my direction. "Everyone signs an NDA."

Shocker.

Who knew what he ran through here. Everything about him shouted mayhem. That his darkness went so much farther than skin deep. That his hands were dirty.

Nerves roiled in my belly.

Was I really doing this?

He rocked back, an elbow propped on a chair arm and his head rested on those fingers. Somehow, he'd lost his jacket in my moment of stupor, as if I'd lost a period of time, lost in the insanity of what I was doing.

And there he sat like some wicked king. His arms a portrait of depravity. Those eyes a vacuum to the sins deep within.

I guessed it was that moment that I remembered my father's words. When he'd say we're all brought to the altar of temptation. We either kneel at it or turn our backs on it, but we can never, ever straddle it.

Call me a fool, but I was going to try.

I lifted my chin. "I won't do anything illegal."

He cocked a salacious grin. "Don't worry, Kitten. I have something much more fun planned for you."

Was he serious?

He had something *much more fun* planned for me?

I gritted my teeth, scrubbing the last of the pots that had been piled high in the industrial sink and fighting tears. I'd never been so offended in my life.

I'd told him I was qualified.

I may never have been a cocktail server before, but I knew how to take care of people and how to do it well. Caretaking had been what I'd done my entire life.

Instead of telling me to come back for training, he'd handed me a freaking apron and sent me into the kitchen, still wearing my heels and skirt, mind you.

Jerk.

Music vibrated the floors, rumbling from the depths of the bar while I fought an irrational rage.

Or maybe it wasn't irrational at all.

He'd wanted to insult me. Put me down. Shame me into subjection.

The fact I wouldn't let him was the only reason I hadn't walked, not that I was ever going to return.

I glanced at my watch.

Two a.m.

I had to be to my *real* job by seven.

Crap, I was going to be a zombie come tomorrow. A very irate, disgruntled, broke-ass zombie.

I would have gladly lost sleep for some actual money.

But this?

I swiped at the tear that got free.

Damn it. I wasn't going to let him see me cry. That's what he wanted. To belittle me. But more than that? I had been relying on this being a break. Had hoped to find some sort of blessing, but I should've known better than to look for it in a place like this.

Maybe it was a sign. My salvation. A gift hidden in the mirage of mockery.

I didn't belong here. Didn't want to be. We all had choices in how we lived our lives, and I knew the choices I wanted to make for mine were out of tune here. The fact the fine hairs prickled at the back of my neck when I felt the shift in the air was proof enough.

The way my stomach flipped at that seething intensity that rippled through the air and covered me from behind. The way they wrapped me in these chains that I refused to become hostage to.

"Kitten." His voice was a rough scrape.

My teeth ground harder. "What can I help you with, Sir?"

I spat it like my own insult.

"Your shift is over. Tom will finish loading the washers and cleaning the floor."

I tried to draw a sane breath into my lungs and not lash out. I pinned on the fakest smile ever faked, but I was sure I still looked like a lunatic when I whirled around and shot it his direction. "Great."

I started to wind around him. He grabbed me by the hand.

Fire streaked.

Flames that screamed up my arm and jumped into my veins.

What the hell was wrong with me?

I froze, barely looking at him, and then my brow curled when he extended an envelope for me to take.

A very fat envelope.

With a shaking hand, I warily accepted it. "What is this?"

"Your portion of tonight's tips."

Confusion flashed so quickly I couldn't keep it out of my expression. "What?"

"Servers and bartenders share a cut of what they make with the rest of the staff. What you do allows them to do what they need to do. That's how it works around here."

Stunned, I blinked, still held by his hand on my arm. The whisper coming from my mouth was shocked. "Thank you."

He leaned in closer, his aura taking me whole, the words a rough threat when he uttered them an inch from my jaw. "Don't thank me just yet."

Then he turned and stalked for the swinging door, not bothering to look back when he said, "See you tomorrow night at nine, Kitten."

I swore, I felt the ground shake beneath my feet.

Tentatively, I peeked at the contents of the envelope. My heart nearly seized. Inside, there had to be at least three hundred dollars in cash.

Oh god.

My hand went to my chest, and I struggled to take in a cleansing breath.

To make sense of this stupor.

This feeling that I should run against the temptation that whispered I should *stay*.

And as I peeled off the apron and went into the locker room to get my bag, my head still spinning, I wondered if I'd finally, finally caught a break, all while praying I wasn't being lured into the deepest pit in Hell.

Chapter Three

Trent

G ROANING, I BURIED MY FACE DEEPER INTO THE PILLOW when my mattress was hit by a Richter eight. So much energy comin' from the pint-size tot it was a wonder he didn't bring down the house.

"Dad, Dad, Dad! You've got to get up and hurry it up quick." He jumped at my side, his little feet creating a cataclysm on the bed. "It's the very first day of school, and no way can we be late because I don't want to go gettin' into trouble. Gettin' into trouble is bad, right, Dad?"

I hugged that pillow and willed myself to shake off the fog. The exhaustion. Because truth be told, three hours of sleep just wasn't gonna cut it.

But he was the one thing that made it worth it.

One love.

One loyalty.

One reason.

"Right, Dad, right?" He kept bouncing away.

That time, I buried the groan into the down feathers before I forced myself to roll over, peeling my eyes open to the dawning day.

And there he was, the kid all sunshine and love and exuberance smiling down at me.

Gage.

My son.

Only thing brilliant and big enough to fill the crater burned through the middle of my black heart.

Only thing bright enough to give me a glimpse of the light.

He was the one good thing I had in my life. One thing I protected with that life, too.

He was dressed in jeans, a short-sleeved button up, and his checkered Vans. Looking like the budding badass that he was.

Except the skin of his arms and neck were covered in squiggles and lines and crude shapes drawn in ink.

What the fuck?

Sitting up, I stabbed my fingers through my bedhead, squinting through the blinding light. "What's goin' on there, little dude?"

I gestured at the shit he'd scribbled all over his body.

He stretched his arms out—far too proud. "What d'ya think, Dad? You like 'em a lot? Now I look just like you." His caramel-colored eyes widened in anticipation. "'cept not as big yet, but I'm gonna be soon! Right, Dad, right?"

He started jumping again, little legs propelling himself as high as he could go, arms raised above his head with all that golden hair bouncing around his chubby face.

Kid cute as fuck.

A slight chuckle rumbled out, and I snagged him around the waist and tossed him onto his back on the bed. I started tickling his sides. "You think you're gonna be as big as me, huh?"

Gage howled with laughter, clutching his stomach and kicking his feet. "You know it, Dad! I got to be."

"You gotta be, huh?" I kept tickling him, but soft and with all the love I had for him.

He batted at my hands, laughing and squirming all over the place. "Yes, Dad, yes! I got to be! Otherwise, my uncles are gonna call me shorty for my whole life!"

"Rude." I widened my eyes with the tease.

"The rudest," he said with a jerk of his chin, resolute.

I slowed, unable to do anything but gaze down at this kid who was looking at me like I was his hero. Most precious grin spreading across his face, so massive it dimpled his cheeks.

Wanted to be that for him.

His hero.

His rock.

Kind of dad worthy of someone looking at him the way my boy did.

Like I wasn't covered in scars and sin and shame.

Like my soul wasn't shrouded in the blemish of the things I'd done.

I ran my hand over the top of his head, pained affection bleeding out. "I do know it. You're gonna be so big. So strong. So good," I promised.

Caramel eyes shined. "Just like you."

Old grief clutched my chest, and I forced a smile. "No way. You're going to be way better."

"Those seem like really too high standards, Dad." He said it all kinds of serious.

Laughter fumbled out, and I ruffled my fingers through his hair.

Fucking Logan.

"Sounds to me like you've been spending too much time with Uncle Logan."

He sat up, more of that earnestness infiltrating his voice. "You crazy? There's never too much Uncle Logan time."

My grin was wry as I sat back and hooked my knuckle under my kid's chin. "I bet he told you that, too."

Gage scowled. "Bettin's bad, Dad, don't you know?"

Kid was a stickler for the rules.

The irony wasn't lost on me.

I shook my head, my lips softening as I stared at the child who I'd do anything for. "You look super cool, man, but I think we're gonna have to ditch the tattoos for your first day of school, yeah?"

A pout took to his face. "Oh man, how come?"

"Because I doubt your teacher is going to appreciate how dang awesome you are." I shot him my most playful grin, though I was one-hundred-percent serious. Last thing I needed was some rigid bitch on my back.

Judging me.

Judging my kid.

"Go on and have Uncle help you get cleaned up. I'm going to grab a shower and I'll be downstairs in a minute."

"'Kay, Dad!"

He scrambled off the bed and went blazing out my bedroom door, his footsteps banging down the stairs.

A heavy sigh heaved from my lungs, and I tossed the covers and went for the massive shower in my bathroom. I scratched at my chin as I shuffled in, trying to stave off the desire to faceplant back into bed.

I turned the water on hot and let steam fill the room as I twisted out of my underwear so I could step into the spray.

My eyes dropped closed at the warmth.

In an instant, her face flashed behind my lids.

Shit.

Seemed no matter what I did, no matter how hard I tried to walk the straight and narrow, I always ended up chasing trouble. Hunting it, like I didn't know how to stop.

Because there I was—struck with it—an errant bolt of lust that didn't belong.

Eden Murphy.

That feisty little kitten who'd wanted to claw my eyes out last night.

Except she was the key to an entirely different type of trouble than I normally sought, and I was just fool enough to want to turn the lock.

No doubt, that was why I hadn't kicked her to the curb. Why I couldn't get her off my mind for a second last night or the fact she'd shown up in my brain first thing this morning, too.

I'd fucking eaten up the way she blushed and fumbled and lifted that chin. The way she came off so innocent but was clearly a fighter underneath.

My dick jumped, hard at the thought of her sitting there all prim in my office, nothing but her thundering heart and fumbling hands and tempting sweetness.

Way she'd gone straight fire in the kitchen before she'd softened like silk. Way her breath had skittered across my face and her honeyed scent had invaded my senses.

I'd bet that's exactly what the girl would feel like—silk.

Like dipping my fingers into sweet honey.

My tongue lapping up the pure.

And I knew better than that.

Before I let the girl get me off track, I quickly washed, rinsed, and was out in less than five. I dried and tugged on some jeans, still rubbing the towel over my hair as I bounded downstairs.

House was one of those luxury cookie-cutter types. A one-in-four chance that your house was gonna be the exact same as the neighbor next door, but that shit still cost a small fortune.

Ceilings were high and the counters were quartz, floors a mix of gray hardwood and carpet.

Like the original Stepford wife herself had drawn the concept *and* done the decorating.

That shit didn't matter, though. Only thing that did was it was a safe place for Gage. Place to raise him right. A big backyard. Kids to call friends. A park across the street.

A million miles away from where my brothers and I had grown up. A lifetime away from the sleazy city. From the depravity. From the grief.

From all the sordid bullshit we'd left behind.

I just hoped to fuck that world would never catch up to us.

Only goal I had in my pathetic life was to keep my brothers and my son safe.

One of those brothers was in the kitchen with Gage as I ambled in.

Logan, the happy motherfucker.

Dude cocked me a smug grin from where he stood at the island in front of where Gage was propped on the counter. With a wash-cloth, Logan was doing his best to erase the marks the kid had lit-tered on his body.

"Ah, look it there, if it isn't Princess Buttercup," Logan called.

Since Gage was facing away, I took the opportunity to give Logan a finger.

My asshole brothers had been calling me that since we were kids and I'd tripped and rolled down a hill, shouting the whole way.

He cracked up.

"What's wrong, sunshine? Someone seems…tense." He pursed his lips like he was in deep contemplation as he dabbed at the ink on Gage's arms. "Lonely, maybe? All the ladies hanging around the club ignoring you? That's sad, brother. Better get some so you can stop moping around here being such a d-i-c-k. Just looking at you is rui-nin' this glorious, sunny day."

I sent him another finger. "And you can F-off, dude." I whispered it, too.

You know, since we were pros at letter cussing.

"And you know I don't touch anyone at the club." Spat that one because that rule suddenly tasted sour.

I was on a no-name basis.

No ties.

No attachments.

No chance of dragging someone into the ugliness of my past or them getting close enough to drive a knife into my back.

"My, my, someone is testy," Logan tsked.

"I'll show you testy," I grumbled as I moved for the coffee maker. Dude gave me shit every second of his life, and I was the sucker who loved him for it, anyway.

Considering he sacrificed his nights to take care of my kid while I was at the club, he got away with it. Truth was, this life we'd built here wouldn't work without either of my brothers. The support they gave. Only two people in the world I could really trust.

"Testy?" Gage piped in, his little voice rising as he tried to catch on to the topic of conversation. "Oh, oh! You think I'm gonna get to do a test at school?"

Clearly, he was failing miserably at catching on, thank fuck, since Logan the loudmouth didn't know when to keep his pie hole shut.

But I guessed it was worth it because my kid was lighting up, thrilled at the prospect of a test. He whirled around to look at me as I filled a massive mug to the brim with steaming hot coffee.

A light chuckle rolled out, and I turned to rest against the counter while I took my first sip. "Think they're gonna be testing you on the first day, huh?" I asked.

Gage grinned my way, all dimples and adorableness. "I hope so. I gotta get straights As. I got my pens and my pencils and my coloring crayons in my new backpack. I'm all ready." He turned to Logan. "You wanna see, Uncle?"

He tried to wiggle out from under Logan's washcloth. My brother looked at me from over his head. "Who is this kid?"

Gage tipped his head back to fully meet his eye. "I am Gage Michael Lawson."

I choked out a laugh around my coffee.

Logan shook his head and tapped Gage's nose. "Gage Michael Lawson who is from Mars."

Gage scrunched up his little nose under his finger. "Mars. No way, Uncle. I'm from Redemption Hills, California, and I was born on August 17, 2016. I even got a *burf* certificate. Right, Dad?"

He was back to looking at me for approval. Way he always did. My heart pressed against my ribs. The love I felt for him nearly too much.

"That's right, Gage."

He turned back to Logan. "See, Uncle. You don't know nothin'."

Logan tossed a dumbstruck glance my way.

I hiked a shoulder. "What can I say? Kid has the smarts."

Logan scratched at his shaven jaw. "Yeah, and apparently, I'm the one getting schooled around here."

"Maybe you need to come with me and get some educations," Gage said with a little shrug.

"I just might," Logan tossed out as he fought laughter, his green eyes dancing with mirth. Asshole ran stocks for his clients. Made a ton of them millionaires, same as he'd made himself. Pretty sure he was stacked with the *smarts*.

My baby brother had the same black hair as me and our middle brother, Jud. But he'd gotten our mother's eyes, these crystal-cut emeralds that sparked and played. Always bright and shining. Got her soft spirit, too.

Same as Nathan had possessed.

Grief tried to squeeze its way through, guilt twisting through me like the gutting of a blade.

I wrestled it back so it could fester where the demons writhed within.

I watched Logan with my son. With all the shit we'd been through, how my brother had turned out halfway normal, I didn't know. Going through his life like every day of his childhood hadn't been jacked.

It was the reason he was the only person I trusted with Gage. Reason the poor sucker had to play babysitter to a five-year-old every fuckin' night where he lived three doors down.

Jud?

He was like me, through and through, though bearded and twice as thick. He owned a bike shop in the warehouse out behind the bar, living out an old dream the best that he could.

Two of us had built a small empire out of the rubble.

"Well, we better get going then if we're gonna be to school on time, Uncle," Gage told him. "We can't be late. School starts at eight o'clock, on the dots."

Anxiety rolled my spine. Hated the idea of my kid being in someone else's care.

But I'd promised myself he would have as close to normal of a life as I could give him, and keeping him home, hidden away like some recluse, wasn't going to give him that.

Logan lifted him from under the arms and set him onto the

ground. "Sorry, shorty, but I think I'm gonna have to pass on school today. I might get in trouble if I don't show up at work."

"Then you might have to go to time out?" Kid asked it like the punishment might be a war crime.

That was the way I wanted it, and I was going to spend my life making sure he never knew about the cruelties of this world.

One life.

One loyalty.

One reason.

"And I don't want that, do I?" Logan answered, voice deep. Like he got it, too. "Now get over here and give me a big hug before you go off and have your best day ever."

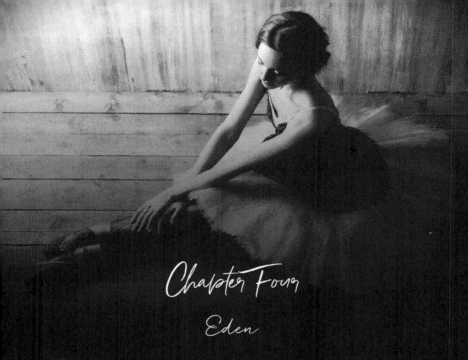

Chapter Four

Eden

RAYS OF AFTERNOON LIGHT STREAKED FROM THE SUN-kissed sky, the heavens the bluest blue. It wrapped our mountain town in a warmth that chased away the cool breeze that blew through the towering pines and oaks.

Lifting my face to it for a quick second, I inhaled and drew the crisp air into my lungs. Appreciating the things that I had and refusing the grief that wanted to squeeze out through the wobble in my spirit.

Squeals of joy rang out, and I returned my attention to the playground where my kindergarten class ran and played. I tried to hide my smile when Tessa started to saunter my way as her class joined mine for their last recess of the day.

My best friend was all sly smiles and curiosity as she sidled up next to me where I stood on the quad close to the playground.

"Someone looks like death warmed over." She'd angled in close to my ear and whispered like it was a horrible secret.

"Wow. I appreciate that." I drew it out with as much sarcasm as I could muster.

Tessa laughed, her strawberry ponytail swishing around her shoulders. "Hey, remember when we promised we would always be honest with each other? What kind of best friend would I be if I broke that pact now?"

"Um...a nice, good, sweet one?"

With a scoff, she knocked her shoulder into mine. "Hardly. You know you love me because you can count on me to tell it straight. And believe me, I'm telling it straight."

She gagged like she was repulsed, all through the smile she was trying to suppress.

I laughed through the exhaustion. "Fine. Considering that's exactly what I feel like, I'm not surprised in the least to know it's showing."

Last night I'd known I would be a walking zombie today. A very irate, disgruntled, broke-ass zombie.

But thanks to the guy who still had me feeling rattled—one who'd left me tossing and turning all night, unable to escape that strange energy that had seeped into my bloodstream—I was just a smidgen less broke.

I had no idea what to make of my new boss, other than the plain truth that I needed to stay as far away from him as possible. Yeah, I was a fool because I already knew I'd go crawling back there again tonight.

"But you got the job? That's good, right?" she pressed.

No doubt, she'd been dying to ask me the details the entire workday, but we hadn't had a second to ourselves. The first day of school was always chaos.

Parents late. Children crying and confused, while others refused to listen to the rules and tested just how far they could push it. Lunches were forgotten and little hearts were broken because some of them had been left for the first time.

I'd poured all my love and energy into each of them, showing them that this was a safe place. A place where they were going to learn and grow and have a blast while doing it.

It was what mattered.

Instilling hope and knowledge into the children who were offered into my care.

It was my greatest joy, the greatest gift.

My heart tremored with the thought of losing it. For this place to just be…shut down. Gone.

Tessa and I taught at a private Christian academy in Redemption Hills. A school my father owned. We had a wait list a mile long since we had a reputation of offering the best private education in the area. No, the tuition wasn't exactly cheap, but we barely ran a profit since my daddy poured most of it back into the community.

I was proud to share in it. I helped out in every area that I could, but none of us were exactly raking in the dough.

We'd always made it work.

Dread wrapped around my ribs and squeezed tight.

Stretched thin was one thing. On the verge of losing it all was another.

The real possibility of it was what had sent me crawling into Absolution last night, even though I had doubted my meager efforts would really make that much of a difference.

But God, that stack of cash sitting in my purse was whispering that maybe I could pull it off. Earn enough to get us by until my daddy figured out what he was going to do.

How to recoup.

How to restore.

How to rebuild both his finances and his spirit.

Tessa nudged me out of the reverie. "Um, hello, Eden? You actually worked, right? I've been dying for the details."

"Yep. I started last night." I fought the flutter that buzzed in my chest. Every thought filled with the memory of the sharp angles of his face. As if they'd somehow cut in and taken hold.

Impossible.

Maybe it was a cruel side effect of sleep deprivation, the fact I couldn't take my mind off the man.

I didn't believe in insta-love or even insta-infatuation or…I guessed I had to admit I'd even given up on the belief of attraction. In the possibility that I could feel it.

I'd come to believe my devastated heart no longer beat quite right.

Tessa's brow rose around her ice-blue eyes, and the freckles that matched her hair danced when she curled her nose. "And it left you looking like this? That sounds...brutal."

Air blew from between my lips. "I didn't get home until two-thirty, and then I was too wired to sleep. This is all your fault, you know," I ribbed.

Anything to take the attention off me.

She gasped, all feigned offense. "And how is that?"

"You're the one who suggested I apply there when you saw the ad, saying it was where I could make the quickest money in Redemption."

You know, without having to take off my clothes, but the second I'd stepped inside that bar, I'd started to question that. Which was why I'd suggested...

Heat flamed my cheeks at the memory. At the way I'd tossed out dancing like it would be my own lure. Like it would sway him or make him change his mind.

Ridiculous.

Except...it had, hadn't it? It was what had made him stop and sit back down. Now I was wondering if I was a fool for being thankful he had.

Disbelief filled Tessa's expression. "Um...I was joking. I never thought you'd have the balls to do it."

"I'm pretty sure balls don't have a thing to do with it. It's called desperation."

"Nah. I think it's called my BFF is a badass."

"Or stupid," I tossed back.

She shrugged. "Only time will tell."

I swatted at her upper arm. "I hate you."

"You can't hate your favorite person in the entire world. Your bosom buddy. Your number one homie. Your ride or die." She sang them, getting louder with each one.

I was giggling by the time she got to the last.

"Fine, fine, I don't hate you. But close." I pinched my fingers close.

She grinned. "So, give me the goods. Is it wild in there? Did you make any money? Get hit on? I mean, you definitely got hit on, right? Tell me you got a few numbers. It's about time my girl got herself some action."

I almost smacked her again, only to stop when a little boy who'd been coloring by himself at a small table came racing our way—basically saving my life because...Tessa.

He waved a piece of paper over his head while his backpack that was three sizes too big for him bounced on his tiny shoulders. "Miss Murphy, Miss Murphy, look it what I made for you!"

He was all golden hair and sweet eyes and the cutest thing I'd ever seen. I swore, my heart had trembled in my chest the first time I'd seen him sitting at his desk.

Tessa called it a sickness—the fact I got attached to every child who came through my classroom door. But there were some kids—some who worked their way in so deep they would forever hold a piece of me. The part of me who longed for it so desperately, knowing it was likely impossible. My chance passed.

"What did you make for me?" I asked him, my voice light.

He skidded to a stop, beaming at me as he held up the paper. "This! What do you think?"

I knelt in front of him, taking the picture. My eyes caressed the crude drawing, a stick-figure depiction of what was clearly meant to be the two of us holding hands beneath a giant sun, standing on jagged grass.

Affection pulsed through my chest, a throb in the void. "I think it's beautiful."

His smile only widened. "Did I pass my test?"

Bewildered laughter filtered free. "Pass your test?"

"I have to get all As, Miss Murphy! Don't you know, As are the best, best."

I couldn't stop it, my hand moved to run over the top of his head. "Don't worry. You're doing great."

His grin widened. "That is really great news. I gotta tell my dad. Did you know my dad is the best dad in the whole wide world?" Somewhere in his ramble, he'd threaded our fingers together and had taken to standing at my side, a jumble of words flying from his mouth as he swung our hands between us. "He took me to the store and got me papers and pens and colors and all'uv the things I need so I can get all the As. I got new shoes, too."

He kicked out his left foot.

Amusement flitted around my lips.

"He sounds like a good dad."

"Yup. He is the best. But my uncle said he needs to get some so he can stop moping around being a d-i-c-k." He lowered his voice when he uttered the letters like he was mimicking the way he'd heard them in the first place.

Tessa choked on the laughter that ripped from her throat, and I whipped around to give her a warning glare. She tossed her hand over her mouth to try to cover it, her eyes blinking furiously as she fought it.

She busted up, anyway, turning away for a beat to hide it.

I did my best to hold mine back, swallowing down the amusement that bounced around my chest.

Tessa turned back toward me, still snickering.

I straightened out the sundress I wore like I could stave off the giggles I could feel building between us, sure she was going to be rolling on the ground if I didn't put a stop to this.

"Maybe you should go swing some more before school's over?" I suggested. "I'm sure your dad will be here soon."

He just tightened his hold. "Nope. That's okay. I like it right here."

Right.

Okay.

Tessa kept giggling.

I widened my eyes at her. "*Would you stop it,*" I mouthed.

"What?" She shrugged. "That was hysterical. And seriously, *get some?*" she mouthed back. "Um, did you see his dad? He dropped him off this morning, and *oh my god.*" She fanned herself. "I'm sure he's getting plenty."

I swatted at her with the hand that wasn't wound with the child's. "What is wrong with you?" I hissed.

But I guessed it didn't matter because the little cutie had started to sing to himself, oblivious as he belted out his ABCs.

She shrugged again. "Like I told you before, I'm a teller of the truth. But did you?" she baited.

Exasperation filled my sigh. Tessa was relentless. "No. I was in a meeting with my daddy."

Trying to save this school and his house. Not scoping out the new crop of dads.

That was enough to make Tessa frown, her voice lowering farther. "How is your dad?"

Sadness gathered tight in my chest. A sadness that struck me, lash after lash. Still unable to believe it. "Worried. Heartbroken. Not sure how we're going to come up with the money, all while struggling to accept she would do that to him."

I thought he still was in denial. Making excuses for my sister. Refusing to call the police even when we had clear proof that she was responsible.

My father was the most generous man alive. He had his ginormous heart set on saving the entire world, friends and strangers alike. Unfortunately, that meant he got trampled on, more often than not.

But when it was blood? His daughter? My sister? It'd been devastating. A blow neither of us had been prepared for.

Sorrow curled through my spirit, an ache so intense I felt it like a wound. Deep and throbbing.

With everything—with all we'd suffered—I didn't understand how she could come here and inflict more pain. How she lived with herself after what she'd done.

What hurt the most was how much I still loved her. How much I missed the relationship we'd once had before she had lost herself.

But my daddy and I? We still had each other, and I was going to be sure I could make it right if I could. Hold some of his brokenness the way he'd always held mine.

I swallowed my own anxiety. "I promised him I was going to figure it out." I made sure to keep the conversation between Tessa and myself since none of the other teachers knew the situation we were in. "I told him I would try to scrounge some money together to keep the foreclosure at bay at least until we can figure out a longer-term solution."

How we were going to manage that, I didn't know.

Tessa sighed. "You can't fix everything, Eden. I'm worried about you."

"Says the one who sent me into the lion's den." Voice wry, I sent her as much of a tease as I could.

"Well, since you would have tried to figure it out yourself, no matter what I said, I thought I might as well point you in the right direction. What was it like, anyway? Seriously, I still can't believe they started you immediately. That's a big break."

I huffed out part of the disgruntledness I'd felt last night. "It was pretty clear the reason I'd had to start immediately was the owner was testing me."

Speculation arched her brow. "How so?"

"Let's just say he took it upon himself to prove I didn't fit in."

A flash of annoyance darted across her face. "And how exactly was he trying to do that?"

I squeezed the little boy's hand who was still belting out his song, the child grinning as he stood there watching the other children play, as content as could be. I angled toward Tessa. "Some hunters love to play with their food before they go in for the kill."

I let my brows raise for my hairline, letting her connect the dots.

"Ah…" she grumbled, picking up what I was laying down. "That kind."

"Yup."

"Let me guess, he's ridiculously hot and thinks the world revolves around him?"

I vented out a raw sound. "That doesn't even come close to describing whatever he is."

Hot.

Gorgeous.

Terrifying.

A total jerk and somehow…protective, in this weird, overbearing way.

"Speaking of hot guys…" She angled her head in the direction of a white Porsche Panamera that pulled into the parent pick-up line on the other side of the wrought-iron fence. "There he is."

And I wondered if I was seeing things.

Hallucinating.

If this was some kind of cruel, sick joke or if I'd just done something really terrible in another life and this was my punishment.

Because there was no mistaking the smoldering eyes staring me down through the windshield where he came to a stop at the curb.

The way shock blanched his unbearably gorgeous face before his jaw clenched in what appeared hatred.

Or maybe glee.

With the man, I was sure they were one and the same.

My hand tightened on the child's.

Instinctual.

A gut reaction to protect him.

Shivers raced. This unsettled feeling that something was coming. Something I didn't understand, but something I should fear.

The man climbed from the driver's seat of the flashy car that I wouldn't have thought would fit him at all but somehow right then looked like the perfect accent piece.

He straightened to his full, menacing height.

"There he is! There he is!" The child started jumping up and down and waving his hand in the air. "Hi, Dad, hi! Over here!"

That seething intensity flashed through the air. My head spun and my knees knocked, my mouth going dry.

Trent Lawson strode toward the gate, all dark swagger and don't-give-a-shit attitude, even though there were at least fifteen signs asking parents to stay in their cars and their children would be escorted out.

I got the sense the man wasn't exactly one to follow the rules.

Because there he was, dressed a lot like he'd been last night, black jeans and a black v-neck tee and black boots that were unlaced. All that exposed, inked flesh somehow appeared obscene.

I had the urge to wrap the child up and take him into hiding. Run to the rest of the children and usher them to safety.

Emergency evacuation.

But I just stood there.

Dumbfounded.

Finally, I mumbled, "That's your dad?"

Gage Lawson.

Of course.

This really was some cruel, sick joke, and I was the very brunt of it.

"Yep! That's him." Gage was jumping and pointing. "Tell him I got an A, Miss Murphy! He's gonna be so proud!"

Trent Lawson strode toward the gate with the clear intention of barging in.

Finally, I found my voice, calling out before he made it through the barrier. "Sir, you need to wait in your car. School isn't over for a couple minutes, and we will bring your child to you. Parents aren't allowed in this area without signing in at the office first."

With his hand on the gate latch, he paused, an arrogant smirk ticking up like a threat at the corner of that plush mouth. "That so?"

I lifted my chin, still clutching his son's hand. "Yes."

He eyed me as if I were the enemy. "So, let me get this straight. I pay an ungodly amount of money for my son to come here, and you get to tell me when I can and cannot pick him up?"

"You're paying for your child's education, Sir, not for me to order you around."

"Huh…would have been mistaken."

My chin lifted higher. "It seems you are very, very mistaken."

A war waged in the exchange. That same tension that had existed last night clear and present, his outright animosity unchanged. But there was something else lining it, too.

As if I'd gained some sort of power as we stared each other down.

"You've got to wait, Dad! I told you I got to get all the As, and you're gonna ruin it by not followin' the rules. Sheesh."

Tessa giggled beside me.

One second later, the bell rang. It jarred me out of the trance the man held me under, my entire being jolted with the sound, as if time had been set to pause and it'd begun to speed to catch back up.

Children screeched their excitement and ran to grab their bags that were lined up against the wall.

"Please remain in your car tomorrow," I called out, the words roughened shards as I reluctantly released Gage's hand.

"I'll see what I can do," he returned, just as smug and cocky and infuriating as he'd been last night.

Gage went running that way, that giant backpack bouncing all over. He glanced at me, running backward for two steps, nothing but grins and belief. "Don't worry, I'll be back to see you tomorrow, Miss Murphy!"

When the child made it to him, Trent stretched out a hand for Gage to take.

For a flash, his entire demeanor shifted when he looked down at the child and the child smiled up at him.

Soft. Kind. Protective.

I had to be seeing things.

Then he turned to leave on those ridiculous boots, but not before he tossed out from over his shoulder, "See ya soon, Kitten."

Anger rushed, my cheeks hot and my pulse wild and that irrational rage taking hold.

All mixed up with that *feeling*.

That impossibility.

They walked back to the Porsche, and I remained rooted to the spot as he helped Gage into the backseat and into a booster before he rounded the front of the car and slipped into the driver's seat.

The man glared at me before he tossed his car back into drive and pulled from the curb.

Fingernails curled into my upper arm. "Holy shit, Eden Jasmine Murphy," Tessa hissed. "What was that? And you better fess it up now, because I can already feel your denial coming on, and there is no denying whatever the heck that was."

She waved a turbulent hand through the air as if she could capture that feeling.

Something unattainable but real.

"That?" I let my eyes follow the car that whipped out of the drive far too fast. "That was my new boss."

Chapter Five

Eden

LIFE IS A SERIES OF CHOICES. SOME ARE EASIER MADE THAN others. Some take days or weeks or even years of contemplation, while others are made in a split second. Some are destined to be mistakes and others are made of sound judgement and mind. Fueled by wisdom and foresight and discernment.

Black and white.

But sometimes?

Sometimes they are grayed. Blurred. Obscured in a hazy cloud of smoke.

Vapors and mist and uncertainty.

That's exactly what it felt like as I slipped into the murky shadows of the hall outside the dressing room where I'd just placed my bag into a locker and pulled a clean apron over the jeans and tee I'd opted for as attire tonight.

I felt as if I were stepping into uncertainty.

Into a different world where I didn't know the rules. Where I questioned the unsteady terrain on which I traveled.

Or maybe subconsciously I knew full well I was making a mistake by following this path. That I was begging for trouble.

Maybe I sensed it as a premonition as I edged down the confined passageway toward the kitchen. An omen that whipped and whirred through the dense, thickened air that held fast to the cramped quarters of the hall.

I was standing at a clear line where I had to make a choice. Keep moving forward or turn and run.

I supposed I was the fool who continued to edge toward that destiny.

I was almost to the turn that hooked into the kitchen when I felt the dark presence emerge from behind.

As if he'd felt me pass by his office.

Or maybe he'd just been watching.

Waiting.

The hunter who wanted to play with his prey before he went in for the kill.

My heart skittered and my flesh prickled, and I inhaled a shaky breath as I slowed and turned around.

Trent Lawson hovered at the doorway of his office, those sooty eyes taking me in like he wanted to see deep inside. Sift through my makeup.

More than likely, he'd read everything written inside, anyway. Had already picked up on the scent of who I was. Smelled the desperation. Sensed the vulnerability.

But the thing about vulnerability? It didn't always make you weak. Sometimes the only thing it did was make you fight harder. Make you more determined to go after what you needed in your life.

"Well, well, well, if it isn't little *Miss Murphy*." He tsked it like it were a sin. "You came, after all."

My chin lifted in defiance. "You thought I wouldn't?"

He chuckled a rough sound and moved to lean against the wall outside his door. He stuffed those tattooed hands into his pockets and slung himself back so nonchalantly that one might mistake him for blameless. But I wasn't fool enough to believe he wouldn't strike at any second.

"I would have thought you'd think it a…conflict of interest." His head cocked to the side.

I tried to ignore the way my heart raced, thrumming so hard it had to be a palpable thing. "Conflict of interest?"

Undeniably, him coming at me this way was the *conflict of interest*. The dude was my boss. Clearly, he didn't give a crap about that.

I got the sense he didn't just ignore the rules, he made his own.

Coarse assumption flowed from his wicked mouth. "I have to admit I was shocked to see you standing with my son's hand in yours when I rolled up this afternoon, but I shouldn't have been, should have I? A place like that is exactly where you belong."

Just like I'd known he would, he struck. Only it was slow. Like a wolf stalking…prowling…slowly stealing in closer until its target was cornered.

Nowhere to go.

My back hit the wall, and he was right there, invading my space, the man pure masculinity and greed.

Energy crackled.

A seething intensity that lashed through the air.

I inhaled a shocked breath, a mistake because the only thing it achieved was a rush of his essence sucked deep into my aching lungs.

Leather and nutmeg and the faint vestiges of cigarette smoke.

Only a fool would have the urge to lean closer and inhale.

But I did.

I had the sudden desire to press my nose to his hot flesh. To drag it up his throat over the tattoo etched there—a baby owl in full flight, its wings stretched wide around his neck, though its face was a disfigured skull.

My fingers itched with the need to trace it.

There had to be something wrong with me.

But I couldn't help it.

The way my eyes traveled, so close, unable to stop myself from devouring as much of the exposed skin as I could.

Tonight, his tee dipped low enough that I could make out the words hidden in the whorl of colors and designs on his chest—Live to Ride, Ride to Die.

My mind spun, no clue why I felt compelled to understand. Why I wanted to ask him to explain. Who he was and why he was. How this hardened, terrifying man was the father to that adorable little boy. And why I cared so much.

I'd only met him yesterday, and the few interactions had already left me caught up. Swept away in a torrent.

"Aren't I right, Miss Murphy?" He angled in closer, his voice dropping to a lure. "You're meant to be there…with those children. Amid all that innocence."

His lips were suddenly at my jaw.

Touching.

Igniting.

Destroying something inside me.

Chills streaked, and my head rocked back as sensation rushed across my skin and desire leapt in my belly.

Those lips murmured the words like an accusation as he ran them up to my ear. "I bet you even teach Sunday School."

God.

What a dick.

I forced myself to pull back. "And what if I do?"

I totally did.

But I didn't owe him a single explanation. Funny, how I wanted one from him.

Trent chuckled a menacing sound. "It would prove exactly what I'd recognized about you the second I saw you last night. You don't belong here."

I crossed my arms over my chest to put some space between us. "You don't know anything about me."

"One look at you, and I know everything I need to know."

"What is your freaking problem?" I hissed.

He shocked me by suddenly moving to the other side of the hall, taking my breath with him as he went. He propped his back against the wall, smirking the whole time.

Even with the three feet separating us, he filled the space. Everything about him overwhelming.

Intoxicating.

I knew better than letting myself get drunk on this man.

"My problem? Not the one with a problem here. I'm doing you a solid, Kitten."

"Wow, aren't you ever the knight in shining armor?"

He scraped out a raw laugh. "Nah, not even close, but for you, I just might try."

Was he serious? I had no doubt this guy would gladly rip me to shreds.

He roughed a hand through the longer pieces of his black hair, and for the first time, something genuine filled his tone. "Listen...this isn't a good place, Eden."

The air shifted, and I swore I saw the slightest edge of vulnerability slip into his features, and I found myself digging again. "And you're not a good man?"

There was no missing the bare truth of the question.

Another of my sicknesses claimed by Tessa. I dug around to find the good bits in everyone. Believed it was there. That we all had something to offer, no matter what we'd done in our pasts.

And I felt desperate to find his.

His voice twisted into a threat, that moment of softness stiffening to steel. "What do you think, Miss Murphy?"

"I think we've all made mistakes, Mr. Lawson."

His nostrils flared, and he was moving again, edging my direction, eclipsing me in his towering frame. He stopped right before he plastered his body against mine, and he angled in so close our noses almost touched.

That energy sizzled.

"Tell me, is it a mistake if you make the choice to do it, again and again? If the sins you've committed make up the foundation of your life? If they make you who you are?"

Involuntarily...instinctively...stupidly—I didn't know—I reached out and let my fingertips flutter over the words imprinted on his chest.

"Are you…a biker?"

Like, a real biker? Was this bar a front? Doubt and fear thrashed and boomed, banging through my brain in a flashfire of warnings while I stood staring up at him as if the question had been a plea.

A shuddered breath left him.

A moment held.

Then he reached out and snatched me by the wrist as if it took him those stilled seconds to realize I was trying to dip my fingers inside and discover a little of who he was, the same way as I could feel him doing to me.

Fury filled his expression. "What do you think you're doing?"

My head shook, and the words left me like confusion. "I honestly don't know."

Severity twisted his brow, and his fierce jaw ticked in restraint. In need. In dark desperation. "You should stay away from me," he growled.

"Should I?" It was out before I could stop it. But I knew there was something there. Something unseen. Something I could feel pulsating in the atmosphere that I'd never felt before.

It stretched between us.

Keening and alive.

Something my spirit warned would ruin me in the end.

"I think you already know the answer to that."

Gathering my courage, I asked, "Then why is it you have me pinned to the wall?"

"Ah…" A single fingertip trailed down the angle of my face, and he was watching me with those eyes, devouring the way a shiver raced across my skin.

Trent tipped his head to the side, raven hair pitching that way. "Now that is the question, isn't it? Why I couldn't look away from you from the start. Why once you were outta sight, I still went to bed thinking about you. Wondering just how soft your skin might be." His mouth moved closer to my ear. "Wondering how you'd taste."

He edged back again. "Guess it makes me the fool who woke up this morning still wondering the same."

Give Me a Reason | 47

Attraction.

It flickered and flared.

A vapid dance in the heated air.

It was such a terrible idea. Giving in to whatever this was would be a crime. A *choice* I knew full well I shouldn't make.

Black and white.

But I felt it.

Desire.

And for me, that was a miracle. My own impossibility.

"You're a dad." It came out softer than it should as Gage's sweet face filled my mind.

With a child like that? I refused to believe this man was only carved of wickedness and greed.

Affection left him on a breath. "Yeah."

"Gage…" His name heaved out of me like a stone. Like a prayer. I guessed that was exactly what it was. "He's…"

I'd felt a connection to the child immediately. In an intrinsic way. In a way that I should ignore.

"Adorable? A handful? Sweetest fuckin' thing you've ever seen?" Trent said each one like he was checking off the child's list of As, the slightest smile tugging at the corner of his mouth.

Sweet. Sweet. Sweet.

My heart fluttered in an entirely different way.

God, I really was traversing dangerous ground.

"He is," I murmured, a smile of my own threatening my lips. "Probably one of the sweetest, most adorable children I've ever met."

"Only good part of me." He said it like he'd heard me ask the question aloud. Saw it written all over me.

"It seems he sees many good things in you."

Trent scoffed out a rough chuckle. "Kid's always singing my praises."

I glanced away before I brought my gaze back to his handsome face. "Are you…"—I gulped before I forced it out—"…married?"

I realized I was shaking. My breath locked in my throat, terrified of what he might tell me.

Trent grunted, angling back just a fraction so I could meet the brutal expression on his face. "Look married to you?"

My teeth clamped down on my bottom lip. Was I supposed to answer that?

He shook his head a little. "Only commitment I've got is to that kid. To this club. To my brothers. Ends there."

Right.

Okay.

It was another warning.

It also felt a whole lot like a rejection.

I blinked, trying to process what I was feeling.

This tingling in my belly. This fullness in my chest.

Was that what this was? Did I...want him? Did I want him to touch me? Want to touch him? For the sake of what? Dipping my fingers into forbidden waters? To experience something unlike I'd ever experienced before?

To sate the feeling that suddenly washed through me?

Something that was hot and sticky and twisted my stomach into a thousand knots. A feeling I hadn't felt in so long.

A flash of guilt clutched me. Admitting it to myself felt wrong, but if I were being honest, it was something I'd never experienced before. Never before had I felt something as powerful, as inescapable, as this.

I gasped a little under the pressure of it. With the shivers that raced down my spine and spread down to throb between my thighs as he edged an inch closer.

Nothing but man towering over me.

Trent chuckled. Dark and deep. As if he'd witnessed every thought that had played out in my mind.

He reached out and stroked the pad of his thumb down the length of my cheek. "Ah, playing with fire again."

My jaw dropped open at his touch, and he went to brushing that thumb across my bottom lip.

Fire.

Flames.

"So fuckin' sweet," he whispered. Those ashen eyes sparked, black flames that searched me in the night. We got held there. Just…staring at each other.

Want.

Need.

Fear.

I saw it in the fraction of a second, gone when he ripped himself away and every line of his gorgeous face went rigid. Pure, unrelenting steel. "You should get to work."

Cold ice slicked down my spine, and my knees nearly buckled with the sudden change in his demeanor.

My chest squeezed tight.

Tied in hurt and confusion.

When he started to edge back, I reached out and grabbed him by the wrist. A fool. A fool. But I couldn't help the way my entire body felt as if it'd come alive.

Sparked into existence after I'd been numbed into nothingness for so long.

"I…don't understand."

He wrung himself out of my hold and held his arms up at his sides. "Not much to understand, Kitten. I'm a bad guy and you're a good girl. You'd do well to keep your space. Simple as that."

My head shook. "It doesn't feel so simple to me."

Grimness lined his lips. "Have a way of turning pretty things ugly."

Another warning.

Though this one rang with regret.

My attention darted left to right, to the ground, before I forced myself to look back at him. Unsure of his life, but sure it was dirty, unsure why I couldn't seem to keep myself from delving farther.

Searching for a way inside.

"Does that apply to Gage? Do you think you're a danger to him? That you could hurt him?"

I didn't even care that my voice shook when I asked it. My students would always be my first priority. But I knew with Gage, it was more than that. That feeling that had taken me over the first time I'd seen him sitting in his tiny desk in the front row.

In a flash, the wolf struck. Trent pinned me to the wall. My palms flew behind me to keep me steady.

His hands were planted on either side of my head, and the entirety of his being vibrated with brutality.

Caging me in. A vicious, obliterating force.

The words that fell from his mouth were daggers. "Am I a danger to him? Miss Murphy…make no mistake…anyone who even thinks about hurting that child? There isn't a soul on this Earth who could save them from me. From the pain I would inflict. From the hole where their body would lie. The only danger is to them."

My throat tightened, and I struggled to swallow around the lump that gathered thick.

My knees knocked with the clear implication.

I knew most parents would easily claim it. Claim they would destroy anyone who hurt their child. It was only normal to want vengeance if they were faced with that horrible circumstance.

With Trent Lawson? It was clear it was no idle threat or exaggeration.

This man had blood on his hands.

I could smell it.

Taste it.

Felt it radiating around him.

An aura of iniquity.

"I pray neither of you are ever put in that position." I meant it.

Stepping back, he released me, but not from the snare of his spirit. Our gazes were a tangle of questions as those fiery eyes glowed and glinted, calling me deeper.

Deeper and deeper.

"You really should go home." That time, he was pleading with me.

I swallowed around the emotions locked in my throat and gave him my own truth. "You're not the only one who has trouble in their life, Mr. Lawson. You're not the only one who would do whatever it takes to protect their family."

I had to wonder if we were really any different at all. If we were all only trying to figure out how to give those we loved the hope they deserved.

Harshly, he searched my face, as if he were looking for a lie. "That what this is? You need money…for your family?"

My nod was jerky.

His lips curled in distaste. "You married?"

Grief trembled, that empty space howling its sorrow. Closing it off, I angled my head to the side, my voice soft surrender as I turned his words back on him. "Do I look married to you?"

Only my commitments ran deep. My promises. My love. My soul's innermost ache.

He wavered in the moment, like he was going to ask me why before he seemed to come to a resolution. He nodded. "Okay, then."

Forcing a brittle smile, he stepped back.

It was as if he had made the decision to put a wall between us. Neither cold nor hot. Indifferent.

It left me feeling as if I'd just been tossed ashore after being drowned in turbulent, tormented waves.

Floundering and coughing and searching for air.

I stared at him for a beat.

At his beauty.

At his intensity.

At this man who for the first time in years made me want to look closer.

My spirit warned I might not like what was written inside.

It didn't matter.

That hunger had lit.

A hunger I would never act on. Would never be so reckless. I knew full well my heart would never recover from the kind of breaking this man would bring.

But I guessed…I guessed I relished in the idea—in the feeling— in the simple fact he made me feel alive for the first time in so long.

"Thank you, Mr. Lawson. Truly. I needed this job."

Peeling myself from the wall, I forced myself to turn and start toward the kitchen.

"Kitten."

That ridiculous nickname coming from his tongue wrapped me like a sinful caress, and I stopped moving, but didn't turn around.

"Your probationary period is over. Go change. You'll start training as a cocktail server tonight."

At that, I whirled around. "What?"

Trent cocked that arrogant grin. "Everyone starts off washing dishes here. Didn't you know?"

Then he spun on his heel and disappeared into his office, slamming the door shut behind him.

I just stood there.

Stunned and confused and grateful.

My heart in my throat and my head spinning.

Whiplash.

Chapter Six

Trent

OUT BACK, I LIT A CIGARETTE AND LEANED AGAINST THE grimy building. I inhaled, filling my lungs full, one boot planted to the ground and the other to the wall.

I looked to the blackened sky smattered with stars.

Trying to get my shit together. To figure out just what the hell I thought I was doing. How I was supposed to maneuver this.

Was basically hiding out back of my own bar, for fuck's sake.

But it was getting harder and harder figuring out how to be in Eden Murphy's space and act like she hadn't gotten under my skin. Like I wasn't constantly watching her. Wanting something I most definitely shouldn't want.

Last week, back on the first day of school when I'd discovered she was Gage's teacher, I'd made the firm and fast decision that I had to draw a line. A clear-cut boundary, one in which eradicated that mesmerizing presence from my bar.

Knew it had to be done with the reaction that'd shaken down my insides when I'd pulled into the lot and saw her holding Gage's hand.

A motherfuckin' arrow straight to the heart.

Piercing.

From out of nowhere had come this *longing* that was pure insanity to acknowledge.

Might have known that I could never have it, that I'd ruin it, but I still hadn't been able to shake the sense that I was looking on something right. Something good. What was missing.

Belief and beauty and hope.

Yup.

Straight fuckin' stupidity.

That shit wasn't in the cards for me.

I'd already fucked it all. Had committed too many wrongs. Most importantly, I couldn't lose sight. Couldn't jeopardize what I was living for by going after something I couldn't have.

Only thing it'd be was another sin mounted on the others.

It didn't help that after the first day of school Gage had climbed into the back of my car and chattered the whole ride home about the greatness that was *Miss Murphy*. How pretty she was. How she had to be the smartest teacher in the world. How he was certain he was her favorite but that *he wouldn't tell the other kids because he didn't want them to be sad.*

My damned chest had felt like it was going to implode as I'd glanced through the rearview and witnessed all that joy lit on his precious face.

It was the only thing that mattered.

Wasn't a stretch to come to the resolution that I had to end things here at the club before it got messy. Boundaries set.

She was my kid's teacher, and that was going to be the end of it.

So, I'd confronted her in the hall. I'd had every intention of cutting her loose, but then I'd been consumed all over again.

Hit with the urge to get closer.

Fingers itching to sink into something pure.

Drawn to that unique, unfound beauty.

Like a prick, I'd gone to tossing who she was in her face, not that I knew how to be much else. Thinking I was going to chase her away when the only thing I'd done was draw her closer.

Her body backed to the wall, her breaths shallow and her heart flying.

My dick steel and raging at my jeans.

Somehow, in the middle of it, we'd exposed ourselves, different boundaries set than the ones I'd imagined, and it'd ended with her *thanking* me for the job after I'd promoted her to server.

Yeah. Girl'd flipped that shit on me, hadn't she?

Now I was left floundering.

Tiptoeing.

Pretending like night after night I wasn't dying to trace my fingertips over every line of her body. Get lost in those autumn eyes and that honeyed flesh. Felt like I was losing my goddamned mind with how bad I wanted her.

No-name basis.

No connections.

No chance of a knife driven into my back.

Apparently, I needed that shit drilled into my brain.

Chuckling at my stupidity, I rocked my head back on the coarse brick and exhaled, blowing the smoke from my lungs and watching it disappear into the nothingness.

Right along with my common sense.

"Yo, brother."

A grin slid to my mouth as the gruff voice hit from the side, and I shifted around to peer into the night. Jud's giant frame emerged through the hazy shadows where he trudged up the walk between our establishments.

Both buildings had been abandoned on a single lot, neglected and crumbling. The roof over at his bike shop had been caving in, and the inside of the bar had been nothing but rotted wood and a mountain of trash.

A bonafide dumpster dive.

My brother and I had pooled our dirty money and vowed to do something clean. Make a change before we ended up behind bars or dead like everyone else we'd run with. Way we'd planned to do before everything had come to a gruesome, horrible end.

As hard as we might try, think we both knew we'd committed sins we could never fully leave behind. Those ghosts slipping through the cracks, haunting our hearts and threatening our lives.

Taking another long drag as he approached, I lifted my chin in welcome. "Where you been?"

Hadn't seen the asshole in days. Dude always got wrapped up in his work. Fully tranced out as he gave old, rusted metal new life.

"Busy," he grumbled before he gestured at me. "Can see someone else is slackin' as usual," he cracked, roughing a massive palm down his black beard.

Low laughter rolled out as I exhaled. "Nah. I'm just getting started, unlike someone else who looks like he's packin' it in for the day," I tossed back.

He grunted. "Considering I've been neck deep in primer and paint for the last ten days, I think it's warranted."

"Big job, yeah?" I asked, drawing one last pull before I exhaled the smoke toward the sky and stubbed out the cigarette with the toe of my boot.

He heaved out a strained sigh. "Yup."

I clapped him on the back. "Then we better get you inside and get some drinks in you."

"Now you're speaking my language."

"Ah, I see what I'm good for."

Jud chuckled and squeezed my shoulder, and I opened the heavy metal side door and we slipped by Milo, the bouncer who guarded the side door and lot.

The two of us moved down the hall that ran along the side of the bar, passing by the employee lounge, storage room, my office, and kitchen.

The whole way, I swore I could scent her. That honeyed goodness wafting through the air. Sweet, sweet temptation. Her spirit flooding the space.

Yeah. Needed to get that shit under lock and key if I hoped not to lose my ever-loving mind.

Jud and I made it to the end of the hall and ducked into the loud thrum of the main bar. Place was already packed, tonight's band set to hit the stage in a half an hour. Lights strung from the second-floor ceiling cast the entire place in a hazy glow. Vibe was seductive and close to slow, though buzzing with the anticipation of getting freed. Of getting lost in the mayhem that was preparing to hit.

We made a beeline for the booth at the back that was permanently reserved for me and my guests.

Did my best not to look around. Not to seek her out.

Jud tossed himself into the left side of the booth, groaning low, his hulking body sagging as he scrubbed his hands over his face like he could polish himself out of the exhaustion.

Dude worked his fingers raw.

I slid in opposite him, waited for him to look up.

"Still worth it?" I asked when he did.

Because of me, we'd be hiding out in Redemption Hills for the rest of our lives.

Jud grunted. "You really still askin' that question?"

"Yup."

"Well, you should stop. Would do anything for that kid." He stretched farther out in the booth, filling the whole thing. He jerked his chin toward me. "For you."

My head shook as I fiddled with the edge of the beer list, peering across at my brother. "Just don't want to hold you back."

He scoffed. "Hold me back? You're the one who made *the* sacrifice, Trent. One who did what you had to do. One who set us free. I'd make a fuckin' million of them to pay you back."

My insides coiled. A clash of anguish and hatred.

This retching, writhing mess of sins that would forever mar my soul.

"Not a debt, man. Other way around."

"Bullshit," he spat.

I pushed out a heavy sigh.

Jud leaned forward, his enormous frame pushed up against the table, his words gruff. "You gotta quit blaming yourself, man. Wasn't your fault."

"Wasn't it?" I challenged.

"Nope." He actually grinned. "Besides, you landed us where we belong. Kinda like it here, if I'm bein' honest. The quiet life."

My nod was slow, sure the cost of it was always going to be too high.

Then I watched his grin widen when he looked to his right. Out into the bar. I didn't have to follow his gaze to know she was there. Thought I could actually sense her moving around the tables as she shadowed Leann through the club. Still in training and learning the ropes.

Could sense that lithe body swishing through the crowd.

Sense her spirit pulsing in little sparks that rippled through the dense, dank air.

Pinpricks prodded at my flesh.

Might have already known she was going to be there, but I looked anyway.

Taking her in as she weaved through the brimming crowd.

Bold but shy.

Confident but delicate.

Eden wore a black Absolution tank that served as our uniform, the thin material stretched tight over her slender curves, these sexy as fuck super short leather shorts that showed off her dancer's legs, and a pair of over the knee high-heeled boots.

She'd look so fuckin' good on the back of my bike.

Jolted at that. Struck by my stupidity. By this want I couldn't shake.

I couldn't go there.

I'd touch her. She'd let me. I knew she would. But she'd hate me in the end, no question about that. I'd taint her. Soil her. But God knew I was itching to get dirty.

Swore, I was a twisted fuck. Salivating at the mouth to tear into something sweet.

That thirst only intensified as she followed Leann over to our table, autumn eyes catching mine for one heated beat before she straightened and put on a professional face.

Considering we were at a biker bar, that only made her seem even more out of place.

All prickly and cute and making my dick twitch all over again.

"Why, hello there…if it isn't my two favorite Lawsons," Leann drawled in her southern accent.

She was so full of shit. Girl nearly creamed herself on the rare occasion that Logan made his way into the bar.

"Aww…now don't go making me blush, darlin'," Jud goaded her because he knew it, too.

I held my laughter.

Dude loved to mess with her.

She'd moved to California from Mississippi with the hopes of finding fame in Los Angeles. Apparently, it hadn't panned out, and she'd found herself in Redemption Hills with the rest of us outcasts instead.

"Are you doing good?" Jud asked, sincere this time.

"I am now that you're here."

Jud grinned. "Charmer."

"Only for you." She touched his shoulder.

The girl definitely knew how to work a crowd. But she was sweet as hell and a good server, too, and she'd become a huge asset to the bar.

She gestured to Eden at her side, like I hadn't noticed her standing there.

Nerves rode out on Eden's warmth.

Girl tiptoeing, too.

"This is Eden, and she's brand new here and helpin' me out tonight," Leann said.

Wasn't a man to miss an opportunity, so I swung my attention to Eden, which didn't take a whole lot of effort considering I kept sight on her from the corner of my eye, unable to focus anywhere else but on the girl who'd stolen every sense.

All trembling fierceness. Stark, gutting beauty.

Her attention jumped between Jud and me. Surprise before some kind of affected amusement played through her features, clearly coming to the realization that Jud and I were brothers.

She lifted her hand in a dainty wave. "Hello."

Jud sat back farther in the booth. His eyes raked her like he was contemplating all the things he might do to that body. "Sure good to meet you, Eden. I'm Jud. This one's brother."

Rage flared.

The irrational kind.

Because right then, I wanted to beat my brother's ass for no other reason than he was eye-fucking the girl.

"It's nice to meet you, too, Jud."

"Why don't you take this one? I think you're ready," Leann suggested, stepping back so Eden could take the lead.

It was basically the last test for a new server before they were let loose—serving me so I could judge if they were ready or if they weren't going to work out at all.

I was in tune with my bar to know well enough Eden was handling it just fine, but still, she inhaled like she was preparing to run a race when she took a confident step forward.

Energy surged.

Could feel her heart beating manic in the space.

I attempted to swallow around the rocks in my throat. To sit still around this feeling in my gut that churned every time she got close.

I fisted my hands under the table, trying to keep it cool when she cast a timid glance at me before she lifted her head and cleared her throat. The way that pink tongue darted out to wet her lips nearly drove me crazy. "Welcome to Absolution. What can I get started for you tonight?"

"You have any suggestions?" Jud, the asshole.

"What do you like?" She angled her head. "You look like a beer guy to me."

Jud laughed. "I think you're on to me."

"I think I might be." Eden was all smiles. A tempting, tantalizing tease.

I itched.

She glanced my way like she was looking to see if she was doing it right.

Only we got locked there, girl staring and me staring right back. That strange energy she emitted zapping me like a shock.

Finally, she jerked, clearing the roughness from her throat again, and turned back to Jud. She started to list off the beers we had on tap like she'd just spent the last five days cramming for a test.

Apparently, she and my son really would get along.

Jud picked his brew, and then she was turning that attention on me, her nerves firing all over the place, but she still had that sweet softness in her eyes. That thing that clearly neither of us understood. "And what can I get for you, Sir?"

Had to grit the words around the need. "Sage knows what I like."

"But I don't." Her voice was doing that wispy, seductive thing, and…fuck, I wanted to fuck her.

It was true.

I wanted to strip her down and lay her out.

I forced a smirk. "Well, then, Miss Murphy, there's a bottle of Macallan back there with my name on it. Like it neat."

Warm, like those eyes. Like that mouth. Almost as good as I knew she would taste.

"Okay." It was a breath. Like she was committing it to memory. This girl doing her best to sink right in.

"Would either of you like to see a food menu?" she asked, glancing between me and my brother.

"Right here, gorgeous." Jud's deep voice bolted through the connection. "This boy's starvin'."

She sent him a tender smile.

Stomach fisting, I drummed my fingertips on the table.

"Well, we can't have that now, can we? I'll be right back with your drinks and a menu so we can get you fed."

"That'd be perfect, gorgeous," Jud told her.

She smiled in relief, like she knew she was in the win before she glanced at Leann.

"That was good, sweetie. I think you're ready to tackle the place."

Eden gave a little nod of appreciation before she started to duck out, though she slowed when her gaze washed over me as she went.

Shy, sweet, curious.

Fuck me.

Something had shifted between us over the last week. This understanding. Like the girl got me. Saw me in a way she shouldn't. Got the sense that maybe I was seeing her, too. That quiet ferocity that kept getting jammed with the sorrow that would swim through her eyes.

Or maybe it'd just been there all along and it was getting harder to ignore.

It was something I knew better than to entertain. Wanting to dig inside and discover who she was all while imprinting myself on that body.

Apparently knowing better didn't matter a bit because I couldn't stop from tracking her as she followed Leann back through the mess of tables and over to the spot at the bar where the servers handed their drink orders to the bartenders, Leann talking with her hands the whole way, giving her instructions.

My attention was glued on that body, on those golden waves that rolled down her back and caressed her slender shoulders, on her waist and the delicious curve of her ass.

A rough chuckle punched me from the side. I jerked back to face my brother. Jud sat there with a smug look riding his face, dark eyebrow arched.

"Wanna tell me what that was about?"

Gave him the most indifferent shrug I could find, asked it like it was obvious. "Training the new girl?"

Jud chuckled low. "Who you think you're foolin', brother? Know you better than you know yourself, and I haven't seen you shit yourself over pussy since you were about fifteen." His forehead pinched. "She doesn't exactly give off the vibe that she fits in around here."

"No shit," I rumbled with a sigh. "But she needs the job, so I gave her a chance to prove herself."

A shock of heavy laughter jolted from his chest, and he shook his head in straight disbelief. "She needs the job? Everyone who applies is in need of a job, brother. That is how that works, in case you missed the meanin'." Every word was a jab.

"Let's just clarify on what you really meant, yeah? Your dumb ass wanted her to have the job. You know... quick access. Think I can't see the greed lighting in your eyes? Think I can't tell you're sitting there imagining exactly how you're going to get her out of those clothes? Thought we agreed not to sleep with the help?"

He looked at me pointed even though he cracked a self-righteous grin.

The two of us had made the rule when we went into business— no dipping our dirty paws into the cookie jar.

These were our employees.

Totally fuckin' off-limits.

I scowled. "Not even considering it."

That time, Jud cackled. "Oh, Trent, you're adorable when you lie."

I frowned at him. "Girl's not exactly my type."

He pointed at me. "Which that, my friend, is exactly why you want her."

Nah, it was more than that, but I sure as hell wasn't going to admit it.

"Doesn't matter. Not gonna touch her. You can count on that."

They were on their way back with our drinks, ripples of intensity coming off her, waves of it as she approached.

Jud and I sat back so Eden could set his beer and a menu in front of him. "There you go," she murmured below her breath, then she turned to slide the glittering tumbler of scotch in my direction.

Slower, though. Like she was relishing in the second she got to be closer to me. Or maybe she was wary of getting too close.

Our gazes tangled.

Questions raged.

Confusion and greed.

"There you go, Mr. Lawson," she whispered.

I reached out, our fingers brushing as I accepted it. "Thank you."

Her nod was jerky, hand shaking as she drew it back, and she straightened herself out and pinned on a smile when she shifted her focus to Jud. "I'll be right back to see what you'd like to eat."

"Sounds good. I'll be right here waitin'." Jud was all burly charm. How the asshole pulled it off, I didn't know.

She peeked at me and that was all it took for that crazy feeling to take hold of the air. A thrum, thrum, thrum in the midst of the music that played and the clamor that was taking to the stage as the band's crew finished their set up.

Ripping herself away, Eden followed Leann to another table.

Couldn't do anything but watch her go.

My smug-ass brother laughed.

"Hundred bucks you have her in your bed by the end of the month. Hell, I'd bet my fuckin' share of Absolution."

I scraped a frustrated hand over my face. "You might wanna retract that bet. She's Gage's kindergarten teacher."

Surprise knocked through his features before he was laughing harder. "This just gets better and better."

"Fuck off, man."

"Look at you over there, squirmin' in your seat."

I started to spout off a response when I stilled, craning my ear and my eye over my shoulder when the atmosphere shifted.

When a disorder descended on my bar.

Could sense it.

Way the hairs at my nape shivered as a roll of corruption and lawlessness filled the room. Tendrils of it rushed through, winding and curling, spreading like a disease.

Supposed it was my past that left me so in tune. Fact I could sniff out trouble in an instant. Scent evil just as easily as I could scent the good.

Same as Jud could do.

We both took note as three guys wound their way through the masses and sat down at one of the only empty tables close to the sectioned off area in front of the stage.

Shady as fuck. Something malicious rolling from their skin.

My eyes roamed the faces in the bar, taking stock, landing on Kult who stood right inside the main doorway. He lifted his chin with a heads-up.

He'd picked it up, too.

I returned the gesture, letting him know I had it covered.

"You seen these pricks around?" Jud asked.

"Nope."

He grunted a hard sound over the clamor of the band taking to the stage. They were local and played rock covers from the 70s to the 2000s. Performed most Monday nights, the crowd eating them up every single time.

My attention swung back to Eden. Fuckin' sweet as sin Eden.

Little Temptress.

Moving through the crowd as she and Leann approached the new table.

Lead singer moved to the mic. Sound crackled through the speakers as the DJ killed his set and gave it over to the band. "Yo, Absolution. We're Deep Under Cover, and we're about to go deeper! Let's go!"

They drove into one of those 80s songs that set off the entire bar.

An injection of chaos.

A dose of unruliness.

Almost everyone got to their feet, and a slew of people rushed to get out on the dance floor in front of the stage where they could completely let go.

This was when we started raking in the dough. When inhibitions were freed. When the chains of everyday life were loosed.

It got crazy busy for the servers and bartenders, too, which had me cringing all over again when Leann motioned for Eden to take the table herself so she could help some other customers.

The girl was clearly ready to stand on her own, but shit, not like this.

Eden nodded and moved for the table.

Nerves rushed. Neck tingling and hands twitching.

Wanted to go charging that way. Send another server over in lieu of her. Maybe get their order myself.

Stupid.

If the girl worked here, she needed to hold her own. I was the one who'd given her the chance and she was the one who wanted to take it.

But I didn't think she had the first clue about the vileness that often came crawling through these doors. And I felt it strong.

A wave of that vulnerability came rushing out ahead of her as she strode for the table, all mixed up with that steely determination as she pasted on one of those smiles.

That was the problem…I wasn't the only beast who took note. Wasn't the only one who sensed her goodness.

Could feel the greed light up at the table.

A flashfire.

I had to swallow down the shock of protectiveness that nearly busted straight out of my body when the slimy, blond motherfucker sat back in his chair and smirked up in her direction. One with the greasy curls and tweaker grin.

Already could see it playing out in his demeanor—the dickbag loved taking what wasn't his.

That overwhelming urge to gather her up and run her to safety took on a new form and shape.

My heart a thunder. A screaming boom.

She leaned in so she could hear whatever he said.

His tongue licked out an inch from her ear.

Fucker salivating at the mouth.

Girl had no clue he'd scented her like fresh, raw meat.

I didn't realize I'd been holding my breath until she stepped away from them and moved back to the bar. The air that had been locked in my aching lungs wheezed out.

But it didn't do much to take off the edge, though, considering the cunt chased her with his eyes as she went.

Jud laughed, but it wasn't amused. He took a gulp from his beer. "Watch yourself, brother."

But no—I wasn't close to watching myself. I was watching her. The way she talked with the bartender and then organized their drinks on her tray once he'd made them. Then she was back to floating through the raving mass.

Beauty and light in the midst of bleakness.

An angel in the darkness.

She started to pass out their order, beers for the two dark-haired guys on either side, before she leaned farther over the tabletop so she could slide the blond prick his drink. Sick bastard took it as an invitation to hook his finger in the neck of her tank and pull it down to get a better look at those tits, like he had the right to touch what wasn't his.

A growl rumbled in my chest, my knee bouncing a million miles a minute as rage jumped into my bloodstream.

She jerked back. Horrified shock curled her gorgeous face in revulsion. She moved to put space between them, but the piece of shit just grabbed her by the wrist, twisting it to the side like he thought she was the one who was out of bounds.

And that was it.

All I could take.

I was on my feet in a flash.

I flew across the room in a blaze of fury.

Not that I wouldn't have kicked this fucker to the curb if he touched any of my girls this way. But it being Eden? Had every intention of ripping out his throat.

Before he knew I was coming, I had him by the back of the neck and was hauling him up.

Eden screamed as the scumbag's chair toppled over and smashed against the floor. Fucker writhed and kicked and struggled to get free.

Jud was right behind me. He grabbed the brown-haired prick who squealed like a bitch, Kult right there in a breath taking down the other.

Asshole thrashed and flailed in the chokehold I had him in as I dragged him back and started wrangling him through the crowd. The band kept playing as I hauled him through the crush and toward the door.

Hands fisted in the back of his shirt, I threw him out.

Literally.

Tossed the skeeze to the pavement in front of everyone waiting in line just to prove a point.

He rolled a couple of feet before he came to a stop facedown.

Fury on his face when he looked up, he licked the tiny droplet of blood from the cut at the side of his lip that he'd gotten somewhere along the way.

My hands curled into fists. Animosity glowered like red destruction, a haze in the murky night. Wanted to bust it wide open.

I leaned over him, up real close, my voice the poison that I wanted to dump down his throat. "You think you can come into my bar and touch one of my girls?"

"Fuck you, man," he spat as he hopped onto his feet just as his crew was getting tossed out beside him. He swiped a violent hand over the cut on his face.

That's right, bitch, let's get violent.

Hands squeezed into fists, I silently begged it. The depravity taking over. The demons clawing through my spirit, screaming to take possession.

The stain of who I was.

Ghost.

It sloshed through my veins in a bout of aggression.

Wanted to beat this fucker bloody for the fact he was the one who'd proven my point.

Eden didn't belong here.

Not in the mix of the corruption that crawled its way to our door.

Not in the mix of the iniquity that was me.

Absolution was nothing but an invitation for sin.

The girl was blameless. I felt it to my bones. Felt it at odds with my spirit.

Goodness.

Grace.

"Don't want to see any of your faces on my property. Not ever again." I pointed between them while I forced myself to remain rooted and not go after what I was thirsting for.

Jud and Kult came to take up my sides, three of us a seething wall of menace.

Blond prick smirked like it didn't affect him a bit, beady blue eyes pinned on me as he cracked a grin. "Not a very nice way to treat paying customers, now is it?"

The tone of his words were mocking, but it was the way he was looking at me that left me unsettled. Something awry. Something more than a junkie prick who'd wandered in from off the streets.

"You're no longer a *paying customer*, now, are you?" This from Jud. His muscles ticked and jumped, dude wanting to tear into the asshole every bit as much as I did.

Rage barely bridled.

Blond fucker laughed. Another mocking sound.

A disturbance rustled through my consciousness.

He cocked his head to the side. "You sure you wanna take that stance?"

I stepped forward, getting in his face, words lowered with the threat. "Get cocky, motherfucker. I've slit throats for much less."

He leaned back, still wearing that smirk, like it was me who was the brunt of a joke. He angled his head to his friends. "Let's go."

They started to walk but not before the guy lifted his chin with a sneer when he said, "See you around."

They spun and strode out into the lot, and we watched until they piled into a pickup truck, engine grumbling to life and the headlights cutting through the haze. They whipped out of their spot and gunned it when they hit the street.

"Fuck," I hissed, whirling around and storming back inside, ignoring the eyes that were watching us from out front. Didn't draw much of a crowd from inside since it wasn't exactly rare for someone to get kicked from the bar.

There were plenty of assholes who got too handsy or unruly, and it was a rare night when some beefed up douches didn't end up in a fistfight.

But this...

"Somethin' doesn't sit right." Jud was at my side, angling in so I could hear him over the roar of music.

"Nope."

"You're sure you've never seen them before?"

"Positive."

"Prick was glaring at you like he knew you."

"I know."

Dread curled in my chest as I shouldered through the mob, heart slamming at my ribs as I scanned the throng.

No sight of the girl.

Jud kept pace, words shards. "You think someone is looking for us? Old debt?"

Foreboding stirred the adrenaline into rage. How many enemies had we made over the years? "Don't know. Fuckin' hope not, but I think we both know better than to stop watching our backs."

Jud exhaled a heavy sigh. "Ghosts don't ever stay dead, do they?"

My chest tightened. "Not in our world, brother."

Terror gripped me. Thought of my son getting in the middle of a crime I'd committed. A sin I'd perpetrated.

Ghost.

I could almost hear my piece-of-shit father hissing it in my ear. Branding me who he wanted me to be. Forming me into a monster.

And a monster I'd become.

Vicious.

Merciless.

Didn't matter how far I ran, I could never outrun who I was or what I'd done. My debt was deep. Ugly and cruel. And I knew one day, I would have to pay.

Exact reason I knew better than giving into this *feeling*. The feeling that spurred me across the packed floor and sent me stalking down the hall. The feeling that this girl meant more than she should.

I tore into the employees' lounge and locker room.

And there she was, sitting on the bench with Leann kneeling in front of her.

So goddamned beautiful.

So fuckin' wrong in this place.

Knew it the second I'd seen her.

"You okay?" I demanded, moving her direction.

That severity surged.

Goodness and light.

Eden barely nodded, her throat trembling as she swallowed, though she was lifting that defiant chin again. "Yes, I'm fine. It wasn't a big deal."

Leann rubbed her knee. "I feel terrible. I should have taken that table. Had I been payin' closer attention, I would have seen those guys were total jerks before I sent her over there."

Eden forced a smile. "I told you it was fine. You don't need to feel bad. I know it's just a part of working at a bar."

The growl that'd been building from the beginning ripped from my throat and cracked like thunder in the heated air.

"My exact fuckin' point," I spat.

Awkwardly, Leann stood, clearly getting the message that she needed to get gone. She wound around me, casting me a curious glance before she slipped out the door. I glanced behind me to see Jud hovering out in the hall, hands running through his long hair.

I turned back to Eden who'd stood on shaky legs. All sexy as fuck body and a halo of glowing light.

She backed away, seeing the rage coming off me in waves.

I moved forward.

Unable to stop before she was pressed against the wall of lockers. She hit the metal with a thud, her breath heaving from her lungs and caressing over me.

My dick jumped.

"Assholes are gone," I grunted around the rage. "Tossed them and they won't be coming back."

She nodded, her words a forced, jagged tease. "How am I not surprised by that?"

"Fuck…I'm sorry." Wasn't good at apologizing, but this…

She shook her head. "For what?"

My insides curled. "I let that prick touch you."

Or maybe I was just apologizing for the fact I wanted to curl my hands around her waist in possession.

Taint this girl with the darkness that writhed in my soul.

Let her light in for a minute.

Soothe the ache.

Knew she could.

Autumn eyes blinked slowly, taking in my face like it was she who was trying to make things right. "It honestly wasn't a big deal."

I lifted her hand, fury igniting all over again when I saw the red ring around her wrist. "Bullshit."

She trembled.

My mouth watered and my blood drummed.

She straightened herself out like she hadn't been affected, yanked her hand free, and put on that ferocious façade. Kind I knew well. Kind that promised you'd do anything to make it. "It's fine, Mr. Lawson, I'm completely fine." She angled herself so she could slip out from where I had her pinned. "I need to get back to work."

She started for the door.

I choked out a sound of disbelief as I whirled around. "Are you kidding me? You're done. No chance I'm letting you back on that floor."

This time, Eden laughed an offended sound as she swiveled to march back in my direction.

Stealing my breath.

Rocking my sanity.

Shooting daggers as she got up close to my face.

"You hired me, Mr. Lawson, now let me do my job."

With that, she spun and stormed out into the hall, leaving me standing there gaping at the empty doorway.

What the actual fuck?

I started to follow her into the hall, only to have Jud step out in front of me from where he was hidden in the shadows, smirk on his face as he gave her escape. When her footsteps receded, he cocked his head. "Not gonna touch her, huh?"

Had to keep myself from shoving him against the chest.

"Nope," I spouted.

"Come now, Trent, tell me your tiny dick isn't hard as steel right now. Now that's some sweet temptation right there."

Little Temptress.

And I was just the fool who might get lost in her siren's song.

Chapter Seven

Eden

THE SECOND MY SHIFT WAS OVER, I FLEW INTO THE employee locker room and grabbed my things like my life depended on it.

Maybe it did.

Maybe the threat I'd felt the first time I'd walked into this bar had finally manifested itself in human form.

Ice slipped down my spine at the memory.

There was something about the jerk that had left a sick feeling in my stomach. Sticky fear that had prickled across my flesh and had become panic the second his grimy fingers had curled around my wrist.

I think what spun my head the most, though, was how quickly Trent and his brother had descended.

The ferocity.

The hate.

Evidence of what I'd suspected since I'd met him. Every muscle in his beautiful body had rippled with brutality. Thirsty for blood. Hungry for vengeance.

More dangerous than any scummy patron could be.

My body trembled, struck with the image of the way he had

looked at me right after it'd happened. As if he were begging for forgiveness, guilty of dragging me into Hell. At the same time, he'd been vibrating so fiercely I'd been certain he was a second from going on a murder spree.

Puffing out the strain, I gave a harsh shake of my head, and with trembling hands, fumbled to shove another fat envelope of cash into my bag. More tonight than I'd ever made since I'd taken a few tables of my own.

It was the kind of money that made my head spin.

It was adding up quick. Quicker than I ever could have anticipated.

Hope filled me, pressing and pulsing, while my heart hammered like a war drum that warned of a coming destruction.

No doubt, I was in over my head, but I was praying with all of me that I could swim.

The only thing I had to do was keep coming here for a few more weeks, six max, make enough to chip away a little of the debt, then I would walk.

I'd earn enough to buy us time. Get the creditors off our backs and the overdue payments up to date.

Then I'd leave this place and never look back.

Still, my spirit warned if I continued to work here, I would never be the same.

If I stayed, I would be changed.

Changed in a vital, fundamental way.

Maybe I was only fooling myself, anyway. It wasn't like I could outrun Trent Lawson any time soon. The man haunted my nights here at the club and assailed my days at the school.

Worse was the way he'd begun to infiltrate my dreams.

The darkest hours spent tossing in my barren sheets aching for something I shouldn't want.

I gulped, my head dropping against the cold metal locker as I struggled for a breath. It had to be the loneliness. That was it. The first attention I'd received in years had me contemplating crazy things.

It wasn't real.

It couldn't be.

Pushing it aside, I tossed my bag over my shoulder and headed out of the locker room and down the hall.

Milo, one of the bouncers, held open the big metal door, standing guard over the employee parking lot and ensuring each of us made it safely to our cars, the same way as he did night after night. The man was truly terrifying at first sight, but as nice as could be when you got to know him.

"G'night, Miss Eden, you drive safe, now."

"Goodnight, Milo. Thank you, and you, too."

"Always, sweetness," he said, his enormous, tattooed body leaned against the door.

I slipped out and into the darkest, quietest night. The heavens were aglow with the vestiges of city lights and the mountain air had cooled to an almost cold.

Even though I knew Milo watched over me, I still felt unnerved as I walked toward my car parked on the other side of the lot.

My boots crunched on the gravel, and my heart beat too hard, too fast, my nerves alight. Trembling, I rushed a little faster. That sensation was only amplified when I was impaled with a sudden streak of energy.

With a rush of raw, unbridled intensity.

I was the fool who found some sort of comfort in it. In the way my thudding heart raced. A desire for more as I heaved a breath and stole a glance back at the dingy backside of the club.

I already knew he would be there.

That he'd be waiting. Watching.

The man stood against the wall to the devil's lair. Hands shoved in his pockets and a single boot kicked back against the wall.

Casually king.

The ruler of that wicked kingdom.

In the shadows cast by the building, he seemed even darker than normal, his eyes like black daggers that gleamed through the night. They were trained directly on me.

I felt suspended for a moment, my feet no longer touching the ground. My stomach in knots and my knees stupidly weak.

Somehow, I managed to tear myself from the grip of his stare. Pressing the lock to my car, I fumbled to get inside, threw my bag to the passenger seat, and jammed at the ignition button. I attempted to control the way my hands shook when I put my car in reverse, feeling frantic when I backed out of the spot.

Hating that maybe Trent was right. I didn't belong within those walls.

I whipped my car out onto the street and accelerated in the direction of my house.

What had to be less than ten seconds later, a single headlight appeared in my rearview mirror. Coming close, eclipsing sight.

As if his darkness had turned into a blinding light.

In an instant, my pulse thundered, this pounding mayhem that rushed.

Faster and faster.

"What is he doing?" I wheezed it aloud, my hands gripping the steering wheel like it could keep me steady as I glanced in the mirror again, unsure if I should welcome this or flee.

My soul and spirit warred.

Any sane person would know the clear-cut answer would be to run.

Put as much space between us as I could.

I sped up and took the next turn a little sharper, knowing it was useless because there was no chance that I could ditch him. I wasn't even sure if I wanted to.

A thrill lit with each turn that we took.

I made a right and then a left, winding my way through our small mountain city.

The forest rose high on every side, a hedge of protection as evergreens stretched for the blackened heavens, a slew of stars littering the sleeping sky.

The bike tailed me over the hills and curves and turns.

Smoothly.

Effortlessly.

As if tracking me was what he was meant to do.

My spirit thrashed and anxiety gripped and this flicker of that something I didn't want to voice ignited anew as I drove toward my little house in an old, quiet neighborhood on the opposite end of town.

By the time I made the last turn onto my street, where the tiny, more-than-modest houses were eclipsed by towering, ancient trees, I couldn't breathe.

Couldn't process the push and the pull.

The gravity that paraded as repulsion.

A fluttering of erratic wings flapped and danced in my chest.

I whipped into the single-car drive, threw my car into park, and tore out of the door just as the motorcycle rumbled to a stop on the street behind me.

Menacing, dark, and intimidating. Every part of it was matte black. Custom and cold and hard.

As wicked as the man who sat at its helm. His head was turned so he could stare across at me while those tatted hands still gripped the handlebars.

"What the hell do you think you're doing?" I hissed, storming three steps in his direction. The words came out so low there was no chance he heard it over the loud rumble of the powerful engine.

Though it was clear he knew exactly what I'd demanded.

The longer part of that raven hair whipped in the wind, and that sinewy muscle tightened and flexed beneath the designs that covered his arms.

My belly quivered where I froze. I couldn't move, but those butterflies flew.

Slowly, he reached over and killed the engine.

In an instant, a burning silence consumed us. The only sounds the whisper of the trees.

In it, we were held.

Captured.

Finally, he kicked the stand and balanced the bike, and my heart did a flip when he swung off it and straightened to his full, towering height.

The man a fortress.

An inferno.

And there he was, standing at the end of my drive as if he didn't understand the reason for it any more than I did.

"I asked what you're doing here." I demanded it again, though this time the grating of my voice cut through the air. Confusion and need.

Did he feel it, too?

He gruffed a hard sound. "No fuckin' clue, Kitten." He dipped his head toward his heavy boots, those hands shoved back in his pockets before he was peering at me with those penetrating eyes. "Other than the fact I needed to make sure that you're alright."

Warmth filled my chest, but I forced myself to lift my chin, sure I needed to protect myself, that I was probably in more danger in that second than I'd been in my whole life.

"I told you I was fine."

"That was a lie, though, wasn't it?" It was a soft accusation from that wicked mouth. Ripping me in two and fracturing more of my chinked armor. "You gonna stand there and pretend like that was just another day for you?"

I swallowed around the lump that had taken a seat at the base of my throat. "Isn't that the only thing I can do?"

His chuckle was disbelief and speculation, and for the quickest flash, the hardness slipped from his features. "Is it, Eden? Is it the only thing you can do? Because it seems to me you have more important things in your life than wasting it away in my club night after night."

Broken laughter heaved from my chest. "Yeah, you're right, Mr. Lawson. And saving the school is one of them."

My students. My joy. My father's legacy.

My life.

I almost toppled with the truth of it. It was all I had, the same as my father. That and our devotion to each other. And I had no idea who either of us would be if we had that stolen from us.

Trent wheeled back.

Caught off guard.

"That school tuition is a small fortune," he argued as if my claim was absurd.

I scoffed around the fullness that had suddenly clotted off my throat, so thick it had become difficult to breathe, cutting myself open in front of the very man I should be protecting myself against. "Tuition that goes right back into every program that is run out of that school and church, Mr. Lawson. Given to the families that come to us for help. Not everything is done out of greed."

He scrubbed a hand over his face, frustrated and concerned, and…and, God, who was this man?

He was conflict and contradiction. Everything that I didn't understand. And the scariest part was how much I'd begun to want to.

"Money run dry?" he asked.

A pained sound escaped before I could stop it, the confession gushing right out. "My daddy has always run it right up to the edge. Giving and giving and giving to the point of breaking. And someone he trusted most, loved the most, my own sister…" I clutched my chest when I admitted it. "She came in and stole from him. From us. It wiped us out. Knocked out the last leg that had kept that fragile balance."

"Your father?" Doubt flooded those words. I could see him rearranging more of what he'd assumed of me, trying to figure me out, see inside, just the way I continually seemed to do with him.

But the truth was, the last week of working with him had wrapped him in a shroud of mystery. The man at the bar was at complete odds with the man who picked up his son day after day.

This man who called to me in a way he shouldn't.

My nod was jerky. "Yes, my father owns the school and is the pastor of the church there." The words shook, my own sadness taking over. "And if he loses them?" My shoulders slumped. "We lose everything. The school. The church. The dance studio. All the things we love."

Things that were so incredibly important to me.

"And my daddy will lose his heart," I whispered because the thought of it broke more of mine.

In an instant, that wraith was moving my way, a dark storm that eclipsed.

Cold and hot.

A burn that would scar.

My thready pulse skittered and shook. I inhaled, trying to fill my aching lungs, only to have my senses inundated with the man.

He smelled like alcohol and leather.

Like metal and oil.

Like trouble served straight-up.

He leaned in and inhaled, too, his nose brushing into my hair. Shivers raced, and I was afraid this man would possess me if I allowed him to get any closer.

"Goodness." He rumbled it as if it were a sin.

"We all have good, and we all have bad, Mr. Lawson."

"Nah, Kitten, we don't. Some of us? Only thing we've got is darkness. Sin and lies and shame. And my club has a bad way of sucking all the goodness out of people. That prick—"

The words were blades.

I trembled with the slice of them.

"What'd that bastard say to you?" Trent demanded, edging back so he could read my expression.

I hugged my arms over my chest as if it could protect me from the invasion that was this man.

"He didn't say much." My tongue swept across my dried lips as I thought back to what had happened. "He...he'd given me a gross feeling from the beginning. There was...something off about him. I'd pushed it aside and took the order for their drinks, but when I came back, right as I was passing him his, he'd asked if all the Absolution girls were whores."

A snarl curled Trent's mouth, and his hands suddenly gripped my sides. Close to circling all the way around.

Heated and fierce. Powerful and relentless.

Flames licked through my body.

I was sure of it then.

It was Trent Lawson who was the danger.

Vicious. A cruel protector. A wicked savior.

A sweet warrior.

I'd seen it in his expression back at the bar. But I felt the fullness of it then, firing from his fingertips and searing my skin in possession.

I was the fool who wanted to open myself to it.

Let him brand me with his touch.

"And?" He demanded it like he knew. "That's not all, is it, Eden? What did that *motherfucker* say then?"

I heaved out the words as a chill blew through. "He said he heard that's the way the owner likes them, and he hoped you shared."

Rage blurred his features in malice, and his fingers curled tighter. "And what do you think, Eden? You think that's what I demand of my girls? You think that's who I am?"

My head shook, and I attempted to swallow around the shards of glass that sat at the base of my throat. "No."

He exhaled. Heavy. Tortured. "When he grabbed you? When I saw his hand on your wrist?" The words were a raw confession. "Wanted to end him, Eden. Wanted to put him in the ground just for touching you."

Chills raced.

Fear.

Revulsion.

Attraction.

Feral eyes flashed, black, seething flames. "Why's that, Kitten? Why did I want to claim you as mine?"

My mouth went dry, and he was tugging me closer, his head angling to the side as he murmured the words close to my mouth. "Why do I want to climb into this sweet little body and get lost there?" He shifted to run his nose along my jaw, inhaling at my pulse point, those full lips at my jaw when he whispered, "I bet your pussy is so sweet. Heaven. Paradise."

Desire flashed with his brazen words.

A blight across my soul.

I struggled to breathe. To see through the haze of seduction he was lulling me into. To fortify the walls I knew better than to let down.

"I do my best not to gamble my heart, Mr. Lawson," I forced out as I inched back enough to meet his eyes, my voice a thin wisp.

Shadows played across his striking face as he pierced me with that gaze. His cheeks sharp and his jaw sharper.

He reached out and splayed a tattooed hand across my chest. Everything raced.

"But it's beating so hard, isn't it? This beautiful heart of yours. You feel it, Kitten?"

Dragging in an unsteady breath, I attempted to stave off the attraction. To wade through the onslaught of sensations. To get myself to solid ground before I went under.

But the only thing I could focus on was the energy that bounded between us. The thunder that raged. I was just asking to get crushed when I let my shaky fingertips reach out to brush across the strength of his chest, lost to the magnet that pulled between us.

To the boom, boom, boom that crashed in the space. "And so is yours."

He let go of an incredulous sound. "That is the problem, isn't it? This feeling? I've ignored the thousand fuckin' times I've told myself to turn my back, to kick you from the club, to grab my kid and run in the opposite direction. And instead of listening to reason, I've run straight toward you. Now I'm standing right here imagining the fastest way to get you out of these clothes."

"We would be a mistake."

"Makin' it would be fun, though, wouldn't it?" A smirk kissed his mouth, plush lips tweaking at the side.

"I'm sure you have plenty of fun." I couldn't keep the edge out of my voice. The questions. The fact I hardly knew him but still was certain that our lives were lived in opposition.

A big hand splayed across the side of my face, warmth invading, the pad of his thumb brushing across my bottom lip. "When is the last time you let go, Miss Murphy? When is the last time you did something just for the sake of how good it would feel?"

That energy rushed. Pulled and prodded and compelled.

Images flashed through my mind before I could stop them.

His hands. His mouth. My legs wrapped around his waist as we writhed.

A small gasp parted my lips as I was slammed with a shockwave of need.

Dark eyes blazed in a torrent of greed. "Let go with me. Just once. Just tonight," he rumbled, both hands gripping my jaw.

I blinked with the harsh impact of what he said.

With the reality.

Of what he had to offer.

The truth that we really didn't match. That I didn't *fit* and I never would.

I knew better, knew better, and there I'd been, a second from giving in.

Shoving down the pain of the rejection, I forced myself to take a step back, to hedge myself, because he was asking me to go somewhere I couldn't go.

A place my spirit would never survive.

"You're my boss, Mr. Lawson, and I'm your son's teacher."

His hands squeezed tighter. "Don't give a fuck."

"I don't…" It popped out before I could stop it, and I trailed off when I realized what I'd nearly said. The last thing I should do was give this part of myself to him. He'd throw it in my face. Belittle me for who I was.

His nostrils flared as he edged back to stare down at me.

Ruining me with a look.

"You don't what?" His voice was the rough scrape of a command.

I wet my lips and pushed out the little I was willing to give him. "I don't sleep with random men."

Trent reached out and ran the tip of his index finger along the line of my jaw.

Electricity crackled.

There was more pleasure in that moment than I'd felt since I could remember. My lips parted and I struggled to stand on my weakened knees.

"Why's it we don't feel that random?" he muttered.

Don't fall.

Don't fall.

"I don't have any room for any more breaking," I whispered on an uneven breath, giving him another piece of myself.

No doubt, he saw the sorrow written all over me, anyway.

He dropped his hands like I'd burned him and stepped back. "Only thing I'm good for, though, isn't it?"

He didn't want my answer. He'd already answered it for himself.

Sadness filled my chest. For him. Maybe a little for me. Still, I said, "I can't believe that."

He may as well have been climbing inside me.

With the way that gaze flared and deepened and dimmed.

Terrified of trusting me, maybe the same way as I was terrified of trusting him.

"You should. All I've got is for my son."

"He's your world. Exactly as he should be."

"And I still don't deserve him," he gritted. Self-disgust clogged his expression in misery.

A place unseen.

A place I was one-hundred-percent certain he wouldn't share with me.

Still, a little more truth came riding out. "I have a feeling you're exactly what he needs."

Agitated, Trent shoved his hands in his pockets, vulnerable for the first time. "Tryin' to be, Eden. Tryin' so fucking hard. Most days, I have no idea what I'm doing."

Everything ached.

My heart and my body and that vacant place.

"As long as you never stop trying, you'll both be just fine."

For a beat, rage hardened his features to stone. Something I didn't understand. It was the part of him that terrified me, and I had a feeling it was for good reason.

"Will give it all for him, Eden. Whatever it takes. He's my life. My *reason*."

My spirit clutched, taken by this man's devotion, by the goodness he couldn't see.

For a minute, we stood there staring at each other, unsure of what to say. Of where to go from there.

One thing I did know was it was time to clear the air. For him to understand me the way I needed him to.

I angled my head, hoping he'd receive it. "I need you to know I'm not as fragile as I look. I can handle myself at the bar."

I just wasn't sure I could handle myself with him.

"Know that."

"Then I need you to stop treating me like I'm helpless or weak."

Trent blinked like I'd offended him. "Never thought that. Not once."

I looked away, into the weaving whisper of the night that crawled through the mountains and the trees before I gathered myself enough to look back at him. "You've been trying to get rid of me since I walked through your door. Telling me I don't fit."

Air puffed from his nose, and he anxiously ran his fingers through his hair. "That's not because I think you're weak, Eden. Just know you're better than that place. Knew it the second I saw you, and I don't want to be responsible for you stepping into a world that you don't believe in. A world your heart shines through. Desperation tends to force people to make choices they regret for the rest of their lives. Don't want that for you."

I got it then.

Saw it.

His wounds. His scars. His fear.

A sweet warrior.

A wicked savior.

This terrifying man who was somehow tender. Goodness in his spirit and demons in his soul.

"I know who I am, and I'm not going to lose that there."

Warmth filled his expression, his voice a soft caress. "And I think that might be the best thing about you."

My chest squeezed, and the only thing I could do was give him a shaky nod.

"I need you to treat me like any other server there, and know I'll be okay."

That time he grinned, his gaze raking me, head to toe. "Not possible."

I rolled my eyes. "Like I'm any different than any of those other women."

Like he hadn't propositioned any of them before? Hadn't touched them? Taken them?

I fought the welling of jealousy. The way my eyes wanted to pinch to block out the vision.

I guessed he saw all my thoughts through the silence because he was in my face again, leaning down low and forcing me to meet his eye. "Never. Not once."

My head spun and my insides twisted, and again, I had no idea what to make of this man. How to protect myself from who he was.

I hugged my arms across my chest, more to guard myself from him than the cold wind that whipped through.

Rough fingertips found my arm. They fluttered down, chasing the goosebumps or causing them, I wasn't sure.

"You're cold," he rumbled, glancing at my face before back to the chills as if he were infatuated by the response.

Backing away, I glanced over at my house. "I am, and I really should go inside. I need to get up early."

"Could think of plenty of ways to warm you up." Another smirk. A play and a trap.

Whiplash.

Constant and unending, no way to decipher where I would land with him.

He'd managed to toss my quiet, safe life into chaos in the short time I'd known him, and I was the fool who was a few errant seconds from allowing it to spiral into full anarchy.

Every rule, everything I knew about myself, everything I demanded for myself, lost to the riot.

Because his offer sounded so good.

One night.

One night.

For one night, it would feel so nice not to be alone, that loneliness screaming out to be filled.

I hugged myself tighter and took a step back.

Because I wasn't aching for the sort of comfort that only ran skin deep.

"And you, Mr. Lawson, are the type of *mistake* I can't afford to make." One I would never recover from. "I know who I am, remember?"

His smile was reluctant. "Okay, then, Kitten. Get yourself inside where you belong."

He started to move down my drive, still facing me, hands right back in those pockets like that was the only way he could control them. Then he slowed, his hair billowing in the breeze and that wicked face filling with severity. "Heaven. It'd be Heaven, gettin' you for one minute while on my way to Hell."

I felt the ground shake beneath.

I had no idea how I'd ended up here.

My stable world shaken off path.

Without another word, he spun and strode for his bike.

All big body and towering force and dark allure.

I stood there frozen, watching him as he climbed onto his bike. He balanced the metal, boots planted out to the sides, and he pushed a button that brought the deep, gurgling engine to life.

Moonlight rained down and struck across the sharp, distinct angles of his face.

A devil who'd wormed his way into my life.

He lifted his chin in a gesture toward my door, and I realized he was waiting for me to go inside before he left.

My pulse skittered, and I tore myself from the spot, hurrying up the little walk that ran from the drive to the door. My hand shook like mad as I fumbled to find the right key, my heart in my throat as I turned the lock and let myself into my small home.

Reaching in, I flicked on the light and stepped inside, glancing back at the man who watched me.

Energy flashed.

A shockwave that I could almost see rippling across my yard.

Electric.

I ripped my attention from him and quickly locked the door behind me. I leaned against it, trying to catch my breath, to find my way back to who I was.

Dropping my purse on the couch, I moved to my bedroom, sank down on the side of the bed, and picked up the picture that sat on my nightstand.

Tears instantly stung.

It was one of Aaron and me. His arms were wrapped around me from behind, and that unending *goodness* radiated from his smile.

That hollow place howled, old grief tumbling through.

Deep and aching and unending.

Guilt came, too.

Wanting someone else for the first time, and in a way I never had before. In a way I didn't know existed.

Those tears broke loose.

They streaked down my cheeks, and I lifted my face toward the ceiling.

God, give me wisdom, why did you bring me here? Is it wrong? Is it wrong?

Because I no longer knew what I was supposed to feel.

Chapter Eight

Trent

A TORRENT OF RAIN POURED FROM THE TURBULENT SKY AS Trent fumbled across the lot.
Ground pitted and cracked.
A crater through the middle.
Everything slowed.
Spinning. Spinning. Spinning.
World coming off its hinges.
Confused.
Disoriented.
Wrong.
So wrong.
The eternal lights of Los Angeles gleamed and glinted against the heavens, his sight blurred and bleary as he searched through the smoke.
Desperate.
Frantic.
Trent dropped to his knees at his side.
A sob ripped up his throat, and his hands searched his body, like he

could reach inside and stop it, take it away, keep it for himself the way it was supposed to be.

"No. No. No," trembled from his mouth.

Blood covered Trent's hands, the rain washing it away only for it to soak them again.

Tainting.

Destroying.

Wrong.

So wrong.

"No," Trent choked, pressing down on his wounds. "Please, no."

His hand fisted in Trent's shirt, dragging him close, the words a gurgled rasp at Trent's ear. "One reason. One reason."

Tears streaked Trent's cheeks, burns where the wind lashed at his face. Agony slashed. Cutting him in two.

He slumped down, his soul released, and with it, Trent felt a piece of himself go missing.

He lifted his face to the heavens and screamed.

One reason, one reason, one reason...

I jolted upright in bed, eyes flying open to the darkness that cloaked my room, air screaming in and out of my lungs in long pants and my heart thrashing in old pain.

The physical kind.

The kind you felt when you were always going to be missing something in the middle of yourself, and there was nothing you could do to get it back. It was going to ache and moan and bleed forever.

Truth that I was the one responsible for it in the first place? It boiled like poison in my spirit and coiled my stomach in nausea. In this disease that just kept festering. Rotting and decaying and somehow healing with the gift I'd been granted in the middle of it.

I heaved around the strain—the regret—the shit I could never take back—and I tried to get my bearings.

Rain pelted at the windows and wind howled through the trees. Every single time that shit brought the dream. A fuckin' constant reminder of who I was, of what I'd done, not that I was ever gonna forget.

Exhaling heavily, I roughed a hand through my hair, trying to calm my battering heart, trying to jerk myself out of the past that would forever hold me hostage.

Distance and time didn't matter.

But one thing did.

I tossed my sheets and climbed from my bed, easing out of the room and into the hall. I nudged the door open farther.

Nightlight aglow, his room was cast in stars, a galaxy hanging from the ceiling, his little body tucked under his covers and serenity on his face.

I edged inside, sat on the side of his bed, and brushed the golden hair from his forehead. I pressed a kiss to the skin.

One reason.

That's all I had.

And I needed to remember that was all I was ever gonna need.

Chapter Nine

Trent

Los Angeles, Twenty-Five Years Ago

THE SOFT, SOFT VOICE PULLED HIM FROM SLEEP WHERE Trent was tucked in his bed. Their mommy sang her favorite song she liked to sing, *Amazing Grace*, her voice the prettiest voice in the whole wide world.

It touched his ears and whispered across his heart.

He felt light and heavy, his chest achy when his mommy sang like that.

He eased out from under the covers, sitting up so he could see where his mommy knelt beside the bed on the other side of the room. His whole body felt itchy as he stood up and shuffled across the carpet to where Nathan was asleep.

Her fingers brushed through Nathan's hair as she kept singing those words like they would make everything better.

"Is Nafan sick again, Mommy?" he whispered, hatin' when his mommy got sad, hatin' more when his twin brother didn't want to get out of bed to play some days.

She shifted her attention toward him, the smile on her face making his chest expand again. He loved when she looked at him like that. Like he was so, so special.

"He had a little bit of an asthma attack when we were playing out back earlier. That's all. He'll be just fine."

His brother wheezed and coughed, and Trent eased in closer, worry filling him up, his heart doing that achy thing again. "You sure, Mommy? You want me to call the doctor?"

"Ah, my little protector, come on over here and see for yourself."

Trent kept edging closer, peering down at his twin brother who was asleep. He was smaller than him by just a little. Other than that, they looked almost exactly the same. Their other brother, Jud, slept in the room right next to them, and everyone always made their mommy laugh when they asked if they were triplets.

But Jud was a year younger. Four and not five like Trent and Nathan. Except Trent was older by fifteen whole minutes, which meant he had to be the protector of 'em all.

"See, he's just fine. Just like the rest of us are going to be."

She reached over and set her hand on his cheek.

Trent's chest felt so full.

"I'm the man now, right, Mommy?"

"That's right."

She pushed to standing, grunting as she straightened, her big, big belly poking out in front of her like a basketball.

Trent knew that was where his new baby brother was hiding until he was big enough to come out to play.

His mommy leaned over and brushed kisses to his brother's forehead before she was wrapping her hand in Trent's.

She squeezed it. "My big boy. Let's get you back to bed."

He followed her to his bed, and she pulled down his covers and tucked him in. Trent snuggled down into the warmth. The warmth of the blankets. The warmth of her green eyes.

Oh, he loved his mommy's pretty eyes. The way they shined when she looked at him.

She leaned down and kissed him on the nose. "Such a kind

protector," she whispered, the edge of her mouth tilting up. "My sweet little warrior."

"I'll always save you," he promised, grinning wide.

"I know it. And your brothers, too," she teased, tickling him under his chin.

He giggled. "Of course, Mommy. You got nothin' to worry about."

"You get some rest now." She pushed to standing, moaning all over again as she wobbled out the door. Trent sank into the comfort. The quiet. Until the rumble started to vibrate the floor and the sound of the loud motor shook the walls.

Fear clamped down on his heart, and he hugged the blanket tight, prayed for it to go away. For him to stay away.

But the sound got closer before it stopped and the back door in the kitchen banged open.

Trent squeezed his eyes shut like he could hide from it. From what was coming.

Because his daddy?

He was a bad, bad man, and he didn't like it one bit when he came around.

Chapter Ten

Eden

Do you remember…

> *Do you remember when we were little?*
> *How we'd spend our days out playing in the backyard? Barefoot in the grass? The sun on our faces and hope in our hearts? We'd dance and dance. Make up our own ballets for Mom and Dad to watch. Momma would clap and Daddy would pick us bouquets from Momma's flower bed. They'd promise we were the best dancers in the world, and he'd take both of us into his arms, tell us he was the luckiest daddy alive to have two daughters like us.*
> *Do you remember how he'd take Momma's hand and pull her out onto the lawn to dance?*
> *He'd hug her tight beneath the summer sky, and we'd skip circles around them. We'd laugh and we'd dream, and we all knew life was going to be amazing, just as long as we had each other.*
> *Do you remember when we were still a family?*
> *Do you remember when I was your best friend?*
> *I remember. And I wish I could go back.*
>
> *Harmony*

Anguish crushed and beat and slayed. I felt them like physical blows as a gentle breeze flittered through the branches of the trees that surrounded my backyard.

I'd sunk to the porch steps when I'd been sifting through my mail and found a letter from my sister hidden in the stack. Unable to remain standing while I'd ripped into the blue envelope.

There'd been no return address, but it had been postmarked in Washington.

What was this? An apology? An explanation?

Tears blurred my eyes as I clutched the letter to my chest. I inhaled deeply and looked up to the same blue summer sky my sister had been talking about. I wanted to reach into the letter and go back to those days. To remember the way she was begging me to do.

God. I felt almost desperate to see her face, to know she was okay, to ask her why.

All while struggling with so much anger, I didn't know how to process it.

Her desertion.

Her betrayal.

The lies she'd cast.

I didn't understand and I wanted to.

But I doubted very much there was a way to get there. No way to undo all the wrongs that'd bound our lives. The trust that had been so brittle years before had been completely shattered after she'd come back three months ago.

She told us she'd changed, that she'd wanted to make amends. Then she'd turned around and delivered the harshest blow—she'd stolen everything we had then disappeared again.

I peeled the letter from my chest and looked at the handwriting that was so familiar.

Hating that I missed her so badly.

Hating that I loved her so much.

Hating that I hated her for who she'd become.

Because I did...I remembered when she was good. And I'd do anything to go back there, too. To change it before she'd spiraled.

I jolted when I heard a car slowing out front and the crunch of tires in the gravel drive. I swiped the moisture from my cheek and stood. I folded the letter and stuffed it into my pocket before I moved around the small yard and to the side gate. It opened to the single carport, and I saw that my daddy's Honda was parked behind my car.

The door opened just as I stepped through the gate.

He stood.

My chest squeezed at the sight of him.

So handsome at his 57-years, his once brown hair now gray. His history—the joys, the sorrows, the achievements, the tragedies— were written in the deep-set lines that were carved into his kind face.

I wouldn't so much as call him rugged, his soul quiet, his demeanor unthreatening, though there was something powerful about him, too.

He was my savior. My rock. Strong and capable. But my spirit also recognized his. How he'd been broken down by the losses he'd been dealt.

"Hey, Daddy. What are you doing here?" I latched the gate behind me.

He smiled, so soft, the corners of his eyes creasing as he looked at me with the same warmth he'd watched me with my whole life. "Just came to see my best girl."

We both ignored the sting of what he'd said, and I swore, that letter I'd hidden in my pocket felt like it just might catch fire.

"You did, huh? You just saw me yesterday," I teased. I moved his way and welcomed the feel of his arms as he wrapped them around me.

Tight.

Ripe with affection.

Pulling back, he held me by the outside of the arms. "That was work and it doesn't count…besides, I feel like I haven't talked to you in ages. I've missed you."

Okay, so maybe I'd been avoiding him a bit.

It was better to hide rather than to face the questions that would inevitably come.

No, I wasn't ashamed of working at that club. But my daddy? He would instantly go into protector mode. He would tell me it wasn't my concern. Say I didn't need to worry. Claim it was his burden to bear. That it was insane for me to get another job even when I'd promised him that I was working on trying to find a solution.

But when he found out where I was actually working? He'd go nuts. Worry himself sick. Be concerned I'd be in harm's way.

So far outside of my element. Of where my devotion lay.

Of where I belonged.

"Do you want to come inside and have some tea?"

"That'd be really nice."

We moved up the front walk, and he followed me into my little house that I loved. It wasn't much, but it was a safe haven.

Peaceful.

Quiet.

My heart ached a little when I admitted it was lonely, too. Sometimes the peace that radiated from the walls echoed with sadness. With a hollowness that reflected the hole burned through the middle of me.

We entered into the small living room stuffed with a cozy couch and a ton of pillows and a slew of pictures of my momma and daddy. Some of my students. Tessa and me, too.

There was a hall at the far end that led to the two bedrooms to the right.

On the left was an arch that dipped into the old kitchen. There was a nook with a small round table surrounded by four chairs, but my favorite part was the sunporch to the very back.

I made us each a cup of Earl Grey and eased out onto the screened porch that could have been mistaken for a greenhouse with the number of plants and shrubs I grew in there.

My daddy was already sitting on a rocker that overlooked the forest that hedged my backyard.

"Here you go, Daddy."

"Thank you, sweetheart."

I sat in the rocker next to him, sighing, letting go of the strain, the questions, and fell into the comfort.

I guessed I really did like the simple things.

Trent's face flashed through my mind. Contrary to everything I'd ever imagined for my life. And still, I couldn't shake it—this feeling that I wanted something I shouldn't. Every night that I slipped into his club and pretended like he didn't affect me made me want him that much more. Every day he picked up his son intensified the ache. Each time he looked at me like he was feeling exactly the same made me light up.

A fire burning bright where everything had gone dim.

But I knew better…knew he was everything that would scar me in the end.

I shook it off and turned my focus on my daddy since I could feel him peering my way.

"How are you, Eden?" he asked. Genuine and true.

"I'm fine," I peeped, not so honest.

The creases deepened at the corner of his eyes. Slashes of concern. "You've seemed…distant lately. Tired."

I took a sip of the steaming tea and fumbled through what to say. "I'm sorry. I've just…been worried. Wondering how we're going to make it through this mess."

He blew out a strained sigh. "The last thing I want is for you to worry about it, Eden. I'm going to figure it out. You just need to take care of your students, take care of you."

I gazed across at him. "And who's going to look out for you?"

He exhaled, devotion in the heavy sound. "You're not supposed to take care of me, Eden. It's the other way around."

I reached out and touched his hand. "Aren't we supposed to take care of each other? I told you I was going to help. That I'm trying to find solutions, too. You can't ask me to ignore this."

Sadness filled his expression. "You've already been through enough."

My head shook as sorrow swam. "We both have, Daddy."

My daddy swallowed, his throat bobbing as he gazed at me.

"How'd we end up here? I never imagined it, Eden...the two of us alone."

I could feel the loss of my momma radiating from him on a torrent of despair. Could feel his grief for me.

Losing Aaron had devastated me. Left a crater that throbbed. But my daddy's? My daddy's was a chasm. An abyss. Bottomless and forever.

I'd thought mine was...

Guilt streaked. Clawing through my consciousness and cleaving through my spirit when a dark, destructive face flashed through my mind.

"I'm sorry that you lost Momma. That you lost Harmony after. Hate that you're hurting so badly now."

When Momma had died, Harmony had lost herself. I'd watched her tumble. Spiral. Lose hope.

The letter felt like ten-thousand pounds in my pocket. Sucking me down. Because I remembered before...before we'd lost it all.

"That's what makes this so hard...fighting for the little we have left when I'd gladly trade it all for your sister if I were given the choice," he admitted.

"Daddy." It was a plea.

He squeezed my hand. "It's true. I love those kids, I love the church, I love it all." He gulped and his eyes swam with his truth. "But to have her back...I'd sacrifice anything for my family, Eden."

Overwhelming love squeezed every cell in my body. This was exactly why I'd do anything for my father. Give it up. Sacrifice. Because of what he was willing to sacrifice for the rest of us. "I'm still digging into some things, Daddy. Trying to find a way to stave off the creditors."

The shake of his head was grim. "I'm not sure we can support another loan, Eden."

I swallowed down the confession, the way the words wanted to rise up and get free. "Just...give me a little time."

"I need you not to worry, Eden. I'll figure it out. Things always have a way of working themselves out. I have faith in that. That we're not alone in the middle of it. I don't want you to walk around with these burdens…I want you to live."

"And I want that for you, too."

His fingers threaded through mine. "The students are my joy, Eden. Our congregation. Helping those who walk through the doors. But the one thing I want? The one thing I pray I get to see before I die? That is to see you happy. Truly happy." He reached up and brushed his thumb under my eye. "Without the sadness I see right here. One day, the one thing I want, is to see it go away. I want to see everything you're missing fulfilled. Given to you a million times over."

"Daddy." Emotion warbled through the word.

Misery tried to seep out from that wound. To crawl out and stake a claim.

"Someday, your heart will break free." He chuckled low, his words turning to a dreamy wisp. "It'll get stolen, more like it. Some man is going to storm into your life when you least expect it, and he's going to steal this amazing, beautiful heart. You might not think yourself capable, but you'll love again."

For the first time in years, I believed it. Believed I could love again.

And I wanted it in return.

To be loved.

Held.

I wanted a family to call my own.

But what I was terrified of was the *storming* part.

Terrified of the one who'd captured me in a way I shouldn't allow him to.

I smothered the feeling, the need, the fear, and I forced a smile. "Don't worry, Daddy. I will. We both will. Heck, I bet you'll find someone before me."

He fumbled out a laugh. "I don't think so, sweetheart. I think I'd prefer to live in the memories."

But sometimes it was the memories that hurt us most.

Chapter Eleven

Trent

Fucking Juna Lamb.

I glanced at the clock on the dash again. She was forty minutes late, which meant I was going to be even later to pick up Gage.

Was she really going to pull this bullshit on me?

My eyes scanned the visible part of the obscured path. It led to a meadow hidden in the dense forest just off the road where I waited about an hour outside our mountain city.

Place we always met.

Secure and unseen.

Didn't matter. Anxiety gripped me in a vise, ribs clamping around my heart that was a thunder of disorder and old rage.

Thing was, it wasn't all that old, either. It was the kind that grew. Amplified and blistered. The kind that would never abate.

The dread. The worry.

The grief and the guilt.

The stark, unrelenting hatred I held for this woman.

Most of all, the devotion I had to my son.

All of it roiled and thrashed and overflowed.

Crashing over me.

Wave after wave.

Knew she couldn't be trusted, but what the fuck else was I to do?

I met her here once a year, and every single time, I was on edge, wondering when it was gonna be the time she fucked me. When she betrayed me all over again. Pulled the motherfucking trigger.

And still, I somehow thought I owed her a debt. Came here year after year because there was one reason I was living my life, so I buried the rage and the animosity and did what I had to do to protect it.

Knew full well it was a precarious line I was treading.

Blowing out a sigh, I grabbed my phone, checking for a message or missed call.

Nothing.

Shit.

I sat there contemplating for a beat before I gave in, decided to ask for help because the last thing I wanted was to leave my kid waiting. Make him think I'd forgotten about him. Like he would ever in a million years slip my mind.

I tapped out a message to Eden, praying she'd get it, understand, praying harder that she wouldn't ask any questions.

> **Me:** Eden, hate to ask, but I got sprung with something messy. Can you cover Gage for 40? I'll owe you big.

I was unable to stop the way my heart stuttered with thinking about her.

Seemed there was no chance of her slipping from my mind, either.

The girl's face twisted through on a constant invasion that I couldn't outwit or outrun.

I would have thought my reaction to her would have faded with time, but thoughts of her seemed to be coming on stronger with each day that passed. With each night she moved around my bar, possessing the air and fucking with my sanity.

More than two weeks had gone by since I'd followed her to her house and had spouted a bunch of shit I shouldn't have.

A clear proposition.

Truth was, after that fucker had touched her, only thing I could process was the overwhelming need to gather her up and make sure she was whole.

Preferably without her clothes covering that tempting, delicious body.

I'd been half mad with the desire to drag her into her house.

Touch her and taste her and take her.

Problem was? It'd gotten clear really fast that need was more than just wanting to get lost in her tight body.

Knew there was a real problem when I wanted to start making her promises I had no business making.

Tell her I would never let anyone harm her. Tell her I'd fight whatever war she was fighting. Fix whatever in her life had gone bad, patch it back together because I'd come to crave those sweet, innocent smiles.

I wanted to dig around inside her to find why those eyes would dim, then set to work at filling whatever had gone missing.

The way I got the sense she might be able to fill a little of what had gone missing in me, too.

Stupid.

I had one reason.

One reason.

I couldn't risk getting distracted. Couldn't risk another heart. Another life.

My chest tightened in that spiky dread when I saw the flickers of red coming through the trees, and I tossed my phone to the opposite seat as Juna pulled into the grassy field.

The air thinned and my spirit groaned.

Hatred. Hatred.

Distrust and this debt and a thousand fucked up things in between.

I was quick to climb out of my car, standing behind my open door with my gun burning a hole where it was holstered at my side.

She came to a stop, staring at me through the windshield, her brown hair twisted in a knot on her head and falling around her face as she clutched the steering wheel in her own fear and agitation.

She was stunning. Not a fuckin' lie.

But she curled every cell in my body in revulsion.

Finally, she killed her engine, warily clicked open her door, and stood.

"Juna," I said through gritted teeth.

Her mouth trembled, and she gave me a timid smile. "Hi."

My head shook in a fierce gush of disbelief. "Don't hi me. We both know why you're here and what you want. No reason for pleasantries."

She blanched. "Trent…I—"

I shook my head again. "No bullshit, Juna." I ducked back into my car and grabbed the duffle bag. I tossed it at her from across the space.

She caught it with a thud, her arms curled around the fabric and hugging all that money to her chest.

"You got what you came for, now go."

Her expression twisted like I'd slapped her across the face. "That's not true."

"No? It was always about the money. Don't deny it."

"I never meant for it to happen."

A blistering scoff left my mouth, and I had to curl my hands around the top of my car door to keep from crossing the space and choking her out. "You did. You set the whole fuckin' thing up. You just got cold feet."

Didn't want my blood on her hands, so she'd left me with my brother's on mine, instead.

My fault, too.

Wasn't like I'd wanted her. Only thing I'd wanted was revenge on an enemy, and the girl had been an easy target.

She looked into the distance, her chin quivering before she tentatively looked back at me. "How is Gage?"

My chest tightened, throat closing off, and my hands were cinching down tighter.

"Safe." That's all she got from me. Only thing she deserved. One thing in this deal she'd given.

Gage.

She chewed at her bottom lip before she whispered, "That makes me happy."

My insides twisted in a thousand knots, that hatred and a flash of gratitude making me feel like I might lose my mind, and she dropped her shoulders and started to climb back into her car.

Guess it was the panic, that paranoia that had been hunting me for the last few months that had the words shootin' from my mouth. "Anyone have a clue where you are?"

Juna looked up at me with surprise riding her expression before she frowned and her brows drew tight. "No. You know I'd never go back there."

My nod was clipped. "Good. Keep it that way."

She didn't say anything else before she ducked into her car, though she watched me with some kind of sadness as she started it, backed up, and whipped around so she could drive back down the bumpy lane.

I watched her go.

On guard.

Always on guard because I didn't trust a damned soul.

Not when the ones I'd cared about most had betrayed me.

Betrayed *us*.

Slayed when they should have protected.

But that's what happened when you lived the kind of lives we'd lived.

When we'd been brought up in depravity and wickedness.

Only exception were my brothers. Gage.

Knew better than letting anyone else into that fold.

I sat there for another ten after she left just to make sure I was in the clear before I grabbed my phone and saw that the message that I'd sent to Eden had still been left unread.

Agitation stirring, I glanced at the clock. School was already out.

"Shit," I mumbled as I dialed her number and hoped she'd answer.

It rang before that sweet, sultry voice came on the line. "This is Eden, I'll get back to you when I can."

I hit the road and gunned it, hating that I had the sick urge to *trust* her with this. I had to stop the truth from sliding out and give her another fuckin' lie to bury the mound of others.

"Eden, hey, I'm on my way but had an issue at the bar. Really sorry. Will be there soon."

I took the curvy, winding mountain road at top speed. Engine flying, but it was my anxiety that was soaring.

This unsettled feeling taking hold, way it did every year right about this time, but I guessed that was something I would be battling for the rest of my life.

I made the hour-long trip in forty-five minutes, barely slowing as I made it to the edge of the tiny city where the dense hedge of trees thinned, and the trendy shops and restaurants tucked underneath the short office buildings and apartments came into view.

My eyes kept darting for the clock on the dash as I sped through town. I beat a path in the direction of the small private school that sat smack dab in the middle of it, really fucking late and still not a word from Eden.

My hands curled tight around the steering wheel. I was doing my best to get the bitterness under control, the regret and the shame, before I got to my kid. Last thing he needed was to see me like this.

The ghosts writhing beneath my skin.

Teeth gritting around the bullshit that bitch always tried to cram down my throat.

No question in my mind that Juna Lamb's favorite game was manipulating me. Hell, I bet she got off on it. Knowing she had me by the balls and all she had to do was squeeze. One year she'd show up making demands, threatening, next sweet as pie and full of feigned regret.

But Gage was worth it.

One love.

One loyalty.

One *reason*.

All I had to do was keep throwing cash at that bloodsucker to keep her out of our lives and pray to God she didn't bleed me dry.

That I could believe her now after she'd committed the ultimate disloyalty.

Tires squealed as I took a right onto Oak View. Gunning it, I came up fast on the entrance to the school. I downshifted, barely slowing as I skidded into the student pick-up circle.

Circle that was completely empty considering how late I was.

School had been over for almost an hour.

Fuck.

My guts clenched when Eden jerked her attention from where she was out on the playground by the slide, she and Gage its lone occupants. Rest of the children were long gone.

Hell, half the staff parking lot was vacant, too.

Even from the confines of my car, I could feel it.

The crash of energy.

Confusion and need.

But it was different this afternoon. The air was hot with anger.

She and I had been tiptoeing since the night I'd followed her home. Skirting each other, our interactions nothing but restraint and civility after our boundaries had been set in stone.

I was her boss at the bar, and she was my son's teacher here at the school, and it ended at that.

Except that was a farse, wasn't it? With the way those autumn eyes flared and flashed. Way that golden color sparked beneath the glittering rays of sunlight that burned through the sky, lighting her up in a fiery show of disappointment.

Protectiveness bled out as she straightened herself in front of my son.

Yeah, I was a twisted fuck because my dick went hard at the sight.

Thirsting for something sweet.

For something innocent.

Something far too good.

The monster who wanted to dirty it. Dirty her. Delve into the sanctuary of who she was.

Get a taste of the light when my entire life had been lived in the shadows.

Her jaw was clenched.

Her demeanor stone.

The tires squealed to a stop, and I jerked the car into neutral and jammed at the button for the brake. I was out in a second flat, doing my best to quiet the disturbance rattling my ribs.

The way I was struck with two different emotions at once.

Disenchantment and a straight up thrill.

Gage whirled around at the sound of my approach, that golden hair bouncing around his cherub face, kid the perfect mix of Juna and me.

Only good thing either of us had ever created.

He looked at me with this huge-ass smile on his face that cut right through the middle of my spirit.

One reason.

One reason.

He pointed my way. "See, there he is. Told you, Miss Murphy, told you he was gonna come and we didn't have nothin' to worry about. My dad is the best." He started jumping, waving his hand in the air like I didn't notice him standing there. "Hey, Dad! Over here, Dad. Where ya been? Miss Murphy thought you mighta forgot me, but I told her never, no way. Not my dad. Right, Dad, right?"

He grabbed her hand and started to haul her my direction as my boots ate up the ground in a desperate bid to make it to the gate as fast as I could.

Fuck the signs posted every two feet.

Wasn't anyone around, anyway.

Eden glowered at me. Fucking gorgeous, sweet Eden who was watching me like I was the devil.

She wouldn't be wrong.

Fire and disgust flooded from her spirit.

Made me a damned fool that in spite of it, I couldn't help but drink her in. Her body and that face and those eyes. I'd gladly drown in her wrath if it meant getting washed in who she was.

One time.

One time, I wanted to make her mine.

Take what couldn't be.

She wore a modest sundress, this creamy soft thing with a touch of lace at the neckline, fabric swishing just below the knees. Still did crazy-ass things to me.

Eden tightened her hold on Gage's hand and lifted that chin in a clear warning.

That did crazy-ass things to me, too. A little rage and a lotta awe, my fiery little Kitten going to bat for one of her kids.

My kid.

And I got that fucked up sense again—one that I was looking on something that was right. Something that was *good*.

I shook that bullshit off because you didn't get *good* when you had no good to give.

"Dad, guess what?" Gage shouted as he pranced my way.

"What is it, buddy?" I asked, though most of my attention was locked on the woman who looked like she wanted to punch me in the throat.

We were all standing at the fence by that time, staring at each other through the wrought iron rods keeping us apart.

"We had pigs in a blanket for lunch. You know what's that? That's the tiniest little hot dogs you ever seen." He giggled it while

clutching to Eden's hand. "And they have bread for blankets! See…
pigs in a blanket."

He cracked up like it was the funniest thing he'd ever heard.

My chest tightened, and I glanced his way, love pouring out,
that flood way more fuckin' powerful than the deluge of anger
Eden Murphy had flowing on me.

"No way," I exuded through the clusterfuck of emotions.

"Yes way!" Gage grinned. All dimples and tiny teeth. "They
were deeees-licious. And that's with a capital D. You think we can
have some at our house for dinner? Is it okay if I be the chef, Dad?
I'll make 'em so good."

"We'll see what we can do, buddy."

The whole time, Eden itched at his side.

"See, Miss Murphy. My dad's the best dad in the whole world."
He was gazing up at her with that expression on his face. One of
sheer belief. Affection took the place of her anger as she looked
down at him before she turned her attention back to me.

Autumn eyes narrowed in hostility and some kind of hurt I
couldn't pinpoint.

Something haunted. I was the idiot who wanted to touch her
face. Ask her what it meant. Beg her to get it. To understand the
lengths I had to go. The position I was in. But I couldn't let anyone
go there. I was a fool for even thinking it.

I reached up for the latch on the gate.

Eden huffed and muttered, "Typical," under her breath.

"What's your problem?" I hissed even lower, tripping on the
mess of emotions that threatened to knock me from my feet.

"What's my problem?" She gritted her teeth. "I think that
should be obvious."

"Gage, why don't you show me how you can go down the
slide?" I suggested through the affliction.

"Really?"

"Yup, do it fast."

He untangled his hand from Eden, and my boy was making

a beeline back toward the playground, shouting the whole time, "Watch this, watch this!"

"Watching," I hollered as I flicked the latch and pushed through. Eden stumbled back, a surprised sound coming from her mouth.

"What's your problem, Miss Murphy?" I demanded again, a knife twisting through my chest, eyes flicking between her and the kid because I wasn't going to miss him going down the slide. "Just say it."

"You're more than an hour late." The words shook.

"Didn't notice." Sarcasm dripped from my voice.

Yeah. Couldn't help but get pissed, too. That she was over there making assumptions and she didn't have the first clue.

She scoffed out a broken sound. "That...that exactly right there," she begged below her breath. "That little boy was sitting over there by himself waiting for you...watching every other kid get picked up on time because their parents actually make them their priority. I had to drag him over to the playground to keep him distracted while you were off doing God knows what."

Was she serious?

I was in her face. Towering over her. Rage snapping my teeth.

Fear and uncertainty stuttered her chest, and her gaze was darting all over my face, like she was looking for who I was. For a worthy explanation. For a reason to *trust* me.

"You don't have a fuckin' clue, Miss Murphy." It was all I could give her and that sucked, too.

Gage shouted, "Here I go!"

Eden stepped back, her arms crossed over her chest as she stood there and warred. The two of us watched him hop into position and use the handles for leverage to propel himself faster. He threw his hands in the air and laughed hysterically the whole way down. He toppled off into the dirt at the bottom, and the second he hit it, he hopped up and had his arms thrown above his head. "Touch down! How was that, Dad? Did you like it? Did you see how fast I went?"

"Perfect ten," I bellowed, trying to keep the anger out of my voice, but it was back full force when I looked at his teacher.

My employee.

At this woman who had me in motherfuckin' knots.

"You have no idea what I do for that kid."

Eden shifted on her feet, her chin quivering. Sadness streaked through those eyes. She tried to hide it by dropping her gaze to the ground, but I saw the moisture rise to the surface.

My chest tightened.

How had she gained the power for that single look to destroy me?

"You should have been here," she whispered on an exhale. "We were—" She clipped off whatever she was going to say, her lips hard when she forced, "He was worried."

In longing, she looked at my son.

"Yeah, I should have been, but it wasn't because I don't care. Wasn't because I simply lost track of time." I angled in closer, letting the words grate from my tongue. Or maybe it was just my defenses sliding out. "Wasn't like I was gettin' my cock sucked by one of my *whores* or doing *God knows what.*"

An earthquake rocked me.

I couldn't stop this feeling that was taking me over.

She didn't understand and I fuckin' wanted her to.

Fuck. I wanted her to.

Her throat tremored when she swallowed. "I didn't say that."

I moved on her, coming closer, swallowing up her breaths and sucking down her aura. My mouth moved close to her ear. "No, but that's what you were thinking, wasn't it? That I'm a shitty dad?"

"No." She blinked, and she angled so she could barely see my face. "Trent…I—"

Eden was cut off when Gage came skipping our way, singing *The Wheels on the Bus* that he'd been driving me out of my damned mind with for the last week, but because I loved the kid so much, I typically just sang along.

She jumped back when she realized how close we were. That energy rushing and whirring and winding us tight.

Magnetic.

Neither of us knew how to stay away when it was clear that was exactly what we had to do.

I looked back at her. "I'm sorry I was late. I texted. I called. Left a message on your cell letting you know. It was out of my hands. Next time, I'll be sure to call one of my brothers from work so I don't put you out."

I wasn't about to lose my son over some closing bell, and that was just the way it was when Juna Lamb was in control. But if it was gonna cause this kind of reaction in Eden, someone I'd been fool enough to think I could rely on with a bit of this bullshit, then I'd figure something else out.

"You ready, Dad?" Gage swiped up his backpack from where it rested against the fence, swung it on, and took my hand.

Little fingers curled around mine.

The anxiety that'd been racing the entire day eased just a bit.

I gave him a gentle squeeze. "Yeah, buddy, I am."

I started to turn and walk but swung back around to meet Eden Murphy's eyes. "Think what you want, Kitten…but I would claw my way through Hell to get to my kid."

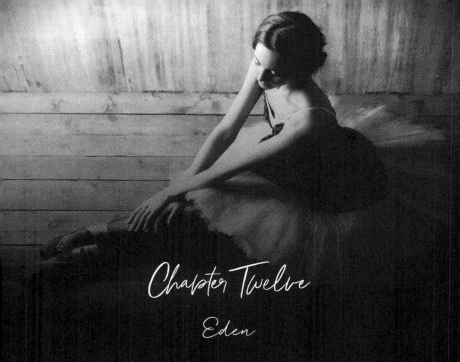

Chapter Twelve

Eden

I STOOD ROOTED BY THE GATE, HUGGING MY ARMS OVER MY chest with my eyes locked on the two of them moving to Trent's car. Gage had his hand wrapped in his father's, prattling away as he skipped at his side.

While a war waged within me.

God, my heart was nothing but a mottled, bleeding mess.

The barely healed over scars were trying their best to rip open wide.

There was a huge piece of me that wanted to chase after them like they were where I belonged.

All while old memories raged against it.

Waiting and waiting and waiting. The sky turning from blue to pink to gray before a Sheriff had pulled into the lot.

Gage climbed into the backseat and into his booster. His sweet voice was still a chatter that drifted on the warm air, even though I couldn't make out what he was saying.

Trent leaned his towering, dark frame over his son, wisped a kiss to the child's forehead.

The man was so tender and so rough that my knees wobbled where I tried to stand firm.

It was a vain attempt with the shockwave of intensity that ripped through the space when the man straightened and moved around the front of his flashy car, slaying me with a look that was a cross between anger and an apology.

His back against a wall.

I knew it.

Could feel it. His desperation in the way he'd flown into the lot, as if he'd been trying to outrun a ghost that had been chasing him down.

His eyes wild and his spirit frantic.

And I guessed I'd been trying to dodge a ghost of my own. Standing in this spot and waiting for someone I cared about to show and terrified they wouldn't.

Care.

The realization punched me in the stomach.

I did.

I cared. So much and too fast, and I knew I was nothing but a fool for allowing myself to feel it.

So what had I done?

I'd let my own anger and confusion tear him down.

Accusations I shouldn't have cast.

But I was having a harder and harder time making any sense of what I was feeling.

The outright protectiveness over a child that had long since crossed over the line of prudent. Beyond a student/teacher relationship.

How I felt tied up and bound to his father.

His father who stared at me from where he whipped open his car door, the man so tall and ominous and intimidating.

But those fierce eyes were filled with something I'd never witnessed before—hurt.

Hurt disguised as rage.

I'd hurt him with my assumptions because his protectiveness was wrapped up in his son, too.

Regret clamped down on my heart, and I hugged myself tighter as Trent slipped into the driver's side and started the car. The engine was loud and powerful and filling the quiet with the chaos that he was.

Those wicked eyes watched me through the glass, glinting daggers that destroyed and decimated.

Regret slipped down my spine like a block of ice.

Cold.

I had to force myself to stand still. Force myself to remain in the spot instead of rushing out to beg him to stop so I could try to explain.

Explain I was believing too much. Seeing too much. Wanting too much.

That I was scared.

That I was broken.

That I was terrified he might be the only one who might be able to heal some of that.

God. I was terrified of it all. That it was wrong. A sin. That I was asking for the pain a man like Trent Lawson would bring.

His tires squealed as he jerked from the curb, like he needed to get away from me as desperately as I needed to get away from him.

Because I could feel myself stumbling in a direction I shouldn't.

Dangerously close to tumbling over an edge and into an abyss that I knew nothing about. No idea of what I would find there. No idea what awaited at the bottom.

Hope or heartache.

And if it was the latter? I wasn't sure I would survive that kind of fall. I had no solid piece remaining that could withstand that sort of breaking. I swore, I was barely holding it together as it was, these healing fractures more fragile than I wanted to admit.

There was no looking away when the car whipped out onto the street and accelerated. The white car disappeared long before the sound of the engine did, so I found myself standing there staring into the nothingness where they had been for far too long.

Long enough that I jolted like a lunatic when a voice suddenly shouted, "Boo," close to my ear.

My heart leapt out of my chest, and I whirled around with my arms flailing.

Tessa, my so-called best friend, cracked up, bent in two and holding her stomach. "Oh my god, you are too easy, Eden Jasmine."

I shook myself off, straightening my dress and the mess of emotions jumbled inside. "Ha, ha, ha, you're hysterical." I rolled my eyes at her.

She laughed harder. "You jumped like five feet in the air."

"I did not."

"Um...yes...you did, you know, since you were standing out here staring after your boss's car for fifteen straight minutes after it disappeared, mouth watering like someone was dangling a piece of chocolate obsession cake in front of you and you couldn't quite reach it. You were all grabby hands."

Her hands grasped for thin air.

I grumbled a sound of denial. "I was just making sure my student got safely on his way home."

Disbelief shot from her mouth. "Are you really gonna stand there and try to pull that off? Act like your belly isn't growling for a little of that *cake?*"

"He's a man, not food."

She jostled her shoulder into mine. "So, you're saying you want him."

"I didn't say that at all."

"You don't need to when it's written all over you. Your eyes are hungry, Eden. Real hungry. Like crazy hungry. Ravenous. Clearly, you've gone without for far too long. I'm actually concerned you might devour that poor boy."

It was an all-out tease.

I scowled at her. She was worried for him? Had she seen him? No doubt, it was me who was in danger.

Her smile softened, her gaze taking me in, expression turning knowing. "You like him," she prodded gently.

My lips pursed in a thin line, not sure how to respond.

"There's no shame in that, Eden."

A frown pinched my brow. "Isn't there?"

I didn't know why I thought it prudent to ask. What answer I wanted. I wasn't even sure there was a correct one.

Tessa scoffed. "Um...half the population would be guilty if it were a sin. The man is stupid hot."

I cringed.

With a wry grin, she nudged me again. "But you want him for more than all that delicious cake."

I did my best to hold back my amusement, and my teeth clamped down on my bottom lip. "I have no idea what I want," I admitted.

The teasing drained from my best friend's face. "I think you do, Eden. I think you're just afraid to reach out and take it."

Emotion clogged my chest, and I had to look away, into the distance. I inhaled a cleansing breath and tried to keep the tears from brimming to my eyes.

A tender hand wrapped around my wrist, dragging me back to the here and now and out of the past that seemed as if it would never let me go. I swiveled my gaze to Tessa. To my best friend who'd been there for me forever. Through my joys and my sorrows.

"What if it hurts?" I wheezed the question, unable to hold back the heaviness of it. "What if I take a chance, and he doesn't take one on me?"

What if he didn't feel the same? What if he wasn't spun up right then, wondering what it would feel like to give in?

What if he was as horrible as he claimed and destroyed me in the end?

Tessa's lips tipped in affection, and she reached out and played with a lock of my hair that whipped in the gentle breeze, her voice as soft as the whisper of the wind. "And what if you don't try, Eden? What if you never let yourself feel again? What if you spend the rest of your life guarding yourself from experiencing what you want, what you need, because you're afraid, and you miss out on all the things waiting for you to take hold of them? What if you keep this beautiful heart from the rest of the world? What if you don't take a chance? What then?"

My throat burned with it. With sorrow. With hope. "He and I are..."

"Opposites?" She grinned. "All wrong? He's everything you shouldn't want?"

I jerked an agreement. "I don't even know him."

And I had a feeling the list she'd checked off went much deeper than that.

That he was dangerous.

That there was a real part of him that was bad. Wicked. Unjust.

That his life was at odds with everything I wanted for mine.

All except for the way he was with that little boy. Except for the way he made me feel. The way he made me believe in something he kept insisting wasn't there.

"Don't let anyone tell you who you should love or what you should want, Eden. You get to decide that, and don't you dare forget it. He may or may not be the one..."

She gestured her chin in the direction of the empty street before she flitted her eyes back to take me in. When she did, the blue was overflowing with emotion. "But you won't know that until you try. Until you open yourself up. Until you go after what you want."

I chuckled out a soggy sound. "That's the problem...I don't know what I want."

"Liar," she razzed, grin playing across her whole face. She leaned toward me and mock-whispered, "You want cake."

I choked over a shock of laughter. "You're ridiculous."

Tessa tugged at my hand, walking backward as she started to haul me back toward the school. "You wouldn't want me any other way. Now come on, your daddy asked if I'd seen you...he wants to talk to you."

Crap.

It'd been more than a week since he'd come to my house saying he missed me. When he'd begged me to let him take on the burden. It'd been two days since I'd completely ignored that and taken all the cash I'd earned and put it against the outstanding debts.

Oh, was he going to have questions.

I had the urge to jump in my car and go hide under my covers. Maybe come down with a sudden, severe flu.

Tessa threaded our fingers together and pulled me up to her side as she swiveled around. Swinging our hands between us as she started to lead me back toward the offices in the main area of the school, she leaned in and murmured, "But I'm not letting you leave until you admit it...tell me you want cake."

She was relentless.

Redness streaked to my cheeks, and I barely peeked her way, letting the confession slip from my tongue. "Okay. Fine. I might want a tiny taste."

She gasped and slammed a hand over her heart. "You hooker."

Playfully, I shoved her. "You jerk."

She laughed like crazy until she sobered and took my hand again, pulling me close to her side. "I love you, Eden. I just want you to live again. Larger and freer than you did before. For your heart. For your happiness."

I nestled my head on her shoulder and held on tight.

Faith brimming up from a spot I'd once thought dead. "I want that, too. So much."

I was just terrified I was looking for it in the wrong place.

I was setting myself up for heartbreak. I knew it. I could feel it shivering around me, a low rumble of thunder in the distance as a storm gathered on the horizon.

As the wind began to stir and my heart began to beat.

I knew it in the barest touch. Knew it when I was held prisoner by those eyes.

I knew it, and I still didn't know how to stop from chasing it.

After today? Trent Lawson just might hate me for implying he didn't care about his son. And I wasn't sure that was a fate I could bear.

I knocked softly at the door and peeked in through the crack. "Daddy? You wanted to see me?"

My stomach tightened as he looked up from the stack of papers where he sat behind the messy, cluttered desk. A weary smile took over his entire face. "Eden. Come in and have a seat."

He gestured at the chair.

I entered, clicking the door shut behind me and moving to sit across from him. Somehow feeling like I was a little girl who'd been called to the principal's office.

Nerves clattered through my being, and my movements were slowed, like any flinch or twitch might give me away.

I was pretty sure I'd already been incriminated.

Daddy removed his glasses and tossed them to the desk, rubbing his eyes before he rocked back in his chair and stared over at me, taking me in as if he hadn't seen me in an age. "How are things, Eden?"

My chest squeezed. "I'm great." I chuckled an indifferent laugh to throw him off whatever scent he'd picked up. "Same as I was this morning when you popped into my class."

There.

Act like nothing was different. Play it off and things would turn out just fine for the both of us.

"How are things with you?" I asked. I fought the urge to fidget like I was guilty of a horrible crime. I was just afraid to my father, that's exactly what it would be.

Still, he studied me with that kind, knowing gaze, though there was no missing the uncertainty that swam in the warm pools of green.

It was…unnerving the way he could see right through me.

He'd always had a way of sensing people's distress. Of feeling it. Watching for it. Always there to offer support. A gentle ear and a kind word and so often the shirt off his back.

I imagined Harmony's deception had hurt all the more since our daddy would have gladly given her his last dime had she asked for it. If she'd come to him and told him she was in trouble and needed help rather than swindling the roof from over our heads. Broken trust was one of the hardest things to mend.

He rested his hands over his stomach in a casual way and hooked his ankle over the opposite knee. "Things are looking up, Eden."

I would have exhaled in relief except for the implication threaded through his words.

I forced a bright smile.

"That's great."

Play along. Play along.

Maybe he just wanted to talk to me about one of my students. Probably Myla who'd painted the kindergarten walls in marker before she'd moved on to poor little Ben's shirt.

Only my daddy's expression shifted in worry, an elbow going to the armrest and propping up his head as he searched me through the bright rays of light that streaked in through the high window. "Yep, they sure are."

He sat forward, all business-like as he started to sift through the papers like he was going to find missing information.

"Such a strange thing, though...I called the bank to talk to them about being granted another extension, and they told me something interesting. They told me they'd already received a portion of the payment and an extension was unnecessary."

"Oh, how wonderful!" I squeaked it way too loud, itching on my seat.

I was a terrible liar. Because my smile was so fake I was pretty sure my face might break.

"Is it?" he asked with a tilt of his head. "I know it was deposited by you, Eden. I know it wasn't some random donation."

Disquiet rustled, and this time I couldn't stop myself from twisting my fingers.

I mean, seriously, did I think he wasn't going to find out? Play it off as a helpful stranger when no one else knew but Tessa, the two of us, and the bank that was breathing down our necks?

"Daddy...I...I told you I was working on it. That I would help fix it. That you aren't in this alone."

The words started to rush in emphasis. In an appeal for him to understand.

It was true my daddy was the best man around, loved every single person, did his best to always look deeper and never to judge, but he was also about as traditional as they came.

Always hoping his children stood on solid, even ground.

And when Harmony had fallen? It'd only made him that much more protective of me.

The creases at the corners of his eyes deepened.

Devotion and worry.

His voice came as a soft plea. "I don't know what that means, Eden. How?"

Dropping his head, he ran a flustered, shaky hand through his hair.

How did I tell him I was working at Absolution?

The club wasn't the real problem, though, was it? The real problem was the path it had taken me down. A dark, dark path with Trent Lawson waiting at the end.

I was flying in a dangerous direction, destined for a collision, and didn't know how or if I even wanted to stop.

He'd get one look at the man and he'd wrap me up and hide me away.

Daddy raised his attention back to me. "There was three-thousand dollars made against the debt, Eden."

"Dad—"

"Money you deposited." The words were thick when he pushed them out, and he started shaking his head. "How? Did you...sell something? Sweetheart, you can't go without for the sake of—"

"I picked up some shifts at a restaurant." I cut him off before he started singing my praises the way he always did. Hell, he'd probably imagined I'd sold a kidney. "I've been working there for a while now."

It wasn't a total lie. Absolution did serve food.

Questions twisted his brow. "And made three-thousand dollars? It sounds like I'm in the wrong business." It was almost a tease.

Affection pulsed through my being, my daddy always expecting the best of me. I clutched the arms of my chair, sincerity in my voice. "I don't think it quite makes the same impact, Daddy. This..." I waved a hand in the air. "This place? It's important. Really important. And I'm doing everything I can to make sure we don't lose it."

Sighing, he leaned back in his chair. "I know you're worried about me, Eden…and God…"

His voice hitched on the emotion.

"I appreciate it more than you can know. I am so thankful I have you. Your support, your belief." His head shook almost as fiercely as his voice. "It means so much to me. Means so much to this school. But this isn't a debt you owe."

"It isn't yours, either." Anger and hurt came out with the defense.

"Eden," he whispered.

"Harmony stole from you, Daddy. From us. From the children here. The families."

Agony spun through my being.

We'd had dreams of going to New York together. Of getting accepted into some prestigious dance school where we'd join a famous ballet.

We'd live our lives dancing and touring the world together.

But then our momma died when she was sixteen and I was fourteen. In a way, I'd lost my mother and my sister the same day.

I'd watched her plummet into darkness. Lose herself. I'd tried… tried so hard to be strong enough for all of us.

To let my daddy have his grief without the worry of my sister, praying I would be enough to see her through.

I wasn't.

She'd left at eighteen. Had gone to Las Vegas to dance. Left me behind.

We hadn't seen her once in all that time. Nothing but a few sparse calls and letters over the years.

Not until she'd shown one day out of the blue three months ago, all smiles and false promises and telling us she was never going to leave again. She'd convinced us she'd made a mistake, casting us aside the way she had, and she was home for good.

We'd believed her. Welcomed her with open arms. The prodigal child who'd been so desperately missed.

My best friend.

My greatest confidant.

The one I'd looked up to my whole life.

A week later, she'd been gone, her things packed, along with every last cent in the school's and my father's bank accounts, not to mention our mama's jewelry she'd heisted like a common, vicious thief.

My spirit shivered with the pain because I'd hoped so desperately that she'd changed.

That my sister was home for good.

My daddy had been devastated when she'd disappeared.

Destroyed.

Ruined on top of it because he'd refused to call the police and turn her in.

And God, I loved her, too, but I refused to stand by and let him lose everything because of her.

It hadn't been the first time money had gone missing from the treasury, either. Maybe I'd lost faith, become cynical, because I'd always secretly believed Harmony had been responsible even when there'd been no proof.

I inched off the chair, never quite rising to standing as I moved around his desk and knelt in front of him. I gripped his hand. "Daddy, your pain is mine, too. Your hurt. Your worry. Your *debt. It's mine, too.*"

He reached out and brushed his thumb across the tear I'd leaked. "That's the whole problem, Eden…I don't want you to hurt or worry. I want you to live the best life you can. Fully and without restraint."

"I am living," I promised, the words choppy. "Let me live a little for you."

"I'm afraid that's all you've been living for, Eden, all this time. For me. For this school."

I wondered how transparent I really was. If he saw so clearly the way I ached. If he knew I tossed at night. Consumed by loneliness.

I squeezed his hand tighter and rushed, "I love it here, and I love you. I love the children. I love the dance classes and the Sunday school classes. All of it. You don't have to worry. I want to do this. I want to help."

"But you deserve more than giving your entire life to this school, Eden, and then turning around and spending your nights working at a restaurant."

He brushed his thumb over the dark bag under my eye. There was no hiding the exhaustion from the lack of sleep. His voice shifted into dread. "I have this feeling, Eden, this feeling that there is something you're not telling me. That you're taking a risk you shouldn't."

"I'm fine." I breathed it.

God. I definitely was transparent.

He ran his fingers through a lock of my hair, tucked it behind my ear, his eyes full of a plea and adoration. "I already lost one daughter. I can't lose another."

"Daddy..."

His anguish speared me.

"You're all I've got left," he whispered on his grief, and I sat up on my knees and hugged him as hard as I could.

"I'm right here, and I'm not going anywhere. You don't have to worry. That's the whole point of me working extra...so you can focus on the people who rely on you. The ones who actually need you."

He pushed to standing, taking me with him. His arms were strong around me. Rocking me and holding me. The same way as he'd always held me as a child.

My hero.

My strength.

The one who had always been there for me, no matter what. No judgement. Just love and belief.

"I want the world for you, Eden."

"My world is right here."

"I know you want more than this."

"I'm happy," I whispered.

He breathed a soft sound into my hair. "You're content. But I know. I know, sweet girl. I know you ache for more. And I pray every night that you find it."

Chapter Thirteen

Eden

TONIGHT, WORKING THE CLUB PASSED IN A BLUR. A BLUR of nerves and energy and worry.

Music thrummed and the lights were dimmed. It felt as if I'd fallen into a daze of the beating bass and rumbling floors and calls for refills.

Cash would be left on my tables, trapped under empties, while most tips were added to credit cards. Alcohol made people loose with their money, which was the whole purpose I was there, but each time I grabbed a twenty stuffed beneath a drink it didn't have the same impact as it normally would.

Tonight, I couldn't seem to concentrate on the debt. My goal. My purpose. The only thing I could focus on was the fact that for the first night since I'd started working at Absolution, Trent Lawson was nowhere to be found.

No sight or intonation.

No wash of that energy or heat from that stare.

I'd drifted through the foggy hours in a state of stupor, my stomach twisted in regret over the way I'd acted toward him earlier that afternoon. I should have been kind…openminded…asked him what was wrong…if there was anything I could do to help, rather than throwing insults and accusations at him.

Now, that was the only thing on my mind.

Was he okay?

Was he in trouble?

Was there an issue with Gage?

My heart stuttered at the thought of that, and my eyes continually tracked the thriving, roiling space.

Searching the darkness.

Wanting to go darker.

Deeper.

Of course, it didn't help at all that in Trent's place was his brother, Jud, the man standing against the far wall with those massive arms crossed over his chest.

A sentry standing guard.

Fierce.

Intimidating.

Every bit as menacing as his brother, though in a different way.

He was sheer size and strength and brute force.

But there was something softer about Jud than Trent. Something playful in the way his mouth twitched beneath his thick beard, though he kept watching me in a way that left me unsettled.

Like he knew something.

Like he was assessing.

Like I was a part of the reason Trent didn't show.

Narcissist, much?

But I couldn't help it. I had to stop myself at least fifteen times from sneaking onto my phone and sending Trent a message. From telling him I was sorry. That I was scared. That I needed to see his face.

That I…missed him.

Awareness slipped across my skin in a wash of chills.

I missed him.

God, I really was in trouble.

I cast another longing look around the bar as the last of my tables left for the night. The hour was late, the club now closed, so I quickly cleaned my area, grabbed my tips from Sage, and started for the locker room so I could change into my regular clothes.

Just before I ducked into the hall, a gruff voice hit me from the side and stopped me in my tracks. "Good night?"

A quiver of nerves slaked through me, and I froze, swiveling around to again find Jud leaning against the wall, hidden in the shadows.

The man this hulking fortress as he stood guard over the bar.

"Yeah, I think so." I lifted the envelope stuffed with my tips as if it were proof. What had to be close to five-hundred dollars was tucked inside. I was never going to get used to the type of cash that flowed through this club.

"Not a lot to complain about when you work in a place like this," he said, inky eyes appraising.

I huffed out a short laugh. "No. There isn't much to complain about."

"Yet, you look upset."

My laughter shifted to disbelief, and I glanced around, trying to gauge his point. What he was getting at. I returned my attention to him and gave him the honesty he was looking for. "I might have hurt someone I didn't mean to earlier today."

Jud lifted his bearded chin. "Didn't mean to?" It was only a partial question, words meant to sift around inside my head for my intentions because he was protective, too.

"Sometimes when we're scared, we say things we don't mean as a way to protect ourselves," I answered.

"And sometimes that's all we can do…protect ourselves. Ones we love." There was a message hidden in his words.

My throat thickened. "I understand that."

Jud angled his head to the side. "Do you?"

My mouth trembled at the edge, and I fiddled with the envelope, my questions floating out on the murky atmosphere. "I want to, but I might be at a disadvantage."

He studied me, warring, before he gave me a little insight. "Guess all you need to know is sometimes good people have to do bad things."

Right.

Okay.

Another warning.

As vague as it was bleak, though it wasn't like I was surprised. It was clear things went so much deeper here at Absolution than the façade of the walls.

The enchantment of this world had convinced me of make-believe things. But this was no fairytale, and Trent Lawson was no knight in shining armor.

"I see."

"Not sure you can handle it, darlin'."

I didn't know if he was looking out for me or his brother.

"I don't break as easily as I look."

His eyes raked me, head to toe. "Not always the physical wounds that do the breaking, though they've been known to cut just as deep."

Everything shivered.

My soul and my mind.

What was I getting myself into? But I'd already known I was straddling that line from the get-go. Teetering a razor-sharp edge that could slice me in two.

Corruption clear. Unquestionable. And still, I was trying to figure out where I might fit.

"Do you include yourself in that company?"

He blew out a sigh. "Think this is a conversation that needs to be had between you and Trent."

"I doubt your brother is going to offer up details." Besides, Jud was the one who'd brought it up.

"Try him. Think he's feeling as confused as you." His expression turned sincere. As if he saw the turmoil burning within.

"I doubt that," I told him, not sure I could believe Trent could ever be as confused as I was right then.

He huffed a soft sound. "You don't strike me as a doubter, Miss Murphy. You strike me as someone who believes. As someone who shines." He gestured back toward the club. "You'd do well not to let this place dim that."

Another warning.

I couldn't tell if this guy was sweet and caring or terrifying. If his advice was meant to give me comfort or drive me away.

Emotion clogged my throat. "I don't have any intention of that."

"Good girl."

I gave him a tight nod and started to walk away, only to slow when his voice called to me from behind. "He deserves someone who will see him for who he really is, Eden. Not for what he's done."

Warily, I shifted to look at Jud from over my shoulder.

Fear spiraled through, twined with the knowledge that Jud was affording.

"I'm worried he's becoming the only thing I can see," I whispered.

His head dipped, and we stared at each other for a moment. A silent understanding weaving between the two of us.

Finally, I tore myself away and rushed the rest of the way into the locker room.

I changed quickly, ridding myself of the leather shorts and knee-high boots, the Absolution tee that felt like some sort of branding, almost sighing out in relief when I pulled on the dress I'd had on earlier that day and slipped into my flats.

I stuffed everything into my bag and headed out through the side door, smiling softly at Milo who was again standing his post. "Goodnight, Milo."

"Drive safe, little dove." His voice was a deep, masculine rumble. The man a burly, brutal monster with the kindest eyes.

Nervously, I glanced around, still unsure, wishing there was a way to go back to this afternoon and handle it differently. With kindness and compassion rather than with knives and whips.

The only other person in the lot was Leann, and she waved goodbye like I was her oldest friend. I gave her a wave in return before I darted in the direction of my car parked across the lot.

The soles of my shoes clacked on the loose gravel pavement, the night all around, the air chilly as it brushed across the flesh of my arms. I increased my pace, almost to the rear of my car when I heard the low grumble of a bike come to life where it'd been hidden at the far end of the lot.

My pulse jumped into a frenzy, and I froze, compelled to turn that way, only to be blinded by the headlight that shined through the darkness.

I didn't need to be able to see to know who it was.

Intensity sliced through the air.

That dark, provocative aura shivering through the heavens. Twisting me in chains and wrapping me in bows.

The bike eased forward, chugging like a beast chained and on the prowl, held back from the hunt. It slowly rolled forward until it came to a stop behind my car. Trent stretched out his legs to keep himself balanced, tattooed hands wrapped around the handlebars and boots planted on the ground as he straddled the powerful machine.

The bike and the man looked like they'd been forged together. Cut of the same steel. Sewn of the same leather.

Peril and power.

I was a prisoner to the awestriking beauty of it.

Held in a trance that made my mouth water and my knees knock.

Tessa was right. I wanted a taste. God, I wanted a taste, and I was terrified of the cost.

The way I lost my breath as those intense eyes took me in, the ferocity that raved verging between anger and that apology.

He was looking at me like I was the only reason he was there.

His purpose right then.

The man on a mission to devour.

Ravage and decimate.

And still, there was nothing I could do but murmur his name in relief. "Trent."

He grunted, no softness about it. "Get on."

Um, what?

My brows shot for the sky as panic took me over. "Are you crazy?" I hissed.

He chuckled a rough sound. "Some would say."

"I'm not getting on that thing," I rasped, taking a step back as if it would keep me safe.

"Oh, come on, Kitten, live a little." It wasn't playful. Not even a little bit.

It was a challenge.

A demand.

My heart raced and my stomach revolted.

"It's not the living I'm worried about. It's the whole splattered across the pavement thing." I tried to keep it as light as I could and not expose just how out of my element I actually was.

I might have even laughed had that dark face not flashed something ferocious. "You really think I'd let something bad happen to you?"

My spirit flailed. A full out war. Because I did—I did trust that he wouldn't let anything harm me, which was crazy considering he was the most dangerous man I'd ever met.

"Need to talk to you."

I wavered, looked left to right as if they'd offer a better solution. "My car is here," I argued.

"And I'll be sure your car gets back to you. Just need you to get on." He seemed to be fighting his own war.

Torn.

This territory unfamiliar because the next thing that came out of his mouth was a grunted, "Please, Eden. Get on my bike."

Those eyes cut me down to nothing.

Daggers and fire.

Wavering, I looked back at my car.

"Give me your keys, and we'll take care of it. Promise to get you home safe."

Flustered, I slammed the keys into his outstretched hand. "Okay."

Then I stared.

Like, I was supposed to just get on?

"Never ridden on a bike before?"

I let out a self-deprecating sound. "I'm not exactly one for danger. Aren't you the one who's been saying I don't fit in?"

"I think the back of my bike might be exactly where you belong."
Trent extended his hand as if he were asking me to join him in it.

Hazard and risk.

While my mind spun with what he'd just said. With the implication of his words.

I guessed the first time I'd stepped into his club was the first time I'd truly stepped into danger.

Now I was willingly diving into it.

Leaping into depravity.

I slung the long strap of my bag over my shoulder, inhaled a shaky breath, and took his hand.

Fire flashed.

I gasped a needy sound.

His arm tensed, too.

I tried to breathe through it as I let this viper of a man guide me onto the back, fighting the heated rush that blistered through my body at his touch.

At the proximity.

God. What was happening to me? Whatever it was, it felt…good.

I relished the warmth that blasted through my senses when I wrapped my arms around his waist. Loved the racing of my pulse, this unfound beat that drummed somewhere out of time. Loved the way my thighs shook when he tucked me closer to all the rippling strength of his body. The way desire quivered in my belly and everything felt as if it was climbing.

Higher and higher.

This need was something I hadn't experienced in so long, and never quite like this.

Because it was different. This wasn't safe. It wasn't sweet. It wasn't a tender love that had slowly been fallen into.

It was reckless and rash.

My heart on the line and my building belief in this bad boy's hands.

My arms were trembling twigs when I tightened them around

his narrow waist, and I pressed my hands to his abdomen that was every bit as hard and strong as I had imagined.

"Hold onto me and keep your feet on the pegs. Don't fight the flow, just follow my lead. Let me do the work and you follow me through it. That's all you've got to do." His hand clenched down on my bare thigh where the fabric of my dress had bunched.

I tried to bury the moan.

His voice was a gruff whisper in the wind. "That's all you've gotta do, Eden. Follow me."

Hugging him tighter, I was struck with the realization that I might follow him anywhere. I sent up a silent prayer that I would make it through this. That I wasn't being foolish. That this wasn't the worst mistake I'd ever made.

Climbing onto his bike as if that was what I'd been made to do. Formed and fashioned to mold to the shape of his gorgeous body.

Like we might become one.

Trent eased the motorcycle through the lot and took to the street. The engine rumbled and growled.

No question he was keeping it bridled. The slow pace he'd taken meant for me. The man trying to offer comfort when I'd never been so far out of my element.

Still, I held tight, completely vulnerable to the open road. The air was cold where it whipped across my face, across the bare flesh of my arms and legs, where it stirred the skirt of my dress and whipped my hair into disorder, but in it…in it I finally understood what so many were looking for.

Freedom.

A feeling of being unchained.

Alive.

Trent only made two turns before we were pulling into another bar.

Though this one was entirely different than the club we'd just left.

It was a small, old brick building with Milly's Place painted on the exterior wall. It was the epitome of a dive. The parking lot out front was darkened save for a few dim lights and the neon beer lights that blinked from the blackened windows. It was long since passed last call, but there were still a long row of bikes parked out front in a symmetrical line and a few cars dotting the lot.

Nerves rattled through my senses, and I clung to him tighter as he eased his way through and swung his bike around. He used his feet to guide us back into a spot right at the front.

He killed the engine.

It suddenly felt too quiet. Only the sound of our hearts and the faint classic rock that seeped through the walls.

"What are we doing here?" I whispered, still clinging to his back, sure I couldn't let go.

I didn't want to.

He grumbled a sound, and the vibration of it rolled through my body. "I'm starving, and Milly makes the best after-hours breakfasts in the city."

He shifted so he could give me his hand again, and he started to help me off. "Keep your legs away from any metal."

I nodded warily, and I fumbled off the bike like a floundering fish. With the slightest smirk teasing at the corner of his decadent mouth, he kept hold of my hand as he swung off the bike and came to tower over me.

This dark, dark fortress that would swallow me whole.

He stared at me through the lapping night before he reached out and ran the pad of his thumb down the angle of my jaw.

So soft.

So right.

"We should go inside."

My nod was jerky.

He tightened his hold on my hand and led me through the double swinging doors. Just like at Absolution, everyone took note of him, dipped their heads as he walked through as if they were kneeling to a king.

It seemed wherever he went, people took note of him.

Compelled.

Fearful and intrigued.

There were only a few of the dingy booths taken, and Trent led us to one at the back. He helped me slide in one side before he slipped into the other.

A woman immediately showed at our table. Her face was weathered and worn, and her gray hair was tied back in a low ponytail. She wore a tight tank with a Harley on the chest, the tattoos on her skin faded with time.

She looked like she'd faced a harder life than anyone should have to. Or maybe she'd just lived it to its fullest.

"Well, if it isn't The Law," she said with pure affection.

The Law?

I had to hide a smile behind the menu she set in front of me.

"How's it tonight, Milly?" Trent asked her. For the first time, his tone was casual.

"Better now that my favorite boy is here."

Trent chuckled and smiled at her. "Sweet talker."

"Not sweet talkin' when it's the truth."

My chest felt light, watching this, seeing the softer side of Trent.

The way he was with his son, though different of course, as if he'd found ease in an old friend.

Milly turned her regard to me, her aged eyes edged in curiosity and a bit of speculation. I got the sense she was calculating, adding up to see if I was worthy to be sitting across from a man she clearly admired. "And who might this be?"

I swore it was affection in Trent's tone when he sat back in the booth and gazed at me as he said, "This is Eden, Milly."

Her questioning gaze turned soft. "Well, it's nice to meet you, Eden."

"It's nice to meet you, too," I murmured.

"Think we're gonna need a couple coffees here, Milly," Trent said without looking away from me.

"Sure thing. Be right back."

She walked away, and the air shifted, the man's nerves real and alive, almost as intense as mine. I was trapped in it. His stare. His trepidation. His fear over trusting me when it was clear he needed it.

A friend.

A confidant.

Maybe…maybe what he needed was me, kind of the way I was coming to need him.

Regret clung to my throat, the words mottled as I whispered, "I'm so sorry about this afternoon, Trent. I—"

Milly was already back with our coffees, sliding them in front of us and placing a bowl of creamers in the middle. "Here we go. Are we eating tonight?"

Trent glanced at her. "Two of tonight's specials."

"Sounds good, sweetheart. They'll be right out."

"Thank you," he gruffed, his familiarity with her clear.

Respect poured out of the woman. I got the sense she watched him like a hero. As if she owed him something.

We watched her go.

Trent was already speaking by the time our attention returned to each other. No doubt, he could feel the questions coming off me.

"Milly got herself into some trouble a couple years back. We fixed it for her."

A shiver rushed at the way he used the word *fixed*.

"I see," I said, the admission quieted like a secret, and I realized why we were here. Trent was opening up. Giving me something I wasn't sure I was ready to hold.

He slung himself back in the booth, an arm over the top, so calm and cool in the midst of what he'd all but just declared.

A jaundiced, yellow light hung above the booth, and a red neon light that hung on the wall blinked against the blunt, severe lines of his cheeks.

It made him appear ethereal. Deadly. Devine.

He cocked his head to the side. "Do you?"

I huffed a muted, disbelieving laugh. "I honestly have no idea what to make of you, Mr. Lawson."

"I think we're passed the Mr. Lawson bit, don't you, Kitten? You should probably call me Trent."

"Not The Law?" Somehow, I managed the tease. Maybe it was the only way I'd make it through this.

He grunted a laugh. "No, not The Law. Not for you."

"And why am I any different?"

Trent shot forward, that wide chest exposed, the words marked there clear.

Live to Ride, Ride to Die.

"What's different about you, Eden? Everything is different about you. Something better. Something good. Something I'm not sure how to ignore."

I gulped, his aura spearing me. Gripping me. Gutting me. "What if I don't want you to ignore it?"

He sat back, disgust lining his words. "Told you I don't have anything else to offer."

"I think that's an excuse. A defense."

"A defense for you. You should welcome it."

My heart wobbled with emotion. I fiddled with the paper napkin on the table, desperate for a diversion, barely brave enough to peek at him from the side. "Yet I'm sitting here."

Trent gave a tight nod. "Need you to understand something."

I lifted my gaze, waiting.

His eyes dimmed and swam and bled. "About Gage."

Anxiety clutched my spirit. The affection I had for that child was so overwhelming I thought it might crush me. "About today?"

Trent dipped his chin. "What you said…implied," he corrected. A wave of severity rushed. "Kid means everything to me, Eden. He's my world. *My reason.*"

"He's why you were late?" I chanced, sure it went much deeper than simply getting caught up in an issue at the club.

"Yeah." Rage bristled beneath his flesh. Something he could hardly contain.

Still, I pressed, "What happened?"

"His mother." He cast the words like a millstone.

A thousand questions raced as I realized how little I actually knew about their situation.

Protectiveness surged. "Does he…have contact with her?"

Guilt flashed. So, I'd peeked at Gage's records on the school system, unable to stop myself from digging around in areas I shouldn't. I was the fool who'd felt relief when Trent and his brothers were the only people listed with permission to pick up Gage.

"No," he shot out. "Plan to keep it that way."

It sounded of his own threat.

"And you were…" I trailed off.

"Dealing with her," he supplied.

I blinked, searching his face, trying to understand.

"Some people are driven by greed, Kitten. Throw a little money at it, and the problem disappears."

I dropped my attention to the worn table to gather myself.

Right.

Okay.

"You paid her off…to stay away from Gage?" I clarified as I looked up.

He stared across at me, needing to see how I'd react. "Once a year. She gets the money, I get the kid. We both get what we want. It's a win/win."

Except his voice was disdain. Hostility and hate.

"She doesn't care about him? Want to see him?"

Trent scoffed out a contemptuous laugh. "She doesn't care about anything but herself. She plays it off, asking questions like she's concerned about how he is, but the second she gets the money, she's gone."

Sadness blanketed my spirit. Unable to fathom it. The idea of turning my back on my child. To me, it was the greatest gift that could be given.

Trent must have mistaken it as my judging him because he draped his arms over the back of the booth, way too casual considering his voice was a low crush of animosity. "Don't worry, Kitten, she was the first to draw the knife. Blade's still in my back."

"She hurt you." It wasn't a question.

He laughed, zero amusement in the sound, the words shards when he grated, "She fuckin' destroyed me, Eden."

I blanched. Jealousy thick. Something I had no right to but couldn't keep from slithering like poison beneath the surface of my skin.

He felt it, those eyes on me, consuming me in their truth. "Not in the way you're thinking. She betrayed me. Sold me out. At the last minute, she got scared and tried to backpedal, but not before it cost my brother's life."

I sucked in a sharp breath, unprepared for that. I blinked, trying to read through the lines and terrified to see.

But his grief and guilt were all that I could see. The way those dark eyes dimmed, and his jaw clenched tight, sorrow bound with the rage, the two together becoming something vicious and vile.

A metal rope that twisted and twisted, chains that bound him in misery.

An eternity of it.

So deep and vast I felt as if I was going under, sucked beneath the waves of despair that radiated from his being.

"Your brother?" I choked over the words, trying to make sense but fearful of pushing it. Of pushing him. But that was why we were here, wasn't it?

"There were four of us, now there's three." His teeth ground as he forced out the explanation. "Nathan."

He broke at that. The word a barb of love and loss.

Those fierce eyes dropped closed when he whispered, "He was my twin."

My entire body pitched with the impact.

"Oh, Trent…I'm so sorry."

The owl on his throat tremored when he swallowed. "The best of us. Always giving and giving. He got in the middle of what I thought was supposed to have just been another job, only turned out this one's end purpose was to take me out."

It left him like a confession. The man might as well have been on his knees praying for forgiveness with the guilt that oozed from his flesh. With the horror and the shame.

I wanted to reach out and touch him. Hold him. Tell him I understood. That I'd lost so many of the ones I cared most about, too.

All while the undercurrent of what he'd said swirled around my feet. Dragging me out into the depths of who he was. A place where I couldn't stand or swim or call out for help.

A job.

A job. I knew what he'd meant because normal jobs didn't leave people dead.

His chin lifted in challenge. "You can stop looking at me like you're surprised, Eden. Already told you I'm no good. Left behind a life that you don't wanna know about."

Milly was suddenly there, allowing me the respite of a breath as she set our plates in front of us, a mountain of biscuits and gravy and eggs and sausage.

"Anything else?" she rushed, shifting on her feet, feeling the strain that blistered between us.

"No, we're fine," Trent said, not even glancing her way.

"Thank you, Milly," I mumbled through a trembling voice, wary as I peeked back at Trent when she disappeared.

I could only take one bite of food before I set my fork aside, my brow curling when I hedged, "The tattoo…"

I let my gaze dip to the words forever imprinted on his chest.

"Was my way of life before I came here."

"You were a biker."

Like, a biker, biker. Like the 1% kind that lived outside the law? That's what they labeled themselves, right? How they were distinguished from everyone else?

Set apart.

A prideful title claiming they did horrible things.

"When I found out I was going to be a father, knew it was time to get out. Get my brothers out from under the life that we'd been forced into."

"Forced into?"

His nod was tight. "Our father was the President of a small but vicious club back in LA. We were raised in the life. Conformed into it. Coerced into it. We were all in deep before we realized it wasn't a good life. But we didn't know anything different. Just seemed our lot. But the thought about bringing a kid into that world?"

His head shook with the severity. "Knew it was time to get gone. Take my brothers and my child with me where we could start a new life. A better life. We had been heading nowhere good, and all of us were gonna end up dead or behind bars if we didn't make a change."

The sound that came from his throat was close to a growl. "Of course, our father wasn't going to be so keen about that. We'd made a plan that we were just going to go. Pack up and split. Get lost in some no-name town and disappear forever. Made a deal with Gage's mom, Juna."

He paused, maybe seeing me gasping. Hanging onto every word. Trying to keep up.

"She'd hooked up with the President of a rival MC, right about the same time she was hooking up with me. She'd be buried if they knew who her baby's daddy really was, so I gave her a solution. A big payoff for the kid. She'd never have to think about money again. She agreed, except what she'd really done was sell me out to our father. Went to him with the plan and earned herself some extra cash." He spat the words, venom in his voice and loathing in his eyes.

My insides withered. Curling with the horror of his past.

This dark, ominous man who held so much pain.

"An ambush was waiting to take me out. She woulda got the cash and the kid and me dead. Except she got cold feet at the last minute—went to my house. My brother, Nathan, was there. She confessed and he came running to stop it. He got caught in the crossfire."

Trent itched. Coming out of his skin as the admission left him, pure misery on his tongue.

Sorrow.

Shame.

Guilt.

They bled and wept from his flesh.

My breaths were shallow and short. Stricken and hurting for this man. Scared, too. There was no question now that I'd crossed onto unstable, shaky ground. Ground that would crack wide open and gobble me up. Where I'd lose myself. Who I was and who I wanted to be.

Everything Trent Lawson had said from the beginning was true. He was dangerous and I didn't belong. But still, my mouth was moving, whispering, "I'm so sorry."

His hands shot to the edge of the table like he needed the support when the devastation fell from his mouth. "My fault."

My head shook. "You said you didn't know what you were getting into."

He chuckled a menacing sound, a snarl wrapped around the words. "Might not have as a kid, Eden, but a man's soul knows. Knows when his deeds have him destined for Hell. Right where he belongs."

My mouth felt dry, my appetite gone. My gaze darted everywhere but at him, knowing I was pushing through a boundary I shouldn't. That I didn't want to know, but I had to.

"But you...still paid her off? After what she did?"

My head spun. Too much to process. This world something I didn't understand. The one thing I did know was this woman's face had become something vile in my mind.

Wicked, evil, and cruel.

Trent swallowed hard. "She warned us, got the rest of us out of there before it was too late, carried my son to term and signed him over to me the way we'd agreed, so I spared her."

Spared her.

There was no more denying it. No more diverting or pretending. No more blissful oblivion.

And still, I needed him to say it. Admit how dark it went. I didn't want some vague foreshadowing. Didn't want to be kept in the shadows. Didn't want him to hide from me.

I needed to know.

Know his truth.

"You've...killed people?" I didn't even know how I'd managed to push out the hushed plea. Praying for a different answer than the one I was sure to get.

Vengeance flashed through his fierce eyes, and he gave me a tight, short nod.

My guts revolted. Nausea twisted through my stomach and bile rose in my throat.

Oh god.

I hitched forward, clinging to the table the same way as Trent had done.

I wondered if we did it for the same reasons?

If he was haunted the way this would haunt me?

This man who I'd come to crave.

My knees trembled and my spirit warred.

From deep within, I had the urge to get up and bolt. Turn my back. Hide away before I got any deeper.

Before I saw any clearer.

While the other part felt frozen. Chained to the spot. Like I couldn't get away from this man if I tried.

Jud's words flooded my mind. *"He deserves someone who will see him for who he really is, Eden. Not for what he's done."*

Did this change anything?

I'd already known, hadn't I? Sensed the aura of iniquity? Knew he had blood on his hands?

And still, I was sitting across from him tonight and seeing something different than the man he was describing.

My eyes squeezed tight as I forced out, "How many?" I peeled my lids back open like I could handle his response.

He scoffed a disbelieving sound, demons playing as shadows over the sharp edges of his face. "Not gonna answer that, Eden."

Everything stung. Tears building and my throat full and the world spinning.

Trent hardened. Stone ridging his spine. "Know what you're thinking right now, Eden. Told you I didn't have anything else. That I'm no good. Warned you. But there is a piece inside me that needed you to understand this. *See* this. *Know* that I've got one reason. My son. Everything I have, I have for him. Every choice I make, I'm making it for him. And I'm trying, Eden...I'm fucking trying to be the father he deserves. To leave the man I've been in the past. That's all I've got to give, and I will do anything, absolutely anything, to ensure he is safe. To see to it that he gets a good life."

He inhaled a long, pained breath.

"And with the way you reacted this afternoon? Seemed I couldn't go on without you really understanding why I went missing earlier today, and I won't apologize for that."

I felt numb.

Floating through a nightmare.

This couldn't be real.

Because I'd guess there was this stupid part of me that'd started to hope. To hope in this feeling. To hope for something better.

For something simple and beautiful.

A chance at a new life. To experience something big and bright and unanticipated with him.

But a man like Trent Lawson was anything but simple.

He would only bring destruction.

The promise of pain.

I'd thought he was dangerous the first time I met him, the ruler of that wicked kingdom, and now, I knew the truth.

I needed to stand up and go.

Run as far as I could.

Miles and space and an eternity.

But I sat there, unable to move. Unable to see anything but this menacing man who had steadily wormed his way into my heart.

I sat there terrified but unafraid.

Sickened but undaunted.

Because I wasn't sure how to want it any other way.

How to run from this man who was looking for his second chance.

Chapter Fourteen

Trent

SHE SAT ACROSS FROM ME, FIGHTING TEARS, FINALLY SEEING me for the monster that I was.

Funny how I'd warned her, needed her to get it, then when she did, it made me want to crawl out of my skin.

Shame thick.

Hatred thicker.

But guys like us? We didn't get to rewind or rework our pasts. We didn't get to make amends because you couldn't right wrongs this bad.

We didn't get a second chance.

Even when we ran, the demons would be right there. Our sins written on our souls. The horrors emblazoned on our minds.

Unforgettable nightmares that would never let up.

When I couldn't stand her discomfort for a second longer, that gaze dipping and ducking and landing everywhere except for on me, I pushed out of the booth to stand. "Let's go."

Surprised, Eden jerked her head up. Long, blonde locks swished around her shoulders like a play of soft seduction while those autumn eyes swam with moisture. With a sea of distrust. A well of fear.

And still, deep within, there was something that shouldn't remain.

The girl was always looking at me like I was better than I was. Like there was something there, buried deep. Something that could be resurrected.

Not possible.

Because any goodness inside me had died the first time I pulled a trigger in the name of the club. In the name of surviving. In the name of my piece-of-shit father.

"What?" she whispered, confused. Unsure and uncertain, and fuck, I had the intense urge to gather her up. Hold her. Tell her I'd never hurt her.

"Looks to me like you lost your appetite."

Her gaze dipped again, like she didn't want to admit it, and I dug into my pocket and pulled out a hundred. I tossed it onto the table.

She remained sitting, her head downcast before she tipped that pretty face in my direction. "Trent—"

I stuck out my hand. "Don't, Eden. You don't have to say anything. Already know."

Already knew I was bad. Wrong. Exact thing she needed to keep far, far away from.

A frown curled her brow, her lips parted on a denial that she couldn't cut loose because she and I both knew it would be a lie.

A lie that said maybe the two of us could be.

Like this want could be sated.

The sight of her that way tied my guts in knots, the chaos of thoughts that roiled through her mind tossing my body into overdrive.

Lust bottled. Need barely bridled.

Tentatively, she accepted my outstretched hand.

Motherfuck.

She singed me. Slayed me. Fire raced my flesh, this girl the kind of flame that could do me in, consume me in a flash.

Knew better than traipsing in the direction of something good. Wanting to dip my dirty fingers in the pure. Would ruin us both when we were done.

That knowledge didn't seem to make much of a difference,

though, with the way I twined her fingers through mine, not wanting to let her go, way my heart trembled in my motherfucking chest.

I led her out, and Eden cowered close to my side, although there was something brave about the way she kept squeezing my hand. Like she was the one giving me encouragement. One giving me reassurance.

Her belief.

Her goodness that shined.

We dipped out of the bar and into the sweeping darkness of the night. Sky so close where it hugged the earth. Heavens smattered with stars strung like ribbons of hope through the night. Beneath it, it was easy to get swayed into thinking there might be a bigger purpose to all of this.

A purpose I wouldn't be graced.

Wind howled through the towering trees, stirred the ground, the night air cold where it breezed against our skin.

Eden shivered where she stood frozen at the side of my bike.

Like she had no idea where she was supposed to go from there.

Lost.

And I was the idiot who thought I could maybe show her the way. Give her a direction, a way out of wherever she'd go when her features would go sad.

To her sister who had fucked her over.

But I got the sense it went way deeper than that.

This girl's heart strewn all over the place.

I shifted, overcome with the need to touch. To trace the goosebumps on her flesh. To watch this beautiful girl light up.

"You're cold," I rumbled, voice barely audible with the strain.

Eden looked at me with those eyes.

Open.

Wide.

Terrified and still giving me the kind of trust I didn't deserve.

Her tongue swept across her lips, cautious and slow, and she was huddled so close to me that when she forced out the words, I felt the stutter of her heart. "I need to know something...is...is Gage in danger? Are you in danger?" Her head barely shook, her attention jumping around to search the silence of the shadows, at war with her fears. "Are we in danger?"

Images streaked through my mind.

Flashes of darkness.

Drums of light.

Begging. Pleading. Blood. Splatters. Shame.

Could barely breathe by the time I came back, nothing but a fuckin' fool when I reached out and traced the chills that had pebbled on her arm, that dress whipping around her legs and her hair thrashing around the angles of her gorgeous face.

My fingertip dragged the length, and I leaned in close, figuring I had nothing else to lose. "The man who was supposed to be my father? One who wanted to send me to Hell? I sent him there first."

Eden's eyes pressed closed, and she exhaled a shattered breath, her sweet soul shivering with the truth.

"Only reason I'm still here in California. But that doesn't mean we're ever going to fully outrun it. That we'll ever fully be safe. I made a lot of enemies back then, Eden. Did a lot of bad, bad things. But I'll spend my life making sure that Gage won't be affected by that bullshit. That he gets to live a semi-normal life."

"Okay," she whispered, giving me more of that unfound trust.

"Let's get you home. It's late."

Warily, she nodded, and I swung my leg over my bike, helped her get on the back. My insides twisted in a rush of want when she shocked the shit out of me by curling those arms around me like that was what she'd been made to do. When she hugged me tighter than she ever had before.

When she held on and buried her face in the back of my neck like she needed it. Like she needed to get closer. Mold herself to my fashion. Sink inside and become one.

Invade.

Possess a piece of me the way she was possessing me.

Like she fit.

Stupid.

Couldn't go there. Neither of us could afford it, that was clear enough.

Opposites.

Goodness and greed.

Purity and depravity.

Plus the fact that I couldn't let down my guard. That I had to focus. Be true to the promise I'd made.

One reason.

I started the engine. The roar ricocheted through the thin air, and I struggled to get my shit together as I eased out of the spot and took to the road that was all but deserted this time of night.

I headed in the direction of her house.

The headlight from my bike speared through the lazy darkness as I zigzagged down the sleeping city streets.

Her arms were wrapped tight around my waist. So fucking tight. The heat of her body saturated mine. Soaked me through.

But she was shaking, too. Shaking so bad that on the straight-aways I kept putting one of my hands over hers that were locked at my stomach. My hand curled over hers like I could hold her fears. Make it right. Be someone good enough to stand by her side.

I made the last turn into her neighborhood. Her house came into view, cream-colored with light-green eaves, shrouded in a hedge of giant trees.

Should have just dropped her at the curb.

Let her off and let her go. It's what a good guy would do.

But that was the whole problem with who I was, wasn't it? I wasn't a good guy. Not even close.

So I pulled into the single-car drive at the side of her house. I eased to a stop, killed the engine, and kicked the stand.

No words were said when I reached down and unwound her trembling fingers and helped her slip off the bike, but I couldn't find the strength to let her go.

She wobbled where she stood, her fingers locked on mine, girl looking at me with those earthy, autumn eyes. Watching me like I was something different. Like I might be worthy to touch her. Hold her.

I wasn't, but still I climbed off the bike, my frame towering over her fierce, sweet body.

So fuckin' pretty.

Different.

Brave and bold and kind.

Better in every way.

"Trent." She whispered my name like a prayer.

Honey dripped from her tongue and glided into my senses.

My free hand came out and cupped the side of her face, my thumb running the angle. "Eden."

Heaven.

Paradise standing there beneath the night sky.

Her throat tremored, and her fingers fell free of the clasp of mine when she turned and started up her walk. Nothing else was said as she walked toward the front door.

Didn't know if it was an invitation. Only thing I knew was I couldn't do anything but follow her.

Powerless to her lure.

That connection zapped.

The draw that was this girl.

Electricity crackling and blistering like a storm.

A heatwave that shocked through the cooled night and strummed my nerves into a frenzy.

I stalked behind that goodness, that vulnerability, wanting to dip my fingers into the warmth of it.

Get lost.

Forget.

Maybe be the guy this girl clearly deserved, even when I didn't know a whole lot about who she was, which was a mindfuck considering the information I'd just dished for the first time.

But I guessed I already knew everything important.

The truth that there was nothing corrupt about her.

That she cared.

Fuck, I got that sense that she might even love my kid.

Thing that was really messing me up was this reaction. Fact that my cock was stone, guts tangled in need, fingers itching to fist in that blonde, blonde hair.

Wanted to take her.

Taste her.

Vanish in that body and that heart and those eyes.

Eden fumbled into her bag to pull out her keys that she must have forgotten she'd surrendered to me. I dug them out of my pocket and leaned around her to unlock her door. "There you go." It was a breath against her ear.

A shiver raced her, and she reached in and flicked on the light before she glanced back at me, nerves rattling through her as her gaze swept me like I wasn't a nightmare that'd shown up at her door.

She widened that door and stepped inside.

Energy lashed.

Swallowing it down, I followed, entering her house for the first time.

I took it in as I clicked the door shut behind us, chuckling low when I realized it looked exactly like her.

Fit her to a T.

Pure.

Humble.

Sweet.

Everything cozy and warm and bright.

Like it couldn't help but glow with her light.

Slowly, she turned around in the small space, wearing that same modest dress she'd been tempting me with this afternoon. In it, the girl was still the sexiest thing I'd ever seen.

My sanity's demise.

Maybe my heart's, too.

Because fuck.

I got the sense Eden Murphy might undo me.

Obliterate the fortress I'd had to build around myself to survive.

Unravel all the dirty threads that were barely holding me together.

Retwine them until I was complete.

Make a broken man whole.

She stared at me with questions rushing over that stunning face. I inched forward.

The air shivered, and Eden's chest heaved.

God, I had no idea what I was still doing standing there.

I roughed a hand through my hair, dropping my attention to my boots. "Listen, I'm sorry if it was too much, unloading all that shit on you."

Rejection twisted through Eden's expression, the curve of her jaw appearing harsher than ever. "Don't you dare apologize to me for that."

My heart nearly stopped at her ferocity.

She stepped forward in a plea, her fingers raking down the front of my shirt. "Don't apologize for trusting me with that."

My stuttered heart started to pound. This thunder that I couldn't contain.

"Not a whole lot I'm proud of in my life, Eden." I took a step her direction. Enclosing. "But I'm fuckin' trying to be something for my son."

Those eyes flitted over my face.

Searching.

Seeking.

"None of us are whole, Trent. None of us are without blame."

I scoffed out a bitter laugh. "Baby, my blame is disgrace. Unconscionable. Unforgivable. I think I made that much clear."

"I don't believe that." Her voice was a whisper. "Not for a second. Do you think I don't see your grief?"

Eden edged back another step.

Temptation.

Raw, innocent seduction.

Or maybe she knew exactly what she was doing to me, the way her pulse thudded in the bare space. A space that called out to be filled.

My soul thrashed.

"Do you think I don't see the goodness you don't know how to show?"

Fuck me, I wanted to dip my fingers into the pure.

Into all that blamelessness radiating off her like a dream. The belief.

"You think I don't see you?" Fingertips traced down the side of my face as she murmured that. "Absolution. I think you are looking for it, too."

Affection in her touch.

Affection in her eyes.

Could barely see. Could barely think.

The only thing I could focus on was the whoosh of the blood I could sense racing through her veins. A thrum, thrum, thrum that bounded and banged and made me feel like I was going insane.

I inclined closer, my nose running the length of her jaw, breathing the words as I went. "I ruin everything I touch, Eden. Ruin it. Destroy it. I'm terrified of doing the same to you, just like I'm terrified I'm going to be wrong for that little boy."

The last I choked out as my hand cinched down on her waist.

Guessed this time, I was the one who was vulnerable. The one who was putting his mangled, ugly heart on the chopping block.

Her palm found my cheek, soft and warm. "Trent." Her gaze moved across my face, her words low and wispy, laden with emphasis. "You have the choice. You have the choice of how you live your life, no matter how you've lived it in the past. You have the power to decide who you are now. The kind of security you give. The kind of father that you want to be. You have the choice to love him with everything you have."

My hand curled around her wrist, two of us sliding into a trance. "I do, Eden. Never thought it possible, the way I love him. Things I would do for him."

But it'd cost.

It'd cost my brother.

It'd cost my soul.

It'd cost our security because we'd be running for the rest of our lives.

"I can't lose focus, Eden. Can't start deluding myself into thinking I've got anything else left after that."

Her throat bobbed when she swallowed. Her voice a snare. "I see it, Trent. Feel it when you look at him. You're different than you are with anyone else. Beautiful in a way I doubt that you can see in yourself. But I see clearly. You have more to give. More to share."

She pressed that hand over my heart that raged. "Right here. I see it living right here. You deserve love just as much as anyone else. You just have to be brave enough to let it free. To give it. To receive it. You have to trust that you deserve it even if you think you've failed."

My forehead dropped to hers.

This girl who believed in me the way few others had. My brothers. Gage. It ended there. Felt impossible to ask for more.

"What if our failures are already too great? What if we've lost too many of the ones we love? Destroyed our chance at ever feeling whole and right again? Who the fuck are we then?"

Sorrow gripped me by the throat. My mother's sweet voice. Nathan's face behind my eyes. Could hear both their ghosts screaming in my ear. Only reason I'd made it through that was because of Gage.

Eden gasped, grief clutching her in a fist. She grabbed at her chest like she was fighting to capture the answer. Lost, too.

"I don't know," she rushed, so low I could barely hear her. "I'm still trying to figure that out."

Her entire being wept, like she had her own ghosts screaming in her ear. She twisted away, haunted in a way that caught me off guard.

Thought she was trying to escape it, too, her past, with the way she moved down the short hall at the back of the living room.

And I was the goddamned sadist who followed her. Unable to stop chasing down the pain. Knowing I'd inflict it. That I was destined to fuck this up.

I'd promised—promised I wouldn't lose focus or direction.

One reason.

One reason.

My chest nearly caved in when she got to the bedroom doorway and her hand shot out to the threshold. She bent in two, holding her stomach and trying to catch her breath.

She stumbled the rest of the way into her room.

I came up short at the doorway.

A bloodsucker who needed an invitation to enter. I stretched my arms over my head and hung onto the top of the doorframe, air heaving from my straining lungs.

Eden sank down onto the side of the bed, woman a seductress and she didn't even know it. Soft and graceful and sexy as fuck.

Blonde curls hugging her shoulders, that dress draped around her body and showing off every delicious curve.

Little Temptress.

But there was so much confusion and sadness shrouding her as she watched me.

That gaze devouring.

Consuming.

Ruining.

"I should go, Eden, I know it. But I don't fuckin' know how to stay away from you."

Electricity zapped through the air.

Crackles of lust.

An explosion of need.

Her lips parted, and a tiny sound slipped from her lush mouth. I took a step inside.

"I'll hurt you, and I won't even mean to," I told her, voice raw and rough with the warning.

She fidgeted on the bed, her knees pressing together.

Part in need.

Part in protection.

"I don't even know what I feel, Trent." She stared across at me. "I don't understand this feeling you've created in me." She pressed her hands to her chest.

Pleading.

She laughed a helpless sound. "You're probably the last man I ever thought I'd want. The last man I should want. So different than anything I ever pictured for my life."

I didn't even take offense to it. She wasn't saying anything different than what I'd been saying all along.

"But I do." The admission bled free like an appeal. "And I don't know how to come to terms with that."

In some kind of shame, her attention drifted to the bedside table.

Like she was drawn.

I followed the path.

To the picture that was there.

Every muscle in my body flinched.

It was of Eden wrapped in the arms of a guy.

A guy who shined the way she did.

A nice guy.

A good guy.

Kind of guy she deserved.

Two of them a mesh of perfection.

Two rings were leaned against the frame.

Old hopes lost.

My stomach suddenly rebelled.

Flailed with her sorrow all while I was overcome with this surge of possession.

Fuck, I really was getting in deep.

So fuckin' deep when she heaved out a breath and the force of it had me inching closer, her words the softest lashes that struck through the room.

Long, fading echoes that bounced from wall to wall.

"My husband's been gone for six years."

No question, this wasn't a case of a marriage gone bad. The dude hadn't walked out on her or left her of his own choice. This abandonment was the kind where no blame could lie. The kind that left you ripped open with questions. Bleeding out for the rest of your life.

I slowly eased to my knees on the carpet in front of her.

Overcome again. This time with the need to wrap her up. Hold her pain. Rewrite the sadness from her spirit with something good. "I'm fuckin' sorry, Eden."

Affection ridged her face, and she was touching mine again. "Funny how we've both told each other the same thing tonight."

There was no stopping it, the way my hand curled around her

wrist, and I was bringing her palm to my mouth, laying a gentle kiss to the soft, soft skin.

"Not the same," I whispered.

I stared up at her, unsure how to handle this. How to deal. Not when I was aching. Aching for this girl who was clearly aching for someone else. "What happened to him?"

Her head shook, and she warily peeked at me, her voice thin, taxed with sorrow. "Nothing glamorous. A car accident in the middle of the day."

I squeezed her knees. Why I was encouraging her to continue, I didn't know. Didn't need to know any of this shit.

But I wanted to hold her pain, too.

Her tongue darted out to wet her lips. "He was supposed to pick me up after school that day." Her expression deepened with the memory, her gaze focused on the picture, her voice far away. "I remember waiting and waiting and waiting. Watching for him to come around the corner. I knew he'd make a big joke about bein' late. Make up some crazy story to make me laugh and take away my worry." She shifted her sorrow back to me. "But he never came."

I reached up and brushed a lock of thick blonde from the side of her face. "I'm so sorry. So fuckin' sorry."

I needed to stand up. Get gone. Because this was so far outside what I was equipped for. I was a prick just for kneeling there at her feet. Girl so high above me that I was a fool for wanting to reach out and touch.

Hold it.

Worse was the jealousy. This sick, sick feeling that someone'd had what was supposed to be mine.

Never said I wasn't a twisted fuck.

Emotion tweaked the side of her face that shined with the tears that streamed, girl looking at me again like I was different. Like she was the one in awe when she was the only thing I could see.

My hand was still in her hair, brushing it back. Stirring that energy. That connection that didn't belong.

We were opposites.

All wrong.

But I couldn't shake the sense that I was supposed to be there. Right then.

"You miss him?" Why I couldn't help from asking it, I didn't know. But it was out there in the air. A stumbling block that was sure to trip me up.

Old affection whispered through her words, broken and real. "I always will."

Had to end this right then. I was in way over my head. There was nothing I could do to compete with that kind of love. That kind of devotion. That kind of loyalty.

Knew full well that's what she needed.

I started to push back and stand.

Eden scrambled to keep me there, her hands on my cheeks and that look on her face. The one that connected us in a way that it shouldn't. Bond so fierce but destined to break.

Her words filled the room. Wonder and a plea. "He was my best friend, Trent. I loved him. After he died, I thought I would never feel anything again. I succumbed to being numb. A prisoner to the vacancy that I thought was a life sentence."

Get up. Get lost. Get gone.

Was chanting it while I knelt in front of her, every rational part of my brain telling me to go. Rest of me?

I was stuck.

Tied.

Bound.

Her features twisted in the same confusion they'd been watching me with from the beginning.

"Then I met you...I met you and I felt something for the first time. How is that, Trent? After all these years, after all this time, I meet you and something inside me lit? Something dead for so long, and the sight of you sparked it, this piece of me alive again for the first time?"

My insides twisted with her confession. A mangle of emotions swept up in a storm.

"Eden, fuck, don't wanna hurt you."

"I think I'm already past taking that chance. When you didn't show today..."

She trailed off.

The implication hung in the air.

Her true fears and anger coming to light.

No doubt, waiting for me had brought all those bad memories spiraling back.

A groan rumbled in my chest. "Eden, baby, I'm sorry."

"I'm sorry, too...for the way I reacted."

"Don't apologize. I get it."

"Do you? Do you get what I'm feeling? Do you feel it?" Eden tipped her face to the side.

My throat felt like the Sahara. So dry. On fire.

Could barely nod as I brushed my fingers along her jaw. "Is he the last man that touched you?"

There I went, flying down a hazardous, perilous lane.

But I needed to know.

She tucked her chin, the pants ripping from her lungs hard and haggard, her voice rough when she returned her eyes to mine. "He's the only man who's ever touched me."

Air heaved free on a ragged grunt, and my hands moved to her knees, cinching down tight.

"Fuck...Eden."

"I don't know how to stop this. Fight this. What I feel from you. What I want from you." Need and desperation fueled the words. "It's...different from anything I've experienced before. This...want. This ache I feel all over when you're near. It's more, Trent. More."

My laughter was low. Dry. Close to being unhinged. "You think it's any different for me, Eden? Fact I never told a soul about how I ended up here? How I ended up with Gage? What's it about you that makes me feel safe for the first time in my life?"

Trust her when I'd sworn I'd never trust an outsider again.

"It's this...this feeling." Frantically, she gathered one of my hands and spread it against her chest. Against the boom, boom, boom that thundered manic at her ribs. Uncontained. Reckless and out of control. "It's this. Do you feel it? Tell me you do, too, because I'm so tired of being alone."

"I'll fuck it up." Didn't need to answer it straight. Admit it. Fact this girl had me on my knees made it clear enough. But she needed to know one thing. "I'll ruin you. Don't fuckin' mistake it."

It was a growl. A warning I already knew this girl wasn't going to heed.

Because neither of us were immune to this.

She pressed my hand down farther. "It's okay because it's the loneliness that hurts the most."

For a few minutes, I was going to take it away.

Greed rumbled up my throat, and my hand she had pressed against the raging of her heart spread wider, pressing tight up against all that gorgeous, honeyed flesh before I was pushing forward, my face pressed to her dress, against the fabric that covered her stomach.

"Eden."

It was a grunt.

A plea.

A warning.

Because I didn't know how either of us were going to come back from this.

Should walk.

Hell, I should fuckin' run. Get on my bike and put a state or two between us. End this before it got any more complicated.

But those fingers drove into my hair, hanging on tight to the point of pain, and I was grumbling the promise into the fabric of her dress, "Gonna touch you, baby. Gonna make you feel right."

She whimpered, and I pulled back a fraction so I could take her in. So I could get a good look at this timid seductress sitting propped on the edge of her bed.

Her breath all around, her heart beating out of control, her chest writhing in desperate heaves.

I glided my hand down her trembling belly, around the curve of her hip, all the way until I was back to holding her by both knees. Dipping down, I pressed my nose to the inside of her left thigh.

Slowly, I dragged it up.

Inhaling as I went.

Sucking down that sweet, honeyed scent.

She shivered, and her hands tightened in my hair. "Trent."

"I've got you. I've got you."

I had this precious girl in the palm of my hands. Ruinin' her the way I did.

Couldn't stop. Couldn't stop.

And I swore to god, she would like it tonight.

The ruining.

The destroying.

She trembled as I slipped my palms under the material of her dress and glided it higher until she was all exposed, quivering, silky thighs.

Lush and curved.

A perfect fantasy.

Lust pounded through my bloodstream, seeing her this way. So damned sexy. So fuckin' sweet. Everything I shouldn't have. Shouldn't want. What I was going to take because I didn't know how to stop.

"You're beautiful, Eden. Fuckin' heaven," I murmured against the flesh, nose riding the length of her inner thigh until I was pressing it to the lacy white fabric covering that sweet spot I was dying to get lost in.

"Little Temptress."

I ran my nose through the seam, tongue stroking out.

Just the faintest taste of this girl and I was about to boil over.

Lose control.

Eden gasped. Gasped as her chest arched. A hiss from her teeth. "Trent...I-I..." Words scraped from her tongue, lost and desperate to find landing.

"Know what you need, Kitten. Tonight, I won't even make you beg for it," I grunted at the fabric, edging back enough that I could meet the weight of those eyes as I wound my fingers in the edges of her panties. I began to drag them down the length of the toned, smooth skin of those long, long legs.

My gaze ate up every inch of her as I went.

Those eyes and that face and her quivering, needy body.

Her desire.

Her need.

Didn't forget the fact that this girl needed care, too. Truth of the fear that lingered in her gaze and shivered through her spirit.

I mean, fuck, the last man—only man—who'd touched her, long fucking gone and now a monster like me was in his place.

And I got the sense she'd never been touched quite like this. That I was going to mark her a little in the way she'd been marking me.

I unwound her underwear from her ankles, her dress bunched up around her thighs.

Every inch of this girl was pink and flushed.

I traced the color with my finger, riding up the top of her thigh, girl sucking in a sharp breath.

"So pretty," I muttered.

Those eyes flared and flashed.

"So perfect."

I kept pushing her dress higher.

"So right."

"That's what I feel when you look at me," she admitted. "I shouldn't, but I do."

My eyes were hungry as I spread her knees wide so I could get a look at that perfect pussy.

She whimpered, her hands going out to fist in the comforter that covered her bed.

Possession wound through my being, seeing her like this, an angel with a devil at her feet.

Only for me.

My gaze devoured her, every inch, most of her covered in that modest dress while I had her exposed in the most explicit way. Weaving my wickedness on the pure. Tainting this perfection.

And when I did, I was going to be sure she never forgot about me.

"Paradise…haven't even tasted your cunt, and I know that's what it's gonna be."

Eden wheezed, her ass wiggling a bit on the bed because she was needy, too. Her slit drenched for me, and I was diving in, tongue delving deep between her lips.

Sweet.

So goddamn sweet.

She whimpered and jerked, jolted by the impact, the starstruck moan coming from her whipping me into a dream.

Gripping her by the outside of her thighs, I held her open wide, tongue roving, exploring her from clit to ass and back again.

Lapping and sucking.

And Eden was writhing.

In an instant.

In a heartbeat.

With a stroke of my tongue.

Losing her mind when I turned to focus on that swollen notch that was throbbing and engorged.

I flattened my tongue and licked her in long, hard strokes. My hands that had been on the outside of her thighs slipped around as the girl spread herself wide.

Needing more.

My name a chant of confusion and desperation. "Trent. Please. God. I can't…I don't."

"Got you," I grunted, tongue slaking out before I thrust my fingers in real fucking deep.

Her pussy was hot and soaked. I wasn't even in her, and she was still the best thing I'd ever felt.

My dick strained. If I didn't get inside this girl, I just might die.

But I knew better. Knew better. And I was going to give this girl one thing.

So I ate her up. Tongue and soul and teeth.

She writhed. Jerked and moaned. Little mewls, so good I thought I just might come.

Eden was gasping, her arms curling around my head. "Do you feel it?" she rasped.

Her spirit was all around her.

Her goodness in the air.

Her belief.

Her trust.

I did.

I fucking did.

I felt them all.

And I drove my fingers deeper. Stroking her just right until she was a bundle of nerves about to go off.

Winding and winding.

Girl riding higher.

Felt it when she split.

Her head flew back, and her heart raced wild, and her walls tightened and throbbed against my fingers.

On a moan, she whispered my name.

A dream.

A claim.

"Trent. Trent."

And I could feel her goodness taking us whole. Whispers of a life like this.

A girl and a boy.

A boy who wasn't dirty. One who wasn't vile.

A man worthy of standing by her side.

That man couldn't help from moving, kissing up over the fabric of her dress, riding higher.

Over her chest and up her throat.

Fingers in her hair and his mouth on her lips.

He kissed her.

Kissed her slow and desperate and with every little bit he had to give.

Soft strokes of tongues and a frantic plea of whimpers and groans.

Fingers sinking into his shoulders and a whisper on her soul.

"Trent."

Trent. Trent. Trent.

Except that man didn't really exist.

But maybe neither of us could recognize it right then.

Because Eden was kissing me back.

Her mouth making a path down my throat, hands under my shirt. She ripped it over my head.

Autumn eyes stroked me like a caress, her breaths shallow and jagged and her hands shaking when she brushed the statement tattooed on my side.

Ghost.

Her gaze flashed to mine in some kind of recognition.

The man I could never leave behind.

And I swore it was trust and affection that lit the room when she slid off the bed and onto her knees.

I held her by the sides of that unforgettable face. "Baby…not necessary…you don't owe me a thing."

But she was at my fly and shoving my jeans down my hips, cock twitching like a fiend when it sprung free and she took me in her hand.

"You're so beautiful," she murmured as she looked up at me.

Somehow it was the same for the both of us.

Maybe for a beat. For a second. That's the way I felt beneath the grace of those giving eyes.

She stroked me soft. Timid. I hissed and curled my hand tight around hers.

"Like it hard, Kitten," I grunted. "You don't need to be shy. Not with me."

Eden whimpered, kissed down my chest and over my stomach.

And I was gone.

My hands on the side of her head and my dick buried deep in her throat.

Fucking drowning in the sanctuary of her mouth.

And I didn't ever want to come up for air.

Chapter Fifteen

Trent

Los Angeles – Eighteen Years Ago

"CUTTER, LET HIM GO. YOU CAN'T DO THIS."

His mother raced out behind them where his dad dragged him by the neck of the shirt toward the truck parked at the curb. The blood in Trent's veins pounded so hard. He felt it in his ears. In his chest. His stomach sick.

It'd been so long since his dad had come there, he'd thought maybe he was gone for good. No longer comin' around makin' his mom cry. His mom who said he wasn't welcome. That she didn't want nothin' to do with his bad, bad life.

His dad spun around, in her face, growling the words. "The fuck, I can't. Know your place, woman."

Trent's mom blanched and turned red all at the same time, her worry wrapping him in dread, her green eyes washing over him like she would be willing to fight to get him freed.

"My place? I never agreed to any of that nonsense, and I sure as hell am not gonna stand by and let you drag my son into that mess."

Trent's chest felt funny. Like it was buzzing and full and going to explode. Like his hands were tingling with anger.

His dad shook him. "About time this boy learned some respect. All of 'em. Get where they're goin'. Who they are. We start with him."

Trent flailed and tried to break away. "Let me go. I don't wanna go nowhere with you."

His dad smacked him on the back of the head.

His mom raged, pushed forward. "Don't you dare lay a hand on him."

Trent's dad had his mom by the throat.

Trent wanted to weep.

To fight.

His throat locked up and moisture filled his eyes.

But he couldn't do anything but stand there frozen while the monster hissed, "I'll do whatever the fuck I want. Should have ended you long ago, bitch. Think you can talk to me like that? Get a say in what I do with my boys? They might live here, but they belong to me. You got it? You're lucky I let you breathe."

She whimpered and scratched at his hand.

He squeezed tight. "Do you understand?"

Her head jerked in a spastic nod.

As much as he fought it, a tear got free of Trent's eye. His mom saw it, flinched, stumbled back when his dad shoved her away. Then he was shoving Trent into the front seat of the truck and slamming the door shut.

Trent slumped down. A nasty feeling boiled in his belly as he looked out the side window at his mom who stood in the middle of the yard while his dad rounded the front of the truck.

Horror and shame on her face. He pressed his fingertips to the glass.

Tears streamed down her eyes.

He was still looking at her when he was smacked again from out of nowhere.

Trent jolted forward, warily peeking over at his dad who looked at him with hate.

With the same kind of hate Trent felt deep in his soul.

The ugly, ugly kind.

The kind he thought might turn black.

"No son of mine is gonna be a pussy," his dad snarled as he turned the ignition and pulled out onto the street. "Twelve damned years old. Bad enough your pathetic twin is always sucking on that air like he can't breathe on his own. Your momma made you all spineless. Weak. I'll knock those tears right outta you, boy. You wanna get cut? Dumped in a canal? You show weakness in this world, and you're done. Now man the fuck up because you have big shoes to fill. One day when I'm gone, you'll sit as President of the Iron Owls, and it's about damned time you start to learn what it's gonna mean to take that position."

Trent sank deeper into the seat as if he could disappear.

He didn't want nothin' to do with the man his mom feared.

The one who left her eyes blued and her mouth bloodied.

But how could he get away from a man like that?

Footsteps treaded quietly into his room. Trent buried himself deeper under the covers. Like he could hide. Pretend he didn't exist. That what he'd seen never happened.

It was just a bad dream.

The edge of his mattress dipped, and that tender voice filled the air. His mom was singing her favorite song. The one about forgiveness when you'd done bad things.

But he was pretty sure what his father had forced him to watch was not one of those things. Something that could ever be covered or forgotten.

He knew he never would.

He shivered, his stomach sick, his head spinning.

Blood.

So much blood.

He'd thrown up then, and his dad had smacked him again.

His mom pulled back the covers and brushed her fingers through his hair.

Softly.

Gently.

Like she'd done when he was a little boy.

Like he was still good.

Like he hadn't had that blood splattered on his shirt when his father had dumped him on the lawn and told him he'd be back soon.

"It's okay, my brave boy. You don't have to hide from me. I'll never hurt you. Never judge you."

Trent shifted, barely peeking out from under the sheet he had pulled over his face. "I don't wanna go back, Mom. I don't want to be like him."

"Shh…" she whispered, leaning down to brush a kiss to his forehead. "I know, baby. I know. I'm gonna find a way. Find a way for us to disappear. You, and your brothers, and me. Does that sound nice?"

He fiercely nodded his head.

"It's our secret, okay? Until we go, you don't tell anyone."

He nodded again. "I'll take care of us, Mom. Wherever we go."

"I know, my sweet warrior, I know."

Chapter Sixteen

Eden

THE SECOND TESSA TURNED HER ATTENTION AWAY, I ducked my head and tried to sneak out of the teachers' lounge without being noticed.

"Um, excuse me? You stop right there, Eden Jasmine Murphy. There's nowhere you can hide. I know where you live."

I should have known I'd never be fast enough.

Whirling around, I found myself backed against the long prep counter. Two feet from the door. So close to my escape.

Trapped.

Tessa pointed at me as she advanced.

I swore, she was part bloodhound. Scenting out a secret like it was what God had created her to do.

I itched, gave her the most innocent, faked expression I could find. "Um…excuse me, what?"

There.

Play it off.

Act like I had no clue what she was talking about.

I was so not prepared for her inquisition this morning, but of course, I'd only made it worse with all my fumbling, rambling words and heated cheeks when she'd asked how my night was last night—in front of five other teachers, mind you. Then I'd gone and tried to sneak out without saying goodbye.

I might as well have tossed a yellow flag in the air.

Called a foul.

Pointed out my questionable, bad behavior.

I mean, at the time, it hadn't felt wrong, but the moment he'd slipped out my door, every question and reservation I possessed had begun to invade.

My night had been spent twisted in my sheets.

Overheated.

Overwhelmed.

Overcome.

My heart thudding with the shout, *What had I done?*

Tessa cocked her head, purebred hunter that she was, her eyes widening and her mouth dropping open. Her words were held on a hissed whisper as she looked around to make sure the rest of the teachers weren't paying us any attention. "You had s-e-x."

Yeah, like she was speaking in code and there was no one else who could decipher what she said if they were to overhear it.

"I did not," I hissed right back.

Her blue eyes narrowed. "Liar."

I crossed my arms in defense. "I didn't...exactly."

She crossed hers in speculation. "Didn't exactly what?" she pressed, brow shooting for the sky.

Ugh.

"I didn't officially." I tossed it out all offhanded like.

No big deal.

Like my best friend didn't know me inside and out. Like she didn't know it would be a *really big deal*.

Her jaw hit the floor, and she snatched me by the wrist, glancing behind us once before she dragged me into the large storage closet. The door snapped shut behind us at the same second the demand slung out of her mouth. "What did you just say?"

I fidgeted, the words so quiet I doubted they had volume. "I said, not officially."

Her hand curled tighter around my wrist. "Oh my god...I was joking. Trying to get a rise out of you...and you did?!" The shriek she let go was barely contained.

"I already told you I didn't."

"But you did...you did. Like there was hot, hot *nekedness* going down? Tell me it's true." Her voice hitched like she'd been granted her greatest wish.

I smacked at her, wrangling out of her hold. "What is wrong with you? This is my daddy's school and there are five other teachers on the other side of that door." In emphasis, I jabbed a finger at it.

I was no little girl, but the last thing I needed was my father to catch wind of what I'd been up to last night. He had enough on his mind without my worrying him more.

And oh, would he worry.

"Um...our school, too. And newsflash, your dad just wants you to be happy, the same way as I do."

"Ha. He'd get one look at Trent and lock me in a closet with lined padding."

Certain I'd lost my mind.

I probably had.

"Look at you...our little Eden sleeping with her boss." She said it like it was salacious. A straight-up scandal. All with a twinkle in her eye.

"Again, I didn't sleep with him."

She angled back in clear appraisal. "Well, whatever you did, the man clearly blew your mind."

My teeth clamped down on my bottom lip, my chest nearly exploding as I was thrown back to it. I dropped my gaze, warring, before I peeked at my best friend. "I don't think I've ever felt the way I did last night."

Beautiful.

Wanted.

Something different than adored. Beyond it or maybe at the opposite of it.

An encounter so desperate that it verged on criminal.

A decadent sin.

It'd felt as if the man might die if he didn't get a taste of me, the same way I'd felt about him.

A man who held the ugliest of secrets. One who'd let me take a peek into the skeletons buried in his closet, invited me into his confidence.

Trusted me.

Even then, I was betting I'd only scratched the surface of how corrupt it got.

In the end, it still hadn't mattered.

The fact he was all wrong.

That he was dangerous.

Everything I shouldn't want.

Everything I should fear.

I'd still surrendered to the pull.

"And you feel guilty?" Tessa surmised, softness winding into her tone.

"Shouldn't I?"

Her expression deepened in profound encouragement. "It's been six years, Eden."

Old agony tightened my chest, all mixed up with this new beginning that I wasn't sure could be real. Something I needed to snuff out before it burned me alive.

"But I always thought..." I trailed off.

Tessa inched closer, all her teasing gone, her understanding firm and fast. "What?"

The words rushed out on a shamed whisper, "I always thought if I felt something again...wanted someone again...loved someone again, it would be secondary. Less."

"And you're afraid this Trent guy could overshadow your memories of Aaron."

I heaved a breath and gave her the bare truth. "I'm afraid he could consume me. Destroy me with a glance. And I know this time, I'm not going to come out okay on the other side."

"He's your wild card."

My brow curled.

"The one you didn't expect. The one you couldn't have anticipated. The one you could love so much, you're afraid to try. The ace. The winning number." She leaned forward, and her tone slipped back into a tease. "Eden, he's the cake."

Her lips twitched at that, and tears blurred my eyes while an unamused laugh slipped up my throat. "What I'm afraid of is that he is a broken heart."

I couldn't bear to tell her the rest. His history. The evil that lurked. That he was doing little more than running. Hiding from his sins. From his pain. From his loss.

No question, willing to fight—to cut down—anyone who might get in his way. And somehow, I'd become the woman who wanted to stand with him through all of that.

Tessa reached out and wiped a tear that streaked down my face. "It's the ones we're afraid of that end up meaning the most."

A heavy breath escaped my lungs, the words firm because I wasn't going to start deluding myself. "I'm pretty sure he doesn't want a life with me, Tessa."

I doubted the man even knew how. He had one focus, and he didn't know how to look outside of that. But last night…last night it'd felt as if maybe he could. As if maybe both of us could look outside ourselves, beyond what we thought we were destined for, and find each other.

Collide in the middle.

Her smile was soft. "Of course, he doesn't think he would want that. I have no doubt he's afraid of you, too. Of what you could mean."

My heart shivered and shook, as fiercely as my head. "I let him touch me, knowing he was going to break me in the end."

I could already feel it, trembling around me, the coming devastation.

Her lips thinned. "You let him touch you because you were taking a chance, Eden. Opening yourself up. Stepping out in your belief. He'd be a fool not to do the same for you. And considering his kid is like the smartest five-year-old I've ever met, this guy has to have something going for him."

Playfully, she grinned.

I managed an awkward giggle. "Well, he has a couple things going for him."

Her eyes widened with glee. "Oh, and I hope one of those things is a really big dick."

She singsonged it.

I choked over the laugh that sputtered from my mouth. "I hate you."

"No, you don't…you love me. Like…mad love. Mad, mad love." She gushed it as she wrapped her arms around me and pulled me to her chest. Her voice dropped. "Crazy, mad love, Eden. The kind you're going to find, whether it's with Trent or someone else. You aren't done yet. I won't let you be."

My chest squeezed. Adoration thick. "I do love you, Tessa. Mad, mad love."

I felt her grin against my head, and then she jumped back when the bell buzzed through the speakers. "Oh crap. We're late."

She spun around and jerked open the door, trying to hide her laughter when two fifth-grade teachers jumped in surprise with us bursting through, Tessa still towing me behind her. She let go of her laughter the second we busted through the lounge doors and out into the corridor.

"That was close," she tossed out from the side, her hand still snug on mine, pulling me along and looking behind her as if we'd just gotten away with a jewelry heist.

"Just a warning, if my daddy needs to *talk* to me today, I'm blaming you and sending you in my place."

"Pssh…" She waved me off. "Bring it on. That man adores me."

Gratitude filled me as I squeezed her hand. My wild friend

who always stood for me. Went to bat for me. Cared for me, no matter what.

"Of course, he does. How could he not?"

She gave a tight squeeze. "Back at you, baby," she whispered right before we parted. Tessa went right down the intersecting hall and I went left. "Hope you have a great day, BFF," she shouted out ahead, her voice fading the farther she went.

"Oh," she hollered over her shoulder, slowing me. She had a glint in her eyes when I looked back. "Don't think just because we got sidetracked you're going to get off with not telling me about that cake. I want all the details. Just how yummy it was and how much you ate."

I hate you, I mouthed.

She formed her hands into a heart, making it pound. Her smile turned into this massive, ridiculous grin.

A giggle slipped free, and I gave her a tiny finger wave before I turned on my heel and rushed in the direction of my classroom. One of the aides who'd been watching my students on the playground had them in a line and was leading them inside the room.

I followed right behind.

The clatter of children laughing and excited for their day filled my heart with joy. With a chaotic peace.

I'd always thought their little faces were the promise of something better. That they were the hope of this world when it felt like everything might fall apart.

But it was one little face that melted a crater through the middle of me. One that made my feet falter and my heart swell to overflowing. His giant backpack bounced all over his back as he came bounding for me through the classroom. "Miss Murphy, Miss Murphy!"

Gage had his arm in the air, waving his hand over his head, his precious smile dimpling his chubby cheeks and his caramel eyes dancing with his joy. "Look it, Miss Murphy. I made something for you! You wanna see? You wanna see?"

I knelt in front of him.

Unable to stand.

I swore, I could feel my spirit twining with his, the magnet that was this child winding me with his.

Spinning, spinning, spinning.

Until I no longer recognized myself anymore.

"You did?" I whispered. Affection rode out. Fierce and unstoppable.

I was in trouble. So much trouble.

He beamed up at me. "Yup. My dad even got up really, really early and helped me 'cause I told him it had to be way extra super special."

He stuck out his tiny hand that he'd been waving in the air. In his palm was a thin bracelet made of blue string with beads tied haphazardly along it.

"Look it, Miss Murphy!" He scrambled to get closer as he hovered over where I held it. Excitement blazed from his little body as he started to explain. "It's got a book because you're a teacher and teachers love books, right, Miss Murphy, right?"

He looked at me for approval.

I gave him a soft nod.

Unable to speak.

"And then it's got a ballet slipper for all your dances, and I think maybe I wanna go to one of those after school."

My chest squeezed.

I could hardly breathe.

He pointed at the last. "And this one is a star because my dad said you're like heaven and the stars are way, way up high in heaven, right?"

With that one, he looked at me, his eyes creased in question. Not quite sure.

My heart thudded. My breath short. My throat locked.

His nose scrunched up. "So, what do you think? You think it's the best ever? Because you're the best teacher in the whole worlds, and I want to stay right here with you forever! Would that be okay, Miss Murphy?"

Affection crushed through my being, tearing everything apart.

Destroying everything I'd known.

Rearranging.

Refiguring.

Restructuring.

I touched his face.

Overcome.

My favorite. My favorite.

Only it was more than that.

Terrifying and true.

I was falling for both Lawson men.

And I had no idea what I was supposed to do.

Chapter Seventeen

Eden

CLASSICAL MUSIC ECHOED THROUGH THE HALL, THE hardwood floors of the studio familiar beneath my feet. The lights were dimmed, only the barest glow emanating from the recessed coves and glowing through the rambling space. The walls were mirrored, and the barres had been pushed aside after my last class of the day.

It was just after six, and I should have been at home grabbing a quick nap before I went in for my shift at the club tonight.

But I needed this.

To dance.

To let my body flow with the tempo.

To be entranced by the moves.

Entranced by the music.

To let my heart rise and fall with the beat.

Where it was just me and the beauty of the movement.

I dipped into a plié before rising up and jumping into a grande jeté. I glided from one move to the other. A mix of graceful and harsh. The music hushed and held in anticipation before it would rise to a thrill of mini-crescendos.

It was funny how ballet was such an intrinsic part of me, yet it still felt incredibly private.

It was where I found myself. Where I lost myself. Where worries and concerns drifted away into the nothingness, and the only thing that mattered was the feeling. The sensation coursing through my veins.

As if I were flying.

Free.

Alive.

It was a little unnerving how that feeling could be so closely compared to Trent Lawson.

In the moment, all rational thought gone. Sane judgement slayed.

When dancing, the only thing I was living for was the high. The rush.

And in the heat of the moment with Trent, the only thing of any consequence or consideration was the ghosting of his fingertips across my skin. The sizzle of those eyes and the impact of those hands.

An entirely different high. An entirely different rush. One I wasn't sure I could ever stop chasing.

Which was why I'd needed to come here and hide myself away. Get lost somewhere else.

Nothing but the charge of adrenaline and the march of the composition.

Art.

Where I understood what I wanted. Who I was and where I stood.

Where there weren't flickers of fear or a blaze of need.

I moved into a pirouette as the music rose to its highest height. I spun and spun, alternating between point and demi-point. Round and round and round. My pulse thundered, and my chest stretched tight with the exertion as every muscle in my body flexed and extended.

Bound with the beautiful exhaustion of this labor of love.

Shivers raced.

That feeling lifting.

Sensation flashed across my flesh.

Growing and compounding.

In it, I let myself completely go. All inhibitions floored. Crushed under the thunder of my feet.

I spun and spun. The mirrors were a blur of streaking ribbons and light. It felt as if it might be the only way for me to fly. To rise to the surreal. Where these impossible questions might hold answers.

It only amplified. Increased. And I was gasping when the song hit its end and cut off with a sudden, jarring high-pitched note.

One second later, a softer, more somber song filtered through the overhead speakers.

But I didn't feel somber or at ease.

Warmth spiraled down my spine, overheating my already sweat-slicked skin.

Tingles raced.

Prickles of need hitched in my spirit.

A glitch in my soul.

Panting, I stilled, shocked out of the trance. My eyes adjusted to the dimly-lit dance studio. Through the mirror, I caught sight of the silhouette at the back, already knowing he would be there.

That menacing, intimidating man stood just inside the double doors with his hands stuffed in his pockets.

A wicked temptation.

A beautiful wish.

Hungry eyes met mine through the reflection, a tangle of greed and awe. A shockwave of that energy blistered through the air, nearly knocking me from my feet.

"What are you doing here?" I could barely force out the question between the surprise and desire that lit.

"Needed to see you," he grunted.

"Did you sign in?"

He cracked a grin. Sweet but at my expense.

"Always following the rules, aren't you, Kitten?"

Redness clawed up my neck and splashed my cheeks. I was pretty sure I broke a thousand of my own rules last night. Gave in and let go.

I couldn't begin to find a way to regret that now.

Not when Trent took a step forward and the ground trembled beneath my feet.

A tiny earthquake.

A warning of coming destruction as he advanced.

Darkness swept like shadows across the dance floor as he edged my direction. Slow. Measured. The hunter circling his prey. His eyes wild and his mouth watering.

My already heaving breaths turned jagged. Short and choppy. Nerves jumping into my bloodstream and wreaking havoc on my senses.

Excitement and confusion and desire.

Because he was every single thing I'd never thought I'd want. The exact type of man I'd never go after.

I'd wanted security.

Safety.

Peace.

Hell, I'd never even had to run from a man like him before because I'd never let myself get that close.

But there I was, my spirit thrashing and whipping and begging him to come near.

He stole forward. A dark, dark storm that gathered from the corners of the room.

Encroaching.

Invading.

Overtaking.

His breath hit the back of my neck, and it sent a rash of shivers racing across my flesh, goosebumps lifting in anticipation of what was to come.

He ghosted his fingertips down my right arm, chasing the thrill, the heady breaths jutting from his lungs curling through the air and inundating my senses.

Leather and nutmeg and man.

Lust pooled in my belly, and I couldn't look away from that fierce, unrelenting gaze that held me captive through the mirrors.

"Think I just walked into a dream, Eden, you in here owning that floor. A fucking superstar hidden away in a mountain town, only for me to see." He murmured it at my bare shoulder, those eyes watching me as he did. "Look at you."

His lips barely brushed my flesh.

So soft. A tender caress.

But those eyes were hardly tender when they took my reflection in.

They were raving.

Roving.

Half-mad.

"What do you see?" I let the question free, the words wispy tendrils that curled through the dense, heated air.

His intense eyes flared, and he exhaled as he splayed a big hand across my belly covered by my leotard and moved his mouth to my ear. "I see the most gorgeous woman I've ever seen. Kind of beauty that knocks the breath from my lungs every time I catch a glimpse. So goddamn sexy I can't think straight. So sweet I forget my name."

The words were a heave and a hook.

I trembled beneath them, barely able to breathe as he continued, "I see a treasure. I see a vision. I see light and goodness and grace. I see *Heaven*. I see everything I shouldn't want. Everything I don't deserve."

He pulled me tighter against the strength of his body. We'd begun to sway, this slow dance that twined our spirits as one. Our bodies melting into the other.

"But I also see a tragedy, Eden. Pain waiting out ahead to devour us both. I know I can't take what I want because that kind of selfishness is only going to ruin us all in the end. And here I am, the greedy bastard standing with you in my arms because I don't have the first clue how to stay away from you."

I gulped. Struggled to remain strong. To stand for what I'd stood for all my life.

But somehow…somehow that image had changed. Brushstrokes painting a new picture. Something so stunning you couldn't help but stare.

So often it were the most haunting canvases that created the most priceless beauty.

"What is it you see, Kitten, when you look at me?" It was a gruff challenge. I got the sense he wanted me to admit I was afraid after what he'd revealed last night. He craved my disgust because it was the only thing he knew.

Part of it was true. The truth that my entire being quivered with the dread. With the ideas of what his life might have looked like before. The violence and brutality.

But more, I wondered how that might spill into the here and now. What he might be capable of.

Who was the man currently wrapped around me? The one who held me like a hedge of safety? A shield? Hope in the bleakness that had dimmed both our lives?

"I see a man who's held me from the moment I met him. A man so devastatingly gorgeous he tripped up my feet and set my heart on fire. Made it burn for the first time in years. In a way it never had."

Against better judgement, I let that confession out.

Possession left him on a grunt, and he curled his arms tighter around me as my whispered words filled the atmosphere, "I see a man who holds the power to spark to life what once was dead. I see a father. I see a protector. I see a warrior. I see someone who is good and kind when he has no idea that he is. I see a kind of beauty I've never recognized before."

Every muscle in his towering frame flexed.

Peril and perfection.

"Eden," he muttered.

We were rocking. Swaying and drifting. Our limbs tangled as we fell into a slow slide of sensation.

Still, I pushed, giving him more of my truth the way he'd given his. "I also see my heart shattered all over the place if I let this go much farther. I see your fear, Trent, and I see what it's become. It's become savagery. A threat of devastation."

The man exhaled, those arms unwavering. "Always been that, Eden, from day one. That's what it's been. Savagery and devastation.

Only thing that ever softened it was Gage." He pressed his nose to the back of my neck, running it up the length until it was buried in my hair. "And you. You are the only thing that could make this evil heart go soft, and that's probably the most dangerous part of all. Fact you make me want to let my guard down. Give in when I've been given one thing to live for. Don't know how to live for two."

Despair wound with his admission, his voice cracking with an old grief that he would forever possess.

I wanted to wrap him up. Tell him we could try. That we could be good together.

That maybe if we just met in the middle...

"It would never work." He gruffed it like he was answering a question I'd asked aloud.

"I know," I whispered. "There are things I want for my life that I'm pretty sure you don't."

Love and life and stability.

I didn't need a white-picket fence, but I wanted a family.

A home.

Children to fill it.

To be cherished, loved, and a priority to a man who crawled into bed with me night after night.

It seemed like a no brainer with Gage built in, but that vein of scars might have cut too deep. And with the little he'd exposed about his childhood growing up, I didn't get the sense he'd had the healthiest of experiences.

And more than that, I wanted—I needed—safety. For my children to have it.

Gage filled my mind. Those eyes and those cheeks and his sweet words. My heart felt like it would implode with my love for him. This protectiveness zapping me straight through.

And somehow, I knew—trusted with every part of me—this man would do everything to protect him.

"And still, look at your face. Those eyes watching me like they know me," he rasped against my flesh. Everything beat. Pounded and shook.

"I don't know how to look away," I whispered.

"View ain't pretty, Kitten."

"You're wrong. It's stunning."

He gave a harsh shake of his head. "Nah. My view is much better."

His lips brushed along the slope of my neck. My knees nearly buckled. "It's torment getting a peek at Heaven from the vantage of Hell. Maybe that's the real meaning of eternal punishment."

My brow furrowed. "Is that really what you think? That you're condemned?"

A low grumble of disbelief rumbled in his throat, and his hand glided up my neck, fingers digging into the tight twist of my hair. "If there is an afterlife? Believe me, baby, I know exactly where I'm going."

My chest ached. "I don't believe that."

"Because you believe in what's not there."

Wow. That hurt.

"You believe in me," he clarified.

My eyes were pinned on his through the mirror. "Don't you think it's time someone did?"

The twitch of a smile kissed the edge of his sinful mouth. "There we go, trying to figure out how this would work. How two opposites could be when we know we don't fit."

"It'd be fun trying." My voice was the tendril of a plea as I repeated the same thing he'd said to me the first time he'd followed me home.

Although this—it no longer felt like a mistake.

He let go of a rough, jagged chuckle.

Warmth and light.

It flooded me.

Filled me full.

And he didn't even know.

His hand caressed down my left arm. It left a trail of flames in its wake. He didn't stop until he was tracing over the bracelet that his son had made. The one I wore around my wrist. One I doubted I would ever remove. "We need to end this now before it hurts too much. My son is already half in love with you."

I'm already half in love with you.

I didn't dare say it.

Emotion gathered in my throat, my words thick and soggy when I admitted, "I care about him so much."

Too much.

My eyes glistened in the bare reflection, and Trent watched me like he didn't need me to say it. That he felt it. Saw it. The way I saw something shine in him, too.

"Would give anything to be a different man for you."

But that was the thing. I didn't think I wanted anyone different. I wanted him.

Reckless.

Another chip stacked against us. A push to admit he was right. We would never work.

My nod was jerky. Pulled out of me against my will.

Trent's was slow and resigned.

Then he pressed the softest kiss to the underside of my jaw. His mouth rested there.

Lingering.

I could feel him squeeze his eyes closed as he savored.

Relished.

As he remembered.

He held me tight for another moment before he peeled himself away, then the man stalked back across the room.

I could physically feel him taking the storm with him.

The whooshing of the receding wind and the void it left behind.

My breath and a piece of my heart I never should have let him have.

My lungs shuddered with the impact, my body frozen in position where I stared at the man walking away through the mirror.

He paused at the door, and he tossed me a tender grin from over his shoulder. "See ya around, Kitten."

Wistfulness tugged at my lips. Not quite a smile, though it still held more adoration than either of us could afford.

One second later, Trent opened the door and was gone.

Right along with a piece of me that I would never get back.

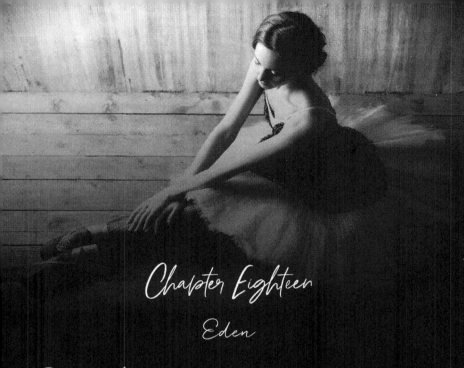

Chapter Eighteen

Eden

Do you remember...

Do you remember when Aaron moved in next door? Do you remember how you two gravitated toward each other? The two of you were the meaning of fast friends. Like you'd known each other your whole lives. Like you knew each other inside and out.

Do you remember how I was filled with jealousy?

I didn't mean to be, but I think there was a selfish streak in me all along. The part of me that wanted everything to go my way. Exactly how I wanted it. You all for my own.

Do you remember how I lashed out? How I threw fits and accused Aaron of being mean? That he wouldn't let me play or lied and said he'd ripped my doll's head off when it was me? Do you remember how I'd go to Momma and cry?

Or maybe you don't. Maybe you were too good and kind even then that you still saw the best in me.

Do you remember how sometimes I took it out on you? How I'd push you down or laugh in your face, and then at night when you were sad, I'd crawl into your bed, wrap my arms around you, and apologize?

I remember, Eden. And I wish I could go back to those days and mean it when I said I was sorry. I wish I could start over then.

Harmony

Chapter Nineteen

Trent

I TRIED TO KICK THE BOX OF TEQUILA OUT OF THE WAY WHERE it was sitting on the floor behind the bar. Admittedly, with more force than necessary. But there was no way to control it. The way irritation swept through my bloodstream, reaching every cell, making me feel like I was coming unglued.

Glass clanked as the edge of the box caught on something, keeping it from sliding into the spot where I was trying to wedge it.

Like it was going to solve something, I kicked it harder with my boot.

It didn't budge.

I kicked again.

Then I was kicking it over and over.

Until I was holding onto the barback and fuckin' wailing away on the piece of shit, like I could beat this feeling out of my system.

Ruin something else instead of letting it ruin this bit of me.

"Whoa, there, bossman. What the fuck is going down with you? Those bottles of Milagros aren't gonna make it better unless you pour them down your throat and not onto the floor. You catch my meaning?"

I was jolted from the anger by Sage's teasing voice, and I kept holding onto the countertop, head cast down and panting for air, trying to find my sanity before I turned my aggression on him.

"Nothing is going down," I grated. Straightening, I scrubbed a palm over my face to chase away this stupidity.

He scoffed. "You've been a surly motherfucker for the last week."

"Maybe that's because all this shit is lying around where it isn't supposed to be. Get it cleaned up, yeah?" My teeth ground with the words, the frustration still getting out no matter how hard I tried to stop it.

Sage lifted his hands in surrender. "Hey now, delivery came in this afternoon and we were short staffed tonight, as you well know. Todd's doin' his best at getting it stocked before we lock up. Now how 'bout you let me pour you one while we get it cleaned up? Take the edge off? You know, before you go Godzilla on this shit."

I swiped the back of my hand over my mouth. Dude had no fucking clue what a rampage really meant.

The rough chuckle hitting me from the side had me whipping my attention to the right.

Jud was standing there, fucker laughing under his breath like he thought this shit was funny.

He glanced at Sage with a jut of his bearded jaw.

"Why don't you pour us both one?" he shouted over the din.

The bar wasn't quite packed, but at just before closing, the vibe was still unruly and wild since the band playing tonight had nearly incited a riot with how rowdy they'd been.

"It'd be my pleasure. Wait. Let me correct that. It'd be for my safety," he cracked, and he jumped back and out of the way when he saw my jaw clench, asshole laughing, too.

Fuckers.

I gave them both a finger.

Jud slipped into a barstool and patted the one next to him. "Sit down, Big Bro, before you go boom. Look like you're about to explode, and we put too much effort into this place to let you burn it to the ground because you're in a pissy mood."

Pushing out a sigh, I rounded the end of the bar and slipped into the stool next to him. Sage was already passing us our drinks by the time I got there.

"On the house." He winked.

Dude really wanted to get his ass kicked.

Jud laughed and tipped his glass to him. "Perks of ownership, my man."

"Life goals."

I wrapped my hand around the glass and brought it to my lips, prayed the burn would soothe.

Because my entire being itched. Fucked from the inside out.

Because this girl. This girl.

This girl I couldn't get off my mind, no matter what I did.

The last week had been torture. Watching her walk through the doors of Absolution night after night and not being able to go to her. Touch her and hold her. Straight misery when I'd pull up to the curb to pick up my son, and she'd be there with his hand in hers. Two fitting like they'd been made to match.

Seamless.

With the glaring offense that was me ripping them apart.

Each night, I thought it might abate, but it'd come just as strong tonight when I'd caught sight of her coming in through the side door. When that sweet heart had thudded out ahead of her like a brush of those hands, touching me from across the space.

Her body right there, so close, but just out of reach.

Guessed it was another penalty. Another cost to pay.

And shit, it pissed me off.

It was a vicious cycle. One I'd hopped right on again tonight.

Spending the entire shift trying to ignore the pull. This draw that I couldn't escape. It only grew stronger the more I tried to look away. To pretend like her presence didn't affect me. Trying to respect the boundaries we'd tossed up like we should have done in the first place.

The only thing it'd accomplished was that energy would strike me like a lash every time she got within a mile of me, which considering we'd been stuck within the confines of the bar, I'd felt like I was getting my ass whipped the whole damned night.

Cut the fuck up and wholly slayed.

Could feel the force of Jud's stare blazing into me from the side. "Wanna tell me what climbed up your ass and died? You've been a salty prick for a straight week."

I scoffed out my annoyance as I took another sip. "Nothing."

Jud rumbled a laugh, watching me as he took a gulp of his brew. "You are legit the worst liar, Trent. You might be hard as stone, but you wear it all right there on your sleeve. Rage. Anger. Love."

He tapped my shoulder with his fist to punctuate each one.

It jostled me, dude always telling it exactly like it was. My head shook in affectionate annoyance. "You know nothing."

"I know everything," he mock-whispered as he leaned in and cracked a wise-ass grin. "And I'm bettin' all this has to do with a certain hot as fuck server who keeps floating through here like some kinda daydream."

A dream.

A sanctuary.

Heaven.

My teeth clamped down on my bottom lip. "She's too much, Jud," I admitted, staring ahead as I brought the tumbler to my lips. The scotch was warm on my tongue, a caress down my throat.

Could feel the questions coming off him in waves. "Too much?"

"More than I have. More than I can give."

He scowled. "That's bullshit, man. Why don't you do all of us a favor and stop with the self-imposed misery."

"Self-imposed?" It was anger. Hate for the past. For everything we'd been pushed into. The atrocities we'd witnessed as fucking little kids and convinced it was just the way. And *the way* was what it'd become.

"Just admit what it is, man. You're fuckin' scared that you care about someone other than yourself. Other than your son. Other than us."

One reason.

"I promised Nathan." The words slashed from my tongue. Pure bitterness and straight anguish. In this oath I would never forget.

Jud flinched and then leaned closer. "You know that's not what he meant."

"He gave up his life for it. I'm pretty sure he meant it."

A big palm landed on my shoulder, and he squeezed tight. "Yeah, he meant for you to live. Not to fuckin' hide away."

"He did it for Gage."

Grief clutched Jud's face. "He did it because he was the best, Trent. Because he was nothing but good, sacrificing himself for the rest of us. Way he always did."

Agony gripped me.

My twin.

My twin.

One who was so good.

One who was kind.

One who had no blood on his hands, yet he was the one who'd died.

My lips pressed into a thin line. "Those bullets were meant for me."

Jud clamped down on my shoulder. "Yeah, because you were the one taking the risk to get the rest of us out of there."

"And Nathan ended up dead because of it."

Shots.

Screams.

Blood.

Pain poured its wrath into my soul.

Drowning.

Felt like my chest was gonna cave with the misery.

Jud's voice shifted in desperation. "You've got to let it go, man. The guilt. This wasn't what Nathan wanted. Hell, he'd be destroyed if he knew the way you've carried this."

I whirled on Jud, words low and razor-sharp. "Destroyed? You're right, Jud. He is. Destroyed. Gone. Because of me."

My fist slammed down on the bar as I fought against the consequences of the choices I'd made.

All because I'd gone after a piece of forbidden ass.

A bid of retaliation that had ruined my brother and given me the greatest gift.

Gage.

One reason. One reason.

Frustration blew from Jud's mouth, and he spun away, his elbows planted on the bar as he took a swig of his beer. Finally, he cut his eye my way, his tone softer than it'd been.

"Yeah. He is gone. Fuckin' gone and it fuckin' hurts. All of us hurt, Trent. All of us loved him like mad, and there's a big fuckin' hole in the middle of us where he used to be. But it isn't your blame, brother. And until you give up that guilt, stop condemning yourself like you were the only one involved? *That bastard* won that piece of you. Stole it."

He angled in closer, his voice his own animosity. "I bet he's holding it like a parting prize where he's floating at the bottom of the sea. You gonna let him keep it?"

Jud might as well have punched me in the rib cage.

Way the breath hurled from my lungs.

An assault of emotions that broke me open.

Fracturing and fraying.

Anguish and hate. Loss and this hope.

Fuck.

I fisted a hand in my hair.

Sage appeared in front of us and leaned on the bar. "Hey, it's getting quiet, so I cut Eden loose. She's been running the entire night and I know she was at her other job early this morning. Sure she'd appreciate some extra sleep tonight."

Could barely nod and force out, "Good."

Needed her out of my sight. Out of my thoughts. Out of my fucking heart.

Didn't know how I'd let her get there in the first place.

Why this was tearing me up.

Couldn't go there. Couldn't. I knew better.

But it didn't matter because I was already there when I felt the shift wrestle the atmosphere. The ripple of morbid interest. The rush of fear as a storm of shouts came from down the long hall that was off-limits to customers.

Still, a bunch of people rushed that way like they wanted to get a better look at what was going down.

I jumped to my feet. Jud was right beside me, dude casting me a worried look as we started to shove through the throng that was pushing and gawking.

I tossed them aside, desperation lighting in my blood, sinking deep into my bones as I fought to make it to the hall.

Eyes searching for a glimpse of Eden through the mayhem.

Heaven. Heaven.

I finally made it through the crush of bodies at the head of the hall just as Kult came barreling out, his eyes wide, the giant shaken.

"What's going on?" I shouted over the clamor.

Rage burned through his expression, every muscle in his hulking body corded. Ready to strike.

He jerked his head backward. "Employee lot."

"What is it?" I demanded, angling around the corner, glancing at him as I stalked down the long corridor at close to a jog.

"Some fucked up shit, boss."

"Who?"

"Eden—" was all he got out before I broke into a sprint at her name. I flew the rest of the way down the hall and burst out the door that was already sitting partially open.

A stir of activity seethed on the far side.

My attention jumped through it, landing on Milo who was across the lot by Eden's car.

Eden who was bent in two, gasping and sobbing, her head shaking as her body rocked with horror.

I faltered for the barest flash of a second before I was darting across the lot, nearly stumbling when the front portion of her car came into view a foot before I got to her.

The world crashed down around me.

Rage and disgust and heartache that pounded and tumbled.

Vomit pooled in my guts while fury spun through my mind.

Her windshield had been smashed in, and a slaughtered pig had been tossed onto the shattered glass. A broken pool stick had been driven through it, and blood had gushed down the hood and side of her car.

My eyes fucking blurred over, and my body rocked in revulsion.

Because written in the blood was a message.

A message for me.

Not even ghosts are immortal.

Chapter Twenty

Eden

FIERCE ARMS WRAPPED AROUND ME FROM BEHIND. A fortress. A shield.

At the contact, a deep, guttural sob ripped from me, this agonized cry as I turned and buried my face in his chest.

"Why would someone do this?" Horror heaved from my mouth. "Why?"

Trent only curled his arms tighter around me, tucking me close, though I could feel him trembling. Trembling with rage. Trembling with his own fashion of fear.

"I've got you, Eden. I've got you. No one's going to hurt you. No one." Trent's voice was carved in stone. It still cloaked me in solace. In relief.

God knew I'd been missing these arms for the last week. And right then…I needed them…I needed them more than ever.

I sagged into his hold and tried to block out the atrocity that had

Who would do such a thing?

A slaughtered animal—for what? To scare me? To scare someone else? Was it random?

Trent ran his palm down the back of my head, holding me close, whispering, "I've got you, I've got you," over and over.

"Trent, I don't understand."

"I know, baby." With that, his breathed words turned soft, but I could feel the ferocity of his stare. Of whatever his harsh silence was conveying to those who'd gathered around us.

"Call the police." I recognized Trent's brother's voice issuing the command.

"On it," someone said.

"Bring me a blanket," Trent grunted.

A flurry of activity whirled around us. A blanket was wrapped around my body before Trent was taking me back in his arms and leading me over to the exterior steps. He sat me down next to him, never letting go. He just tucked me closer.

His mouth was a constant caress at my temple. In my hair. Along my cheek. "I've got you."

Four officers arrived on the scene.

They fired a thousand questions, their flashing lights breaking over the darkened lot.

It all felt blurred. As if I were experiencing it from afar. Through a foggy mirror. Lifted high above it where I didn't have to take part.

I answered the officers the best that I could.

"I arrived at work at quarter to ten."

"I didn't notice anything out of the ordinary when I arrived."

"No, I hadn't been out to my car until I came out and found it this way at one-thirty."

My face twisted in grief when I answered one that I really didn't know how to, my head shaking fiercely. "No, I don't know anyone who would do something so awful."

Didn't know anyone who'd want to hurt me this way.

Anyone who could possibly hate me this much.

I'd continued to cling to Trent as if he could be the solution to it all.

As if I didn't recognize the word painted in my car.

Ghost.

The rest of the staff had answered everything the officers threw at them.

No one had seen anything amiss.

Not even Milo since he kept the employee door locked unless he needed to accompany someone outside. "Makes it safer that way," he'd grunted.

Worse was the way Trent responded to his. Direct but vague. As if his explanations had already been planned.

Or maybe I just knew him in a way no one else could. Sensed the strain that lined his muscles and ate at his soul. I knew that this was going to be another burden that he carried.

The police left with access to the security video, though they weren't hopeful they'd be able to see anything definite since my car was parked on the opposite side of the lot, up close to the woods where the cameras barely reached.

The entire time, Trent hadn't left my side. Rubbing my back. Whispering promises I knew he had no intention of keeping.

Won't let anyone touch you.

Not gonna let you out of my sight.

I've got you.

Two hours later, the last cruiser finally pulled out of the lot. They'd towed my car for evidence, and everyone except for Jud, Milo, and Kult had already left. The three beasts had been on a constant prowl of the full perimeter, ready to take out any threat.

Exhaustion weighed down, pressing into my consciousness, but there was no chance I could settle, either, the anxiety still wringing through my system.

Trent pressed a kiss to my temple. I leaned into it. Savoring the sensation. Wanting to wrap it up and keep it forever even when he'd made it clear we were never going to work. That it couldn't happen. That our lives were too at odds for them to ever fully come together.

When Milo came to stand in front of us, Trent hardly shifted his attention from me. "What else can we do, boss?"

"Inside clear?"

"Yup. Everything is secure. All doors are locked except the one behind you."

"Thank you. You've done everything you can tonight. Go on home."

"Yes, Sir," Milo said, though he and Kult seemed less than eager to leave us behind as they climbed onto their bikes and rode into the night.

Jud remained, hesitating, hands stuffed in his pockets, so much like his brother yet so entirely different. "You good, brother?"

There was nothing but care in his voice.

"Yeah. We'll be fine. We'll talk about this tomorrow."

A silent conversation transpired between them. The two of them wired. Worried. They were keeping something to themselves. Either something they both knew or suspected.

Dread shivered through my being.

I couldn't shake the word from my mind. The one I'd discovered inscribed on Trent's side last week. The same as had been written in blood on my car tonight.

Ghost.

"You get her home safely." Jud cast a glance at me when he said it. His onyx eyes were soft. Filled with sympathy.

"I will," Trent said, voice hard.

Nodding slowly, Jud backed away before he swiveled on his boot and disappeared at the end of the lot toward his shop.

In an instant, Trent and I were alone. Secluded in the silence that consumed. The arm he had draped around my shoulder pulled me close. "Come on, let's get you home."

Warily, I nodded, and we stood. I had my bag I'd left with earlier, back when I was trying to get away from Trent Lawson as quickly as I could.

Back when I thought I couldn't stand under the pressure of his presence for a moment longer.

I hated the way we'd tiptoed for the last week.

Avoided.

Did our best to pretend as if the other didn't affect us at all.

Now, he refused to let me go. His arm was wound tight around my waist as he turned and locked the heavy side door behind us. That arm only tightened when he led me down the three steps and toward his motorcycle where it was parked at the front of the lot.

Energy rippled.

That connection fierce.

Unrelenting lashes that struck us as the wind whipped through the trees and howled through the air.

It was as if it were shouting that we were fools. Fools that we'd thought we could escape the pull.

Trent let his arm slip from my waist, though he didn't go far. He threaded his fingers through mine so he could swing his leg over the bike. Balancing it, he started it. Those eyes raked me like a caress as he shifted to pull me to straddle the mass of cold metal behind him.

But his body was warm.

So warm as I curled myself against his beautiful, tragic form. My arms bolted around his narrow waist, and for a beat, he set both his hands over mine.

A promise.

An oath.

God. What was he doing to me? Who was I becoming? Because I knew, even after tonight, I'd never felt safer than I did right then.

I exhaled the heaviest sigh, pressed my cheek to his back, and let his heat chase away the cold.

Trent took to the road. The roar of the engine filled the dense night air, the world vibrating around us as we flew down the deserted street. Claimed it as our own. The stars seemed too close, dangling just above our heads like wishes strung up on hooks, just out of reach.

And I guess I was barely aware that we weren't heading in the direction of my house. It took us only a few minutes before he was slowing and guiding us into a much newer, nicer neighborhood than my own.

I sat up a fraction, taking in my surroundings, an antsy confusion curling my brow when he made a left into a driveway. He stopped the bike, his legs planted out to the side to keep us upright as he thumbed into his phone and tapped something on the screen. The garage door began to rise.

He eased his bike inside, next to the car I recognized as the one he picked Gage up in each day. He cut the engine. In it, the silence was almost deafening.

I hugged him for a second, not wanting to break the trance, before I whispered near his ear, "What are we doing here? I thought you were taking me home?"

He huffed out an incredulous laugh, dark hair flopping to the side as he angled around enough to meet my face. His jaw was set in a hard clash of teeth. "You think I'd take you home to stay by yourself after what just went down tonight? Not gonna happen, Kitten."

"Trent—"

He cut me off with a harsh shake of his head, and he unwound my hands from his stomach, guiding me off his motorcycle so I was standing. He continued to straddle the metal, though he never let go, the man clutching my hand as if it were a lifeline as he pulled me to stand beside him.

He stared up at me.

Ruthless, savage beauty.

Every inch of him this sinister seduction that I didn't know how to look away from.

And he was gazing up at me like I was the sun. The breaking day. A light in the darkness.

I shuffled my feet, trying to rearrange the broken bits of my heart. The pieces I'd already given him that he'd crushed a week ago. All while I felt him stealing more.

All of it.

All of me.

Whiplash.

With Trent Lawson, I never knew if I was coming or going. If he was going to push me away or draw me near. If he was going to ravage me or destroy me.

I guessed with the man, it was one and the same.

Dark, desperate eyes sparked beneath the dull light of the garage, a collision of blunted and bright, desperation carved in the sharp angles of his face. He squeezed my hand. Almost too hard. An apology. "No question that was a message for me, Eden."

I gulped around the thickness in my throat. "Why?"

He scoffed and looked away, giving the words to the lapping night. "A million reasons why. Uncountable enemies. Innumerable wrongs. All of them on me."

Sorrow had etched itself into his expression when he looked back at me. Deep, bleeding wounds from the depths of his striking, gorgeous face.

And I was struck again with what Jud had said. With his brother's belief.

"He deserves someone who will see him for who he really is, Eden. Not for what he's done."

And I did. I saw him for something so much better. Something so beautiful I was staggered.

I shouldn't have, but with a trembling hand, I reached out and cupped his cheek. Like I could hold a piece of it when the only thing he wanted to do was shield me. "All of them in your past."

In a flash, he was on his feet.

Towering.

Obliterating.

"It happened tonight, Eden. Right now. In our city. That doesn't seem much in the past to me. I fuckin' won't..." He choked on the words, as if everything had gone sour, pain leaching into the threat. "I fuckin' won't let anyone touch you. Touch Gage. I won't."

The rigidness of his jaw promised it wasn't an idle threat. Just the same way as I'd known it before. This terrifying man with the aura of iniquity. Blood on his hands. A tainted spirit with a beautiful soul.

"I'm not your responsibility."

"Bullshit," he spat. His face pinched in sharp rejection while the next word came soft as his hands latched onto my upper arms to draw me close. "Bullshit."

It was a whisper.

A breath.

I shook, looked away, managed to force out, "I shouldn't have come here. After last week…" I trailed off, revealing too much.

That it'd hurt. I hadn't meant for it to. For it to come to that. For him to hold a part of me. That I'd been giving in and letting go.

Welcoming the coming devastation.

He only tightened his hold. "Wouldn't let you be anywhere else."

Big hands slid up my arms and over my shoulders.

Riding up until he was holding my face. Until I was trembling and trembling. My heart in his hands. "Don't know why they delivered that message through you, Eden. Hell, I don't even know *who* they are or what they want. But until I do? Won't let you out of my sight."

I thought maybe that was more dangerous than anything else.

My throat tremored when I swallowed.

Trent followed the movement. First with his eyes and then with his fingertips.

Tattooed hands gliding down my throat. Fire and flames.

Chills streaked as my head dropped back, and he continued down, his palms spreading over my shoulders and gliding over my arms.

As if the man could hold everything.

Desire flooded through me. Head to toe. Everywhere. Everywhere.

My eyes dropped closed, and I forced out the shaky words. "You know we can't do this. It's going to hurt too much when you let me go."

At least I still knew that much about myself.

Intensity flashed from his body. A shockwave. A serrated inhale through his nose. A growl in his throat.

Then he ripped himself back, dropping his hands like the topple of stones.

My hands moved to take the place of his, rubbing the cold spot on my arms, aching for his warmth and his comfort and knowing asking for it would be all wrong.

He took another rigid step back. "Let's get you inside where it's warm. Where you can sleep knowing not a soul is gonna get to you. I'll keep you safe, Eden. Promise you that."

I should tell him no. Call my daddy and ask him to come pick me up. Even though he would be worried, it'd be a lot safer than this.

For my heart.

But no.

I gulped down the doubt and gave Trent an erratic nod. "Okay."

Tattooed fingers wound with mine. Looser than they had been before, as if he were trying to keep himself restrained.

"Come on."

I warred, glued to the spot.

He angled in close. "Don't make me toss that pretty ass over my shoulder." It was a snarl. The unmitigated truth that he'd meant what he'd said.

He was going to keep me safe. Whatever it took.

Warily, I followed, shuffling along behind him as he punched a button and the garage door closed. He pushed open the interior door and led me into his and Gage's home.

Why it felt surreal, I didn't know.

As if I were stepping into something private.

Something sacred.

My eyes were wide as I took in everything. Desperate to know a little more of this man. As if maybe looking at his possessions would give me a clue.

We'd stepped into a great room of sorts, a living area with a modern kitchen to the back. Everything was clean and contemporary, decorated bland, though there were a few toys strewn about.

It was so different than what I'd pictured.

I thought maybe the man was trying to blend into the gray walls. Fade away and become a backdrop.

Impossible.

"This way," he grumbled, slowly pulling me toward an arch in the wall that led into the formal living area. He moved directly for the staircase. I followed him, continually dropping my gaze each time he glanced at me from over his shoulder. Each time he stole my breath. Each time his big boots shook my simple, easy world.

Our hearts were a thunder in the quiet, sleeping space.

Drum, drum, drumming against the walls.

Shadows that crawled.

Intensity that whispered.

A building storm in the night.

I doubted either of us knew how we were going to make it through this.

Because I could feel every inch of Trent bound in tension. In want and restraint.

We hit the deserted landing. To the right was a long hallway with a bunch of doors. To the left were double doors that clearly led to the master bedroom.

"Where's Gage?" I whispered.

Trent turned around.

A demon in the night.

Beautifully terrifying. All hard, savage lines.

"At my younger brother, Logan's. He sleeps there when I'm at the club. He'll bring him home early in the morning."

I could barely nod. Could barely think.

Could only feel.

Trent walked backward, tugging me along toward the double doors. He angled around enough to open the right side, dipping through the doorway as if it were a passageway into another world.

I wondered if it were.

Because everything shivered and shook.

Different than last week.

As if we'd bridged a new beginning.

Or maybe we'd just been tossed into Hell. Like he'd warned. And I had no capacity to put on the brakes. No idea how to turn around and make a run for it like I clearly should be doing rather than following him into his bedroom.

His bedroom that was shrouded in shadowed silhouettes.

As if those ghosts crawled his walls and forever haunted his dreams.

This room was more like him.

On the far side of the room, the giant bed was made in a plush black comforter. The fabric headboard was tall and took up almost the entire wall, black and studded. Large pieces of art were hung along the wall closest to me, authentic paintings done on twelve-foot canvases that captured the man as if the artist had a tap into his brain.

Like it gave me one, too.

Each were a depiction of those ghosts that screamed and howled. Demons that climbed from Hell and roved a forsaken Earth. But there was also eternity. Beauty written in the starry skies.

Each piece was poignant and unforgettable. Breathtaking and hair-raising.

Or maybe it was the hand gliding up my forearm that lifted the chills, returning my attention to the man who towered in his room.

A dark refuge on a shore of treacherous waters.

Or maybe…maybe it was all a trap. The daunting phantom waiting to pull me under.

"I should get cleaned up," I forced out through my thickened throat. The air was so dense and deep I swore I could see the words float on it.

Trent stepped back. "Bathroom's this way."

He gestured to the door at the far left side of the room, between the foot of the bed and the wall of images. He led me that way, stopping at the door and leaning in to flick on the light. He shifted to the side to let me in ahead of him.

I blinked against the stark intrusiveness of the blinding rays, hugging my arms over my chest like it would protect me from whatever this power was.

Whatever was happening.

Rising higher.

Coming closer.

Trent edged by, watching me as he reached into the shower and turned on the showerhead to let it heat before he slipped back by and ducked into the cabinet to pull out a fresh towel and washcloth.

He stole my breath as he went.

He set them on the counter. "There you go."

The only thing I could do was nod.

"Let me grab you something to sleep in."

I felt short on oxygen. "Okay."

He moved back into his room, and I sucked as much air as I could into my lungs. I hoped it would give me clarity and strength.

The only thing it did was amplify the energy that crackled through the confined room when Trent dipped back into the bathroom with a tee and a pair of boxers. "Probably gonna be a little big on you."

He gave me a smirk at that, those eyes raking over me as if he were picturing me in his clothes. Or maybe without them.

I trembled.

Stepped back.

Tried to hold onto what he'd told me last week.

We'd never work and taking more of what I couldn't have was the most reckless thing I could do.

It didn't mean those vacant places didn't throb. That I didn't ache. That I didn't want to be touched.

Adored.

Wanted and cherished.

Trent seemed held in it, too. Entranced. Unable to move. That lure a rope that bound us in the space.

Finally, I found enough strength to snap us from the hazy fog, the steam from the shower heating our flesh and filling the room. "I should get in."

Trent's eyes were the hardest, softest things I'd ever seen. The contrast of the man the very thing that was going to be my ruin. Because I wanted both sides.

The brash and the bold. The loyal and the sweet.

"Okay."

He spun and went for the door.

"Thank you," I rushed before he was able to step all the way out. Apparently, I wanted to cling to the connection for one second longer.

Trent twisted around to look at me. That man who'd done me in from day one coming out to play, a wry smile on his sexy face. "Don't thank me just yet, Kitten."

Then he stepped the rest of the way out and snapped the door shut behind him. The click tossed me out of the stupor.

I jolted with the impact.

My body bowing that way like it didn't know what else to do but follow after the man.

Foolish.

I gulped it down, tried to find my footing, to seek out a little common sense in the midst of this insanity.

But I didn't know how to find it. Not when I angled into the spray, so hot it was close to scalding, as hot as Trent's touch.

And I was assaulted with it.

Image after image from last week when he'd followed me into my bedroom.

From the days leading up to the moment when I'd let another man touch me for the first time since I'd lost Aaron.

More from the afternoon in my dance studio.

The days without his touch.

Fear traveled my spine when I thought of what I'd walked out on tonight.

The truth that Trent Lawson's world was so far removed from mine.

But I knew, right then, I didn't care. I'd step into his if he would let me.

I gasped at the realization, my body lathered in suds that smelled so much like the man, the nutmeg that'd always overwhelmed me. I held it to my nose, let it infiltrate, let it consume.

I rinsed, turned off the showerhead, and grabbed the towel that he'd left folded on the counter.

I wrapped it around my overheated body.

Every nerve ending was alert.

As if one touch would burn me alive.

Steam fogged over the room, and I did my best to dry, though my flesh remained sticky and hot. I dressed quickly, his clothes engulfing me.

I rubbed the towel through my hair, anxiety lighting me up when I moved to the door and slowly opened it to the darkness waiting on the other side.

Because Trent was right there.

Two feet away.

His chest heaving with greed.

A storm gathering strength.

Every promise I'd ever made myself ceased to exist.

"Eden." He said it like I might be his saving grace. Electricity crackled, ferocity in the bob of his thick throat. "What if I wanted it, Eden? What if I wanted it to work? What if I wanted it all? What if I don't want to let you go?"

And I knew right then I was in too deep.

No longer walking on solid ground.

Because the towel slipped from my hands.

"Then hold onto me, Trent. Hold onto me, and don't let me go."

One second later, Trent prowled my way.

Falling.

Falling fast.

His mouth crushing against mine with zero hope of recovery.

Chapter Twenty-One

Trent

GREED CRASHED THROUGH MY SENSES AS I STALKED through the bathroom door and drove my fingers into Eden's wet hair. In an instant, my mouth descended, capturing the sweet plushness of hers.

Eden whimpered as she opened to the kiss.

Bliss streaked down my spine.

Intense.

Blinding.

While my mind began to spin with the impossibility.

Words on repeat.

What if I don't want to let you go?

What if I don't want to let you go?

Wanted to make it real. Hold her forever. To be the guy who could be right for her. Be good enough for this amazing woman who looked at me like I could be something better. Even after the evil that'd gone down tonight.

Fuck. I wanted to trust in this. For her to trust in me.

Guilt constricted at the thought. So tight. But I couldn't do anything but shove it down when Eden whispered against my lips again, "Don't let me go."

She breathed the plea through the kiss. Tender fingertips ghosted over my shoulders and across my chest, like this girl was asking for permission. Begging for that invitation I wasn't quite sure how to give. She broke away to peek up at me. Autumn eyes sucked me right down into the depths of who she was. "Don't let me go."

This feeling speared through the middle of me. Something bigger and brighter than I'd ever felt before.

My palm spread across the side of her head, fingers dipping into her hair, my thumb tipping back her chin.

Eden pinned me with the raw truth of who she was.

"Because I'm right here, and I'm going to hold onto you, too," she promised.

Her gaze traced over me through the steam-hazed light in the bathroom.

My chest tightened in this war of need and loyalty. Who I was, the promise I had made, who I had to be, up against this goodness I wanted to get lost in.

But how did a sinner, a demon like me, stand in the light?

My thumb brushed against the delicate angle of her jaw. "Want to be right, Eden. Wish that I was." The confession was gravel.

"And what if you're exactly what I need?" Eden's words were a breath of desire mixed up with this gush of adoration that I didn't deserve. "What if you are what I've been waiting for?"

I spun her around. A gasp of surprise raked from her throat when I had her belly pressed to the counter, my body pinning her to the stone. I took a fistful of her hair and leaned over her shoulder so I could swipe the mirror. Our reflection came to life through the heated mist.

Eden's face was flushed. Flesh kissed in pink. Those eyes so real and that face so pretty.

Goodness spilled out, shrouded by the darkness of who I was as I hovered behind her.

"Look at us, Eden. Look at you against me. Don't you get it? I'm no good."

My free hand splayed across her trembling stomach, pulling her back against the rigid planes of my body, my mouth pressed to her ear, "And still, I want it. I fuckin' want you. Want in you. To be with you. To live and die for you."

Blasphemy.

At the greatest expense, I was given a second chance.

And there I was, slipping into treason.

Eden's expression deepened. Every line slashed like a sworn oath. "It doesn't matter who you were or what you've done, Trent. It matters who you are now. And that man? He already has me."

She took my hands, weaving our fingers together and stretching our arms out wide. A perfect picture of who we were. Darkness getting ready to swallow the light.

And she lifted her chin.

Succumbing.

And I was done. No reserves left. Nothing to do but spin her around and hike her up, her perfect weight in my arms. "Eden... baby...what have you done to me?"

A tiny jolt of a moan escaped her as she wrapped her legs around my waist. Her arms curled around me, way up high as I held her sweet body against my chest.

She gazed down at me, those eyes nothing but a soft caress. "I'm yours."

And it was Eden who kissed me, girl slanting down to consume my mouth. To consume my soul. Calling me into a sanctuary. A minute's reprieve.

Heaven.

Knew I was holding it in my arms.

I kissed her back, our tongues a tangle of need. Of desire. Of something bigger than the both of us.

Because I could feel it pressing against the walls as I carried her back out into my room.

The energy that lashed.

Shocks of intensity.

Sparks of life.

I carried her toward my bed while the girl writhed over me. Tiny whimpers of need slipped between our mouths and whispered from our tongues.

There was no rational thought left. No restraint. No good sense.

The only thing that was going to happen right then was a claiming.

This girl was mine.

A frenzy made its way into our kiss.

Eden kissing me like it was what she'd been born to do. Like this moment was destined. Like she wouldn't go back if she could. Like she wouldn't change the mistake of ever walking into my club.

Or maybe it was all me. This feeling like I couldn't be anywhere else. That this betrayal was inevitable.

This girl fate.

In my arms because she, too, didn't belong anywhere else.

"Eden," I mumbled between the collision. Nothing but tongues and teeth and screaming souls. "Eden."

Couldn't deny her. Not any longer. It didn't matter how wrong it was.

"I won't let anyone touch you. I promise you," I growled.

Eden swept her fingertips down my face, so soft compared to the madness of our mouths. My chest squeezed at the action, overcome with who she was. "I trust you."

God. She shouldn't. She shouldn't. But I wasn't sure I'd ever heard sweeter words than those right then.

This girl ruining me.

Breath by breath.

Whisper by whisper.

Touch by touch.

"I'm yours," she said again.

Decimated.

Done.

No longer knew who I was. What I wanted. What I stood for.

One reason.

One reason.

Was it possible that this girl crashing into my life could change what that meant? That I could be better?

The demons thrashed at that. All the vileness of what I'd done clawing to be exposed. Like she could hold those, too. Believe in me even through all the atrocities I'd committed.

Our frantic movements slowed as I eased her onto the bed, laid her out in the middle, the girl the most gorgeous thing I'd ever seen.

All that blonde, lush hair spilled out on my black comforter like a halo of light around her head.

She watched me like she could see all the way to the depravity of who I was.

Jud's paintings covered my walls while this beauty was laid out in the center of my bed.

Felt like I was standing in the middle of a juxtaposition of evil and light.

I knew taking her was exactly that. A devil descending on an angel. Feeding from her beauty. Glutting on her grace. And I didn't know how to be anything but the monster who was aware of it and did it anyway.

Emotion crested those lips that were swollen from my kiss. "I can't believe I'm here…with you."

"Feeling is mutual, Kitten." It was a harsh exhale.

Shame.

I tried to put up a wall. Some boundaries. Mute this connection that was so loud I could hear it screaming in my ears.

She shook her head against my mattress, refusing it, like she saw that, too. "I never thought I'd feel this way again. Feel this way at all. Alive. Alive in your touch. Alive in your eyes."

"Shouldn't be the one."

"But you are," she breathed. "No one else, Trent…no one else has ever made me feel this way."

There was sorrow in her admission. Meaning that shouldn't exist.

Felt the proclamation bounding around my room. Banging through the dense, dense air.

Lust and need and something more.

"You're so fuckin' beautiful, Eden. You have any idea? Any idea of the way I feel when I look at you?" It was a grunt as I took in the treasure lying on my bed.

She writhed, her breaths heaving and hips jutting. My insides twisted, watching over that sweet body that was nothing but a needy plea. "You make me feel that way." Her words filled the space. "I feel like I found the one person who can see me after all this time."

My chest tightened. Greed and a bit of that jealousy, thinking of her with another man.

So fucked up that I wanted her as my own.

And still understanding what she was giving me. What she was saying. There was something between us that neither of us had felt before.

My hands fisted as I cast out the confession. "I've been hiding in the darkness for all this time, Eden. Until you came and shed your light on me. Lit up something that's never existed. Not ever."

Her chest pitched, like she'd been impaled by the words. "And I don't believe that's by chance. Not for either of us. That's what this is, Trent...this is our chance."

God. She believed that because she was goodness. Because she couldn't see anything else. No clue of the danger that might be waiting for her by tying herself to me.

"Terrified of it, Eden, what you could do to me. The way you make me feel."

Fact this girl had a hold on me in a way no one else ever had.

The things she had me contemplating.

Autumn eyes danced in the shadows.

My brow curled. "Don't wanna hurt you, Eden. My life—"

"Is scary," she supplied, cutting me off. "It's scary, Trent. I know it, and I'm still falling for you."

Wanted to tell her not to do it. To stop right there. To give us tonight. That we could hold each other through all the bullshit that'd gone down at the club and then let this foolishness go.

But I was the dumb fuck who couldn't seem to make those words form on my tongue, the ones I let go wholly reckless and faulty. "You're mine, Eden."

The tip of my index finger found the inside of her knee at that, and I dragged it down her slender leg, all the way to the delicate curve at her ankle. I found myself kneeling, pressing my mouth to that spot, rumbling, "You're mine."

I let my mouth follow that path back up, kissing along the silky soft flesh of her leg. Inhaling as I went because fuck the girl smelled like me.

Mine.

Wanted to mark her with it.

A brand.

Tattoo myself on her flesh.

Sink right in until we were nothing but one.

Where we existed in a place that only belonged to us.

She whimpered, bowing off the mattress as I kissed along the inside of her knee and rode up the top of her thigh. Her fingers dove into my hair and yanked like she wanted to mark herself on me, too. "God. Trent."

I pressed my face into the fabric of the boxer briefs she wore, girl swimming in them, looking sexy as fuck and destroying another bit of my mind.

"Little Temptress," I whispered.

Eden sighed, clutched at my hair, and I moved to straddle her at the waist, my knees on either side.

That time, it was a gasp, passion seeping from her pores and spilling into me.

Taking in the delicious sight, I gathered the hem of the shirt she wore and dragged it up that lush body, never slowing until I was peeling it over her head.

Chills lifted across her skin as she sank back down to the mattress.

All that hair spilling out.

Had to bite the inside of my cheek with how fuckin' stunning she was.

Her tits were these tiny, perfectly perky things that made my mouth water. Nipples pebbled up and begging like the rest of her body.

"Beautiful." I murmured my praise as I brushed the pad of my thumb over the left bud.

A whisper fell from Eden's lips as she arched into my touch. "Please."

I guessed it was the faith coming off her that did me in.

Way a shockwave of energy burst from her body.

The way that unfound connection blistered through the air and bounded against the walls.

Ricocheting.

Amplifying with each pass.

Intensity building and building.

My heart beat a riot, a fuckin' battering ram at my chest.

This boom, boom, boom that promised the two of us were about to combust. No care to what might be left in the aftermath.

I edged back so I could slip off the bed. I dipped my fingers into the waistband of the boxers as I went, not slowing as I dragged the fabric down and twisted it off her ankles, unable to look away as the girl shivered and shook where she gazed up at me.

Completely bare.

Just heart-stoppingly gorgeous.

Truth.

Because my goddamn heart skipped an erratic beat.

Tried to catch my breath. To stop the avalanche of need that plowed right through the middle of me. Maybe regain a little control.

Impossible.

One glimpse and I was done. Gone.

Reaching up, I tugged my shirt over my head and dropped it to the floor. My teeth clenched in a bid to keep from losing my cool while every muscle in my body flexed.

Bowed in restraint.

Ticked in want.

Eden whimpered her desire, taking me in, doing a little of that devouring, too.

Every angle.

Every inch.

She sat up, that gaze rushing across the nightmare written across my body. It went sliding to the one that judged and condemned. She traced her fingers over the script.

"Ghost."

She said it like she understood what it meant. Like she was accepting it. Accepting me. And fuck, there was nothing I could do to stop the feeling that rushed through my veins, filling me to overflowing.

"Who I used to be," I grunted out.

One to be feared.

A reaper sent to slay.

Someone I didn't want to be any longer.

"The only thing that matters is who you are now." She repeated it. Her voice nothing but belief.

Didn't want to tell her she was wrong. That I would never outrun it. Could never rewrite the sins on my soul.

Not when she was looking up at me when she said it. Not with the way she meant it.

She had her body angled just to the side, a single shoulder curled in. The tiniest bit of shyness pinked her flesh, and all those blonde locks fell down around the temptation of her body.

"Don't hide from me. Not now," I told her. Not when she was seeing right through me.

Eden lifted that chin. No defiance left in it. It was surrender. Welcome. An invitation. "I couldn't if I tried," she admitted.

I trailed my fingertips down the trembling of her throat, words grit. "Gonna own this body, Kitten. Gonna score myself in you so deep you aren't ever going to forget me. Tell me you're good with that."

She gulped, and then she scooted back and leaned back on her elbows, her knees bent and rocking in anticipation.

Fuck.

She was a vision.

This trembling vision where nerves and anticipation had her pressing her heels into my bed.

"I'm more than good, Trent. What I'm feeling right now cannot be defined."

I'd already taken off my boots while she'd been in the shower, and I jerked through the buttons on my jeans and shrugged out of them, kicked them aside, watched as those wide eyes rounded farther.

A mesmerizing swirl of greens and golds and browns sucking me down. My dick was stone, bobbing at my stomach, begging to get lost in her.

In that moment, every single cell in my body existed for her.

She flicked her attention up to my face and whispered, "You are the most magnificent thing I've ever seen."

I crawled over her, pressed her down onto the mattress, and dove for her mouth. My tongue sought possession. I kept my weight on my right hand, and with my left, I reached down to take a handful of her lush ass.

I squeezed, lifting her against my aching cock.

Eden whimpered, dug her nails into my shoulders. "Trent. Oh god. I need this. I need you."

That sweet mouth dripped with honey. Those words. Those lips.

In a blip, two of us were nothing but passion.

Fire.

Flames.

Combustion.

And I was rubbing my cock through her bare lips, her pussy soaked as she rocked against me. Begging for friction. Her thighs squeezed the outside of mine.

We were a blur of darkness and light.

Opposition trying to mesh and meet.

Clashing and yielding.

My teeth nipped at her bottom lip, her jaw, tongue stroking down her neck. "Eden," I murmured against her pulse point, this girl's heart thrumming like a song.

Eden's hands slipped down my back. Her palms were perfect chaos. Her touch sweet tragedy. "You are everything I didn't know I needed."

Her words were panted into the thick air. That connection a glimmer in the room. Throbbing. Consuming. Binding us whole.

I burrowed my face under her chin. My confession was pressed to her skin. "And you are everything I will never deserve."

Something I was taking anyway.

A man on his way to Hell, but I was gonna live in this sanctuary while I had it. Before my life—who I was—inevitably cast me out. A sinner who was going to pretend for a minute he could be right. Protect her. Keep her.

I knelt back between her quivering thighs.

The girl was an ocean on my bed.

Writhing and undulating.

A tide that'd swept me up in her undertow and knocked me from my feet.

I gripped her right knee in my hand like I could hold her steady, keep her from floating away, and I leaned over to grab a condom from the nightstand on the left, never looking away from the girl as I edged back and was quick to cover my dick.

Lust billowed in the space. Our breaths short, the crashing of our hearts jagged.

I slipped my arms under her knees. "Yeah?"

Last ditch plea for this girl to come to her senses and run like she should have done from the beginning…before she got herself permanently tangled with me.

Her hips bucked, her cunt urgent against my cock. "I'm yours."

I took her in one swift thrust, clutching her by the outside of the thighs as I did, burying myself so deep her body bowed off the bed.

My entire being pitched.

Canted to the side.

"Trent," she cried on a ragged breath.

"Say it again," I demanded hard, nearly passing out from how goddamn amazing she felt.

Way her throbbing pussy hugged my cock in a perfect vise.

"Trent."

Wanted to hear her shouting it forever.

She squirmed, struggled to adjust to me. To the feel of me owning that sweet, tight body.

"Heaven." The praise rumbled up my raw throat, and I clutched her legs tighter as I pulled out to the tip and gave her another deep, deep dive of my dick.

She arched, only her shoulders touching the bed, though one of her hands was reaching for me. "I need you."

A fissure.

A crack.

A cavern running right down the middle of who I had been.

A crumbling of all restraint.

Of all loyalty.

Of what I knew.

A pile of rubble laid at her feet.

Because I shifted, angled forward, and planted both hands on either side of her head.

And I stared down on the girl. Her hair was all around and that look was on her face. I leaned down enough that I could brush my lips across hers. "You have me."

It was the goddamn truth.

Moisture filled her eyes, emotion cresting, riding high. I kept one hand pressed to the bed, the other cupping her precious face.

I began to rock.

Slow at first. Measured thrusts as the girl's mouth parted and her honeyed gasps filled the air.

Mesmerizing.

Intoxicating.

We moved together.

Our bodies in sync.

A treacherous dance.

Faster. Deeper. More.

Nothing but heaved breaths and desperate hearts that were just learning to beat. And I wondered…wondered if this girl could really beat for me.

She watched me with those eyes the color of fallen leaves. The color of the earth. The color of redemption. She lifted her hand and touched my face. I kissed across her fingertips. "Eden."

"Trent. Sweet, sweet warrior."

I felt like I'd been impaled by her words. Fact she'd call me that. While she looked at me like she recognized me.

She cut right through me. The girl splayed me open until there wasn't a single place I could hide.

She met me thrust for thrust. Our bodies slick. Arching and begging.

And I felt myself getting caught up.

Lifted.

Elevated from the depths and dragged into the light.

Where it was bliss.

Where it was beauty.

Where only me and this girl could exist.

Twining. Knitting.

My spirit getting loose and weaving with hers in an intricate web.

A piece of myself I no longer possessed.

Euphoric.

Terrifying.

I panted and she gasped, and her nails dragged and scraped against my chest, clawing for a way to get closer. "Do you feel that?" she whispered.

But it was her.

Feeling me in a way no one else ever had. In a way no one else could. "It's you, Eden. It's you."

She whimpered, her legs dropping wide, taking me deeper. I hooked her leg over my shoulder.

Fuck. So good.

A hard exhale burst from her lungs. "More."

"I know, baby. I know."

My hand drifted, squeezing her thigh, her ass, fingers dragging through her cleft before I angled so I could brush my fingertips over her swollen clit.

Eden was already right there.

On the brink.

Her body bowed.

Her nerves alive.

Could see them in the room.

A glow of colors and shapes.

And I stared down at this girl as I drove her to ecstasy.

Stared at her through the haze of this faltering reality. As the promise I'd made to my brother echoed in my ear.

One reason.

One reason.

I took her.

Found her.

Eden whispered, moaned, dragged me deeper into the well of that sweet, sweet soul. "Trent...I'm..."

She scratched her fingers into the stubble on my jaw.

Awe.

Adoration.

And I felt it, too.

The crumbling.

The crashing.

The fall.

But I doubted there was much I could do to keep either of us from tumbling over the side. Girl going over.

Falling.

Falling.

So, I jumped with her like I could be her safety net, pressed my forehead to hers and whispered, "I won't let you go."

A faulty, foolish promise.

One that slipped like finality from between my lips.

My lips that took hers as I felt her body hit that highest point.

When she broke apart, that energy whipping and lashing, kissing every inch.

It set me off. Every stroke bliss.

Pleasure raced my spine.

Tingles and fire.

One thrust later, I split. Coming apart.

Lost in her body. Her eyes. That heart.

I clutched her as I came, shouting my praise. "Eden."

Felt so good I nearly blacked out. Pleasure rushed out through every nerve. An explosion in every cell.

I could no longer see. Could no longer make sense of the mess I had made.

Instead, I heaved for air in a bid to come back down, to remember who I was, but at the end of that fall was her arms.

Her sweet arms that she wrapped around my body like that was where they belonged.

Couldn't do much else except wrap her in mine, and I shifted us so I could tuck her to my side. I pressed a kiss to her sweat-drenched temple and brushed back the blonde hair that clung to her stunning face. I gazed at her through the shadows of the ghosts that haunted my room. "Won't let anyone get to you. Not ever."

And I prayed it wasn't the greatest lie I'd ever told.

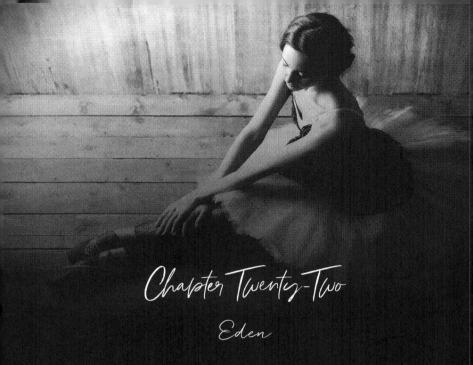

Chapter Twenty-Two

Eden

I STARED AT HIM THROUGH THE BLEARY DARKNESS, MY fingertips running over his swollen lips.

Awed.

Floored.

Unsure if any of this was real or if I'd lost myself to the shock from earlier and had slipped into a dangerous fantasy. One where I was his and he was mine.

His body burned me up where we were tangled, our flesh slicked with sweat and our muscles still ticking with aftershocks.

He kissed my temple in this adoring way that made me want to come apart all over again. "Be right back."

Trent climbed out of his enormous bed. Completely bare. Almost every inch of his body was covered in colors and designs. Strength rippled from his sinewy, imposing form, the man this stunning work of art that I got to fully appreciate as he walked into his bathroom.

I didn't know whether to hide my face or ogle his beauty.

I was miles away from what I knew. So beyond my comfort zone. Treading far, far outside the bounds of familiarity.

He disappeared into the bathroom. The faucet ran, and I clutched the sheet and brought it to my nose.

Trying to figure out where I stood. Wondering if it was possible for us to remain here—where we'd met in the middle.

Two people so different crashing together, joining, like we were made to fit.

There was no stopping the redness that streaked across my already overheated skin when he reappeared in the glaring light of the doorway.

An outline of power. An etching of desolation. A pen line of hope.

He sauntered out, no shame, just all that rigid, fierce cockiness carved in every muscle. I had to bury my face farther into the sheet when I saw his huge penis was still partially hard. I thought if I asked him to take me, he'd be ready for me all over again.

Still, I peeked out as he approached. That redness heated to a flashfire, the sheet fully pressed to my face by the time he made it back to me.

A rough chuckle filled the air, and he tugged the silky fabric away, peering down at me through the dusky light. "You hidin' from me, Kitten? If you run, this time I can't promise that I won't go chasing after you."

The words were a tease, but they were weighed down with a tenderness that had never been there before, the way he gently nudged the sheet down far enough so that he could take in the entirety of my face.

Trent hovered above me.

All that fierce, unyielding intensity staring down like he'd uncovered a treasure.

Darkness that blazed the brightest light.

My teeth clamped down on my bottom lip. I nodded against his pillow, my throat thick when I admitted, "I wouldn't get very far. I'm pretty sure I would only come running back to you."

Emotion rippled, and Trent climbed onto the bed, a massive palm splaying across the side of my face. "How did we end up here? How's it possible the two of us match like this…because that…"

He trailed off, his tongue swiping out across his full bottom lip as if he were trying to process what we'd just shared.

Something different.

Magical.

Extraordinary.

I didn't need to have been with a bunch of different men to know it. To understand it. This connection that bound us in some intrinsic way.

"Perfect," I supplied on a whisper.

Trent dropped his forehead to mine. "Want to be that for you, Eden."

My fingertips scratched into the stubble that covered his strong jaw, urging him back enough so I could meet his eye. "You are perfect, Trent. You're perfect in your flaws. Perfect in your strengths. Maybe you believe you're all wrong, that you don't have anything to offer, but I can't help but believe you're perfect for me."

I guessed it was right then that I finally accepted its truth. When I no longer was afraid of his past, of the pain he could cause, but knew I wanted to stand at his side in spite of it. Hold him the way he was holding me.

I just prayed he would find his way through his guilt to me.

On a needy moan, Trent pressed his mouth to mine in a close-mouthed kiss. His eyes squeezed tight. Like he was savoring. Committing us to memory. Then he curled his arm around me, and a squeak of surprise ripped up my throat when he flipped our positions, rolling us until I was on top.

The two of us were chest to chest, though I was angled, my legs off to the side. The sheet barely covered me where it was twisted around my bottom. Trent pushed his fingers into the fall of my hair. "You really believe that, Eden? That I could be perfect for a girl like you?"

A tease wound its way into his tone.

"You act like I haven't made a mistake or two."

"Doubtful." Affection flitted through his grin.

"Of course, I have."

He arched a dark brow. "Let's hear it."

I chewed at my bottom lip, trying to think of the worst thing I'd ever done.

Tattooed fingers brushed through my hair, and he held back a sound of amusement. "You can't even think of one thing, can you, Kitten?"

"No, it's just there are so many I can't settle on one."

I hoped right then wasn't one of them.

"Come on then." Playfulness ridged his mouth.

"Okay…so when I was a junior in high school, Tessa and I snuck my daddy's car and went to a concert in Tahoe that we'd been forbidden to go to. I was grounded for four weeks, but it was totally worth it."

Trent gasped with a mock waggle of his brows. "Scandalous."

Giggling, I smacked at him, a giddy sensation rippling beneath my skin. "You're a jerk."

He softened, his fingers still running through my hair as he sent me a tender smile. "And you're sweet. Love that about you."

His gaze darted across my face, and then he moved to tip up my chin. "Guess you aren't completely innocent, though, going and seducing me like you did. Little Temptress."

"Seducing you?" I scoffed, my chest pitching in a riot of excitement and need. "I think that was all you."

I mean, six years and not a flicker of a feeling. And then there was this man.

Potent.

Provocative.

All consuming.

"There was no resisting you."

This dark, dark defender.

He huffed a breath through his nose. "And I wanted to get you out of your clothes the first time I saw you…see all that sweetness hidden underneath."

"You felt it then?"

"Didn't you?"

My nod was wary, a frown pinching my brow as I thought back to the way I'd felt that first night. "Yeah."

He ran his knuckles along the apple of my cheek. "But you were scared."

Another nod. "I felt that part of you, too."

"And now...after the shit back at the bar?" I could tell he was trying to suppress the fury when he pushed out the question. To bring us back to the moment that had brought us together this way, though I had a feeling that we would have ended up here, anyway.

We were bound, fated to this moment.

"And now, none of it matters. None of it matters except we're both here. Right now. Together."

Trent released a low growl, and his hand was fisting in my hair. Possession.

Power.

A shiver raced down my spine, that dark aura taking me whole. Wicked possession.

"Oh, Kitten, it fuckin' matters. Matters that someone would be so foolish to send me a warning through you. Pussy is gonna pay."

Pain leached into his rage. Worry and dread. I wanted to wipe it away. Tell him it was fine. That we were safe. Clearly, that wasn't a promise I could make.

"It means they're watching, Eden. Pinned you as a vulnerability. As a weakness." His voice only got harder with each phrase he spat.

Part of me wanted to look away, to find reprieve, to fight the flash of terror without him witnessing it played out in my eyes. But I couldn't move. I was held by his intensity.

The man a hook and a snare.

"Will they try to hurt me? Try to hurt Gage?" I could barely force out the questions.

His lips thinned. "They might try, but I won't let them get close to either of you. Promise you that."

"I'm not weak, Trent. I just need to know what we're up against."
We.

The proclamation rang through the air.

I was in this with him.

Trent swallowed hard. "No, Eden, you're not weak. I see your goodness for what it really is. Strength. Resilience. But you also don't understand where I come from, how ugly it gets, and it's the last thing I want to involve you in. Don't want to taint who you are, and that world has a bad way of doing just that."

He glanced away, unable to look at me as he gritted the words. "If something were to happen to you…"

My head shook. "I won't say I'm not afraid, Trent, but everything…it's led me here to you."

Shame blanketed his expression. "Last place you should be."

"Don't say that." It was a plea. "I wouldn't want to be anywhere else."

His fingers threaded deeper into my hair, as if he felt the need to hang on. "You sure about that?"

"Don't ask me to regret you."

"I'm bound to mess this up, Eden." He repeated the same thing he'd told me in my bedroom last week—a night that felt a million years away from right then. As if all that time had passed and we'd been caught up in it.

Becoming one.

Not knowing the details but understanding each other in a way few ever did.

"Not if you choose not to, Trent." I hesitated, then pressed. "Ghost?"

The word was a question. Different than when he'd been undressing. It was acceptance, then. Now, I was asking him to let me farther inside. I wanted a view into who he really was. The part he kept shrouded in the shadows.

"Who I used to be," he reiterated. He took my hand in his and pressed my knuckles to his lips. "So much shit I don't know how to leave behind. I've done bad things, Eden. Really fuckin' bad things."

Dread slicked down my spine. I could feel my spirit being crushed by the malignant, haunted desperation that churned in his eyes.

My mind raced, lighting with blips of images of the things he might have done. The blood that stained his hands. My thoughts skipped from one to the next because I realized I really didn't want to envision them.

Because in the end, I only had one truth that mattered. "We all have history, Trent. All of us. It's how we live on the other side of it that counts."

He grunted. "How's it you handle yours so well?"

A huff of saddened laughter left me, my past so different than his, but I wondered if they'd somehow affected us the same. My voice was coarse with sorrow when I whispered, "I've been lost for a long time. Looking for my way. Just fumbling through life, day-to-day, wondering if I would ever feel again. If the numbness would ever go away."

A crash of guilt and anger flashed through his expression, and his teeth ground as he forced out the words. "Are you okay with it? Me touching you...?"

He left off the last.

After him.

After Aaron.

Torment twisted through me. Loss. My own guilt. My head slowly shook as I burrowed close to Trent, to the steady, hard pounding of his heart. "I miss him, Trent...I'll miss him every day. I know I told you he was my best friend, but I did love him. But it was a peaceful kind of love...the kind that grew out of that friendship...out of comfort."

I thought back to how it'd been. Aaron, Harmony, and I growing up together. Running through the woods and playing in our backyard. Defending each other and fighting with each other. I guessed until I'd received the second letter from Harmony, I'd blocked out the rest. Her jealousy. The way she'd hated it when I'd played with him instead of her.

I realized my gaze had drifted, lost in thought, and my attention slowly shifted back to Trent. "We grew up next door. His parents went to the same church as ours. In third grade, Aaron started at the school, and he'd sat in the desk right next to mine. He and I climbed trees together, went to the movies together, to prom together, and we just...fell into that pattern. It also became...kind of expected of us."

Nervously, my fingers traced across the words stamped on Trent's chest.

Live to Ride, Ride to Die.

"My parents were comfortable with him, trusted him, so we slipped into the mold our parents imagined."

Trent huffed.

My head shook. "We weren't forced into anything, Trent. It was just...easy."

I glanced at him, chewing at my bottom lip, the admission a breath of old affection. "I always thought he actually had a thing for my older sister."

That time it was a grunt from his delicious mouth, his fingers gliding through my hair, like he couldn't stop touching me. Holding me. "Pretty sure you could never be considered the consolation prize, Kitten."

My shoulders hiked a little, brushing our bare chests together. A tiny flicker of flames lit in the middle. "Harmony was the wild one. The one who was always laughing. Always getting into trouble, too. I think Aaron got stars in his eyes every time she came into the room, but she never wanted him around. She thought he stole my attention from her."

Could feel his muscles bunch in his arms. "She the one who got you and your father into financial trouble?"

My nod was desolate. "Yeah." I swallowed it down and forced a smile. "My momma got sick and passed when I was fourteen and Harmony was sixteen. My sister left soon after."

Grief filled his face. I knew he felt that kind of loss on a personal level. "I'm sorry."

I shook my head as I was hit with a swell of emotion. "I was so broken after that, so alone, that I think I leaned even more on Aaron. After that, he and I fell into what we were."

"And what was that?"

"Happy. Content." A wistful hum rolled up my throat. "We both liked the quiet life. Staying home and watching movies on a Friday night. Working in the yard. We both wanted a big family. We'd just bought our first house a month before he died."

"And you were going to fill the rooms." Trent barely hid the spite in his tone.

I nodded again.

His thumb brushed my cheek. "I'm not that guy, Eden."

No. Trent was Aaron's opposite.

"I loved him, Trent, but I didn't burn for him."

A growl rumbled in his chest, and his fingers fisted in my hair, lifting me higher so I was straddling him and my face was hovering an inch from his. "You burn for me, Kitten?"

"Yes." It left me on a pant. "I never knew I could want a man the way I want you."

"That's a good thing because I've never wanted anyone to have me the way I want you to."

My heart took off at a sprint. "What do you want me to have?"

"All of me, Kitten. Fuckin' all of me."

He angled up to capture my mouth. His kiss rough. Possessive. Mind-bending.

I swore, every single kiss altered who I was.

I kissed him back, crawling over the rigid lines of his body as Trent owned me from below. That hand in my hair cinched down tighter and his other gripped hard onto my hip. He sat up, our kiss turning frantic as he pulled me against his cock that was hard and huge and stealing my breath.

I gasped at the contact. Sensation rushed over my skin as he guided me to rub our bare flesh together.

Sparks that stoked that raging fire between us into an inferno.

I pressed up onto my knees as he licked from my mouth and down my throat, my head dropping back and my entire being arching into his touch.

Desperate for more.

My fingers dug into his shoulders, and needy sounds were slipping up my throat as he kissed along the slope of my neck, his voice a low reverberation, "You, Eden. So fuckin' beautiful. So good. So right. Want it. Heaven."

"You have me," I mumbled back, writhing over him.

So different.

With Trent, it was so much more than I'd ever experienced.

The feeling of being consumed alive.

Owned.

Possessed.

And I wanted it.

"I want it all," I whispered.

He kept trailing down, kissing a path down my throat and to my chest. Every nerve ending came alive as he licked over the top of my right breast and sucked my nipple into his mouth. His teeth raked the sensitive flesh before he bit down.

Hard enough to make me yelp.

Everything fired.

Flashed with desire.

I arched into the feeling of it.

Everything. Everything.

I begged for more.

"Trent."

My nails scratched into his back.

He softened, licked his tongue over my nipple that had pebbled up, so tight and tingly, and he pulled back to watch the action as he ran his thumb over the peak.

Nail raking it.

Back and forth.

Back and forth.

"These tits. Perfection, baby. Knew it. Knew it the second I laid eyes on you. All of you. Every inch. Want to live in this body."

He kept me pinned with that gaze as he slipped his hands farther down. He curled his right into my hip while the other slipped between us, his fingers rubbing at my center, pressing inside.

I was no longer writhing. I was rocking. Begging. Riding his hand in a desperation I didn't know existed before Trent Lawson crashed into my life.

Chasing this feeling that grew and grew.

Pleasure.

The blinding kind.

The kind that would cause me to lose all control.

I was so ready to let it go.

"Do you want me again, Eden?" he grunted, that stormy stare unrelenting as he watched me. Tracing my expression. Waiting for a cue. He didn't need one because he already knew all of them, anyway.

"Yes," I whimpered when he shifted his fingers, hitting a spot that made my sight flicker at the edges. "Always. Forever."

It might have been way too soon to say it, but it was the truth.

I was never going to stop wanting this man.

I could feel his penis twitch between us, and on instinct, I wrapped my hand around it, the fat head throbbing and dripping.

Trent groaned as I stroked him, my fist wrapped tight as I pumped his massive length, and I found myself leaning down to his mouth, my greedy tongue sweeping across his lips.

I dragged my teeth over the bottom one and bit down, as hard as he'd done to my nipple.

He'd said he liked it hard. I just hoped I wasn't a fool aching to discover what that meant.

A dark chuckle rumbled from his chest when his bottom lip popped from my teeth. Sooty eyes turned to black, glittering crystal.

Feral.

Shivers raced, and my pulse thundered.

He wound his hand back in my hair. The words were low and curling through the room like a threat. "Ah, Kitten, you do like to play with fire. On your hands and knees."

He had me flipped around before I could even process the command, on my hands and knees and facing the opposite end of the bed. Just off to the left was a giant mirror propped in the corner of his room, and my sight snagged on the reflection, my eyes wide as I took in the scene framed in gilded black metal.

My hair wild and my chest heaving.

My body bare, slicked with sweat, trembling with anticipation.

And I felt beautiful. Sexy and wanted in a way I'd never felt before.

Then I was trembling anew when Trent got to his knees from behind, that foreboding wraith covering me like a shroud. His body cut and chiseled, vibrating with want. Jerking with need.

He grabbed me by both hips, and his fierce stare found me through the mirror just as he was running both palms over my bottom.

Tattooed fingers squeezed and kneaded.

My heart ravaged my chest with jagged, uneven beats.

"Look at you, Eden. Fuckin' fantasy, right here."

I whimpered.

Ached.

Wanted.

He chuckled again, then he was dipping down to kiss a lusty path down my spine. Chills lifted in his wake and spread over the surface of my flesh.

Emotion scattered.

High and low and coming at me from every direction.

Standing at a precipice. Riding a razor-sharp edge as I waited for something brand new.

His name left me on a gasp when he used his hands to spread my bottom. He never slowed as his tongue stroked through the cleft of my ass, around my hole, before he licked down to my center.

Lapping.

Stroking.

Growling possession as he went.

My sight narrowed, fuzzy at the edges. The wave of pleasure that slammed me made me dizzy.

I whimpered and begged, rocking on my knees. "I need you."

Trent eased back, enough that our eyes tangled in the mirror, and he was dragging his fingertips through my crease again before he was swirling the tips of two fingers around my ass.

Air rushed my throat, my lungs quivering, my thighs shaking as he started to put the barest pressure there.

My knees felt weak as I was struck with a flood of desire. Half terrified, half frantic.

A big hand splayed out across my lower back, pushing my chest closer to the mattress and jutting my bottom out. "Look at you," he grunted, his voice a rough scrape across my skin.

A torch that flamed.

And I was sure this fire was going to consume us both when he started to press harder, as I whimpered and writhed and pulled away and pushed back, my hands fisting into the comforter as he slowly drove deeper.

Because I'd never felt so vulnerable.

So prized.

So panicked.

I heaved a needy, lust-hazed breath when he dragged his fingers out.

The low laughter Trent released dripped sex, and he leaned down and kissed across my shoulder, muttering, "Oh, Little Temptress, we're going to have so much fun."

He pulled away and moved to his nightstand. I was panting like some kind of fiend as I watched him roll on a condom, his outline the most devastating thing I'd ever seen.

Then he was back behind me, pressing the fat head of his penis between my shaking thighs as he hauled me onto my knees that could barely hold my weight.

My back to his chest.

Those inked hands spread across my stomach, splaying wide, like a writhing statement written across my clear flesh. He ran them upward. Cupping my breasts for a moment, his thumbs perfect torture as he teased my nipples before he dragged all the way up to guide my arms over my head. He never stopped until he had my hands locked around the back of his neck.

His mouth came to my ear, and his hand curled around the front of my throat, his fingers fluttering along my jaw as he warned, "Hold on, Kitten, it's about to get rough."

And I didn't care if I fell into his darkness.

Just as long as he met me there.

Chapter Twenty-Three

Trent

Los Angeles, Sixteen Years Ago

AGENTLE HAND STROKED THROUGH HIS HAIR, SPURRING him from sleep. The faintest rays of light bled through his bedroom window, and Trent blinked his eyes open as he rolled over to find his mom gazing down at him. Her voice was so soft as she whispered, "Are you ready, Sweet Warrior? It's time."

Trent's heart jumped into overdrive, and he shot up in his bed and scrubbed his palms over his face. "It is? Where are we going?"

"Somewhere far, far away. Somewhere no one will find us. Somewhere we can be free. Are you ready?"

He nodded hard. "Yes."

"Help me get your brothers."

Gulping, he tossed back his covers and stood. His mom left the room to get Jud and Logan, while he moved across to where Nathan's bed was on the opposite side. He nudged him softly on the shoulder. "Nathan, hey, wake up."

244 | A.L. JACKSON

as Trent's were full of confusion as they blinked open. "What's wrong?"

Trent's chest squeezed so tight. With so much love. His mom said they had a special bond. That they could feel each other even when the other wasn't there.

He thought it was true. The way he felt his brother's heartrate speed up faster. The way he felt his worry and fear take him over.

Nathan was smaller than Trent. Kinder and softer in a way that made Trent sure he would always need to look out for him. Stand up for him when some asshole started making trouble, way the pricks always did at school.

"Nothing's wrong. We're just going to take a special trip."

Nathan's eyes went wide with excitement. "Like...to Disneyland?"

"Better'n that."

Nathan scrambled to get up, grabbing his inhaler from the nightstand next to him, taking a real big puff. "I just gotta get my shoes."

Trent already had them. He set Nathan's favorite sneakers and a pair of socks down in front of him. Leaving them there, he moved to stuff a bunch of their things into a duffle bag.

"Why are we bein' so quiet?" Nathan asked from behind.

"'cause no one else is allowed to know where we're goin.'"

Alarm burned through the space. Pummeling Trent's back. Slowly, Trent turned around as his twin asked, "What do you mean?"

"I mean, this isn't a good place, and we're gonna go somewhere I can take care of you. You and Mom and Jud and Logan. Where it's only goin' to be the five of us."

Nathan gulped.

Trent squeezed his shoulder. "You don't have to be afraid. I'm always gonna take care of you."

⚓

Gunshots.

One.

Two.

Three.

A scream tore up his throat, and he went racing across the lawn. To his mom. His beautiful mom. She was covered in blood.

So much blood.

So much blood.

He turned her over.

Her hair was matted in it, soaked, her eyes full of fear. He pulled her onto his lap and rocked her.

Rocked her and rocked her while he begged, "No, Mom, no. Don't leave us. Don't leave us."

Her fingers found his face, the words barely heard over the gurgling in her throat. "My sweet warrior. Watch over your brothers. Take care of them. Love them with all your might."

"No, Mom. We need you here. Please. Please." He begged it.

Torment rode out with his cries. Tears stung his eyes, blurring everything.

But still, he could see. He watched the man get back on his motorcycle like it was just another day. A man with the leather vest that said *Demon's Day* on the patch on the back.

"Promise me," she wheezed.

He nodded fiercely, and the tears burned so hot as they streaked down his face. "I promise. I promise."

"Love you forever, my brave boy."

He felt when she left them. When her spirit flew away. When her body slumped down and the crater formed in the middle of his chest.

A sob tore free. So loud as it burst against the morning sky. Deafening as the anger rushed to fill its place.

Sirens sounded in the distance, and he had to force himself to move. To get up. To go to his brothers who were huddled behind the car, Jud covering Nathan and Logan like he could be their protection.

Trent stumbled that way.

The ground no longer existed as his world canted to the side.

Nothing made sense except for the rage that burned through his veins.

He dropped to his knees in front of them, and he covered them like he'd promised his mom. Praying he could be brave. That he could be enough. That he would do it right.

"What did it say?" his father snarled as he leaned in front of Trent, demanding the answer.

That anger raged at his insides.

Dark and ugly and vile.

Twelve hours had passed. The four of them were at their father's house. About the last place Trent wanted to be. But this was their lot.

"What did it say?" his father demanded again.

Trent knew he would never forget. Would never erase the memory of that man.

His stomach sick and his soul slayed and vengeance carved on his flesh.

"Demon's Day."

Chapter Twenty-Four

Eden

"Miss Murphy! Miss Murphy!"

I blinked awake, disoriented as I was jarred from the dead of sleep. Clarity was just on the brink of my mind, flittering around the edges as thoughts of last night spun back through like a dream.

Only the jostling continued, the little voice not so quiet as he shouted, "Miss Murphy! Miss Murphy! Wake it up, why don't you?!"

Panic seized me when I realized what had woken me was a child jumping in the middle of the mattress.

Gage.

On a gasp, I scrambled around from where I'd had my face buried in the pillow. I was quick to gather the sheet tighter to my chest to make sure I was covered.

My eyes struggled to adjust as I looked at the bouncing silhouette where he was darkened by the blinding rays of sunlight that speared in through the large gap in the drapes.

"Hi, Miss Murphy!"

Oh my god. If I'd ever traipsed into unprofessional territory, this was it. Twisted up in sheets, bare beneath, with my student jumping on the bed.

Did it make it better that he was grinning down on me like my presence had made his entire day?

All cherub cheeks and flapping arms and joy flooding into the room.

My chest tightened, and I eased up to sitting, praying I was fully covered. That he was still so innocent that he didn't have a clue what'd happened in this room last night.

The thought of it sent heat rushing across the surface of my flesh, a blush lighting every inch as I gulped and tried to orient myself to this reality.

"Miss Murphy! Did you come to see me on the weekend?" He dropped down onto his knees, bouncing a bit, a giggle riding free and wrapping me in warmth. His sweet little voice lowered like we were sharing a secret. "Because I'm your favorite, right, Miss Murphy, right? Don't worry, I won't tell nobody, no way."

Yes. That. For the love of God, don't tell anyone.

I had to stop myself from saying it aloud.

I cleared my throat and glanced around the room like I might find a life vest to keep me afloat, in dire need of rescue because I was really in over my head.

Treading dangerous, dangerous waters. Waters that no longer affected just Trent and me.

Because here was this beautiful child in the middle of it.

An endless abyss of hopes and consequences.

I wondered if it was only me with their heart on the line. If it was only me taking the risk.

All those complications shouting to be heard.

No question, my daddy would lose it if he knew the position I'd found myself in. Worry for me and the trouble I was asking for.

I didn't know which was worse—that or the fact I'd broken the clause in my contract where I'd promised, "I agree to conduct myself in a professional manner with all staff, students, and parents."

I'd broken my oath not to do something so reckless. And our reputation was something the school board took seriously.

I'd meant to be awake and long gone by then.

Slinking out on the shadows on which I'd arrived.

Unashamed but still not having the first clue where I stood.

After last night, there were only a few things that I was sure of…

I'd been changed.

Made whole.

All while setting myself up to get ripped apart.

Gage's excitement drew me back to the immediate issue at hand.

How the heck I was going to get out of this bed without scarring the poor child for life.

"Are you hungry? We're makin' the best breakfast in the whole wide world! You smell it?" He tipped his nose up and inhaled deep. "It's so yum, yum, yum in my tum, tum, tum. You better hurry it up, lazy head, or you're gonna miss out. I thought you were gonna sleep the whole day. Sheesh."

His arms flapped out to the side in emphasis.

Like this was normal.

No big deal.

A sinking dread slithered through my consciousness. Was this normal? Did Gage wake up with random women sleeping in his father's bed? Where was Trent, anyway?

Nope, don't go there, Eden.

I pressed a shaky hand to my forehead and tried to get it together. *Don't panic. Don't panic.*

"Okay." I managed a single word and a feeble smile to go along with it.

"That's so good!" He clapped, and apparently, that was all the response he needed because he started to jump back to his feet, but then his attention snapped to my hand that had the sheet clutched to my chest like a lifeline.

He hopped forward, coming closer, that smile on his adorable face spreading in a streak of joy.

"You wearin' your bracelet, Miss Murphy? It looks so pretty. Do you love it?"

He grinned up at me with so much pride, nothing but dimpled, chubby cheeks and adorable hair framing his face, his gaze darting between my face and the bracelet tied around my wrist.

My heart did that crazy thing. Pounding and expanding and trying to break free of the confines of my chest. The affection for this child overwhelming. More than I could fathom.

The fact his adoration tamped down the turmoil raging inside was proof enough. The way I couldn't help but reach out and touch his cheek.

"I love it, Gage," I whispered, though I might as well have been shouting it.

Proclaiming whatever this was, even though I wasn't sure myself.

All I knew was I had crossed a line there was no returning from. I'd been marked in a way that could never be erased.

I had no regrets, even though it might destroy me in the end. There might be too much going against us. Too many old wounds, secrets, and fears that would tear us apart.

As much as I wanted to silence them, Trent's promises that he would ruin us continued to play on repeat.

On top of it, my job was at stake.

But the truth was, in the end, that wasn't even a question.

I knew I'd gladly accept every risk when Gage's little shoulders hiked up to his ears in pure, unmitigated delight.

"That's really good because I love you." He didn't even give me time to choke over his confession before he was back on his feet and jumping off the side of the bed and blazing out the door. "Gotta go, Miss Murphy! Hurry it up and get your booty downstairs right now, little lady."

Um.

Okay.

Apparently, Gage could give me whiplash as quickly as his father could.

A crush of relief left me on a heavy breath when he disappeared down the hall, his tiny footsteps pounding on the stairs, getting quieter and quieter the farther away he got.

"Ugh," I moaned, pressing my hand to my forehead and trying to get myself together.

To rein in these emotions.

But they were running so far out ahead of me that I couldn't catch up to them. Each so different, so at odds, so big and consuming, I didn't know how to process them.

How did I make sense of what I was actually feeling?

Awakened.

Feverish.

Afraid.

Everything I'd felt since the moment I'd met Trent Lawson, now amplified times a thousand.

My teeth raked my swollen bottom lip as my mind raced back to last night, as my hand smoothed over the rumpled sheets.

Trent and me in this bed. Over and over again. The man insatiable. Blissfully rough. Wickedly sweet.

Turned out I was insatiable, too.

Redness raced as those simmering embers leapt.

Now, I had no idea how to navigate. How Trent and I were really going to fit.

A muted ring echoed from the bathroom, and I realized it had to be coming from where I'd left my phone in my bag on the floor. "Crap," I mumbled.

Pushing out a shaky sigh, I slipped from the bed, taking the sheet with me. I dug through my bag on the bathroom floor in search of my phone that'd stopped ringing, dinged with a message, only to start ringing all over again.

I finally found it and pulled it out. Tessa's grinning face was on the screen.

Double crap.

I rushed to answer it, though I couldn't help but whisper when I put it to my ear. "Hello?"

"Don't you dare *hello* me, Eden Jasmine Murphy. I've called you at least fifteen times in the last two hours…you know…since I showed up to your house with Saturday morning coffees and doughnuts, and your car was nowhere to be found. I've been worried sick."

The heel of my hand pressed to my temple.

All the craps.

"I'm so sorry…I completely forgot."

"You completely forgot that we've had coffee and doughnuts every Saturday morning for the last six years?"

I cringed. "Maybe?"

"You little hooker…you had cake instead, didn't you?" I could feel her glee through the phone.

My attention darted around like I was going to find a bug planted in the room. The bedroom was vacant, no movement about, and I quietly snapped the door shut behind me as I hissed, "I did not."

"You are the worst liar of all liars. I can literally hear the sex dripping off your tongue. You ate it all, didn't you?"

Gah.

"I hate you."

Tessa squealed. "Oh my god, hallelujah."

"Shut up."

"Was it good?"

My back slumped to the wall as I gave, as I let it all rush me. The feeling. The truth that when I looked at my reflection in the mirror across from me, there was something new written in my being.

My reflection the same but different. Stronger and more vulnerable. Wiser but a fool. But I'd known all along if I gave myself to Trent that I would be changed.

That's what succumbing did.

It opened you up to whatever was waiting on the other side.

And I wanted it all.

"It was the best night of my life, Tessa."

She was silent for a second before she whispered, "He's the ace. Your wild card."

"You were right, Tessa. I'm terrified of loving him. Terrified of what it could mean. Terrified of what he makes me feel." The admission bled free. True and whole and devastating.

I was terrified of it all, and I still wouldn't want to be anywhere else.

"Um…the man is terrifying, so there's that. Not sure how you wouldn't be."

I choked on a small laugh, fighting the feeling that came on so savagely it was going to knock me to my knees.

No darkness to keep it shrouded.

The light of day chasing away the shadows.

"Does he treat you right, Eden?" Tessa pressed, worry in her voice, all the teasing gone when she felt the crush of my emotions.

And I couldn't confess to her the rest. What had brought us here. The truth my car wasn't simply parked outside Trent's house because our connection had been too intense, and I'd followed him home.

Couldn't confess that this was so much more complicated than she knew.

With my wild card, the stakes were the highest they'd ever been.

I could only murmur, "I think he would burn the world to the ground for me."

I hoped it would be enough. That in the process of taking down whoever wanted to hurt him, he wouldn't take us down, too.

She swallowed hard. "I'm so happy for you, Eden. So proud of you for stepping out and taking a chance. Are you okay? You sound… weird."

"I'm fine," I told her.

"Um…the word *fine* should have no place in this conversation. Amazed. Astounded. Staggered. Those would all do."

A slight giggle bled free. "Oh, it was amazing, Tessa. I just need to process it all."

She sighed. "I know, Eden. I know you well, and that's why I need to know you're all good. You need me, you say the word, and I'm there. Hell, I might even save you one of these doughnuts."

"Thank you, Tessa."

"Pssh…just be thankful I didn't call your daddy and ask him if he knew where you were. You know, since you left me hanging for two freaking hours, banging on all your windows and doors, having no clue where you were without so much as a text. I was about to break into your house to make sure you weren't going to star in the next episode of True Crime."

Um, yeah, don't even joke about that.

I couldn't say it aloud. Instead, my teeth clamped down on my bottom lip before I addressed the more pressing matter. "Thank you for not saying anything to my daddy. I have no idea how I'm going to ease him into this."

If it would even come to what I could only imagine would be uncomfortable introductions and unpleasant explanations.

A signed release declaring that I was in a *romantic relationship* with one of the parents.

Is that what this was? Is that what Trent envisioned for us?

Questions came faster with each second that I hid away in this bathroom.

"I say rip off the Band-Aid. Sit him down and give it to him straight. 'Daddy, I'm banging the bad boy. Deal with it.' Only thing you can do."

"Are you insane?"

"Um…I think we already know the answer to that."

I pressed my fingertips to my forehead.

"Seriously, Eden, like, you need to talk to HR. You're sleeping with one of your student's daddies…who's also your other boss. And I'm not criticizing, but even for me, that's messy, and it'd be much better just to get it reported and on file so there's no fallout. You know those moms who pretend like they're not secretly ogling the man when they pick up their kids would have a field day with that kind of scandal."

I recoiled at the thought. "I'm pretty sure we're not at that point. Let's not complicate this more than it already is."

She huffed. "Fine…but you can't pretend like this isn't happening."

I blew out a sigh. "I need to go. We'll talk about this later."

"Deflecting," she sang.

"I am not. I really have to go. Breakfast is ready." I flinched even saying it.

Tessa squealed so loud I had to pull the phone from my ear. "Um…you're not at that point, my ass. But fine. Go. Eat breakfast, then eat some more cake and make sure he eats some, too. Don't worry, I'll be a good girl and wait for the details until tomorrow."

Just great.

"Love you!" she peeped before the call went dead.

Sighing, I softly banged my head against the wall before I forced myself into action. I couldn't stay in this bathroom all day. I slipped back on the same clothes I'd worn yesterday, ran my fingers through my mussed hair, and found some Listerine under the cabinet so I could at least rinse out my mouth.

I balled the sheet against my chest, trying not to blush all over again when I slipped back into the bedroom and to the mess of a bed, doing my best to make it quickly, smoothing out the sheets and the comforter and resituating the pillows against the headboard all while struggling not to let my mind revisit every moment that I'd spent with Trent there.

Impossible.

Last night had been branded on me.

Finally, I gathered enough courage to leave the room, and I slinked down the hallway, my ear inclined to the barest noises that filtered up from below. The clanking of dishes and the rumbling of a deep voice. Gage's high-pitched, sweet one was mixed in between.

I stole down the steps, nerves scattering through the room, my heart in my throat and the blood whooshing through my veins.

Fully unprepared for what I might feel when I came face-to-face with Trent again. Wondering why he hadn't at least prepared me for the whirlwind that was Gage. Why he didn't come and ask me to breakfast himself.

All those whys rambled through my brain, my fingers twisting because the whole problem was I didn't know how to navigate this. Where I stood or where we were heading.

The only thing I knew was I felt anxious for those eyes to take me in again.

I made it to the bottom landing.

Sounds filtered through from the arch that led into the great room.

I edged that way, stopping when I got close enough to peek through.

In the daylight, it appeared entirely different.

The enormous room was brightly lit by a wall of windows facing the backyard, gleaming with the rays of sunshine that burned through.

Gage was on a stepstool at the island, pouring orange juice from a giant container into plastic glasses he had set up in a row.

But it was the man with his back to me who stood at the stove that locked the air in my throat. Those frazzled nerves scattered far and wide.

He was all black hair and sinewy body—but not the body I knew.

"Miss Murphy! Yay! You woke up. Sheesh, you take *forever*. I thought I was gonna have to go back up there and drag you down." Gage drew it out like it was a crime. I felt like I was committing one while I stood there shifting on my feet.

Because the man at the stove whirled around at Gage's welcome.

His smile similar but so different. Lacking any malice. Missing the sinister threat. Instead, he grinned, all dimples and barely-there stubble on his ridiculously handsome face. "Well, well, well, if it isn't *the* Miss Murphy I've heard so much about. Sleep well, I hope?"

He was all satisfied innuendo.

Oh my god.

I was going to melt into a puddle of embarrassment right there. My wave was timid. "Hi. I'm Eden."

"Logan."

Right.

The youngest brother.

"Yup…I told my uncle Logan all about you, Miss Murphy. How you're the best teacher in the whole wide worlds and you like me the best and that I love you."

My heart skipped a jagged beat.

"Oh." I whispered it. A soft affection as I looked at the child who'd slayed my safe little world, with a little help from his father of course.

"Uh-huh! Yep. Uncle Logan, did you know she even taught me how to spell orangutan? O-r-a-n-g-u-t-a-n."

He drew out every letter.

"It's the very hardest word in the whole dictionary, you know, and now I'm the best speller ever, and I'm gonna get all As, right, Miss Murphy, right?"

I didn't have the heart to tell him the rest of the kids had learned it, too.

"That's right, Gage," I murmured while sneaking wary peeks at the man who was watching me with a sly grin riding over his mouth. As if he was the keeper of a secret only he was privy to.

"See Uncle, told you, you don't know nothin'."

Logan rustled his hand through Gage's hair, that smile never leaving his face. "Guess not. I really am going to have to go to school with you one of these days."

"So you can get all the lessons." Gage dipped his head in a resolute nod.

"Um...where's...?" Anxiously, I looked around the room.

Logan pressed his palms to the island, his green eyes dancing. "Ran an errand."

My lips pursed as my attention bounced around, looking for a safe place to land.

Right.

Great.

He'd left me there by myself.

"Yup, Uncle Logan said my dad finally got some so he doesn't have to be such a d-i-c-k, anymore. What'd he get, anyway, Uncle?" The question twisted Gage's brow into a knot as he tipped his head back to look up at his uncle who'd moved to stand behind him. Trent's brother was suppressing laughter as he pressed his lips to Gage's forehead.

"Seems he got something really special."

Okay, I took it all back.

Confessing it to my daddy would be way less painful than this.

"Like a new toy?" Gage asked.

Logan laughed as he swept Gage from the stepstool. "Time to eat," he said instead of answering, effectively diverting the topic, thank God.

Gage squealed when Logan tossed him over his shoulder, the man all easy arrogance as he carried the child over to the little nook by the window and plopped him into a chair.

"This spot's yours, right here, Miss Murphy! You wanna sit by me? I told you me and my uncle made the best breakfast ever!" He pounded on the spot next to him, and I glanced there, warily, no clue what I was supposed to do.

My purse was upstairs, and my car was impounded, and Trent...I gulped, whirling around when Trent was striding in through the side door where we'd entered from the garage last night.

Black jeans and white tee and stunning face, so gorgeous he hitched my breath.

All that potent power infiltrated the room.

A flashflood.

My knees went weak.

Then confusion had me frowning when I realized he had my pink carry-on slung over his shoulder.

He didn't slow or explain. He just dropped it by his feet and strode my way.

Purposed.

Those ridiculous boots eating up the floor.

I swore the walls spun when he didn't slow, just took my face in those big hands and kissed me like none of the questions I'd had this morning counted.

Kissed me hard and desperate and with relief.

I whimpered and sighed, holding onto his wrists and wondering if he knew my heart was at his feet.

Gage giggled. Giggled wild and raucous. "Dad's got a girlfriend, Dad's got a girlfriend. It's Miss Murphy! It's Miss Murphy!"

In my periphery, I could see that Gage had stood on his chair, and he was pointing at us like the spectacle we were.

Redness flushed, and Trent dropped his forehead to mine, never releasing my cheeks as he sighed. "Gone for one fuckin' hour, and I already missed you. How's that, Eden?"

I eased back enough to look between him and my bag. "You… went to my house?"

"You needed clothes, yeah?"

"And you…"

"Let myself in. Had to go in through your bedroom window because that teacher-friend of yours was there, eating doughnuts on your porch while taking about fifteen-thousand selfies of herself."

He said it like she was the one who was doing something crazy.

"Which getting in, by the way, was way too easy. Going to send someone over there to take care of that today. Make sure no one is getting through that we don't want in there."

My head spun, still hung back on the spot where he'd broken into my house. "You just went in and got my things?"

"Yup. So you could sleep. Figured you might be a little worn out this morning." With that, he traced his fingertips down the angle of my jaw, his eyes flaring. Chills spread, and my lips parted as a bout of desire leapt into my bloodstream.

God. I couldn't even think straight when I was in his presence.

"We can go back and get the rest of your things this afternoon."

"Trent…I…I have to go home. I can't just stay here."

"Told you last night that I wasn't going to let you out of my sight until I found whoever did this." He growled it, so low that only I could hear. "Meant it. I don't want you anywhere that either me or my brothers aren't there."

Flustered, I stared up at him. "I have things I have to do."

Like clear my head.

"Then I'll go with you."

"Are you serious?"

He had me hauled out of the great room and backed to the inside wall of the main living room before I could make sense of the action. His body towered over mine where he had me pinned.

His chest strained with pained, heaving breaths, a torment woven in that I didn't understand. "Don't fight me on this, Kitten. Promised to keep you safe."

With a shaky hand, I reached out and touched his face. "I have a life, and so do you. You can't—"

He cut me off when he grabbed my hand and brushed his lips across my knuckles, his words grit, "And I'm going to protect it."

"Trent."

"Kitten." He erased the bare space that separated us, his hot body pressed to mine, our hearts beating frantic as he dug his fingers into my ass, hauling me from the wall and plastering me against him.

Every inch of him was hard.

I gasped at the contact.

He took the opportunity to kiss up under my jaw, fully picking me up and pressing my back to the wall when my body softened to putty. He licked the flesh, his lips nibbling at my ear. "Tell me you don't want to live in my bed because I can't wait to be in this body again. I'm going to own it, Kitten. All of it."

I whimpered, then froze when a throat cleared to the side.

We both whipped our attention that way.

Logan stood there grinning like mad. "Breakfast."

"F-off, dude," Trent grumbled, though there was no anger behind it. He reluctantly set me on my feet and gestured between us. "Logan, this is Eden. Eden, this is my pain-in-the-ass baby brother, Logan. Feel free to ignore him."

"We've met," Logan said, all smug smiles and playful welcome. "You gonna put up with this punk?" he asked me, no seriousness to that question, either, clearly trying to get a rise out of his brother.

Like they were just…normal. Two brothers who gave each other constant crap but would do absolutely anything for the other.

Trent smacked him on the back of the head. "Dude. Watch it. I will take you down."

Logan jumped back and lifted his hands in surrender. "Hey, just checking that she knows what she's in for."

Trent grunted at him and threaded our fingers together. "Come on, let's eat."

I was still fighting the urge to hide my face when we walked in to find Gage still standing on his chair, though he was shoving mountains of eggs into his mouth from the fork he wielded. "Sheesh, about time. You been kissing again? How many kisses are you gonna get, Dad? Like a million?"

Trent pulled the chair out for me, guided me to sitting, and pressed a kiss to my temple. Then he looked at his son and said, "More like a billion."

"A billion?! Whew. You sure are gonna be busy."

A flush flashed, and I dipped my head to try to hide the giggle that slipped free all while feeling like I was melting into a puddle of goo.

The room radiated with my confused affection.

The awareness that even though I felt unsettled, it still felt right.

Trent went into the kitchen then came back and set a plate in front of me. "There you go, baby."

My head spun while I did a little more of that melting. "Thank you."

Then he tossed a set of keys to a Mercedes onto the table. "Got you a replacement car while I was out." He dipped down to murmur the plea at my ear. "Promise me you won't leave without either me or one of my brothers."

"Trent." I wheezed it, though I was finally seeing all his rough abrasiveness for what it was.

This sweet, sweet warrior.

Someone who would fight.

For his family.

For me.

I hoped I could be a little of that for him, too. Bring him out of the shadows where he'd lived.

"Always the babysitter," Logan whined when he sat down with his plate across from me, though he was smiling softly, winking to let me know he wasn't serious.

"That's because you're a really, really good babysitter," Gage said, still shoveling in the eggs. "Right, Dad, right?"

"That's right, buddy," he said, tugging his son down to sitting. "Couldn't make it through this life without him."

I looked around.

Taken.

Gone.

My feet no longer touching the ground. Every part of me completely washed away.

Logan was right.

I had no clue what I was in for.

Chapter Twenty-Five

Trent

"**R**EADY TO TELL ME WHAT THE HELL IS GOING ON?"
Logan forced under his breath once we were out of
earshot of Eden and Gage.

The two of them had gone into the great room. She'd wanted
to clean up after breakfast. I'd insisted she relax. And what had the
girl done?

She'd climbed to sitting on the carpeted floor, her knees hugged
to her chest and all that lush hair wisping around her shoulders, and
started to play with my son.

My chest tightened when I took them in. Adoration was written on that stunning face as she watched Gage scramble around on
his knees, showing her every toy in his toy box. No doubt, the kid
was telling her the whole damned history behind each of them, too,
prattling on the way he did.

Nonstop jabbering.

That shit was probably annoying to anyone who didn't know
him. To those who didn't love him like mad, since the only thing that
sweet little voice did was fire at warp speed.

Eden...Eden watched him like he was a treasure. Like every word out of his mouth was precious.

And fuck me if watching it wasn't precious to me.

I roughed a hand over my face to pull myself out of that fantasy. One where I could deserve something more. One where I didn't destroy the ones I loved most.

Gunshots.

Blood.

Loss after loss.

I sucked for a staggered breath as fear rushed. Bottled in my being. Dread sinking into my bloodstream.

A low, disbelieving chuckle rumbled to my side, and I swung my attention to Logan who caught me in the vicious act of trying not to spiral.

"Dude, you have literal fucking hearts in your eyes, all while looking like you're about five seconds from packing up and running for the hills. Quite the accomplishment, if you're asking me."

"Wasn't asking you," I grunted, breathing out a heavy sigh when I moved to join him at the sink. He had the water turned to full blast as he rinsed the dishes, a buffer to hide the conversation we needed to have.

He gave a cynical shake of his head. "Even if I don't say it out loud doesn't mean it's not true. Fact you've got a girl here says it all, anyway, doesn't it?"

My past mistakes gripped me by the throat. Constricting. The lie I pushed around it tasted like dirt. "Just watching out for her until we figure out who was responsible for what went down last night."

Logan scoffed. "Right, brother. Tell me you don't believe the bullshit you're trying to feed me. And while you're at it, how about you fill me in on why we are watching her?"

He tilted his head in the direction where Eden was currently singing a song.

Her voice this soft, lush timbre that weaved itself way down deep.

"You know," he continued, "the one who means absolutely nothing to you, even though she woke up in your bed and is currently chilling with Gage in the other room."

I hadn't had time to give him the low down. The only thing he'd gotten was a vague text late last night warning him to keep out an extra eye. That something went down at the club. By the time he got here with Gage this morning, I was already heading out the door. I'd asked him to stick around until I got back, and that I'd explain everything then.

Huffing through my fear and frustration, I started to load the dishes into the dishwasher like it might distract from the undeniable fact that our past had caught up to us.

"Think we're in trouble, Logan."

Logan stilled for a beat, then moved on to scraping another plate, putting on that casualness he wore like a brand. "And what kind of trouble might that be?"

My voice was a rough warning. "Someone slaughtered a pig and tossed it through Eden's windshield."

His body rocked with the severity before he shook his head and attempted to joke, "Wow, that sweet little thing pissed someone off that bad? Does she have some crazy-ass-stalker ex we're going to have to take down? If she does, sign me up because that shit is messed up."

My voice was grim. "Logan." His name was a warning to prepare himself. "In the blood running down the side, there was a message. A message for me."

Logan hesitated as he glanced my way, his brows lifted as he waited.

"Someone wrote in the blood, 'Not even ghosts are immortal.' Not a chance that shit was random."

Logan froze, and I could physically see the dread race through his system. Way it slithered down his spine and twitched through his muscles. He just stood there, holding the plate under the spray of water as he fought to catch up to the implication. "You sure?"

"Clear as day. Someone knows we're here."

His throat bobbed as he let the plate slip into the sink. His hands pressed to the counter, and he dropped his head between his arms before he looked at me from the side. "Who is it?"

It was a hiss.

Old animosity.

New fears.

"I don't know yet. Jud has some connections digging. We'll find out. End this before it starts."

Logan's hands curled tighter onto the counter. "Before it starts? Sounds to me like it's already started. If someone is here? Throwing threats? Sending messages like that? Someone wants to get messy."

Question was who and why.

Apprehension bounced between us, a sticky awareness that slithered and crawled through the room.

Since last night, my mind had been back on the three assholes who'd been at the bar all those weeks ago. Way the one had left something itching in my consciousness, though I was sure I'd never seen the prick before.

Sultry laughter rang through the air, and my attention was drawn that way, to where Eden laughed while Gage jumped and flailed his arms in front of her, being a goof, girl waving her hands over her head, playing into whatever antics he was tossing her way.

Everything clutched.

My heart and my body and my mind.

How had I gone and gotten so reckless? Let this girl invade? Take up the places inside me that she couldn't?

"We left so we could get a second chance at life, Trent." Logan's voice came as a bid where he stood at my side. "All of us. Stop refusing it for yourself."

I glanced at him with a scowl. "Not sure I get that luxury, Logan. The one thing I need to focus on right now is making sure everyone is safe. I can't get distracted and fail again."

At protecting Gage.

At protecting my brothers.

Fuck.

At protecting *her*.

Eden was the only person I'd ever considered letting in, and the first thing I'd done was put her in danger.

And I didn't know how to stop.

How to resist.

This girl the kind of dream I didn't want to wake from.

"You deserve joy, man." Logan squeezed my shoulder. "Stop fighting it."

The old demons screamed.

Whimpers and pleas.

Gunshots.

Blood. So much blood.

All of it on my hands.

"Not so sure about that."

The sound of a motorcycle out front pulled us from our conversation, and I glanced to the screen on the security system to see Jud pulling into the driveway. He eased to a stop and climbed off. Dude nothing but a goliath who came striding to the front door. He entered the pin on the keypad to let himself in.

At the beeping, Gage hopped up and went beelining that way.

"Uncle Jud, Uncle Jud, did you come to see me, too? This is the best day ever in my whole life!" he shouted as he flew through the archway and out into the main room.

Way I wanted it. My kid completely oblivious to the turmoil that was raging inside me.

"Whoa, there he is. Gage in the cage!" Jud shouted. Inevitably, he was hoisting Gage up and spinning him over his head like he was gonna pile drive him. The two of them were in a constant wrestling match.

Gage squealed and laughed and hung on tight as Jud carried him in through the archway.

"No way, nuh-uh, Uncle, you can't keep a good man down. I'm comin' for you. You won't even know what hit you."

Jud had tossed him onto his back, one hand slung over his shoulder to keep the child from falling, and Gage had gotten him into a chokehold from behind, squirming all over like he was actually going to take Jud to the ground.

My chest stretched tight at the goodness of it. Way my brothers had surrounded me, come together as one, to raise this kid when I hadn't known how to do the first thing right.

They'd sacrificed.

Relinquished a shit-ton of their freedoms and offered them to me.

Then that tightening was turning to a seizing when I felt the pressure in the air.

A zap of energy. A burst of light.

That magnet had me shifting my attention to where Eden climbed to her feet.

She was all nerves and hope and kindness.

So fucking gorgeous wearing a floral dress that hugged her just right.

My mouth watered, and my mind sprinted to the second I could get her alone again.

Little Temptress.

Distracting me in a way she couldn't.

"Eden," Jud said, dipping his chin.

My brother's eyes flitted around to take in the situation. Adding. Calculating. Sliding to me for a quick second of speculation.

She'd stayed, and she wasn't fucking going anywhere.

"Hi, Jud," Eden whispered in that wispy tone.

Sound of it had always twisted me inside out.

After last night?

It was nothing but shackles and a chain.

"How you holdin' up, sweetness?" Jud asked, the man rigid and hard and looking for a fight.

Knew him well.

He wouldn't rest until we put this threat to bed.

Autumn eyes found me. A question. A whisper. A claim.

The connection that bound us thrashing wild.

She looked back to Jud. "Better than I could have imagined."

Possession slammed me, and I was moving that way, the lure

unstoppable. I moved up to her from behind, wrapped my arms around her waist, and fucking stuttered out a relieved sigh.

No use in denying it now.

She leaned back into my hold, exhaling, too.

Jud's lips twitched at the side, dude silently gloating that he'd called it with that bet. Taking the girl to my bed.

Apparently, I owed him my share of Absolution.

Would gladly part with it if it meant keeping this girl whole and safe. My son happy and unharmed.

I dropped a kiss under Eden's ear.

Gage howled from where he was perched on Jud's back like he was witnessing the most scandalous thing. "See, Uncle, see?! My dad's got a girlfriend and he's gonna be kissing her like a bazillion-gajillion times!"

"I see that, shorty," Jud said, voice a tease but his eyes intense and on edge.

"Would you mind taking Gage in the other room so I can talk with my brothers?" I murmured at Eden's sweet flesh, not wanting to let her go, but I needed to find out if Jud had gotten any information.

Eden shifted enough so that those eyes could meet mine. A thousand questions swirled through the fathomless depths. Girl trying to get a read on me.

Piercing.

Cutting deep.

Trying to touch way down in those places I was terrified for her to see.

Instinct had me wanting to put up a wall. To stop this from happening. From her getting any deeper than she already was.

The sick part of me just wanted to give it all, lay it at her feet.

Probably was no use in hiding, anyway. With just that one look, I could feel her crack me wide open.

She got me on a level no one else could.

Both wary and devoted, Eden nodded. "Of course."

"Thank you." I turned my attention to Gage who Jud was flipping over his shoulder, making him laugh as he somersaulted, before he carefully set my kid on his feet.

"Why don't you show Miss Murphy your room?" I suggested.

"You wanna, Miss Murphy, do you wanna? It's so cool! I got a whole solar system and I know all the planets. Do you want to see 'em?"

Eden stretched out her hand and took my son's. "I would love that."

I watched them disappear out the archway, heart wanting to go chasing after them. When I looked up at Logan and Jud, they were both holding their laughter.

"Miss Murphy?" Jud mouthed.

"Shut it, assholes," I grumbled, turning and heading for the refrigerator while the two of them busted up.

"Dude, you're so screwed." Logan was all grins.

"Pay up, bitch." There it was, Jud deciding it was time to collect.

I grabbed a beer from the fridge, shut the door, and leaned against it as I twisted the cap and took a long pull. I rocked my head back on the cool metal, meeting their questioning gazes. "I'm fucked, guys."

So fucked.

Because I was never supposed to let myself get in this far.

Tangled and tied.

Logan shook his head. "Nah, man. You're fucking blessed, so stop this shit. You've got an amazing kid and a woman who clearly adores your surly ass considering she's still here, so suck it the hell up."

"Mom would like her." Jud leaned his hip on the end of the island, looking at me with his beefy arms crossed over his chest.

Emotion locked at the base of my throat. So tight I couldn't breathe. "She would if she was here, but I failed her."

Failed at protecting her like I was supposed to do.

And she was gone.

Gone.

Just like I'd failed at protecting Nathan.

And I'd never outrun that.

Jud exhaled and scruffed a palm down his face. "No, Trent. Would bet my life she's watching down right now, and she's fuckin' proud. Fuckin' proud of who you are."

Shame billowed through my being.

The sins I'd committed.

The awful things I'd done.

"Just…promise me you won't shut her out," Jud pressed. "That you give this thing a chance."

I took a gulp of beer as I tried to process all the shit spinning through my brain.

"She'd be terrified if she knew what I'd be willing to do to protect her." The words slipped out a growl. A warning of what was likely to come. If violence had followed us here? I was going to return it tenfold.

Jud gave a tight nod. Catching my meaning.

"Did you find out anything?" I asked.

"Talked to Ridge." Ridge rode with Pillage of Petrus, which was another MC back in LA we'd had ties with. Worked with. No bad blood. Ridge and Jud were good friends. Went way back. Dude was someone Jud trusted with his life, which meant I did, too.

"There's been some strife within the ranks of Demon's Day."

Mention of that club sent fire lapping through my insides. Singeing. Searing. Burning me alive.

Bad blood was all we had with them.

A war had started with them the day my mother was gunned down on our front lawn. Kind of war that was never going to end. Which was why I'd fucked Juna Lamb in a bid to get back at their president.

No better way to piss off an enemy than to put your dick in his girl.

Grief thudded in my spirit.

It was that mistake that had set the rest in motion. What had led to us losing Nathan. Another score on my soul.

But it was also the one that'd brought me Gage.

And I still didn't know how the hell to balance that.

My throat felt tight, and my ribs clamped around my charred heart. "And how does that relate to what happened last night?"

"Not sure if it does, but Ridge is always keeping an eye out for what's going down in the city. Demon's Day has had some guys go missing. A few jobs gone bad." Jud blew out a strained sigh. "Still not certain the two are connected, but there was also an attempted hit on Keeton Petrus."

"Fuck," I hissed. "Is he okay?"

Keeton was the President of Pillage of Petrus. Which meant if someone was targeting both clubs? Moving through the ranks of both Demon's Day and Pillage of Petrus? Even going so far as to come after us? This was ugly. Dirty. Someone making a play for territory.

"Yeah. Someone shot up the outside of the dive they were hanging at as they were coming out. No one was hit, but the shooter got away. No one got a look at who it was. Ridge is doing everything he can to find out if there is a link to us."

I dipped my head. "Tell him I appreciate it."

"Will do. So what in the meantime?" He angled his head in the direction of the footsteps we could hear banging above in Gage's room.

"We don't let either of them out of our sight."

I wasn't going to let a soul get near either of them.

Would fight. Stand in front of a raze of bullets. Die protecting the two of them.

All of them.

Because I was done losing the people I cared about. And this time, I wasn't going to fail.

Chapter Twenty-Six

Eden

I stood just outside Gage's bedroom door. Trent knelt at his bedside as the night pressed at the window, that potent, intimidating man gently running his fingers through his son's hair as he tucked him in. As he murmured sweet words that made his son giggle.

As he adored him. As he loved him.

As he proved he was made of layers and substance.

Of bone and heart and spirit.

Of beauty and darkness.

Enigmatic.

Mysterious.

Kind and good.

Ferocious and terrifying.

Trent had asked Jud if he would keep an eye on Absolution so he could take a few days off, and after Jud and Logan had left, the three of us had spent the day together.

We'd played out back. Laughing under the tree as we'd pushed Gage on the swing. I'd made them spaghetti for dinner, and we'd eaten at the table before we'd snuggled on the couch to watch a movie as the sun had set.

It'd all felt so natural. So right. Even though I could tell Trent was continually on edge.

Watching.

Listening.

Prepared.

On the sly, he'd check his phone for news, though when I'd asked if he'd found out anything, he'd said he didn't have any information. That Jud was digging, though he gave me no insight or details, only said that he didn't have any idea of who was responsible for last night.

I could feel him wrapping me in a hedge of protection. A wall he kept me girded behind, terrified to let me see to the other side to where I knew his past prowled.

Lurking and waiting to devour.

I could feel it.

Sense it in the air.

Almost as intensely as I could feel *this*.

The love that radiated. So bright and blinding that I felt enraptured by it. Held in its gravity. A force that beckoned and blew and compelled me to take a step forward.

It locked in my throat on a knot of emotion as Trent leaned forward and pressed a tender kiss to Gage's head. "Night, little dude."

Gage grinned. Ear to ear. Those dimples denting and his eyes flashing in the bare light. "Night, night, sleep tight, don't you dare let the bed bugs bite."

Trent chuckled.

Warm and devoted.

"No way are any bed bugs getting in here."

"'cause you'll chase 'em away, right, Dad, right?"

"That's right, buddy. Won't let anything get near you."

"Because my dad is the best dad in the whole world. Just like I got the best teacher in the whole world and I love her so much and she's your girlfriend."

I wobbled at that, my knees weak as I watched the sweet scene.

As they both looked my way and a flood of affection slammed me so hard that I lost balance. My hand shot to the doorframe in an attempt to keep myself steady.

There I stood, so close to everything I'd ever wanted. So close to the dreams I'd all but given up on because I'd believed they were no longer meant for me. That I'd lost my chance.

And I wanted this to be mine.

My chance.

My reason.

Trent looked at me like maybe I could be a part of his, too. Though there was no missing the reservations. The lingering belief that he'd stolen the little joy he had, and it'd be flirting with disaster to ask for more.

Begging for his broken heart to get slaughtered.

I understood it.

I understood it.

And still…

I sucked for air when Trent finally stood.

That imposing body filled the space, and his aura rushed me in a wave of greed.

"One more kiss, Miss Murphy!" Gage called, breaking me from the spell the man cast.

I eased in that way, a smile fumbling on my face as I fought the moisture that kept stinging my eyes. I leaned down and pecked a kiss on Gage's cheek. "There."

He grinned, those eyes so brilliant, so sweet. "More!"

I kept crossing all the lines I shouldn't cross, but I couldn't find it in myself to care. I just started to pepper kisses all over his face, his nose and his chin and his cheeks and his eyes, making smacking noises as I did.

All while I held a sob deep in my chest. This love that wanted to break free.

Gage grabbed my face in both of his small hands. "My turn! I'm gonna give you a billion kisses, too!"

He smacked little kisses all over my face. Turning me inside out. Twisting me in two.

My heart in his tiny, tiny fist.

I wanted to sing.

I wanted to weep.

"Goodnight, my sweet Gage," I finally managed to say.

Before I lost it, I tore myself away, holding it in as I moved for the door as quickly as I could. I rushed out into the hall, my back to the door as Trent rumbled a few more words to Gage before the light flicked off and his footsteps thudded on the floor. The door creaked as he partially closed it, leaving it open an inch.

His presence washed over me from behind.

So big.

So beautiful.

Everything I'd ever wanted, and so much I hadn't known I needed.

His fingers brushed down my arm. Chills lifted.

"Eden?" He whispered it like a question.

I barely managed to peek at him from over my shoulder. "You're such a good father."

There was no keeping the emotion out of it. The way my mouth trembled and my spirit shook.

"I'm trying to be."

"There's no trying to it. That child...he's amazing, Trent. So amazing. I..."

How did I tell him that I wanted it? To be a part of it?

Trent pressed his hand to the small of my back as he rounded to my front. His palm moved up my spine until he was cupping the back of my neck. With his thumb, he tipped up my chin.

Understanding filled his dark eyes as tears slipped from mine.

"I see you, too, Eden, and I wish I could give you everything. Everything you need. Everything you deserve. Wish I could heal every broken part inside you. Hold it. And I'm so fuckin' scared I'm going to be the one to tear you down."

"I don't think that's possible when you're the one holding me up. Sweet warrior."

Pain eclipsed every inch of his face.

"What?"

"My mother used to call me that."

Agony fisted. "Oh."

He edged in closer, his spirit alive. "I wanted to live up to that. Wanted to so damned bad."

"You are for us."

"Eden."

"What happened to her?" I chanced.

His expression hardened, a barrier trying to drop between us. His words were shards. "Lost her when I was a kid."

I didn't push farther, only touched his face. "I'm so sorry. You've lost so much."

That barrier fell for a beat. "No more, Eden. No more losing the ones I love."

"Are you afraid?" I whispered.

"Terrified," he admitted.

"Who is after you, Trent? Who would do this?" My chest ached with the thought of someone that evil. That cruel.

His fiercely beautiful face pinched. "I don't want you to worry about that."

"Trent—"

Desperation flashed. "Please, Eden. Let me take care of you."

"I don't want you to hide from me."

"Couldn't if I tried, baby. I need you. I fuckin' need you."

His forehead dropped to mine and the words scraped from his mouth. "Tell me you need me, too. Tell me that tonight none of this other shit matters. Tell me nothin' right now counts except for me and you."

"Nothing matters right now, Trent. Nothing but me and you. Nothing but *this*."

I wondered if he knew that included Gage. Included this little family that was slowly staking its claim on me. On my heart. On my soul. On who I was.

Because the hand at the back of my neck curled in possession, and the other was splaying wide, gripping me by the bottom and pulling me against every rock-hard inch of the man. "Little Temptress."

I whimpered a needy sound. "It's me who can't resist you."

Trent growled.

Then he hiked me up and into his arms. In an instant, I was pressed to the wall, my legs wrapped around his waist and his mouth devouring mine.

It was a clash of tongues.

Greed.

Lust.

Fire.

My dress was bunched around my waist, and he took the opportunity to burrow his fingers into my bare thighs.

His touch searing me through.

Our movements were a blur.

Impassioned kisses.

Heated hands.

Feverish whispers.

He kissed me as he carried me into his room, pressing me against every surface as we went. Furniture banged and fabric ripped and souls sang.

Hungry caresses and needy touches.

Taking. Taking. Taking.

I was on fire.

Burning.

Dying in the dark haze that was this man.

He blindly fumbled into the nightstand drawer and pulled out a condom.

In a flash, my panties were gone, and Trent's jeans were shoved around his thighs.

No thought but this.

This.

It was the only thing that mattered.

He covered himself then drove into me.

Overcome.

Like I could be the source that sustained life.

I cried out at the feel of him.

At the full intrusion.

At the bliss.

He didn't slow. His fingers sank into my bottom as he thrust, my back pinned to his bedroom wall and my arms wrapped around his head.

He filled me and filled me, his heart running in jagged, erratic beats.

Mine raced and my head spun and my body conceded to the power of his.

He took me hard.

Desperately.

Urgently.

Brazenly.

He grunted and gripped and drove.

Never letting go.

The way he'd promised. The way he'd promised.

"Don't let me go." I whispered it as I gasped. As my fingers clutched in the locks of his hair and my spirit writhed and leapt and called out to meet with his.

Trent took me whole.

Devoured and destroyed.

I felt myself flying away.

No longer touching the ground.

The pleasure too beautiful. Too staggering. Too great.

Gathering and building.

Driving me to the highest high.

I lost myself there. In the peaks of paradise. Where I split apart. Where I floated through ecstasy.

Wave after wave.

Trent met me there as he came, as he grunted, "Heaven. Heaven."

And I clung to him as our bodies bowed and jerked and blazed with this thrill. With the driving sensation. With the bliss that streaked and boomed and sang.

But it was bigger than that. Brighter. This place where we met. Far, far above the middle. In a place that only belonged to us.

My arms curled tight as I slumped against his body.

The two of us drenched, panting, trying to catch our breaths and still breathing the other.

"Heaven," Trent murmured again.

I hugged him so tight.

As fiercely as he was holding me.

Because I wanted it for him.

Heaven.

Peace.

For him to look in the mirror and not see a monster.

To know he was far more than just redeemable.

I wanted him to know.

To know he was precious to me.

Chapter Twenty-Seven

Trent

Los Angeles – Fifteen Years Ago

DEKE SHOVED THE MAN ONTO THE CONCRETE FLOOR. HE skidded on his side, crying out as he scrambled to get onto his hands and knees. Blood dripped from the cut on his mouth and spilled onto the stained floor.

Hatred filled Trent's being. Heart. Body. Soul.

His sight was blurred by the rage. The only thing he could see was the profile of the man's face and the patch sewn on the back of the vest he wore.

Demon's Day.

The same man who'd climbed onto his bike and rode away like it was nothing after he'd slaughtered Trent's mother.

In cold blood.

In front of her four children.

"This the bastard?" his father hissed at his ear. Cutter as he was known. His voice was as vile as the blood that pumped through

Chills skittered across Trent's flesh, and his mouth watered with venom. "Yes," he managed to say.

His father pressed the gun to his hand. It felt cold and heavy. As cold as the hole burned in the middle of his heart.

"You get to do the honors." Cutter's words were close to a laugh.

The man thrashed. "What the fuck? Cutter, you piece of shit. Let me go."

Deke kicked him in the face. "Shut the fuck up, Demon. No one is talkin' to you."

"Do it," Cutter instructed.

Trent's arm shook like crazy as he lifted the gun. His sight blurred and his heart hammered and his soul screamed in chaos.

He killed my mother.

He deserves it.

You can't.

Don't.

Don't.

Don't.

Run. Just fucking run.

Turn your back and never look back, just like Mom said.

A vicious voice caressed his ear. "Do it."

Trent gulped, and his arm shook harder, the gun jumping all over, so heavy he thought it would slip from his fingers and clatter to the ground.

"You remember, son, what he did? You remember your momma bleeding out on the lawn? You remember her smile? Way she loved you?"

Sweat dripped from his hair, or maybe it was just tears that were leaking down his face.

"Just pull the trigger, and all the pain will go away. Do it, do it. It's who you were meant to be. No turning back from it now."

Trent did.

He pulled the trigger, and he prayed with it, it would wash away the pain. The price paid. Justice done for his mom.

But the man slumped to the ground and the hole just got bigger.

With it, Trent's rage only multiplied. The pain growing deeper. The vacuum sucking him under.

His father grinned. "*Ghost.*"

It was the day he gave himself over to the hatred.

To the thirst for retribution that could never be sated.

And Trent kept pulling the trigger.

Ghost.

Ghost.

Ghost.

Wearing that patch in the name of Iron Owls, thinking one day, one day, it would be enough.

That one day, it wouldn't hurt so bad.

But hate made you forget what you were supposed to be fighting for in the first place, and the shame reminded you that you'd already condemned yourself.

Until you woke up one day realizing you weren't any better than the man who'd taken her life.

Chapter Twenty-Eight

Trent

"DAD, DAD, DAD, WAKE IT UP, WE GOT A SURPRISE FOR you!"

I rolled over just in time to find Gage jumping on the edge of my bed before he flew into a swan dive, coming right for me. No caution because the kid knew I would catch him. Wrap him up. Hold him tight.

"Whoa there," I said with a groggy laugh, and he giggled as he landed with a *thunk* against my chest.

I curled my arms around him.

Somehow, this morning, hugging him this way almost felt like it might hold the power to chase away the memories. Ones that haunted my heart and mind. Ones that kept creeping up. Demons thrashing and flailing and vying to be heard when the only thing I wanted to do was permanently silence the atrocities of the man that I'd been back in LA.

Bury him.

Be someone better.

But how could a man like me earn a second chance?

My chest tightened when I felt that presence at the doorway.

Struck by the lash of energy that I now recognized for what it was.

Goodness.

Grace.

I sat up, still holding onto my son as my attention moved that way.

Eden stood just inside my bedroom. So stunning she knocked the breath clean out of my lungs. So kind and full of belief that she had me believing just a little bit, too.

She was holding a tray and had the sweetest smile dancing all over that mouth. Affection and hope all mixed up with the secrets of the way we'd spent the entirety of last night tangled and tied.

"See, Dad, see? We made you breakfast and it might be even better than Uncle Logan's! What do you think?" Gage grabbed me by the face and forced me to look at him, caramel eyes wide and full of joy.

Kid so fucking cute another stake pierced through my heart. I hugged him tighter and nuzzled my nose into his neck. "I think it smells delicious."

Gage giggled then wiggled when I tickled him on the side. "See, Miss Murphy! I told you he was gonna love it so much! My dad says breakfast is the most important meal of the day, and since my dad is my most important person, you gotta have both."

Eden's smile lifted at the side. Warmth riding out. Filling the room and all those howling places in my soul.

"We definitely have to have both, don't we?" she said, so tenderly, autumn eyes watching my son like he held a bit of her light. She carried the tray over to the bed, and I scooted Gage off my lap so she could set it on my legs as I sat back against the headboard.

"What's this about?" I murmured, looking up at the woman who threatened to change everything.

One who I could feel rearranging my insides. A potter reforming all the vile bits.

She reached out and caressed her fingertips down my jaw. Tingles spread. "You deserve for someone to take care of you, too."

Gage bounced on his knees at my side. "Yup, yup, yup! And you better eat it up way super fast because we gotta go!"

Confused, I swiveled to look at Gage who was grinning like mad, my heart thrumming all over again. "And just where are we going?"

"Church!"

What the fuck?

My attention whipped back to Eden. Eden who just laughed this tinkling sound when she saw the shocked horror scored on my face.

Because no. Just no.

She dipped down and pressed a little kiss to the side of my head, and her mouth came to my ear. "I teach Sunday school, remember?"

Well shit.

"Unless you want me to go by myself?" she asked. Half a tease and one-hundred-percent serious.

"You know I don't want you going anywhere by yourself."

"Then you'd better get ready. I don't want to leave my class waiting or have to explain to my daddy why I didn't show."

Then she waltzed across my room toward the bathroom wearing this flowy robe that swished around her gorgeous legs.

While I sat there wondering what the fuck I'd gotten myself into.

I itched. Knee bouncing at warp speed as I incessantly roughed my fingers through my hair where I sat in the last row of chairs at the back of the church sanctuary.

By myself and wondering which second it was gonna be when I caught fire.

Eden and Gage were in the Sunday school class across the hall. A class she'd told me I couldn't stay in with her. I hadn't had a background check and any volunteers in the children's center had to be cleared, not to mention it would draw questions neither of us needed right then.

And I appreciated the effort made to steer the creepers clear of the kids, but what I didn't appreciate was sitting in a church with

Eden's father at the pulpit and feeling like I was gonna crawl out of my goddamn skin.

Didn't like it.

Not one bit.

Men like me didn't belong in a place like this.

Not when Eden's father was spewing some bullshit about forgiveness. About how everyone deserved it and not one would be refused it. Especially not when the band had played that song my mother used to sing. One that had struck me like a chord. A resonation that I'd long since forgotten.

Because men like me earned no grace.

Now I sat there twitching like a fiend. Watching the clock and looking for the closest exit.

Had to admit the place was different than I expected, though. Like anyone could walk through the door and be welcomed. No judgement. Most everyone was dressed casually. It was small, but not so small that I couldn't hide at the back.

Maybe that made it all the worse. Fact a demon had slunk in through the doors and no one had noticed.

Or maybe I was coming unglued because Eden had been itching in about as much discomfort as I was right then when we'd pulled into the lot, and she'd confessed that her father didn't know anything about her working at the club. Instead, she'd told him she'd been waitressing at a diner. She'd whispered he had no clue about us, and she wasn't sure how to approach it.

That I was the first, the only, after Aaron.

Hated the way she'd flinched when I'd suggested we pretend we didn't know each other. She'd pinned on this fake, pained smile, nodded, and said, "Yeah, we should do that."

Like the girl had secretly wanted me to stand up and claim her.

And I was right back to asking how the fuck a man like me had the right to do that? Two of us so at odds. So different. Coming from such different places. Had no right to suck her into my sordid world, and still, I had her there, anyway.

I took it as a reprieve when her father finished the sermon and asked everyone to bow their heads. I dropped mine into my hands and squeezed my eyes shut tight.

The prayer I mumbled was one asking to disappear.

Never should have agreed to this.

Her father finally said, "Amen," and everyone looked up just as the band started to play another song.

People began to stand.

That was my cue.

Only an old lady who'd been sitting two chairs down from me leaned over and patted me on the back of the hand. "I sure hope to see you again next week."

She smiled softly, her eyes appraising.

Right.

Okay.

I went back to roughing that same hand through my hair. "I'm sure you will."

Not happening, but I would say whatever to get out from under this.

I pushed to standing and edged down the row. People were milling around, filling up the doorway. I slithered through like the snake I was.

I was heading straight to Eden's room, getting my girl and my kid, and getting the hell out of there.

Except someone was suddenly standing in my path.

Smiling and appraising, too.

But different.

Like he felt the evil lurking from within me. Felt it radiating from my soul and seeping from my skin.

Eden's father.

He was probably close to sixty. Nothing intimidating about him. But still I stood there shaking in my motherfucking boots.

Though his smile was kind, his gaze still assessed, quick to look me up and down, darting to the glaring sins inscribed on my skin.

His head tipped to the side in speculation. "Hello. I'm Gary Murphy. I don't believe we've met."

He stuck out his hand.

Warily, I slipped mine into his, swallowed down the jagged pill at the base of my throat. "First time here. My son goes to the school, and he wanted to check out Sunday school, so here we are."

Gritted it through clenched teeth.

He shook my hand, chuckling, and that smile was turning into something relieved. Like he'd been worried he was going to have to throw himself in front of his congregation to protect them from the likes of me.

Nope, just your daughter, Sir.

"That's great. Who's your son?"

"Gage Lawson."

Everything about him brightened. "Gage? Oh, he's in my daughter's class. Little spitfire and smart as a whip, that one. You must be proud. He's a good kid."

My chest tightened.

I was.

I fucking was.

Just wasn't proud of the rest.

"Thank you. He amazes me most days. Best part of me."

The green of his eyes deepened. "Our children always are."

Wondered how he handled it? Having a daughter who'd done what she'd done. Betrayed him the way Eden had said.

I forced a smile. So brittle it was gonna crack. "It seems so."

His head angled in question again. "So, you've met my daughter? Miss Murphy?"

Miss Murphy.

Eden.

Little Temptress.

The pill in my throat grew spikes. "Just in passing. Feel like I know her since Gage sings her praises every day."

Awesome.

Lay it on thick.

More of that parental pride swelled in his expression. "She's the best we have, and I'm not just biased. Just don't tell any of the other teachers."

He winked at that, still shaking my hand.

"I'm sure it's not biased at all," I said, playing this game the best that I could all while feeling like a piece of trash.

Standing there having tainted his daughter all while thinking about the next time I got to do it again.

"Well, it was really nice to meet you, Mr. Lawson. I hope to see you again. Our doors are always open. Anything you need." His voice turned emphatic at that. Genuine.

"I appreciate it."

Before I could get any deeper, I slipped through the crowd that mingled near the doorway and rushed down the hall, anxious to get to Eden and my kid.

Eden and my kid.

I managed to refrain from shoving through, the apprehension building, the feeling that my past was right there, so close to finally catching up. I breathed out in relief when I made it to the door that was propped open, though right inside, the room was blocked off by a high counter and a swinging gate where parents signed the children in and out.

Eden was in the middle of a mass of kids who were dancing and laughing.

And the girl...the girl was laughing, too.

So free.

So good.

All that grace shining around her like a dream.

I moved to the clipboard on the counter where I'd signed him in. I was quick to sign him out.

A second later, Eden edged my way, my son's hand clutched in hers as she led him over to the gate. She barely brushed the edge of my hand as she passed Gage through.

It didn't matter if no words were spoken. Those knowing, kind eyes whispered all the things I didn't fucking know how to say. Everything neither of us should feel.

Jutting my chin, I took Gage's hand in mine. *We'll be in the car*, I mouthed, and the tiniest smile tugged at the edge of her mouth before she turned her attention to a woman who came in behind me.

We stepped out, and immediately, Gage started bouncing along at my side as we walked, kid prattling on about how amazing Sunday school was as I led him out the door to where my car was parked at the back of the lot.

I helped him into his booster in the backseat, and I dropped a kiss to his forehead when he stopped for one second to take a breath.

Overwhelmed, I pressed my nose into his hair and inhaled his sweet scent.

Felt myself spiraling. It was all right there. Nipping at my heels.

My son, my son.

I tried to remember the one reason.

The reason my mother had given me.

The reason Nathan had passed on after that.

Failure after failure.

There wasn't much I was scared of in my life.

The only exception was the one that drove it all.

I was utterly terrified of making another mistake that would cost someone I loved their life. Wouldn't survive if I did it again.

I rounded the back of the car and slipped into the front seat. I powered up my phone. It blipped with a message.

I thumbed into the screen.

Jud: Call me.

Anxiety lit. Burning through my insides as I pressed his name to return the call. It rang once before he answered. "Where the hell have you been?"

"Church," I grunted, glancing at Gage in the backseat where he was reading some little book he'd brought out with him.

Disbelief filled Jud's laugh. "You're shittin' me."

"Don't start, man. Just tell me what the hell's up."

I could feel his hesitation travel through the line.

"What is it?" I demanded low, trying to keep the bite out of my voice.

Jud sighed. "Word is, Juna was spotted in LA a couple months ago."

Fury hit me in an instant.

Dread.

Betrayal.

Fear.

"Fuckin' bitch." It slipped from between my lips before I could stop it.

"Ridge's informant didn't know why she was there or who she was seein', only that there were rumblings of her name within the Demon's, but if she really was there…" Jud trailed off.

Neither of us needed to say it.

If she was there, she'd broken the pact meant to keep us alive. A pact she'd made promising to never return to LA since she was the only one who knew where we were.

Juna was the one who'd led us to Redemption Hills in the first place. Other than the money, she had one stipulation to our deal—I had to raise Gage here. A place she and her family had vacationed when she was a child, and she'd conjured some kind of fairytale idea that one day she'd raise a family here.

Was easy to concede to. A random place to disappear.

"Tell him we need details." The words grated from my tongue.

"He understands the severity. I wired him some money so he can see who will roll."

Money always caused people to talk. Secrets confessed for a little dough. Cash the only thing it took for most to sell out.

I'd always wondered when the day would come when the money that I was feeding Juna would no longer be enough, and she'd start sniffing out ways to swindle me in this treacherous deal.

Through the mirror, my gaze found my son. My innocent son who didn't deserve any of this. A son who should have a mother that loved him rather than one that was willing to sell him.

How fucked up was that shit?

He was doing his best to read to himself, sounding out words below his breath, paying no attention to the conversation I was having with Jud.

"Thank you," I managed.

"No thanks needed, man. You know that. This is family. This is *life*."

That bitter pill finally splintered down the middle. Jagged pieces piercing me through. "And I'll do whatever it takes to keep it that way."

"Know you will, brother. Same as me. We're in this together."

"*My sweet warrior. Watch over your brothers. Take care of them. Love them with all your might.*"

My mother's voice whispered in my ear. Like Jud heard it, too, he muttered what sounded like a warning. "Play it cool and be safe, Trent. Promise me you know this isn't all on you."

My grunt was reluctant.

"I'll take that as your oath." Then he blew out a sigh. "I'll call you as soon as I find out more."

The line went dead.

I glanced at Gage again before I was dialing the number that I only dialed once a year.

A number that made bile rise in my throat and hatred boil in my blood.

It rang and rang before her voice came on the line. "This is Juna. Leave me a message."

Was sure my teeth were grinding to dust when I hissed, "You better think twice if you're even thinking about double crossing me because I promise you aren't gonna like the outcome."

Nearly jumped out of my skin when the door whipped open in the middle of my leaving it, and Eden slipped into the passenger seat. My attention darted that way in time to catch her face twist in worry.

"Call me as soon as you get this," I grated before I ended the call and tossed my phone to the console.

"Who was that?" Eden whispered, voice shaking, though she kept it low to keep Gage out of the conversation.

"No one, baby, no one."

Chapter Twenty-Nine

Eden

Do you remember…

Do you remember when Momma got sick?

She fought so hard because she desperately wanted to stay with us. But I saw her fear, the way she watched us each day like it might be her last. Do you remember how she promised that even if she wasn't here, she'd be watching over us?

Do you remember how much it hurt?

Do you remember how Daddy pretended to be so strong? But he'd weep at night, his agony seeping through the walls and into our hearts. He'd beg and pray, ask for them to trade places, and still, she got sicker every day.

Do you remember how brave you were the whole time? You sat at her bedside for months and held her hand. Whispered stories in her ear while she slept and murmured your promises to take care of us in the moments she was awake. At night, though, you'd lean on Aaron. I think that was when you fell in love, in that quiet peace you found with him at your side.

Do you remember how I was jealous all over again?

You were in so much pain, Eden. So much pain, and still you stayed.

You loved. You cared. You were willing to stand in the middle of the storm, your arms lifted high as you shouldered the burden.

Do you remember how I watched it from afar? Detached and floating away? The one thing I wanted was to feel something good or just not to feel at all because I found no comfort in those walls. I found only fear and hurt and the coming loss.

Do you remember when we laid her in the ground? It was so cold that day. The wind bitter and cruel as it howled through the trees. You held my hand so tightly. I'll never forget it, Eden, the way you held on like you were trying to save me, too.

With your other hand, you held onto Daddy. A firm fortress in the middle of us.

You were our rock while I'd never felt so removed and so alone.

Do you remember how I ran? How I turned my back? How I stole? How I lied? How I caused more pain?

I remember, Eden. I remember it all, and I wish I could go back.

Harmony

With shaking hands, I folded the letter and stuffed it into my back pocket where I stood in Trent's kitchen.

Grappling.

Battling.

Rocked again.

Unable to process what she was saying or what she wanted.

I'd felt my world shake when Jud had brought me a stack of mail from my house and there'd been another letter from my sister.

Part of me wanted to find her and shake her. Tell her I couldn't take anything more right then. To just go. To stop the turmoil she caused and leave us behind the way she'd done for years. I was already dealing with enough.

The other? The part that would love her forever? Even when she'd destroyed me and my father again and again?

I wanted to beg her to return. To return the money she'd taken or find a way to help us repay it. Tell her we'd forgive her either way. Tell her she *could* go back and make it right.

"Miss Murphy! Miss Murphy!" Gage came bounding in through the archway, jarring me from the daze. "What are we gonna have for dinner? I'm so the hungriest, and you're the best cook ever, even better than Uncle Logan, but don't tell him that. It's a secret. Can I help?"

Affection burst. The emotion I was trying to contain shifting and reshaping, taking new form.

"You're hungry, huh? What do you think we should make?"

"Pigs in a blanket?" he asked way too excited.

A giggle slipped free, and I ran my hand over the top of his head. "We had that last night. How about we make something different? How about some chicken and broccoli?"

"Broccoli. Blech." He curled his nose.

"It's good for you."

"I already take the vitamins. I'm as healthy as can be." He showed off his tiny biceps.

I laughed. Couldn't help it. He was a whip. A sweet little whip that had me completely wrapped around his finger.

The week that I'd been staying there had passed in a blur of worry and bliss.

I'd leave here each morning in the car Trent had rented for me, and he'd follow me to the school. I'd had to make an excuse to Tessa that my car had broken down and I'd gotten a rental upgrade.

"Lucky bitch," she'd said.

She had no idea.

Trent would drop Gage off at the curb, the man watching me from afar, all that heat and intensity touching me from across the space.

He'd tried to convince me to take off the week like he'd done with Absolution, but I'd convinced him I needed to work. That I couldn't leave my father in the lurch like that.

Besides, I still had a debt I needed to pay.

So, he'd post himself at the coffee shop across the street. Watching. Waiting. Continually on guard.

Then he'd pick Gage up and follow me home.

Home.

To this house that had started to feel that way.

Where we ate together. Laughed together. Worried together.

Loved together.

I gazed down at Gage.

That's what this was, wasn't it? This joyful fear that burned so bright?

The way I sparked and shivered every time Trent touched me. The way my heart felt lighter every time he took me into the safety of his arms. The way my spirit shouted each time I wrapped mine around his son.

It was exactly what I did right then.

I hoisted Gage into my arms, hugging him as I said, "Let's make a deal…you eat some broccoli, and I'll make corn on the cob, too."

His sweet eyes doubled in size. Pure excitement.

"Deal!" Then his voice went gravely serious. "But we gotta shake on it because I don't want you to go trickin' me the way my uncles like to do."

"Smart boy," I teased.

"That's why I got all the As, Miss Murphy." He said it so matter of fact, and I was laughing again, emotion twining through the sound. I squeezed him tight. If I could, I'd just hold him like that forever.

Reluctantly, I set him on the island and stuck out my hand. "This is a binding deal, Gage Michael Lawson. Once I shake on it, I can't take it back."

"Like a promise?" he asked, words twisting up with resolute sincerity. Sprinkled with all that sweet innocence that he exuded. "Because promises are really important. You don't go breakin' those. No way, not ever."

My chest ached. Brimming. So close to being full. "Like a promise, Gage, and I promise, if I make one of those to you, I won't break it."

He slammed his hand into mine, shaking it with all his might. "Then it's a deal. And I promise I love you so much. All the way to the highest mountain in the world."

He stretched his arms as high as he could over his head.

I felt impaled by his words.

Stricken.

Wrecked.

Whole.

And for the first time, I said it aloud. I whispered, "I love you, Gage. So very much. I promise you that."

And I wanted to make a thousand promises right then. That I would love him forever, which was true. But more than that, I wanted to promise that I would stay. That I would never leave him. That I'd be his mommy if he wanted me to.

A fool.

A fool.

Because I could hear the mutterings from the other room. The hushed voices where Trent and his brothers talked below their breaths.

I had no idea how to break through the barriers Trent had resurrected between us this last week.

He treated me like a queen. Like his love. Like his life. Like he would throw himself in front of a train, sacrifice himself, if it meant keeping me safe.

But he was also keeping me in the dark. His fears and demons a writhing, living obstruction that separated us.

He might try to keep the conversations he had with his brothers hidden, but in the low murmurings, I heard the terrifying words.

The threats of retribution I knew they would make good on.

Sickness coiled in my stomach when I thought back to what I'd accidentally overheard when I'd gotten into his car after church last Sunday. The way Trent had jolted when he'd realized I was there, his mouth pressed into a grim line as he lied and told me he wasn't talking to anyone when I'd heard it plain as day.

And with all the chatter? It wasn't hard to figure out who it had been.

Gage's mother.

And he'd threatened her.

I trembled when I thought of it. My own hate that burned and boiled as I stared at the child's sweet face.

How could someone be so awful to put him in danger? So selfish? So unkind?

Her own son?

It made me want to fight, too. Lash out. Protect.

But I didn't know how to do that when Trent was keeping me at arm's length. Behind that wall he'd built like a hedge of protection that shut me out from the most significant parts of him. Where I felt him withdrawing with the strain. With his worry. With his belief that he was a darkness in my life rather than the light that flooded me every time he came into the room.

But the truth was, I'd rather stand in his darkness and see him for what he was than to flounder in his shadows.

"Come on, we'd better get dinner started."

I hefted Gage up from under the arms, swinging him around, and landing him on his feet. He squealed and laughed and filled the vacant places of my heart.

The front door shut, and I could hear Jud's motorcycle start.

Trent sauntered in through the archway. Hard as stone and as beautiful as could be. He walked straight over and pressed a kiss to my forehead.

Eyes dropping closed, I relished in the sensation, this man who thought he wasn't capable of giving me his love cherishing me.

Chapter Thirty

Eden

MY ARMS CURLED TIGHTER AROUND TRENT'S WAIST AS he slowed and eased his bike into the Absolution parking lot. I was doing my best to keep my nerves at bay but pulling into the lot for the first time after the incident had them igniting anew.

Night hovered over the earth like a curtain, a swath of black that pressed down on the blue neon lights that glowed with the promise of indulgence and revelry from the enormous brick building.

The club was packed. More people than ever were standing in a long line at the front door.

A big band I'd never heard of were playing tonight.

Apparently, it'd been in the works for months, tickets pushed to max capacity, and extra security and staff had been brought in to accommodate.

Trent had wanted to cancel it, especially since the band was from LA. I'd convinced him he couldn't. This was his livelihood. What he'd built. Two weeks had passed, and we had to start to move on with our lives, but I guessed when you'd been running for the entirety of yours, it was hard to do.

Even though I knew we had to do this, I felt myself clinging to him so tightly. So tightly I could feel the ferocity ripple through his tense, rigid muscles. So close that I could feel every curve, line, and intonation. Sense the ruthless edge that had carved his spirit into blades.

Tonight, the aura radiating from the menacing man had turned malignant.

Malevolent.

Ready to strike at any moment.

He eased the gurgling mass of metal around to the side lot, and I tried to keep my heart from sprinting away with the bolts of fear that flashed through my mind.

With the images that took hold.

Blinks of the horrific message that had been left.

Trent guided his bike backward until he was parked beside Kult and Milo's motorcycles. Normally, he'd leave his bike at the front and make an entrance, but he wasn't taking any risks.

He killed the engine. In an instant, my ears were filled with a drone of voices and the thudding bass that echoed from inside.

Trent pressed his hands over mine.

Reassurance. For him or me, I wasn't sure.

All I knew was it was a promise that he would never allow anything or anyone to harm me.

And I just kept praying it wouldn't be him. Because that hollow space inside had transformed and shifted and reformed. Refitted to the shape of him.

I'd known after Trent Lawson I would never be the same. What I hadn't expected was for him to write himself on my soul. For him to become the beat of my heart and the blood in my veins.

He unwound my hands that were locked against his stomach and helped me off. He followed, rising to his full, obliterating height, covering me in shadow.

That beat of my heart stampeded.

The man a paradox.

Conflict.

A crux.

Tattooed, vicious fingers were so tender as they unfastened the strap of the helmet from under my chin. Sooty eyes so soft but razor-sharp as they took me in. The defined, distinct contours of his stunning face glinted below the haze of lights.

My stomach pitched with desire and my chest stretched with that feeling I could no longer deny.

"Stay close to me tonight." His words were barbs.

"You've said that a hundred times." I managed a tease.

He grunted. "I'll say it a hundred more. All night. All day. Forever."

The words slipped into a murmur as he wound his arm around my waist and pulled me snug against the hard lines of his body. And I wanted to get lost in the undercurrent of what he'd said. In the promise he didn't know how to make.

The confession danced on my tongue.

I love you.

I love you.

I didn't say it.

He'd clam up and run. Hide behind every reason he couldn't keep me.

He dipped down and pressed a quick kiss to my lips. "Little Temptress…trying to wreck me."

My fingers curled in his shirt. "You're the one who's done all the wrecking, Mr. Lawson."

He smirked, arched a brow. "Mr. Lawson, huh?"

My mouth tugged up at the side. "You are my boss, after all."

His hand splayed across my lower back before he gripped me by the bottom, his face pressed to the underside of my jaw. "I'll show you boss," he grumbled at the sensitive skin.

A giggle slipped free, along with a rush of need. "You better," I whispered back.

He groaned and chuckled. "Like I said…Little Temptress."

He peeled himself back, the slightest smile twitching over his sexy mouth, and he threaded our fingers together and led me to the side door. Milo was there, holding open the heavy metal barricade, though the man would likely be much harder to break through than the door.

"Sir," the bouncer said with a jut of his chin. "Little Dove."

"Hello, Milo," I said with a tiny wave.

"How's it going tonight?" Trent asked, glancing around, gaze sweeping the lot.

"Crazy, Sir. Members of A Riot of Roses are in the dressing rooms in the back, and their crew is setting up. Place is a madhouse. Buzzin' and gettin' ready to bust."

"Extra security is in place?"

Milo's attention dipped to me. "Absolutely."

"Good."

"Nothin' will get by," he promised.

Trent squeezed my hand like he was the one who'd said it.

We angled into the murky dimness of the long hall. I lost my breath there again, with the way Trent shifted to look at me, with the way he pressed me to the wall. "Just want to take you home," he muttered, his body plastered to mine and his heart beating out of control.

I tipped my face up to meet the fear in his eyes, and I scratched my fingers into the stubble on his cheek. "We'll be fine."

My gaze searched the severity of his. *Will we be?*

Taking my hand, he pressed my knuckles to his lips. "No one will get near you."

Thickness filled my throat. "I told you I'm not weak, Trent, I just need to know what we're up against."

And that was the hardest part. He wouldn't give me that.

"I'm working on it."

The same answer he always gave.

I gave him a short nod. "I'm going to go change."

He hesitated. I knew it was a warzone in this brutal man's mind. A battle with every decision.

I pressed at his chest. "We already talked about this. I'm still here to help my daddy, Trent. The reason I came in the first place. You have to respect that."

But I'd be a liar to deny some of those reasons had changed.

"Let me take care of it."

My head shook. "No, Trent. I'm not here for you to *take care* of me."

I'm here because I love my daddy and I'll do anything to help him. And I'm also here because I love you, and I want to stand by your side, too. Support you the way you've supported me.

Yeah, those reasons had most definitely changed.

Did he see? Did he understand?

He stared down at me with that potent, heady gaze. "I know that, but I still want to."

The tiniest smile tugged at my lips. "And that makes you amazing."

He grunted like he still believed he was bad.

"Mr. Lawson."

Our attention shifted to the end of the hall where a security guard from the temporary agency stood.

"I'm sorry to interrupt, but we wanted to go over a few things before the show starts."

Trent lifted his chin at him before he returned his focus to me. He dipped in for a kiss, one that was probably a little too passionate for an audience, but right then, I couldn't mind.

Not when his mouth moved and played, and his tongue danced and whispered.

Stealing my breath and reservations.

But there was nothing left of my heart to take.

He already owned it.

He nipped my bottom lip before he forced himself back a step. The man's entire being heaved. He held my hand between us. "Be careful. I'll have someone watching over you the entire time."

"I'll be fine," I promised.

He nodded, and I pried myself from the wall and headed into the dressing room to change. Leann was there, shoving her purse into a locker. She squealed when she saw me, slammed the door shut, and came clamoring my way on her high-heeled boots. "Oh my god, you're back."

She threw herself against me and hugged me tight. "I was so worried about you."

I returned her embrace. She was truly so sweet. "I told you I'd be fine."

She eased back, holding me by the outside of the arms. She angled her head to take me in. "Are you? That was insane."

I swallowed around the dread. I'd been wading in it for so long. I just wanted to rise above it. To leave it behind us so we could truly find ourselves. But until this threat was ended, I had no chance of scaling a wall as high as the one Trent had built around me. No chance of fully reaching him when his only purpose was protecting me and his son.

Our safety had become the only thing that mattered.

And I needed the man to understand he mattered to me.

"It was really scary, and we still don't have any answers, but honestly, I'm okay."

More than okay.

She saw it. A smirk hitched on her face. "Sometimes trauma reveals what we need the most, doesn't it? It rips away all the questions to expose the raw truth underneath."

My teeth clamped down on my bottom lip in the same spot Trent's just had been. "Oh, there are still plenty of questions."

Her head shook. "I think the only answer you need is the one written all over your face...you look..." Her mouth pressed together in some kind of awe. "Happy, Eden. So different than when you first came here."

Then her expression turned wry. "Which is kinda a shame because oh my god, have you seen the band?!"

She fanned herself.

"I mean, I'm more of a country girl than a rocker, but I'd gladly change my stripes if it means gettin' a little of that. Their lead, I think his name is Royce? He's married to this country singer that I've listened to for years, but the rest of them...seems they're looking for a little fun," she drawled as she wiggled her hips.

A shot of laughter ripped out. "Well, you have *fun* with that."

"Oh, I plan to." Looking in the mirror, she swiped on some lipstick. "Wish me luck!"

She started to walk back out but not before she paused at the doorway, her voice lowered with caution. "I've worked here for a long time, Eden, and I know I don't know you that well, but I've had this scary, intimidating boss for years who I couldn't quite put my finger on. Now there's a light in him that didn't exist before. And I know that's because of you."

Appreciation swelled, overflowed my chest. "I hope so. Thank you, Leann."

Her smile was soft, then she pulled away and disappeared down the hall.

I quickly changed into the Absolution uniform. Oh man, was it so unlike anything you'd ever find in my closet. The tiny leather shorts and high-heeled boots that came above my knees. But somehow, I felt confident in it. Powerful in a way I had never been before.

Or maybe it was just that Trent had helped me see myself in a new light, as well. Broken up a piece of me that had been hidden away. Opened me up, lock and key.

After I was ready, I moved out into the bar, weaving through the crowd. I said hello to a few other servers and tried to answer questions posed by those who asked for details.

Impossible, when I had none myself.

Finally, I got to work.

I figured most had assumed I wouldn't return since there was no missing the way gazes appraised and questioned as I started to take orders and deliver drinks.

Is she really okay? Is she insane for coming back? Was she targeted or was the attack random? Is someone after her?

Others were filled with speculation.

Look, there's the one who's fucking the boss.

Clearly, that's exactly what I was doing since Trent couldn't keep his dirty paws off me every time I passed. I didn't mind. Not at all. I liked it probably more than I should, the claiming he was doing in front of everyone.

The slide of his rough palm down my bare thigh.

The chills it lifted.

The stolen kisses under my jaw.

His hot breath on the back of my neck.

I felt no shame in it. In who we were or what we shared. People could judge me all they wanted, but the only thing that mattered was what was on the inside. Who I was to myself, and how I treated those around me.

But I also knew as I watched him, too, as I felt that dark aura moving through the thriving, living space as the band readied to take to the stage, that I wanted more than just stolen kisses and illicit hands.

I wanted it all.

I wanted forever.

The main floor had been rearranged. The tables and low couches had been moved out, and a large barrier had been set up to create a huge floor in front of the stage. People vied and pressed within its boundaries, trying to work their way closer, while others were happy to snag one of the booths that ran along the walls.

Tonight, I was working upstairs where there was a second bar and pool tables, although there was another big crowd that had gathered on the balcony that overlooked the stage below.

Trent felt that area would be more secure, and I didn't see a point in arguing with him. No reason to add to his stress when I could already feel every molecule in the man's body on guard.

I was delivering a tray of beers to three guys on the balcony when the dim lights flashed and a furor of screams echoed through the cavernous space.

Rising and lifting.

Feet stomped and whistles of anticipation rang through the air.

Everything went dark, the energy held, before it cracked.

Busted wide open when the flashing lights hit the stage, strobing and slashing and inciting a riot that broke through the crowd on the floor.

Apparently, the band was happy to invite exactly what their name claimed.

They drove into a loud, tumultuous song. A driving rhythm and thrashing beat. The singer's voice was rough and smooth and everything in between.

I rushed to keep up with the orders that flooded in as the band moved effortlessly from one song to the next. The singer was all over the stage, screaming his soul out like he was laying his heart at the trampling feet.

And oh, Leann was right—the stage was consumed by these aggressively gorgeous men. Each mesmerizing in their own way.

But none were as striking as mine.

I could feel the pulse of his stare when he'd ascend the stairs. The way my heart would pound a little harder, race a little faster as I pushed through the crush and did my best to keep up with the onslaught of orders.

It was wild in here tonight, in a way it'd never been before, in a way I didn't expect.

Maybe Trent had. Maybe that was why he'd been so on edge. Why he'd wanted to scrap the entire thing because pocketbooks and tongues and hands were freer than they'd ever been.

The faces had become a blur as I was jostled and bumped and knocked around.

At least our glasses were plastic tonight considering half of them ended up on the floor.

I'd force a smile, take their money, ignore the catcalls and the wayward touches and the unwanted advances.

And maybe it was the trauma that remained right there. Something I'd shoved down and didn't want to acknowledge.

Honestly, I knew I'd put on a brave face and hadn't fully dealt with the fear.

There was no missing it in the way anxiety bubbled, buzzed, and gathered in severity as the night wore on. The whole time, I was riding a terrified edge of wanting to be strong and wondering if this had been stupid, after all.

A mistake.

If I'd foolishly put us in a bad position.

An hour and a half in, I felt frayed.

Ragged.

Like I'd crack at any second as I pushed through the throng.

I finally did.

Completely overreacting when some guy who didn't know any better grabbed me by the wrist as I passed. I yelped and my tray toppled to the ground as I yanked myself free of his hold.

"Whoa, just want another beer," he slurred, taken aback by my reaction.

But it was Trent's that none could have anticipated. Or maybe it was exactly what I should have anticipated.

What I'd felt steadily building over the last two weeks.

The man a furnace waiting to blow.

Gasoline dumped on a smoldering torch.

Because he had the man thrown on top of a pool table in a flash so sudden that it made the crowd split.

People scrambled to get out of the way while Trent descended like a phantom.

A vicious storm.

From out of nowhere and everywhere at the same time.

In an instant, he was a blur of fury and fists that rained down.

Dark aggression. Fiery retribution.

Punch after punch on the man's face.

Blood spurted from his nose, and it only seemed to spur Trent farther. As if he could beat any threat out of the guy who had made the mistake of touching me.

I rushed for them, trying to latch onto Trent's arm. "Trent. Stop it. He wasn't hurting me. It's not him. It's not him."

Shouts roared around us, and a few people pushed in to try to stop the madness.

While I fought harder to break through the cloud of hate that surrounded Trent.

"Trent." My hands sank into his shoulder, gripping at his arm. "Listen to me. Stop. He doesn't deserve this. He doesn't deserve this."

Trent kept wailing away.

I begged while the beast seemed removed.

Completely oblivious to anything but the wrath that poured from his being.

Finally, Kult broke through the thrashing wall of bodies. His eyes were wild as he assessed what was happening.

"Kult. Help. Stop him," I pleaded, still trying to pull Trent off the man.

But I got the sense he couldn't see me. Couldn't feel me.

A black veil of antipathy was his driving force.

His demons alive and freed.

Screaming and clawing and begging for destruction.

Kult shouldered through and ripped Trent off. "Let up."

Trent thrashed and flailed while Kult struggled to hold him back. "Cool the fuck down, man. Cool it."

"Oh my god." It left me on a gasp when I saw the guy who lay bloodied and battered on the felt. Coming in and out of consciousness.

Blindsided.

While Trent continued to rage. Those ferocious eyes filled with hate. With grief. With something so dark that I couldn't see through to that level of pain.

One of the upstairs bartenders, Jason, was on his phone, calling for the paramedics.

While Kult dragged Trent back through the gaping crowd.

I rushed to the guy on the table whose wife was helping him sit up.

"I'm so sorry," I barely managed. "An ambulance is coming. I'm so sorry."

A Riot of Roses continued to play downstairs, completely unaware that the owner had just snapped.

It was what he'd warned would happen.

He'd warned that destructive force would one day rise. No longer contained.

Milo was suddenly there, pushing through the people who'd decided the incident was more interesting than the band, though most continued on blissfully unaware. "Let's get him moved downstairs." He lifted his chin. "You'll be compensated for your trouble although it's company policy that patrons do not touch our servers. Security believed she was in danger."

Right.

A veiled threat and a payoff so the cops wouldn't be called.

Taking the employee elevator at the back, Milo led the man down to the locker room and propped him in a chair, and a minute later, two paramedics came through the door.

They tended to his wounds that could have been much worse, and I had to assume that Kult had intervened much faster than it'd seemed when I was trying to break through Trent's anger.

The man's nose was bloodied and he had some cuts littering his face, but it didn't appear that he would have any permanent damage.

Thank God.

While I hovered and paced, a fear bottled deep, that thing that Trent believed raged inside him freed.

Once the man and his wife left, Milo squeezed my arm and walked out, and warily, warily, I eased down the hall to Trent's office.

I pushed open the door to the darkened room save for the small lamp that glowed from the edge of the desk.

Jud was kneeling in front of Trent who sat in a chair in the far back corner. He was bent over at the waist with his face buried in those tattooed hands.

His knuckles bloodied and his being tossed in chaos.

Jud swiveled to look at me, and he slowly rose to standing when I quietly slipped inside.

Unease blistered. A receding storm that threatened to make a rebound.

Jud moved my way, his heavy boots thudding on the ground, his understanding thick. He paused in front of me, squeezed my fingers, and leaned in to murmur so only I could hear, reiterating what he'd told me all those weeks ago. "He deserves someone who will see him for who he really is, Eden. Not for what he's done."

My nod was short and shaky.

He dipped his bearded jaw, edged out behind me, and clicked the door shut behind him.

With it, that intensity struck.

A flashfire of severity.

A wash of hate and wrath.

Trent looked up through the darkness.

All that loathing was directed at himself.

Still, he did that casual thing that he did, slung himself back in the plush seat with his arm draped over the back as he pinned me with that unrelenting gaze.

He angled his head in challenge. "You see it now, Eden? You see me for who I really am?"

"I've seen you all along." The whisper curled through the dense air.

On a scoff, Trent climbed to his feet. A menacing refuge in the billowing night. "And just what is it you see, Eden?"

The last time he asked me it, he walked away from me.

Fear tumbled down my spine, a cold sweat that shivered across my flesh. Not because I was afraid of him, but because I was afraid of the power he wielded.

I lifted my chin and met his steely gaze. "I see a man who's touched me in a way no one else can. I see a man who burns so bright, he might burn me alive. I see a hatred that runs so deep in his veins, and still, I want to dip my fingertips into the flow."

A growl rolled up his throat, and he swallowed hard.

The wings of the owl on his throat flapped as he took a prowling step forward.

"Look at me, Eden," he demanded. He grabbed my hand and pressed it to his face.

Fire flashed.

Streaked my arm.

The sharp contours searing into my being.

Into my flesh.

Branding me.

"Look at me, really look at me, and see me for what I am. A monster."

Everything trembled.

My heart and my soul and my hands.

I shook my head and gulped around the knot that burned in my chest.

"No, Trent. I see my heart. I see my future. I see my life."

He blanched as the admission spilled free, and the man angled back as if he'd been slapped.

"But I also see the man who is trying to ruin us."

The shake of his head was grim. "We were ruined before we started."

"No."

"The things I've done—"

"Stop it, Trent, just stop it. I already know. I already know. And none of it matters. The only thing that matters is right now, and right now I'm looking at the man I love. I love you."

My hands pressed to the thunder of my heart. "I'm in love with you. I love you in a way I didn't know existed. In a way I didn't know was possible for me to love someone. And I'm standing here, begging you to love me back because I don't know how to go on like this."

Shame flashed through his expression, though there was something underlying it that tried to break through.

Vying for space.

For voice.

Then rage came bounding in to take its place.

"And I told you I don't get that. That I don't have that to give you. I have one reason, one fucking reason to live, and you've distracted me from that. Made me lose sight."

He slammed a ferocious fist against his chest. "Made me lose focus on what I'm supposed to be fighting for. I'm losing my mind over you, and because of that, I've gotten careless. Sloppy. And I can't afford that when it comes to my son."

His teeth ground. Or maybe it was just the sound of my heart being decimated.

Destroyed.

Just like he'd promised he would.

My nod was jerky, and I blinked through the tears that rushed to my eyes. I would not cry. I would not cry. Not right then.

Still, my lips quivered and twitched, and I backed away. "I guess I do see now."

Then I turned and rushed for the exit.

"Eden!" he shouted behind me.

I didn't slow.

I threw open the door and flew down the hall, ignoring the bashing I could hear behind me.

His violence spilling out again.

This dark, dangerous devil who'd stolen my heart and crushed it in nearly the same beat.

I didn't take the time to change. I grabbed my purse and rushed to the side door where Milo stood guard.

Sympathy lined his expression when he saw my face, then I cried out in devastation posing as frustration when I realized I didn't even have a car.

My entire life had gotten wrapped up in the man who didn't want me.

Who thought I was a burden.

Who'd built the walls up so high that he couldn't see what we could mean if he'd just slow down long enough to see his worth.

I fumbled to get into an app to call a ride, thanking God that at least a car was nearby. I jumped into the back as soon as the Prius pulled to the curb, trying to hold it together at least until I got home.

A minute later, a single headlight pulled up behind the car.

But that energy didn't slam me.

Need didn't consume me whole.

I choked over a cry, the tears slipping free when I came to the acceptance of what Trent really thought of me.

He let me go but sent his brother in his place.

Like a job that needed to be done.

Ten minutes later, the car stopped in front of my house, and I fumbled out onto my weakened knees.

Agony lashed.

Ripping at my insides.

I swore, standing there, I was bleeding out.

That single headlight eased up as the car drove away. Jud slowed, barely stopped, just looked at me with remorse. Like he wished he could make it right. Like he was the one who was giving me an apology.

My head shook. "You can tell Trent he doesn't need to worry about me any longer. You don't need to waste your time looking out for me."

"Eden." Sorrow filled Jud's tone.

"Please, don't make excuses for him. Just go."

Worry pinched his face, and I turned and stumbled up my walkway. I felt like I was being haunted by everything Trent had said to me.

His need.

His confusion.

Promises that he'd never let go.

Mine.

Mine. Mine. Mine.

He'd claimed it again and again, but more than that, I'd felt it in his touch.

Felt it, even if Trent couldn't.

And maybe that was the saddest part.

Loving someone and refusing to acknowledge it.

I dug into my bag for my keys. I pulled them out, but they slipped from my trembling hands, clattering to the ground.

I choked over a sob as I leaned over to pick them up, and cries were tearing out of me by the time I managed to unlock the door and let myself into the hollowed vacancy of my home.

Loneliness howled from the depths.

Cold and stark.

This place no longer felt like a sanctuary but rather a reminder of what I had been living without.

I let my bag slide from my shoulder and drop to the ground, and I shuffled down the short hall and flipped on the light switch to the lamp on my nightstand.

I blinked against it, through the haze of tears, and I moved to my dresser and pulled out a pair of pajamas.

A whimpered cry slipped out when my fingers brushed against

the metal frame where I'd buried Aaron's picture at the bottom of the drawer.

I hadn't done it because I was trying to forget him, but because it was hard to remember him when I felt the way I did about Trent.

As if it were a slap in his face.

A disrespect.

And I would forever cherish the sweet man for who he'd been.

Harmony had been right. Aaron had been a safety net. A shoulder to lean on. An ear to listen. And I had to guess I'd been the same to him.

I unzipped the knee-high boots, kicked them off, and shoved out of the leather shorts and tank and jerked on the cotton shorts and a tee.

I pressed my hands to the top of the dresser and tried to catch my breath. To stop the tears that wouldn't stop falling. To remind myself Trent had been worth the risk.

He'd jumpstarted my heart.

He'd shown me that I could feel.

That I could burn and need and love.

But it just hurt so goddamn bad I didn't know how to breathe under the weight of it.

No longer able to stand, I sank down on the edge of the bed.

Weak.

Worn.

Broken.

I reached over and clicked off the light, then curled up in a ball and hugged my knees to my chest.

Let the pain bleed out.

The hopes.

The fears.

I had no idea how long I'd lain there, but I'd drifted, lost in the crashing waves of this heartbreak that beat over me time and time again.

Partially lucent, the other lost to a bad dream.

As if I were floating through a reality I didn't want to recognize.

It only made me feel more disoriented when the doorbell rang, and I shot upright, my face still soaked as I blinked through the lapping darkness.

I rolled off the bed and stumbled out into the hall. My hand pressed to the wall to try to get my footing, and I sucked down the shuddering breaths that kept hammering my chest.

My lungs burning and my world spinning.

I made it to the front door, and my heart slammed against my ribs when I peered out through the drapes to the front stoop.

To that dark force that obliterated and shook.

So intimidating and wrong and so terribly right.

He held his sleeping son in the safety of those strong, strong arms. Gage's face was buried in Trent's neck, and Trent held his sweet frame like the treasure he was.

I tore through the lock and whipped open the door.

Then I froze.

Speared by the intensity that cut me to the quick.

Knocking the air from my haggard lungs and piercing me to the spot.

Because all the fury was gone, and the man stood there staring at me.

As broken as me.

Swallowing hard, he tightened his hold on his son. "You ruined everything, Eden Murphy."

Hot tears streamed down my face.

"Everything I thought I knew."

"Trent…"

His head barely shook. "Look at me, Eden."

That time, it was surrender.

Everything clutched.

"Look at me. You think there's a chance that I'm not in love with you? That I'm not gone for you? And I'm fuckin' terrified of it. Terrified of losing someone else I love. Of failing you, too. And I could fight it forever, but I think I'd still end up standing right here in front of you, begging you to love me back."

Sorrow lacerated the words.

His confession.

The same thing I'd begged of him.

"Trent." I whispered his name.

"What happened tonight…" He trailed off, his tongue swiping his lips. "I lost it because of what I feel for you. Because I can't fucking lose you. Because I love you. You said I brought your heart back to life, but Eden, you made mine beat for the first time."

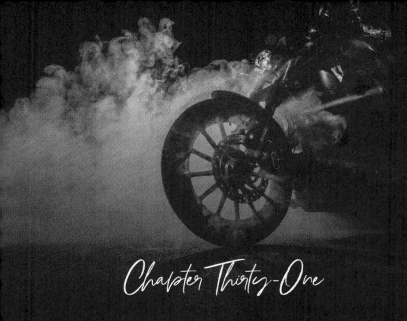

Chapter Thirty-One

Trent

E DEN.

Fucking beautiful, sweet Eden.

She widened the door after the bullshit I'd pulled tonight. After I'd lashed out because I was fucking scared and, rather than just admitting it, had put the blame on her.

Like any of this bullshit was on her.

Forgiveness.

Was something I'd never really believed in. But for the first time in my life, I might have felt what it meant.

Like my confession could wash away what I'd done and what I'd said. Like in her eyes and touch I might be made whole again.

Foolish?

Yeah.

But it was the truth.

I fucking loved this woman, and I didn't know how to go on without her in my life.

Swiveling around, she moved deeper into her house.

One reason.

One reason.

I followed her down that short hall where I'd followed her before, though this time she went through a door on the right. It was a smaller bedroom, and there was a tiny bed against the far wall. She eased all the way inside and pulled down the floral covers.

In silence, I moved that way and laid my son down in the middle. Eden trembled, covered his little body, lowered to her knees and pressed her face into his hair and breathed him in.

I was impaled.

Pierced.

Stricken.

The girl...the girl loved him, too.

Finally, she stood, tears still streaming from those autumn eyes. But it was different.

It was a flood of belief.

Of adoration.

Of love.

Everything I didn't deserve but would be a fool to reject.

She'd cut me down to the core.

To the bare beat of who I was.

Those eyes held mine as she angled around me, and she turned around, walking backward the rest of the way down the hall and into the room where I'd first touched her.

Where I'd known in a flash that I could own her body.

Should have known with it, she was gonna own my heart.

She edged backward, standing in the hazy shadows like an offering.

I stood at her doorway, heaving breaths, no restraint left.

"Watched my mom get gunned down when I was fourteen." It left me like a confession. Guessed that's what it was.

I watched it. Felt it. The way every cell in her body wept. "Oh my god, Trent. I'm so sorry."

My throat felt tight.

Tingling and burning.

Tried to swallow it down.

Bury it.

But I couldn't hide this any longer.

"I was supposed to take care of her, Eden. Was supposed to protect her and my brothers because she didn't have anyone else. Yet she died in my arms, but not before she made me promise to take care of my brothers. Protect them. Ten years later, my twin died the exact same fucking way. In my arms because I wasn't strong enough to protect him."

My eyes burned, and still I forced out the words. "Failed her, Eden. Failed my brother. Keep failing the ones I love. And failing you…failing Gage…it'd be the end of me."

"Trent—"

I took a step toward her, cutting her off. "I've had one reason all these years. One reason, Eden. My son. And you…you've become a part of that reason. I get it now. It's not split in two. Cut in half or divided. You. Gage. My little family I never thought I'd have."

Eden's lips parted, and a whimper slipped out as fat droplets kept leaking from those sweet, adoring eyes.

"I want to give you everything," I whispered. "Everything in this life that you desire. I want to be right."

Eden tremored. "All I need is you."

"Tell me you're mine. Tell me you're *ours*. Tell me you'll protect him right alongside me."

Her spirit flashed. A whip of that energy that cracked in the air. "I love him, Trent. Love him with everything. With my whole heart. A heart I thought would never love again. Just like I love you."

I moved then.

Claiming her mouth.

That sweet little body.

I angled her onto the middle of her bed.

Took me half a second to get her out of the modest sleep shorts and tee.

Girl sexy as fuck and brighter than the day.

A ray of light that cut through the darkness.

She was completely bare when I edged off the side of the bed, writhing and looking at me like I had become her reason, too.

I stood there watching down on her as I undressed, and the girl heaved with pants as I climbed up to hover over her.

The softest fingertips found my face. My eyes, my nose, my cheeks. "I love you," she whispered.

"Never loved anything the way I love you." The words grated from my raw throat, and Eden was sliding those lush thighs around my waist.

I took her bare.

As bare as my heart.

Because I had nothing else to hide. Nothing else to lose.

I moved over her. As natural as the tide. The ebb and flow of our bodies as we gave and took.

As we climbed and lifted.

Propping myself up on my elbow, my hand curled around the back of her neck. I thrust slow and deep because I didn't want this to end.

We were nose to nose.

Our hearts beating out of time and perfectly in sync.

Eden's mouth was full of the softest whispers, her eyes overflowing with our truth.

Because I'd known what it was like to fight.

To fear.

To kill.

But what I hadn't known was a love like this existed.

Chapter Thirty-Two

Trent

Los Angeles, Six Years Ago

YEARS WENT BY THAT WAY. HIS LIFE A BLUR OF BLOOD AND atrocity.

Trent chased a high that always dropped him to the lowest low. He could no longer tell if it was rage that drove him or just duty.

Numbness had frozen over his soul, this detached sense of being each time he pulled the trigger.

But it wasn't the comfortable kind. It was an ocean of disgrace. A sea of shame.

The sins that mounted.

The pleas. The cries. The blood.

The blood.

He was floating in an endless abyss of it. Face barely breaking the surface.

Soon he wouldn't be able to breathe.

Would drown.

But he had one reason to keep going. That tiny glimmer that burned through the bleakness of who he was.

And he'd fight for them until his last breath came.

Only problem was he'd started to wonder what that really looked like. Started to wonder if he were doing it all wrong. Had started to wonder if he should just go, the way his mother had said.

The life they were living was so vastly different than the one he'd imagined. He didn't deserve any better, but his brothers sure as hell did.

He pressed his hands to the dingy table tucked in the back room of the dive where his crew liked to hang. He glowered across at his father.

Cutter, the piece of shit.

He might still be the President, but he wasn't gonna push Trent on this.

"Leave Logan and Nathan out of it," Trent warned, his voice a growl. "No way they're coming on that run."

A smirk ticked up at the edge of Cutter's greasy mouth as he sat back in the chair, his teeth ripping the flesh of the chicken from the bone before he tossed it to the plate. "And how do you have any say about this?" he snarled as he roughed a napkin over his beard.

"They're not like us."

Cutter spat a laugh. "That so?"

"I promised my mother I would protect them, and I won't let them get in the middle of this bullshit."

Jud was different.

He'd followed Trent like that was what he'd been born to do. But as time went by, Trent had started to wonder if it wasn't only because Jud was doing some of that protecting, too.

Nathan and Logan wouldn't survive this world. This vile, disgusting world.

Sickness curled through his stomach, all mixed with the cruelty of who he was.

Cold.

Hard.

Numb.

Years of it.

But lately, the awareness of that depravity kept breaking through the oblivion. His spirit staging some kind of revolt. Truth was, Trent wasn't sure how much longer he was gonna survive it, either.

"Your mother?" Cutter laughed. Pure disgust. "Tell me you aren't still hung up on that."

Trent was in his face, gripping him by the vest before the asshole had the chance to prepare himself. Trent pressed the barrel of his gun to the underside of his chin, aching to put a bullet there.

Cutter might be the boss.

But it was Trent who ran the show.

Cutter might not want to admit it, but most of the men were loyal to Trent. Looked to him for direction.

"Hung up on it?" The words were razors. "She is the reason I'm here. Only reason."

Retribution.

Revenge.

Justice.

His own debt that could never be repaid.

A vicious smile curled Cutter's mouth. "You put that Demon in the ground years ago. It's done."

"Last I checked, there are still a few Demons walking this earth."

And he wouldn't stop until he reached the top. Until Pit was dead. Because there was no way the order for that hit came down from anyone but their president.

Cutter edged back from the barrel, staring Trent down. "And maybe it's time you focused on what you were made for rather than chasing a ghost."

Ghost.

Ghost.

Ghost.

"Only. Reason. I'm. Here," Trent hissed.

Loud and clear.

Except Cutter wasn't one who wanted to hear it.

Cutter's eyes flashed. "You belong to me, Trent. You shouldn't forget it, *VP*." He said it like a taunt as he jutted his chin at the patch on Trent's cut. A reminder of the chains that bound. "You're lucky you have my blood running through your veins or that little stunt would have been your last."

Cutter tipped his attention to Trent's gun, a threat in his eyes. But Trent saw the rest, too. The jealousy. The flicker of fear. Trent had long since become more deadly than him.

Giving for the moment, Trent straightened and tucked his gun back into his jeans. "Wrong again, Prez." He sneered it. "Don't belong to anything but the promise I made my mother. You'd do well not to forget it."

Raging like a beast, Trent strode back into the main area of the bar. Slew of Owls were there, tossing back drinks, sluts dancing on the tables.

He moved to where Jud was at a tall table in the middle, dude sitting back and taking it in. He slid a beer in Trent's direction. "About time. Wanna tell me what that was about?"

"Nope."

No need to draw attention to the monster trying to draw his brothers into the life.

Trent grabbed the bottle, draining it as his eyes scanned the place. It locked on the hazy figure in the far back corner by the jukebox.

Without saying anything, he set his empty on the table and moved across the bar, following her out through the back door and into the dingy lot.

He pressed her to the wall, pulled out his dick, and hiked up her skirt.

Pit's girl. Girl he was making his just for the fact that he could. Girl who kept showing again and again because she couldn't get enough.

She was a good fuck, but the only reason he'd gone after her was to get closer to Pit.

A little acid tossed in his face.

A precursor to the pain that was to come.

Juna Lamb.

Except when he finished, she clung to his neck, pressed her mouth to his ear. "I'm pregnant. It's yours."

Trent's entire being seized.

Shut down.

Before it struck back up.

He jerked back and stared her down. "How the fuck do you know it's mine?"

She dropped her eyes. "Pit only wants me on my knees."

"You're sure," he demanded.

She nodded before terror filled her face. "He's gonna kill me, Trent."

It wasn't an exaggeration. Not something tossed around like regular people did for effect or attention.

Pit would put her in the ground. Along with Trent's kid.

It might have been the first time Trent felt real fear since the day his mother had died.

A spark in his blackened heart.

"I didn't mean…" she trailed off, chewing at her lip.

"Didn't mean what, Juna?" he demanded.

Brown eyes peered up at him. "I didn't mean for this to happen."

"And what do you want?"

Tears blurred her eyes. "I…I can't raise a kid, Trent. I'm not…"

"Kid's mine. You don't have to worry about that."

She blanched. "I'm going to need—

Fucking typical.

It was always money. Always fucking money.

"Come by my place…tonight…after midnight. We'll get you out of town and into hiding. Soon as the kid's born, it's mine. You disappear forever and you don't say a fucking word, and I'll take care of you. I'll take care of everything. You understand?"

Grief, or maybe it was guilt, passed through her expression before she nodded. "I understand."

328 | A.L. JACKSON

"Is this really what you want?" Nathan asked. The face that was nearly the exact same as Trent's filled with uncertainty. Guy would do anything for Trent same way as Trent would do for him.

It was what Trent had been trying to do for years.

Protecting.

Hiding.

Seeking retribution.

Looking at Nathan's face, he finally got that he'd been doing it wrong all along. "This isn't a good life. We stay, we end up behind bars or dead."

Way everyone else did.

And that was not a fate Trent would entertain.

But he'd been fighting for so long, he'd forgotten what he was supposed to really be fighting for. His mother hadn't asked for vengeance. She'd asked for life. It was time he gave it.

"But will you be happy?" Nathan pressed. "Only thing that matters."

A scoff of a laugh left Trent. "You think this life makes me happy?"

Sadness passed through Nathan's expression. "I don't know that anything makes you happy, Trent. Not sure I've seen you smile since the day Mom died."

"You make me happy." Trent looked around where his brothers were gathered in his living room. "Three of you, that's it. And…" Trent choked over the admission, though he pushed it out, done hiding from the rest of them. "And this kid."

A second chance.

Nathan smiled a satisfied smile. "That's because you finally found a reason, brother. A real reason. You fucking live for that reason. Not this twisted shit you're tied up in. Promise me."

Fuck.

Nathan was everything Trent had believed him to be.

Good.

Kind.

Right.

Dude deserved a life so much better than the one Trent had

dragged him into, even though he spent most of his time trying to keep him and Logan out of the throes of it. Trying to give them some sense of normalcy when that was nothing but a pipe dream.

His own lie.

"I promise," Trent muttered.

I promise.

Trent cleared his throat and got down to business. "Have a deal to see through tonight. Big one. I don't show, Cutter will be coming to collect. Don't want to raise any suspicion. Get ready. Pack only what you need. Meet here at four. We roll an hour before sunrise. That is if everyone is with me?"

All three of them stood, hands set on Trent's shoulders as they gathered around. "We're with you, brother. Always have been. Glad you can finally see it."

Nathan pulled him in for a hug. "You're gonna be a dad, man. That's…"

Everything Trent hadn't known could be a possibility.

It was hope. It was a flicker of joy just out of reach.

It was life.

And right then, right that second, he found a new reason.

One reason.

Chapter Thirty-Three

Trent

HAD YOU EVER FELT A JOY SO BIG YOU THOUGHT YOU HAD to be hallucinating? Lost in a dream that you didn't want to wake from because you'd really like to hold onto the fantasy forever? Something you wanted to cling so tightly to because there was no chance of it being real?

I guessed that's the way it felt when I woke that morning to the lazy rays of light streaming through her bedroom window.

To Eden's hair bunched in my face and her sweet body tucked against mine.

That honeyed scent filling my senses and her goodness and grace filling my spirit.

I hugged her tighter, the girl dressed again in the pajamas she'd had on last night. I buried my nose at the nape of her neck and inhaled. Like I could inscribe myself with the moment. Spend an eternity in it.

Then I was grinning wider when I felt the bustle of energy come bursting through the bedroom door along with a stampede of tiny feet.

"Dad, hey, Dad! There you are!" From the foot of it, Gage dove onto the bed, right between us. I shifted a bit to take my kid into my arms.

He grinned down at me, all dimples and light, voice fueled by excitement. "Did we get to have a sleepover at Miss Murphy's house? Like you were hopin' when we left? Because I fell asleep so much in the car and then I woke up and we were here. Did I miss it? Did you get our girl? Did you, Dad?"

Light laughter filtered free.

Last night, when I'd picked him up from Logan's house, I'd woken him a bit, and with those little arms clinging to my neck, he'd wanted to know what we were doing. I'd admitted we were going to get *our girl*. Kid had taken it to heart.

Yeah, buddy, me, too.

"Looks like it," I said, running my fingers through his hair, feeling sweeping over me so intense it locked the air in my lungs, that feeling only stronger when Eden rolled around to face us.

Girl blinking through her sleep with a crush of emotion flooding from that warm, sweet gaze.

And there was Gage, tucked right in the middle of us.

Gage looked at her. "What do you think, Miss Murphy? Did we get you? Did we? Do we get to keep you?"

He wasn't even looking at me, and I could feel the force of his smile. The overwhelming joy. His love and belief.

She touched his face, and over the top of his head, autumn eyes found mine before she shifted her focus back on him. "You already had me."

He threw himself on top of her, hugging her tight. "Now we get to keep you forever."

I wrapped my arms around both of them.

Yeah.

I did.

It felt so right.

Gage howled with laughter, and Eden giggled and looked at me with that face that shined so bright.

Joy. Joy. Joy.

God, I didn't know it existed like this.

Then I tugged them around just a bit, playfully, with all that happiness that washed and spread and glowed. "And I'm not letting go," I claimed, a tease wound in my voice but the words a promise. "Keeping you forever."

Eden wrapped her arms around us, too.

"Imma Gage sandwich!" Gage shouted, though it was muffled in the blankets and pillows and our bodies.

By our love.

"Gage sandwiches are my favorite," Eden played, tickling my son, soft and sweet.

Gage kicked and howled and begged for more. "Your favorite, favorite?" he asked, trying to hold onto his shaking belly.

"My favorite, favorite. Although I kind of like your dad, too."

A tease played all over her stunning face.

My chest squeezed.

So damn tight.

On my side, I propped myself onto my elbow, reached over, and cupped her cheek.

Gage slowed, just smiling up between us as I stared over at the girl. "Kinda like you, too. Kinda a lot."

Eden took my hand on her cheek and pressed it to her mouth, her lips a whisper against my palm. "So much."

"That's called love, right, Dad, right?" Gage asked, close to a shout, looking at me for approval the way he did.

"Yeah, buddy, that's called love." I was looking at Eden when I said it.

Gage giggled. "Yup, definitely love. Whipped. That's what Uncle Logan said."

"Totally whipped," I said.

No shame.

A smile danced over Eden's delicious mouth, and I leaned over and pecked a kiss to it, thumb brushing the apple of her cheek. "Why don't you take a shower and Gage and I will make breakfast?"

"You two better be careful...a girl could get used to this."

"You better get used to it, Miss Murphy. If we're gonna keep you, we gotta make sure we take care of you. Just like my dad takes care of me. That's what people do who love you, you know?"

Her laughter was almost a whimper. Love spilling out. She ran her fingers through his hair. "Then I think you both had better expect me to take care of you, too."

Gage beamed. "Because you love us."

"Yes, Gage, because I love you both."

Scrambling onto his knees, he pecked a kiss to her cheek before he went scampering out the door.

Soon as he was out of sight, I eased off the bed, took her hand and guided her to standing, kissed her deep.

The softest moan slipped from her mouth.

Danced across mine.

Yeah, she wasn't the only one who could get used to this.

"You'd better get into the kitchen before I demand you take care of me in a different way, Mr. Lawson." Playful seduction wound its way into her tone.

A chuckle rolled up my throat. "Ah, Little Temptress. Playing with fire. Don't worry, baby, you'll have plenty of that."

She edged back just a fraction. "That's good because I'll never get enough."

Yeah. I fucking liked that.

Us.

Here.

Now.

She spun around and waltzed toward the adjoined bathroom, those dancer's legs exposed by the tiny shorts. I stayed rooted until she disappeared, and I heard the showerhead turn on, then I adjusted my dick in my underwear because that was gonna have to wait for later.

I dragged on my jeans and ran a hand through my messy hair before I moved back through the hall, the living room, and into the kitchen.

Every inch of it was bright, warm, and inviting.

Eden written all over it.

Gage was already in there, digging through the refrigerator. "Whelp, Dad, we're gonna have to get really super very creative because all Miss Murphy's got is some eggs and nuffin' else in here. Sheesh. We better go to the store so we can take care of her better."

Swore my chest was gonna burst as I walked up behind him and swooped him into my arms. "Sounds like a plan."

Those arms wound around my neck. "'cause we love her so much all the way to the highest mountain, right?"

"That's right, Gage, because we love her all the way to the highest mountain."

"That's called Mt. Everest, you know."

I chuckled. "That's called my boy's got all the smarts."

"I got to get all the As!"

I pressed a quick kiss to his temple before I propped him on the counter, set my hand on his cheek so he'd know it was important, my voice low with the gravity of the question. "You okay with this, Gage? With bringing Miss Murphy into our lives? Her bein' a part of us?"

Kid actually scoffed at me. "Dad, tell me you're jokin'? She's the best thing that ever happened to us." His arms raised to the sides, and he said it with so much seriousness.

God.

Felt like I was flying.

This love so bright.

For the first time since my mother died.

His eyes widened in emphasis. "You get offered something good, you better take it."

There he went again, schooling me at life.

"Well, I guess we better take it then."

"You know it."

Still laughing under my breath, I started to dig around in Eden's cabinets in search of what we might need.

Gage was right.

Only thing in the cabinets were cobwebs.

Then my heart was dropping to my stomach when the front doorbell rang.

Hairs lifting.

Because shit, my gun was locked in my glove box. Eden might have thought I'd overreacted last night when that douche had grabbed her, but in my life? With my past? With the demons that were right there, threatening to take me down? There was no fucking such thing as overreacting.

You reacted quick or you were dead.

Simple as that.

And I realized as I grabbed Gage and pulled him into my arms and carefully crept into the main room so I could peek out the window, that I was done with the ghosts of that life.

So tired of running.

So tired of hiding.

So tired of being afraid.

I had to find a way to put it behind us.

Permanently.

"What we doin'?" Gage whispered, his arms locked around my neck, kid no fool, feeling the agitation that instantly lit across my skin.

"Just seeing who rang the doorbell." I peered out the sheer curtain. "Nothing."

Relief filled me because it probably was just a delivery. Sighing out a strained breath, I tossed off the bad feeling and moved back into the kitchen, where I set Gage onto the counter.

Then my attention was whipping around when the back door rattled then creaked open.

Terror in my heart and vengeance in my hands.

Reaction I didn't know how to stop.

Only the man coming through froze, eyes going wide in shock when he saw me standing there with my kid on the counter, like he was the one who needed to go into protector mode.

There I was, every muscle poised to jump into action, only wearing my jeans that were slung low on my hips, no shirt covering the sins written across my body.

The clear imprint of Eden was written there, too. Like the girl seeped from my flesh and whispered from my pores.

Eden's father reeled in sheer confusion.

Then this creeping horror filled his expression as his eyes darted and raced and took in the scene. Adding it up quick.

"I...uh...um..." The man gulped, warring where he stood frozen in the doorway, his hand clutching the handle like if he backed out and closed the door it wouldn't be real.

Gage shifted on the counter, a smile spreading wide on his precious face. "Oh, hi, Mr. Murphy!" Gage looked at me. "Dad, look, it's my principal and he's so, so nice. Did you know that?"

Gage looked back at him with that excitement blazing from his tiny body. "Did you come over, too? We're just gonna make some breakfast which is the most important meal of the day, but we don't have a whole lot, so we're gonna have to share. That okay with you?"

Eden's father forced a smile. "I...uh..."

Discomfort lined every inch of him when he looked back at me.

I pulled Gage off the counter and into my arms, trying to figure out the best approach.

What to do or what to say.

Because I had no shame in loving Eden, but the girl had every right to be ashamed of me.

Girl who I felt stumble to a stop behind me.

Her gasp.

A lash of that intensity.

But it was different that time. Her own horror rode through her being as her bare feet skidded to a stop. I looked that way just in time to see her tighten the robe she had wrapped around her body.

Her hair wet and her expression full of her own shock.

I shuffled on my feet.

"Daddy." Eden whispered it like an apology.

"I'm sorry, I didn't mean to barge in. I rang the doorbell, and no one answered, and I was..."

His lips thinned into a grim line, his face pinched, and he shook his head like he was going to step back out.

Unease rippled and shook.

He was worried.

Had every right to be.

Fuck.

I should duck and run.

Save Eden the turmoil.

All the questions I'd had from the beginning reared up and hissed in my ear.

A reminder that I was nothing but a devil standing in an angel's kitchen.

Had no right.

Had no right.

Except she was padding forward, all that grace echoing from her skin. The girl came up to my side, took my hand, and weaved her fingers through mine.

A clear statement.

"It's okay, Daddy. Come in. There's someone I'd like you to meet."

Chapter Thirty-Four

Eden

WARM RAYS OF SUNLIGHT SPEARED DOWN THROUGH the summer sky. I sat on the lower step of the porch out back, clinging to a mug of coffee, while my daddy sat on the upper step, the man toiling in questions and confusion and worry.

I was no fool.

I felt it.

I knew what it looked like.

Disquiet stirred.

Heck, it didn't just *look* like it. It was the truth.

My father had walked in to find a virtual stranger standing in my kitchen making breakfast in the early morning hours, barefoot and not wearing a shirt.

His son propped on the counter, who just so happened to be one of my students.

Awesome.

Very awkwardly, Trent, Gage, and I had made breakfast, brewed coffee, sat my daddy down at the little nook in my kitchen while we'd eaten together. Thank God Gage had prattled right through the discomfort.

Masking it.

Or maybe what he'd done was make it better.

Afterward, Trent had pressed the quietest kiss to my lips, said he'd clean up, and gestured to where my father had wandered out back. "You should go talk to him," he'd encouraged.

Because the man was amazing.

Incredible and wonderful and, in that second, he'd filled my heart up all over again.

So, there I sat on the back porch steps outside the sunroom, staring up at the thin wafts of clouds that breezed through the warm air.

I decided to rip the Band-Aid off like Tessa had suggested.

"I love him, Daddy." I whispered it toward the sky, though I prayed my father felt it in his heart. In his big, giant heart that was most likely terrified for me.

He blew out a long sigh. "I see that, Eden. Plain as day. See he loves you, too."

My chest squeezed, and in question, I peeked back up at my father who gazed down at me with a soft but worried smile on his face.

"Not a lot of men who'd stick around through breakfast with some girl's father who showed up out of the blue, unwelcome and unannounced, and keep looking at you the way he was."

"Well, you know what Gage says—breakfast is the most important meal of the day."

Affection poured out when I said it, and I wrapped my arm around my father's leg. "And you're always welcome, Daddy. Please don't ever think you're not."

"But you didn't trust me enough to tell me." There was his disappointment.

I wavered. "I didn't know what to tell you. Didn't know where he and I were going. And it's…"

"Complicated," he supplied.

"Yeah."

More than my father could understand.

Silence drifted around us for a few moments before he shifted, sat forward, and rested his forearms on his thighs. "How? You saw him at the school and…"

That time, I sighed, the sound a confession that wheezed from my mouth. "No, Daddy, the fact that Gage is in my class was a coincidence. My second job…"

My father tensed, and I peered back at him again.

"The diner?" He phrased it as a question. Like maybe he'd known all along.

My head shook. "No. I started working at a club on the other side of town. Absolution. Trent is the owner."

His throat bobbed heavily as he swallowed, his nod slow and full of disappointment. "Why didn't you tell me?"

My head shook. "Because you'd worry. You'd say it wasn't necessary. You'd say the burden was all on you, and I couldn't sit around and let that happen. I needed to be there for you, fight for you, the way you've always done for me. It's not exactly the kind of place I'd typically find myself in."

I wasn't ashamed of working there.

It just was the truth.

Until I got to know the people behind the doors, it'd felt foreign. Removed.

A place I could never call home.

And that's exactly where I'd found myself—home.

"You should have told me, Eden."

"I know, but there are some things we just have to do, and that was one of them."

"And you…met him there. Fell in love with him," he surmised.

"I did."

It might have been messy and fraught with uncertainty, but I had.

"When I found out he was Gage's father, when he realized I was Gage's teacher, we tried to ignore our feelings for each other. Knew it would be frowned upon at the school. We tried to keep in our lanes and pretend we weren't drawn. I think it was impossible for both of us."

Some gravities were too strong.

Daddy scrubbed a palm over his face.

"He's so different…" He trailed off. He didn't say it. Still, I heard what he'd meant.

So different than Aaron.

Everything my daddy never would have imagined for me.

Ruthless and hard and intimidating.

"I know, but that doesn't mean he doesn't fit me perfectly."

At that, my daddy flinched. "I'm happy for you, Eden. You know the only thing I've ever wanted in my life is to see you find the full joy of yours. But I…"

He wavered, hesitated, contemplating if he should say it. "I need you to be careful…there's…there's a darkness inside him. I met him at the church last week, and I felt it then. Felt it just as strong as I did this morning."

I nodded. "He has demons."

"We all do, but I'm not sure his are in the past. There's something, right there, just below the surface."

God, I'd been keeping so much from my father. But the last thing I wanted was to add more to his burden. Deepen his worry. Not when we were barely seeing hope lighting at the edge of our horizon.

And I doubted much that the pain of my sister was ever going to go away, and at some point, I needed to find a way to tell him about the letters she'd been sending. Once I figured out her intentions.

With all of that, there was no way I would saddle him with the weight of what'd happened to my car.

Besides, I'd started to hope it was random. That there was no threat. That Trent didn't need to keep looking over his shoulder.

Weeks had passed and…nothing.

That's the way I wanted it.

I looked back up at the man who'd always been my rock. The one who'd taught me to believe. "We all deserve forgiveness, Daddy. To be loved in spite of what we've done, to move beyond it when we've made the choice to live our lives the best that we can."

Chuckling out a self-deprecating sound, he looked to the sky. "I know that in theory, in God's way, but as your father here in the flesh, it's harder to accept, looking at someone and seeing they might be dangerous. It makes me want to wrap you up and run away with you."

He forced lightness into it. A wistful smile. His love flooding out.

I jostled my shoulder into his leg. "Which is exactly why I didn't tell you. Because I didn't want you to feel like you needed to protect me."

My voice tightened in emphasis. "And I know you'll always think of me as your little girl, but he is a choice I have made. And even if his demons are right there...alive...I will choose to fight them with him. At his side."

My daddy touched my chin. "You've always been such a beautiful, brave girl. Every life you touch, you brighten, and I hope that man is smart enough to let you brighten his."

This time, I curled both my arms around his leg, hugged him tight. "I think you wouldn't worry so much if you understood the way he's brightened mine."

"Uh, think I don't need that information, thank you very much."

"Daddy." I giggled a discomfited sound.

He stood, his smile soft as I followed. "Like you said, I'll always think of you as my little girl, but you're a woman. A woman who's been through hell and back. And I want you to experience the most beautiful things in this life. Have it all. Just promise me you'll demand it, Eden. That you don't fall into a temptation that you'll regret later."

"I could never regret him."

My father nodded, hugged me fiercely, and murmured, "Then love him with all your might."

He stepped back, though he was still holding my hand. "I love you, sweet girl."

"I love you, too."

He started to walk away then he turned back and grinned. "I'll try not to barge in next time."

Affection rippled out and I ran my hands up my arms. "That might be a good idea."

He lifted his hand in parting, and I did the same, and he turned and disappeared around the side of the house. I waited until I heard the gate latch before I moved back up the steps, through the sunporch, and into the back of the house.

Gage was at the little table by himself. Singing and scribbling with a pen and paper. I moved to him, pressed a kiss to the top of his head. "Where's your dad?"

"He got a call he had to take." Gage rolled his eyes as if it was something annoying he heard all the time.

While something inside me pinched.

This feeling that took hold.

That fierce energy suddenly whipping up a disorder.

Pushing against the walls and scratching across the hardwood floors.

I moved out the archway and through the living room before I started tiptoeing down the short hall.

Trent had his back to me, his phone to his ear, and I caught just the end of a plea.

It was indistinct, but I could tell it was a woman's voice.

"Hurry."

"I'll be there as fast as I can."

He ended the call, and I knew when he felt me, when the air shifted and thickened and brimmed with that feeling that pulsed between us.

A compulsion.

He slowly turned around.

The man menace.

Mayhem.

"Who was that?"

He slipped his phone into his pocket and came my way, took me by the face, and dropped his forehead to mine. "Gage's mom. She says she's in trouble. I have to go check it out."

Fear curled down my spine. Compressing. Crushing.

At the same time, I was so thankful he was giving me this. Letting me in. I tipped my gaze up to meet the ferocity of his. "Do you think she's responsible for what happened at the club?"

Trent tipped my face up to meet with his. "I don't know, Eden.

Gut tells me she is. She's not exactly proven herself to be trustworthy, and if she thinks she's going to put my son in danger..."

Cringing, my eyelids squeezed shut.

Trent kissed both of them.

Softly.

Tenderly.

While every muscle in his body rippled and jerked with bated aggression.

"Little Temptress."

I held him by both wrists. "Please, just be safe."

He nodded then peeled himself back. "I'm going to send Jud over here. You and Gage sit tight until he gets here, yeah?"

I'd woken up to the rental sitting in the carport.

Trent had had Logan and a friend drop it off since I had a meeting with parents this afternoon about a student who was struggling.

The man always thoughtful. Taking care of me.

"Yes, of course."

He nodded then blew down the hall. He came up short at the end, pausing, sooty gaze dimmed with devotion. "I love you, Eden."

My heart swelled. "I love you."

Then he was gone.

"Oh please, oh please, can I go with you?" Gage actually steepled his hands together in a prayer.

A laugh tumbled out. "It's super exciting to go to the mailbox, huh?"

I took one of his hands in mine, smiling as we headed out the front door. I'd just gotten a text from Jud that he was wrapping up at the shop and would be on his way to follow us back to Trent's house.

I went ahead and rescheduled the conference so Jud wouldn't have to follow me there.

Since I hadn't been back to my house in so long, I'd tried to get a few things accomplished.

Gage had helped me water the plants on the sunporch, and we'd weeded a flowerbed out back. I guessed I'd put off grabbing the mail until the last. Both hopeful and wary of what might be waiting.

It was strange hating something and wanting it at the same time.

"I just like to be by you." He shrugged it like his sweetness wasn't demolishing every bit of me. All those broken pieces transformed.

Mending.

Healing.

Growing.

I squeezed his little hand. "I just like to be by you, too, Gage."

"I know why because I'm your favorite and you love me so much! Right, Miss Murphy, right?"

"That's right."

Gage skipped along at my side as we moved down the walk to the street, and I realized I was shaking a bit as I dug into the box.

Praying for another message from my sister. My spirit could feel it. Her remorse. That she was asking for forgiveness but didn't have the courage to come out and say it.

And I knew…I knew I'd forgive her. Our daddy would, too. We just needed her to make a move and actually mean it.

No more lies.

No more stealing.

No more leaving.

It was time for her to come home.

My chest swelled. I realized I wanted to share this with her, too. That I'd found a man that I loved with a little boy who I loved just as much.

A family to call my own.

Would she share in my joy? Feel all the things I'd feel for her?

Tears blurred my eyes when I saw the light blue envelope peeking out, the same as she'd sent the rest in.

Relief pressed against my ribs.

I so badly wanted to fix this part of my life. To restore what had been broken down.

"What's the matter?" Gage blinked up at me.

"Nothing, sweet boy. Nothing. I just got a letter I was hoping to get."

"From a friend?!" Excitement widened his eyes.

"From my sister."

"You got a sister? I don't have a sister or a brother, but I think I want to have five of 'em."

A laugh ripped free. Clogged with the emotion. With the love. I ruffled my fingers through those locks of gold-kissed hair as we stepped back through the front door. "Five, huh? That's a tall order."

He shrugged. "My dad says brothers are the best. Obviously, I really need to get me some of those, too. Life's better with the one's you love, you know, least that's what my uncle Logan says."

Love burned. Burned bright with the possibility.

Although *five* was pushing it.

"I think your uncle Logan is definitely right. Sisters are good, too. Let me show you." I grabbed an album that was tucked in one of the shelves in the living room and carried it with the stack of mail into the kitchen. I set it on the table for Gage to look through while I tore into the envelope and pulled out the folded letter.

My eyes raced over the words, knowing they were likely to hurt, but we often had to open ourselves up to the pain, let the wounds bleed, before we could truly heal.

Do you remember...

Do you remember, Eden, after I left? I went to Las Vegas thinking there would be a better life waiting for me there. After all, the only thing I'd wanted to do was dance. I knew I was leaving you behind, closing the door on that chapter of my childhood because it was too painful to keep it open.

Do you remember I didn't call for so long, not until I started calling Daddy for money, manipulating him while he was grieving for Mom? He'd wipe out his bank accounts because I'd convince him I was in need, not making enough, when all I'd really done was put it up my nose.

It was easier not to feel that way. To numb. To hide. To pretend like I could maybe be halfway whole.

Do you remember how you both still loved me then, even though I know you knew? That you saw right through the lies?

I choked over her confession. I suppose a part of me had always known. That she'd slipped so far that she'd begun to numb herself from the pain. But she'd never once come out and said it. Admitted it. And I knew…knew she was opening up, giving me more in a way she'd never done.

Behind me, Gage chattered and giggled at the pictures in the album while I went back to devouring the letter.

Do you remember when you sent me a letter asking me to come back for your wedding? To stand at your side? I said yes, but I didn't show, but I still watched you from afar.

I saw a flicker of your joy, and I was jealous then that you could feel any joy at all.

Do you remember, Eden? When I spiraled? When the drugs became the only thing that mattered? When I started to take off my clothes for money before I started to crawl into strangers' cars where I walked the street?

The next fix.

The next hit.

Do you remember, I hopped on some guy's bike and rode with him to LA where he promised me he would make it better?

No, you don't, because you didn't know me then.

I wheezed over the shock. My brow pinched tight. Pain lanced through me. Pain for my sister. For that life. For all she'd let go. Her confessions felt like a brand-new puncture to my heart.

My mind began to spin with the rest.

She'd gone to LA? When?

In the background, Gage was saying something about me being

a cute baby, but I couldn't focus on anything but trying to process what Harmony was saying.

The depravity.
The sickness.
The endless cycle of pain and numbness that just went on and on.
But I do.
I remember it all.
I remember when I stooped to my lowest low.
I got pregnant there, Eden. Do you remember?

What? The paper curled in my fingers, eyes frantic as I rushed to read the rest.

No, you couldn't remember, because I'd shut you and Daddy out.
I was only supposed to prove some biker's disloyalty to his father. No big deal. All I had to do was lure the son out and he'd set me free forever.
Buy me a diamond and a house and I'd be set.
So I'd seduced that man. Tricked him. Manipulated him.
Except at the last minute, I couldn't do it. I couldn't do it.
They were going to kill him.
I had to stop it.
Only it spiraled. It spiraled and spiraled.
So much death.

My legs wobbled. My body swayed. I blinked. Tried to process. To understand.

Do you remember, Eden, six years ago when I came racing home, terrified for the life of me and my baby after I'd betrayed all of them? Do you remember when all that money went missing from the church treasury? I'd taken it because I was going to disappear.
Do you remember how Aaron caught me as I was sneaking out?

No.

No. No. No.

My eyes blurred and sickness raged.

He'd begged me to stop before he got in his car.

He chased me, Eden.

I ran a red light.

So did he.

But he didn't make it through to the other side.

Do you remember, Eden? Because I remember it all, and there is nothing I can do to take it back.

Harmony

I fell to my knees. Unable to stand. Unable to see. Images struck me from every side.

Knives and arrows.

Impaled and impaled.

She'd been responsible for Aaron.

Aaron.

Oh god.

I gasped, unable to stop the sob from ripping up my throat.

The biker.

The biker.

Gage climbed down beside me, that album in his hands.

The walls began to spin, and I tried to remain sitting up as bile lifted in my throat.

He giggled and pointed. "Look it, Miss Murphy, look it. That's my mom. I got a picture of her at home with a bear she gave me when I was a baby and it said on the back of the picture that she loved me 'cept I don't even know her because my dad says she lives far away. You wanna be my mom?"

Gage.

Gage.

Gage.

I recognized him then. Those eyes. That smile. The way my heart had pressed full the first time I'd seem him.

I felt the dismantling.

The crashing.

The falling away.

The walls. The ceiling. My heart.

My sister.

My sister.

Aaron.

Trent.

My cell rang on the floor beside me.

Jud.

I didn't even know how I managed to answer it through the blur of tears and the clot in my throat. Through the ache and the questions and the pain. "Jud."

Maybe part of it was his. This intonation that crashed through the line.

Agony.

His voice was hoarse. "Don't have good news, Eden. Gage's biological mother was found dead." He hesitated, then said, "Trent was arrested at the scene for her murder."

I couldn't do anything but throw up right here on the floor.

Chapter Thirty-Five

Trent

Los Angeles, Six Years Ago

WIND WHIPPED THROUGH THE BARREN, BROKEN streets of the city, and hazy lights burned down through the heavy clouds that sagged in the night.

Los Angeles.

A cesspool of greed and corruption and wickedness.

Trent wondered if he could really outrun it. Flee from it. Become someone better than the monster that roamed these streets.

His bike grumbled as he slowed and pulled into the deserted lot of the warehouse at the slummy end of the docks. He killed his bike, his eyes keen as he took in the vacancy. As he peered through the howl of the wind that gusted, kicking up debris and trash that tumbled along the pitted ground.

His heart rate accelerated a notch. Not that it didn't every time he showed for a job.

An exchange.

An observer.

An executor if the need arose.

The life he hated.

One he was leaving behind.

His chest stretched tight with the thought. With the possibility. With something new. A chance he'd never thought he'd be given.

He figured that might have been why there was an extra dose of unease that thudded through his veins as he slipped through the chaotic quiet toward the double, sliding metal doors.

One last job.

One last job.

He stilled a fraction as he heard the roar of an engine come blazing down the deserted street. Felt the fear and the disorder that blistered through the air. A connection that stretched tight.

Pulling and pulling.

That bond that screamed.

He whirled around just as a motorcycle flew around the corner and into the lot.

Careless and reckless.

Nathan.

Trent's entire being lurched. A compulsion to get in front of his twin.

Protect and provide and keep.

Nathan braked hard, and the back tire fishtailed as he skidded to a stop. He jumped off the bike, dumping it to its side, shouting as he ran across the lot toward Trent. "Trent! Stop! It's a trap. A fucking trap. Juna. It was Juna and Dad. They set you up. He knows we're leaving. He knows."

Agony shredded through Trent.

His father.

That bitch.

That fucking bitch.

Trent started to run in Nathan's direction to head him off. To stop him before he got in the middle of it.

He made it two steps before a hail of gunshots rang out from the blacked-out windows of the metal building.

Trent stumbled and jumped behind a metal crate, screaming, "Get down! Nathan, get down. Take cover."

Panic lanced. Spears and stakes. Trent grabbed both guns, one from his belt and the other from his boot.

From behind the crate, he fired.

Shot after shot.

"Nathan, get down! Get down!" he kept shouting. "Find cover and stay down."

Screams and shouts rang and ricocheted and pierced.

A barrage of bullets.

A flurry of confusion.

From that spot, he took down two in different windows.

Two assholes came racing out from the main door.

Trent pushed to his feet. Happily a shield for his brother. He fired and fired.

One fell. The second after him.

Another man dressed in all black came running out from the backside of the building.

Trent took aim.

Cold cruelty seeped through his veins. That numbness that always came.

The ruthless monster sent to slay.

Ghost.

Ghost.

Ghost.

Trent walked backward, firing as he made a barricade between himself and his twin brother.

Trent took every motherfucker out.

Silence fell at the same time as the last man.

Fury in his hands and horror in his heart.

Nathan.

He whirled around just as a bolt of thunder cracked and a torrent of rain poured from the turbulent sky.

Fear clutched his throat when he saw the crumpled pile at the far end of the lot.

"No. Nathan! No." Trent staggered forward, tried to move, to get his legs to cooperate, before he began to run.

Running toward the devastation.

The ground was pitted and cracked.

He swore, there was a crater through the middle.

Everything slowed, and he felt the world come off its hinges, splitting in two.

While the sky spun.

Spun and spun.

His mind and his soul.

He was confused.

Disoriented.

Because it was wrong.

So wrong.

Trent's sight was blurred and bleary as he searched through the haze and the smoke.

Desperate.

Frantic.

There was no cover where he dropped to his knees at his twin's side. No safeguard. No protection. Not a fuckin' thing he could do.

A sob ripped up his throat as he rolled him over.

Trent searched Nathan's chest. Blood covered his hands. The rain washed it away only for it to soak them again.

Tainting.

Destroying.

Wrong.

So wrong.

"No. No. No," trembled from Trent's mouth. "No, Nathan, no. Please. Oh God, please."

Trent pressed hard against the wounds scattered over his brother's chest. Like he could reach inside and stop it, take it away, keep it for himself the way it was supposed to be.

"No, Nathan," Trent choked. "Nathan. No. Fuck. Please. Why? Please. Why? Please, no."

Eyes full of fear searched Trent in the night, wide with shock and terror as blood poured out of his mouth.

His hand grappled for Trent's shirt, dragging him close, the words a gurgled rasp at Trent's ear. "One reason. One reason."

Tears streaked Trent's cheeks, burns where the wind lashed at his face. Agony slashed. Cutting him in two.

Nathan slumped down, his soul released. With it, Trent felt a piece of himself float away.

Trent lifted his face to the heavens and screamed before rage took a rebound and he stood.

He strode through the driving rain.

One reason.

He passed by the bodies he'd left littered on the ground, in search of the only one that mattered.

Both guns were raised as he stepped into the warehouse. Shadows eclipsed, only the barest light filtering through as the rain pelted at the metal.

Deafening.

Or maybe it was the hatred that had filled his soul.

He moved.

Searched.

Hunted.

The hairs lifted at Trent's nape when he felt the movement to the side, and he whirled that direction.

Cutter.

That motherfucker who was supposed to be their father.

"You thought I'd just let you leave?" Cutter said, a gun drawn. Hatred blanketed his face, clear in the shadows, as clear as the fear Trent could feel radiating from the bastard's pores.

Asshole was afraid.

He fuckin' should be.

"You thought I'd just let you walk?" Cutter sneered. "Turn your back? Take your brothers? You thought wrong."

Fury ground Trent's teeth, though they chattered with agony.

With sorrow.

With the missing piece.

"You piece of shit. They killed Nathan. He was innocent."

"He shouldn't have gotten in the way. Just needed that slut to confirm what I'd thought so I could get rid of the weak link. You."

Hatred burned.

"You killed Nathan." Trent's teeth ground.

"Nah, his blood is on you. You're the one who went outta bounds, VP. You forget everything I taught you about loyalty? About who you are?"

Torment twisted. Hammered like the deluge that poured from the sky. Violence bled from his being.

Trent scented it. Cutter's fear. The way he kept looking over Trent's shoulder.

"They're all dead," Trent said, so cool, so calm. "Just you and me, asshole."

Trent dove behind a wooden box when Cutter fired. Dust blew, the sound of the shot piercing Trent's ears. He scrambled around in time to see Cutter duck and run.

Fucker thought he was gonna get away.

The pussy coward dipped deeper into the shadows.

Trent chased after him, jumping behind crates as Cutter kept firing over his shoulder. Through the sound of the driving rain, a door clattered open at the back.

Trent followed.

Cutter fired.

A bullet struck Trent's arm.

He didn't slow. Didn't feel. Didn't care.

He stalked forward, to the edge of the water where Cutter stood.

Cutter lifted his gun and pointed it at Trent. "You're no son of mine."

"Thank fuck."

Trent pulled his trigger before Cutter got the chance.

The shot rang out, and Trent stood there with his arm still lifted as the gun dropped from Cutter's hand. As the man clutched at the side of his neck where he'd been hit.

One reason.

One reason.

That was all Trent had.

And he wouldn't let this scum threaten that.

Trent watched as Cutter fell backward into the water.

It was the first time he'd pulled the trigger and felt no shame. No remorse. Not an ounce of it for the man whose blood ran through his veins.

He stood there staring as the sky wept around him.

As the realization that he'd failed his mom came crashing down.

He'd lost her.

Had lost Nathan.

And he knew there was no forgiveness for a sinner like him.

His soul cast to Hell.

Sorrow ripped through him. Knives and blades.

He only had one reason not to chase it down right then. One reason not to welcome his fate.

One reason to breathe.

One reason to live.

And Trent would live it for him.

Chapter Thirty-Six

Trent

Six hours earlier...

I SPED DOWN THE WINDING ROAD, FUCKING HATING THAT I'D
had to walk out on Eden like that.

Only thing I wanted to do was slip back into the sanctuary
of her bed. Into the warmth of her eyes.

Place I'd wanted to cling to forever because I knew it had to be
a fantasy.

Something so good it couldn't be meant for me.

Blips of trees and sky and earth blinked by as I made my way
to the small town about twenty minutes on the other side of where
Juna and I typically met hidden in the forest.

With each mile, the anxiety had built.

Steadily.

Viciously.

Violently.

Until I was nothing but a ball of crackling aggression.

My hands tightened on the steering wheel as I entered the tiny town off the beaten path.

That's where Juna should have stayed.

Off the beaten path.

Hidden.

Forever out of sight.

After I'd put Cutter in the ground, we didn't know what the threat would look like in LA. The rest of the Owls had disbanded, some joining Pillage of Petrus, others falling into the Demons. The immediate threat had been ended, but we'd made enough enemies along the way to know not to be fool enough to think that no one would ever come looking for us.

It'd turned out Pit hadn't even been involved with Juna all that much.

Yeah, she'd hooked up with a bunch of their crew at their club bar.

Got on her knees for Pit, like she'd said.

Inserted herself in the middle of them and made it look like she was something to him when she hadn't been.

Juna had confessed it.

That piece was a lie.

A bait.

A trap.

One I'd played right into.

Turned out, Juna had met Cutter in Vegas one night. She was looking for a way out and he was looking for a pawn. Someone who could worm their way into my life. Someone who could get close enough to dig out my loyalty to Cutter.

Considering there hadn't been any in the first place, it hadn't been hard to do.

"I think I'm in trouble, Trent," she'd said on the phone back at Eden's place. Panic had ricocheted through the words.

But she'd been trouble all along, hadn't she?

Guessed I'd always imagined she'd be the one to bring it back to our doorstep.

And the fucking problem was I couldn't trust her. Couldn't tell if she needed me to stand up to take her back or if she was driving the knife she'd left in mine deeper.

If she was just luring me in.

Setting another trap.

"You gonna let her live?" It'd been Jud who'd asked it outside the hospital room the night Gage had been born.

There'd been plenty of reasons to end her.

Her betrayal.

Her lies.

The manipulation.

Fact she'd fucked me on my father's dollar.

Was no secret the real reason Jud had asked it, though, his own hatred thick, although he'd left that decision up to me.

She'd gotten Nathan killed.

But she'd also come to stop it. Gave the warning hoping she might be able to thwart what she'd set into motion.

Most of all, she'd given the world the gift of Gage, and I'd already had so much blood on my hands I couldn't take any more.

So we'd made this tenuous deal.

I got Gage and she got the money.

We got a second chance and she got hidden away.

One thing she'd demanded was she got to pick the city I raised him in—a place she'd said she'd visited when she was a child and had dreamed she'd raise a family there one day.

Far enough away from LA that no one would find us.

Redemption Hills.

And I'd started to think that maybe...maybe...I'd find redemption there, too.

Wasn't quite sure how that shit was gonna happen when rage burned through my bloodstream.

After she'd shown her face back in LA?

How could she do it?

Risk it?

Or maybe that's what she'd been intending to do all along.

My entire body vibrated with hostility as I cut across the two-lane road and into the long dirt parking lot in front of the run-down, single-story motel. To the left was a diner, the open sign blinking a sad plea in the window.

Dust billowed behind my car as I flew to the far side of the lot and whipped into the spot in front of a faded turquoise door.

Room seven.

Hand was shaking out of control as I fumbled into my phone and dialed her number.

Stomach in knots and my mind spinning out of control.

Just this…feeling taking me hostage.

A thick dread that something wasn't right.

Same sense I'd gotten the night we'd lost Nathan.

Her phone rang and rang before her voice came on the line. "This is Juna. Leave me a message."

"Fuck," I spat, pulling the phone away and glaring at it before I tucked it into my pocket and hopped out. I ran for the door, hammered on it with the back of my fist. "Juna!" I shouted. "Open the fucking door."

Nothing.

I moved to the window, slamming my palm against the pane. "Juna. Where the fuck are you? Open up."

Silence echoed back.

I pressed my face to the glass and tried to peer through the gap in the drapes.

Couldn't make out shit through the glare.

Until I did.

A foot…there was a foot hanging off the side of the bed.

I smacked the glass again.

That foot didn't move.

"Juna!" I screamed it that time. Screamed it and screamed it. "Juna!"

She didn't move. I rammed my shoulder against the door.

Took me two times before the wood split and the thin metal lock busted free. The door banged against the inside wall, and I raced in only to freeze in the middle of the room.

Lungs losing air at the sight.

Juna stabbed at least a dozen times.

Lifeless eyes staring into nothing.

I bent in two. Tried to breathe.

To focus.

To fight.

But the walls spun.

Spun and spun.

I barely registered the sirens. The two cruisers that pulled up behind my car. The stampede of feet and the cock of a gun and one who yelled, "Get on the floor. Face down, hands out in front of you."

Could feel nothing but the truth.

I was a monster. And my sins had finally caught up to me.

Chapter Thirty-Seven

Eden

COLDNESS SET IN.

Bone deep.

It was the kind that caused you to tremble and shake. Your teeth to chatter. No chance of warmth because you were frozen from the inside out.

I sat propped against the kitchen wall while sickness clawed through my system.

Sadness.

Sorrow.

Fear.

Sweet little Gage had made me a cup of tea.

Lukewarm because *he wasn't allowed to get hot water*. Then he'd pushed it across the floor up close to me, then mimicked my stance with his back propped to the wall.

He might be the only thing that could melt the iceberg that sur-

Ruined.

Gage threaded his little finger through mine.

I glanced down.

At Harmony's son.

At the little boy who'd put that bracelet around my wrist. The bracelet that felt like a brand.

My nephew.

How?

And she was gone. Gone. And I was never going to get the chance for her to explain.

Agony clawed up my throat. Talons that cut through skin.

"It's okay to cry sometimes, Miss Murphy. Don't you worry, not at all, not one bit. My dad said we all get sad sometimes and it's natural and we ain't got nothin' to be ashamed of."

Trent.

A blade driven straight through my aching spirit.

How could he…?

That time, I made it to the trash bin, vomiting what was left of the breakfast I'd eaten before Trent had left. Before he'd left to take care of Gage's mother. Before he'd promised his love.

How?

Pain speared and sliced and cut. Soul deep.

I retched over the bin like I could purge it out.

Or maybe I would finally wake up. Wake up from this nightmare.

A fist banged on the front door.

Heavy and hard.

"Eden, it's Jud." The rough voice echoed through the wood and into the kitchen.

I swiped my hand over the back of my mouth and stumbled that way.

Gage darted ahead of me.

I couldn't breathe, couldn't think, could hardly stand.

I struggled with the lock, barely setting it free to let the door drop open.

Jud's dark eyes took in the room, fixed on me as he let Gage jump into his arms.

"Uncle Jud, hi! You came over! Are we still gonna go to our house? Miss Murphy got sad so maybe we should stop and get some ice cream so she feels better."

Sorrow filled Jud's gaze, the man never looking away. The bob of his throat when he swallowed was like a million pounds beneath the fullness of his beard.

"How about you go get your shoes on while I talk to Eden for a minute?"

Gage groaned. "Is that code for no little ears, too, Uncle Jud?"

Sadness billowed from Trent's brother, though there was affection, too.

It seemed the child's warmth wasn't only irresistible to me.

"Yeah, buddy. Need to talk to Eden alone for a minute."

Gage huffed then sighed. "Oh man, fine."

Jud set him down and Gage went racing away, and I stood there with my arms crossed over my chest like it might hold me together.

"Eden." His voice was an apology. His own agony.

My eyes whipped up to meet with his. "She was my sister."

Shock blanched across his face. "What?"

I choked. "Juna. Gage's mother. She was my sister."

"What the fuck, Eden?"

My head shook. "I didn't know. Not until right now. I was showing Gage pictures of my sister...Harmony...he recognized her."

Jud reeled, scrubbed a big hand over his face. The words falling from his mouth were shards. "That's what the attorney said when he called me...Juna...her real name was Harmony."

My stare became fierce. Hardened with the anger I felt. "Did Trent know? Did he know?"

Did he?

How could he?

I gasped, knees weak, my body swaying to the side.

Jud grabbed me, hugged me close. His entire frame tremored. "No, Eden. No. He didn't know, either. Promise you, and I promise you he didn't do this."

My head shook and tears broke free again. I'd been crying so much, I didn't know how it was possible they hadn't run dry. "He...I heard him threaten Gage's mother. He...hated her. She betrayed him."

God.

Had she done it again? Had she driven him to this? Did he do it to protect Gage or had he done it to protect himself?

Love and hate.

Love and hate.

They warred.

This pandemonium that fought for a victory that none of us would win.

Because Trent and I? We'd already lost.

My sister had already lost.

My legs lost strength, and I slumped forward. Jud kept me upright.

"She did, Eden. Juna fucked him over in a way most people will never understand. She destroyed his life, was responsible for our brother being killed."

Torment filled his voice, and Jud shifted, holding me out by the side of the arms. He angled down to get in my face. "And he still let her live, Eden. He let her go, supports her, protects her, after all of that. After the life he'd lived. When killing was the only thing he'd known. He *chose* to change his life. To live it for his son. To do it right. And unless she had a gun pointed at Gage's head... it didn't happen."

He squeezed tighter. "Tell me you see that in him. Tell me you see him for who he really is, Eden. Not for what he's done. Because he's going to need us more than ever."

My mouth felt dry. So dry. My tongue sticking to the roof. "She was my sister."

"I know. I'm sorry. I'm fuckin' sorry. I promise, I know exactly what that feels like. It's fucking horrible. Horrible. But I refuse to believe Trent is responsible for it."

"What's going to happen?"

His head shook. "I don't know. I need to take Gage to Logan's. The attorney is going to meet me at the station in Lamroe so we can get details. Hopefully talk with Trent and find out what went down. Need you to get your things."

My head shook.

I couldn't just…go with him.

Not when…

Agony slayed. Razors of it that just kept lashing.

"I need to go see my daddy before he gets the call. I want to be the one to tell him."

"Eden."

I stepped back. "I need time, Jud. I don't understand any of this. How it's possible Harmony was Juna. How Trent ended up here…"

I trailed off. Couldn't say it.

With me.

With me.

"It's not safe for you to be by yourself until we figure out what's happening."

What if it was Trent? What if the man responsible is already behind bars? What if I never breathe again?

The thoughts burned through my brain faster than I could process.

I guessed all of it had played out on my face because Jud flinched.

Disappointment dimmed his expression. "If that's what you want, Eden."

He stepped away. Offended.

The man was a protector, too.

While that war raged in the middle of me.

How?

What if?

Why?

It hurt. God, it hurt.

"Gage, let's go," Jud hollered, and Gage came racing into the living room, dragging in all that light. This little boy who I adored with all my heart.

With every shattered piece.

I knelt in front of him, unable to stand, my hand cradling his precious face. "I love you, sweet boy, no matter what."

"Of course, you do, Miss Murphy! I'm your favorite! And you're my dad's and my favorite, too! We love you all the way to the highest mountain, don't you know?"

My spirit clutched.

Ached and wept.

Tears slipped free. Hot and fast.

I nodded. "I do know it."

Did I?

My mind screamed to stop being a fool. That I'd been one since the second I'd walked through the doors of Absolution and fallen prey to that man.

To that dark, wicked, dangerous man.

But my heart, it screamed louder.

So loud, it was deafening.

"You said I brought your heart back to life, but Eden, you made mine beat for the first time."

"Get your keys, I'll follow you to your father's house." It wasn't a question. Jud just widened the door.

"I—"

"Don't fight me on this, Eden." He edged forward and hissed under his breath. "My brother fuckin' loves you, whether you can love him through this or not."

My nod was jerky, and I lumbered into the kitchen, nudged my feet into flip-flops, and grabbed my bag.

Tried to dry my face.

To focus.

To process.

For it not to hurt so much.

Following Jud and Gage out, I locked the door behind me. My feet dragged along the concrete as I made my way to the rental.

How was I going to tell my daddy? How could I break his heart like this?

Jud started down the walk that led to where he was parked at the street. He helped Gage into the back of a big truck, buckled him into a booster, shut the door, then turned around to look at me.

Freezing me to the spot. His sympathy so fierce.

"I know you want to know how, Eden. I get it. Wish I didn't. But I do. And I won't act like I have a clue what the fuck is going down, but the one thing I do know? In the deal Trent made with Juna...or Harmony...or whatever the hell her name is, she insisted that Trent raise Gage here."

In contemplation, his teeth raked his bottom lip. "I'd thought it was bullshit. She'd given him some story that if she ever had a family, she wanted to raise them here because she'd come here on vacation as a kid. She'd demanded this was where she wanted Gage to live. She was also the one who'd insisted on the school."

His voice lost its edge, turned soft with understanding. "Thinkin' now it wasn't such a coincidence that Gage is in your life. Think she planned it."

His words decimated.

Slaughtered and devastated.

They also warmed.

This trickle of something through the heartbreak.

Do you remember... Do you remember...

"Thank you," I whispered.

"Please be safe, Eden."

I climbed into the car and started the engine, cried a thousand more tears as I drove to the house where Harmony and I had grown up.

Where Aaron had lived next door.

Where our momma had gotten sick.

Jud followed close behind.

And I could feel Gage's little spirit from where they waited on the other side of the street as I stumbled up the pathway and rang the doorbell, unable to just walk in like I normally would do.

My daddy's face twisted in surprised concern when he opened the door and found me standing there. "Eden?"

"Oh, Daddy. I'm so sorry. I'm sorry." I threw myself into his arms, hugged him as fiercely as I could, prayed I could be enough to hold him up. "Harmony's gone, Daddy. She's gone."

Chapter Thirty-Eight

Trent

THE LOCK BUZZED AS IT DISENGAGED, AND THE HEAVY door swung open. I shuffled out into the light of day after spending more than twenty-four hours in a tiny cell that might as well have been a coffin.

Jud was there.

Waiting for me.

Relief on his face while torment blistered through my being. I stumbled out, down the three long concrete steps, disoriented and trying to find my footing.

Jud placed a hand on my shoulder. "Trent, brother."

My head shook. "How the fuck…?"

Couldn't even finish the thought before I whirled around and slammed a fist into the red-brick wall of the police station where I'd been being held.

Pain splintered up my arm as the skin on my knuckles split. I reared back and did it again. Let the hatred and the sorrow and the confusion fly.

How?

I went to punch it again when Jud grabbed me by the wrist and rumbled at my ear, "Don't, man. Not gonna change a thing."

On a pained groan, my forehead dropped to the rutted wall. I rocked it back and forth, agony slicing through. "Who the fuck would do this?"

Who the fuck hated us so bad that they'd slaughter a woman as bait?

Fucking meat to drag me out from the shadows?

It seemed more than likely, though, that someone had been trying to frame me.

At least, that's what Rudy Espinoza, my attorney, assumed. Way it was set up. Cops showing a few minutes after I got on the scene.

But I got this tremulous sense that it wasn't that.

It was just a harbinger.

A prelude.

Something to fill my guts with fear and loathing.

Something to drive me to the edge.

Taunting me into fury.

Main thing pointing to that truth was it hadn't taken much for Espinoza to get me out.

If someone wanted to frame me?

They would have done a fuckton of a better job than that.

There'd been no evidence to hold me other than my fingerprints on the bag of money where the contents had been strewn across the floor.

Stacks of cash.

Same bag I'd brought to pay her off a few weeks before.

Yeah. That didn't look so good, either.

Because of it, Espinoza had warned I wasn't out of the woods yet. Charges still might be brought against me. He'd instructed me to hang tight and lie low.

What he didn't realize was I was standing lost in a forest where the demons prowled through the trees.

What'd I expect? That I could get away with turning my back

on my sins? Bury my transgressions? Just walk away and act like my fucked-up past didn't exist?

Go on like I deserved to be free?

Find love?

Happiness?

Nah. Karma wasn't a bitch.

She was just.

Only she wasn't always swift.

She had bided her time until I'd almost hoped to believe that I could be something better.

I'd known better.

I'd known better.

I'd had one fuckin' reason, and I'd lost sight of what that was. Got distracted. Got greedy. Wanted for myself what I had no right to claim.

And it ached.

Fuck, it ached.

All of it.

So fucking bad it nearly dropped me to my knees.

Jud squeezed tighter. "Come on, man, let's get you home. Gage has been asking for you nonstop. We keep tellin' him you're working, but he knows something is up."

My chest tightened.

Kid was smart as a whip. Full of life and light. No way he'd be immune to the darkness that had descended.

I climbed into the front seat of Jud's truck, and he took to the two-lane road and headed back toward Redemption Hills.

While I was slammed with a million thoughts. Endless questions.

"Harmony. Eden's sister." It fell from my tongue like a whispered confession.

Harmony was Eden's sister.

Eden.

Sweet fucking Eden who just kept getting in the middle of this.

"She loves you," Jud said.

Tension bound the cab, and I shook my head. "Doesn't matter."

A scoff flew from Jud's mouth. "Doesn't matter? Don't fucking do this, Trent. Know you're getting ready to run. Can feel it."

I glanced at my brother from the side. "Don't see much of another option, do you? Someone's out there, Jud. Someone who has no qualms with shedding blood."

Someone seeking retribution.

Revenge.

Retaliation.

I should have known it in Juna's voice when she'd called. The way it'd shaken. Whoever it'd been? I'd bet my life they'd been there when she'd made that call. Most likely with a gun to her head forcing her to make the call, coaxing her with what to say.

Yeah, I'd spent a lot of years despising Juna Lamb. But I'd heard the desperation. Should have heard the warning, too.

Frustration rippled from Jud. "You want us to pack up and leave? Tuck tail? We all have lives, man. Lives we like. Homes. And so do you."

Swallowing felt impossible, the way my heart had taken up residence at the base of my throat. This thud, thud, thud that suffocated.

Snuffing out hope.

Snuffing out life.

"You think I'm going to stay there? Put my son in danger?"

Air huffed from my brother's nose. "No. We figure this out. Together. But you've got to be tired of running. Of always looking over your shoulder. God knows I am."

I fidgeted with the outside seam of my jeans, gaze tossed out the passenger window at the scene that passed in a blur of browns and greens and yellows.

Like those autumn eyes were watching me.

I forced out the words. "I have to go, Jud. At least until I know it's safe for my son. I won't take that chance."

My cell started to ring.

Eden's name lit up the screen.

My chest felt like it was gonna blow.

Girl had to hate me. Had every right.

Her sister...was gone.

And fuck...that sister was Gage's mother.

The truth of it twisted through my insides until nothing worked quite right.

This fuckery that distorted and destroyed.

This messed-up life bending and bending until it broke.

I let it ring, didn't answer, couldn't bring myself to talk to her.

"Harmony brought you to her, man." Jud's voice had softened.

Harmony.

Wanted to rip my goddamn hair out. Instead, I scoffed out a sickened laugh. "I'm pretty sure she didn't mean for it to go down like that."

No doubt, she hadn't meant for me to fall for her sister.

Fucking fall fast and hard.

My phone beeped with a message, and I was the masochistic fuck who lifted it and listened, put the girl's voice to my ear.

Little Temptress.

"Trent..." She choked over a sob. "I...I don't even know how to navigate this. What to say. The only thing that makes sense right now is...I need you. God...I need you."

Misery thundered through my veins. Poison as potent as her sweet words.

Because I needed her, too, and the only thing that had done was get her wound up in a perversion she didn't deserve.

I tapped out a message, losing life as I did.

Me: Warned you I would taint you. Ruin you. I'm sorry, Eden. Fucking sorry for who I am.

She had to see it now. See me for the monster that I was. For what I'd done.

It blipped back.

Eden: Please.

"You're a fucking idiot," Jud spat as he sped around the winding curves.

My head hit the back of the headrest. "Love her, Jud."

And some things you loved enough to know you had to let them go.

Silence fell over us as he raced back toward the small city that had been our home for the last five years.

Anxiety and apprehension held tight in the dense air of the cab.

Jud's breath harsh and hard.

Almost as jagged as mine.

When he made it to the outskirts of the city, I looked over at him. "Want you and Logan to go with me...just temporarily. I'm not asking you to give up the life you built, but I am asking you to stand at my side until we can end this. Until we find out who wants me dead."

They did.

Knew it to my soul.

And I was going to have to do the one thing I'd promised myself I'd never do again.

Nothing but the fool who'd thought he could outrun who he was. *Ghost.*

"Then you two are free to do whatever you want. I won't ask you to follow me. But I can't lose either of you to this bullshit."

Jud's nod was tight. "I know, brother, I know. Just can't stand to watch you give up on your joy."

I looked back out the windshield. "Never really was mine to begin with."

Because Eden was light.

Goodness and grace.

And a demon like me didn't get that kind of beauty.

Because there was no redemption for a man like me.

"I'm going to grab a few things that Gage will want. I'll meet you at Logan's in ten."

Jud hesitated at the front door. "You sure this is what you want to do?"

"Don't have another choice."

It didn't fucking help that Eden kept calling. Leaving me these messages that she believed in me. Other times weeping over her sister. Others pleading for us.

Warily, he nodded, then he slipped out into the late afternoon and clicked the door shut behind him.

Before I lost my fuckin' nerve, broke down and did something stupid like go after the girl, I bounded upstairs, grabbed a duffle bag, and stuffed it full of Gage's favorite toys, some clothes, his album of pictures, then I moved into my bedroom and grabbed anything of necessity.

Gage's birth certificate and other documents. Some cash from the safe as well as two guns and ammo that I locked in their case.

Did my best not to look at my bed.

Bed where I'd lost this black heart to a fierce little kitten with the purest soul.

Before I cracked, changed my mind, went soft the way she'd been making me, I raced back downstairs, needing to get the fuck out of town.

Get my son where it was safe so we could put a stop to this threat. End it.

Give Gage the best life that I could, even when every step I took felt like I was coming unglued. Surrendering another piece that no longer belonged to me.

One reason.

Needed to remember.

My phone rang from my pocket. I pulled it out as I opened the door that led into the garage.

Eden.

Sweet Eden.

My spirit thrashed. I stumbled a step and squeezed my eyes closed against the assault of need.

Go.

Fucking just go.

You can't have her.

She never was yours.

In the darkness, I jammed at the button for the garage door. It slowly lifted, the burn of the day blinding. I jogged for my car, popped the trunk, and tossed in the duffle bag and plastic case.

I slammed it shut and started for the driver's seat.

Only to freeze.

The hairs at my nape lifted in tiny spikes of dread.

In awareness.

In sickness.

Everything trembled.

My vicious hands and my sickened heart and the hatred that would never end.

Slowly, I turned around, very fucking aware that my guns were locked in the trunk as I squinted through the rays of glaring light at the silhouette that stepped forward.

He edged forward and came into view.

My father.

He cracked a menacing grin. "Good to see you, Ghost."

Chapter Thirty-Nine

Eden

Do you remember…

My eyes blurred over as I held the piece of paper in my trembling hands.

What was I doing to myself?

I wasn't sure how much more I could take. If I could even stand to read my sister's words knowing she was gone. If I could spend one more minute thinking about Trent without breaking apart.

I'd had to get out of my father's house. I'd been there for more than a day since Jud had followed me there yesterday morning.

Church had been cancelled this morning, and where my daddy normally supported and held up and cared for the congregation, they'd come to take care of us. There'd been a nonstop barrage of condolences and flowers and casseroles.

Yesterday, Tessa had immediately come running.

Refusing to leave my side.

Standing for me when I had no strength left.

She'd held me while I'd cried for what'd felt like an eternity. All day and all night.

Throughout the morning, I'd tried to put on a brave face and be there for my father, to smile and thank our visitors. I'd made it until about an hour ago when Tessa had found me hiding in the bathroom.

She'd told me to go lie down in my old room, and she'd cover for me.

Only, I'd slipped out the back.

Needing solitude.

Or maybe an answer.

A balm.

Some kind of hope in the darkness.

So, I'd come back to get the stack of letters from Harmony.

I needed to feel her again.

Find a way to understand.

To catch a clue or a line of information I had missed.

But what had shaken me was I'd found another letter in the stack. One I hadn't noticed yesterday since it was different than the rest.

Rather than being in one of the large blue envelopes, it'd been sent in a small, plain white one.

I'd been frantic, anguished, ruined when I realized what it was.

Now, I had to squint to make out the words, the handwriting messy and rushed and filled with agony.

I could sense it.

Her fear carved into the paper.

Do you remember, Eden? When I was a horrible sister? When I ruined everything? I know you do. Of course, you do. Even though I don't deserve it, I'm asking you to be there for me one last time. To believe what I'm telling you. It's my last truth because I don't have time for any more lies.

The end is coming for me. I know it. I've earned it. And I'm scared…terrified truthfully…but I've dug a grave I don't think I can climb out of.

I've hurt so many people, you and Daddy and Trent.

Trent.

Yes. I saw you with him the other day. I'm supposed to stay away, keep out of sight, but I needed to see my son one last time.

Sorrow raked from my lungs. The pain so great. My knees knocked as I tried to remain standing in my kitchen. Gulping, I forced myself to keep reading.

He was the man I was set to betray, and he was the one who saved me after I committed the greatest sin. I cost him the life of his brother after I'd bargained his.

Money. It was always about the money.

But somehow, I'd found a speck of conscience that convinced me I couldn't see it through. But I'd been too late, Eden. I couldn't stop it.

Even after that, he'd saved me. Spared me. Taken care of me.

In the deal we'd made, there'd been one thing I'd insisted upon—I'd insisted that he move with Gage to Redemption Hills. Trent never knew the real reason, but I needed to know my child was close to the ones who loved me, to the only good part of me, like Gage might be able to feed from your nearness even if he never knew who you were.

But then I'd taken it farther and convinced Trent to send Gage to the school.

What I'd never expected was you two.

But I saw it, Eden.

I saw that you found each other.

I saw that you love Trent, saw that Trent loves you, and I saw that you love my son.

Not as a nephew, but as a child, and I'm begging you to keep it that way. Don't look at him like the child your sister lost, but as the child of a man who deserves to be loved for the father—the man—that he is.

I swindled and stole and took from him for years. Now, it's going to cost me my life because I was a fool and went back to Los Angeles about six months ago. I'd thought enough time had passed. My selfishness never knew any bounds.

Trent's father was dead, after all. What did it matter?

And with the Demons, the drugs were always easy to come by. That place more like home to me than anywhere else. Where someone like me belonged.

But his father wasn't dead, Eden. He survived. He'd been waiting, watching for the perfect moment to come out of hiding and hunt Trent down for what he had done.

And I was that moment.

Easy prey.

A million dollars, and all I had to do is lure Trent out. That's what Trent's father offered.

But I knew better.

That's why I returned and took the money three months ago. I'd tried to lead Cutter and his crew astray, lied to them about where Trent was living, all while planning to disappear. Truly disappear forever. But Cutter and his crew stopped me before I could get lost. Forced me into revealing where Trent and his brothers were living.

They'd forced me into meeting Trent for my payoff.

I should have warned him then.

I should have, Eden, but I was praying for a way to figure out how to survive at the end of this. Yeah, selfish again.

But I'm already dead even though I'm going to fight it to my last breath.

Cutter is set on taking back what he thinks was stolen from him. Rebuilding his MC while cutting down their old enemies…and their friends. He wants supremacy. He wants revenge.

He wants Trent.

Cutter and three others are in Redemption Hills. Plotting and planning. Waiting for the perfect moment to strike Trent down.

Trent doesn't know. Warn him. Call the police and get to a safe place. Please, please, please be safe. These people are not human, Eden. They'll hurt anyone who gets in their way.

My phone is being monitored, and I'm praying these letters are getting to you. I wanted to tell you sorry to your face, but now all I can do is pray that I haven't stolen another part of your heart.

Warn him, Eden.

Save him.

Love him.

Love Gage, too.

And in the end, remember that I love you. Just like I will forever remember your love for me.

Harmony

I dropped to my knees.

Gutted.

Shattered.

A sob ripped from my aching, raw throat, and I tried to find the air to breathe.

It hurt everywhere.

The sorrow had seeped all the way to muscle and bone.

She'd cost so much. But now I understood. I understood.

I scrambled to my purse to get to my phone, half walking, half crawling.

I dragged it onto the floor from where I'd left it on the counter and dialed Trent's number for what had to have been the hundredth time in twenty-four hours.

He hadn't returned a single call other than the one text saying he'd known he would ruin it.

Still, I'd tried. Tried to break through the barrier.

Each time, it would crush me all over again.

But this time, this time I choked on the fear. "Trent. Oh God, please answer."

It beeped to leave a message. "Your father…he's alive."

I ended the call and forced myself into action, dialing 911 as I raced from the house and to the car.

I started it and flew out in reverse, then rammed down the accelerator when I put it in drive.

"Trent, my sweet warrior. Please." I prayed it as I gunned it, needing to get to him as quickly as I could.

I had to warn him.

Needed to see him.

The operator came on and I explained the best that I could, all while my heart beat out ahead of me as I sped in the direction of his house.

And I realized right then, I no longer had any questions about this man. His intentions or who he was or his involvement with my sister.

I had one truth—one reason—I loved him, and I would do anything to protect him, too.

Chapter Forty

Trent

CUTTER STOOD AT THE END OF MY CAR. A GUN IN HIS HAND and hatred in his eyes. He no longer had a beard. My gaze dropped to the left side of his neck where the skin was mangled and scarred.

Distorted and disfigured.

But that wasn't what made him ugly. This nasty, vile creature standing there. No, it was the maliciousness lining his insides.

How the fuck was he still alive?

"Ah, don't look so surprised to see me, son." He cracked it. A taunt. A sneer. "Didn't you miss your dear old dad?"

His body rippled with aggression.

With hate.

While I reeled.

Awareness slowly caught up. Every nerve in my body fired. Muscle binding and twisting.

My eyes scanned. Calculated. Searching for a way to get out of this when I had a gun pointed at my face.

Funny how things turned out that way.

Running and running and running, and I'd ended up in the exact same fucking place.

The wickedness abounding. Clawing and eating and decaying.

Guessed it was grief that slipped down my spine and stirred in my stomach. Fact I'd done it all wrong. All along. Regret after regret.

"Put a bullet in you," I grunted.

Cutter laughed a disgusted sound. "You didn't think I'd go out so easily, did you? Guess you should have been a better shot." He tsked. "And here you were supposed to be the best."

"And what…you crawled out of the sea like the snake you are and waited for the chance to strike?"

He hiked a shoulder. "Was never going to let you get away. Not from the beginning. Not when your bitch of a mother was gonna run off with you or when you decided to run off with that lying whore."

Shock punched me in the chest. A full body blow. Kind that stumbled me back as my head dropped and my eyes squeezed shut for the quickest beat.

As the meaning of his words came to fruition.

Hatred heaved from my throat, my voice twisted with horrified disbelief.

With my stupidity.

With a brand-new grief.

"Mom."

Chuckling, Cutter looked at me like I was ignorant.

Stupid.

I had been.

God, how did I miss it? All those fucking years chasing down a demon when he'd been standing right in front of me.

Had to force myself to remain still. Not to get knocked to the side like a fist had just landed on my jaw. Or just go running straight for Cutter when he'd pull that trigger if I so much as moved an inch.

"You really think that Demon was responsible? Come now." The prick laughed. Playing me. Winding me up.

"I…" Memories slammed me.

I'd been just a kid…a kid who'd been oblivious to the truth.

Oblivious to Cutter's intentions all along.

A smug smile filled his face. "Have no idea how you never realized it…guess you were so blinded by your hate, thirsting for revenge over her death, that you missed the whole goddamn point. You and your brothers…you belonged to me. I didn't mind ending anyone who threatened that."

"You killed her."

"Gladly."

Bile raced my throat, and my hands kept curling into fists. Rage simmering to the surface.

But I had to keep it together.

Stay focused.

Stay quick.

Hope to fuck that Cutter made a misstep and I could take him out.

Needed to play the bastard the way he'd played me for years.

"What does it matter now, Cutter? Why kill Juna? Why all this bullshit? That fuckin' pig? Those pricks at my bar? You didn't have to be a coward…you could have just shown your face. You and me."

But truthfully…why?

He'd already lost everything. His crew. His club. His freedom. Fucker had been hiding for the last six years.

Dread slipped beneath the surface of my skin when I thought back to the intel Jud had gotten through Ridge.

Fact that Demons and Petrus had started losing members.

Shit.

Cutter was making a play.

Reclaiming turf.

Had been rebuilding. Behind the scenes. Growing in strength. Growing in numbers.

No question, those bastards in my bar had been sent by him.

Scoping.

Planning.

Inciting.

Because that's what Cutter had wanted.

My fear.

He gestured wildly at his face with the barrel of his gun, his smile manic. "You didn't think I was just goin' to let you get away with this? Let you live after what you did? Figured I could have a little fun with it in the process."

My teeth grated. "You killed my brother."

"Nah, Trent, that was always on you. Now it's time you finally paid that debt. Think I still have time to get some use out of your brothers and that little shit that started this all in the first place. Your son has my blood flowing through him. Only makes sense. Owls are back, but sorry *VP, you've been demoted.*"

Rage.

It flooded.

The irresistible kind.

The kind that made my mouth thirst for the taste of blood.

It was what I'd done for so long. For so many years.

Ghost.

Kill after kill.

The numb violence that had spilled through my veins before I'd spill blood on the floor.

No chance would I let any of them get dragged back into that sordid world.

Not my brothers.

Not my son.

I choked over all of it.

That man. One who'd gladly kill at odds with the man I wanted to be.

But for Gage, for my brothers…

Mocking laughter rocked from Cutter. "Tell me you didn't go soft on me? Here you were, my pride and joy. Just your name incited fear. Loyalty. But that's what you always lacked, isn't it? Loyalty. Now look at you, standing there shaking. The deliverer of death should always be ready to die."

I blinked.

Tried to see.

To focus.

I had to stop this here because Jud and Logan wouldn't go down without a fight, and I couldn't allow them to be put in that position.

Then I froze.

Awareness slithered.

The breath ripped from my lungs.

Metal clattered off to the side just as I was struck with a bolt of that energy. With that overwhelming intensity that blistered and lashed.

Cutter whirled around to the side.

Eden appeared through the blaze of sunlight that burned through the garage door.

Oh god. Eden.

Sweet, fucking Eden.

Didn't need to slow to feel the terror that radiated from her flesh. To sense the determination that had lined her bones.

This brave girl with the brightest belief.

So reckless as she came into the garage.

For me.

For my son.

I knew it.

I knew it.

"Eden." Fuck. Eden. "Get out of here."

She ignored it. Stepped deeper into the garage.

"Police are on their way," she said with a jut of that fierce chin. She kept moving forward. "They'll be here in a minute. I told them about your guys hiding out here in Redemption Hills. They know you and the three of them are responsible for killing my sister. You're not getting away with this. Not any of it. This is over."

"It's over when I say it's over, bitch."

"Eden, get down." I dove for Cutter in the same second he lifted his gun her direction, tackling him from behind as the deafening gunshot rang out.

An *oomph* jutted from his mouth as I toppled with him to the floor. His arms and legs flailed, and the bullet pinged against the wall.

We both scrambled onto our feet. A war for dominance. A fight for possession of that gun.

"Motherfucker, it's time to die," Cutter spat.

Whole time, I was shouting, "Eden, get down. Take cover. Please, go."

Please, go.

Since the minute I'd met her, I'd refused to let her get in the middle of my mess.

And there she was.

Danger all around.

I refused to let something happen to her. Refused it. This world would be the darkest place without her light in it, and this black, mangled heart would beat its last beat for her.

For my son.

This little family I couldn't keep.

My mother. Nathan.

It all crashed down on me. The lives I'd stood for. The ones I'd lost. The ones that had to burn on.

No matter the cost.

No matter the cost.

Fury and fire singed through my being, my hands grappling to take Cutter down.

The man was a meaty fuck. Full of his own wrath and rage. "You spit in the face of everything I offered you. Everything I gave you. Ungrateful prick of a kid."

But I didn't want it. I never had. Had been manipulated.

Molded.

Exploited.

I was just a kid. Just a kid.

We struggled, banging into the car, the workbench, the wall. While I felt Eden's chaotic spirit rushing through the space.

Punches were thrown, our teeth clenched, one hand around the front of his neck.

He ripped his arm free, the gun cocked.

In a flash, he had it pointed at my chest.

Hatred flared in his eyes. Ruthless victory. "Not even ghosts are immortal."

Then those eyes rounded.

Surprise.

Fear.

Anguish.

He dropped to his knees. Slumped over. Fell to the ground. Blood poured out, and a puddle gathered quickly around his lifeless body.

The screwdriver Eden held slipped from her trembling fingers and clattered to the concrete floor.

Shock filled the air, and Eden stumbled in horror. In the gutting realization of what she'd done.

She lifted her hands that were soiled by my father's blood.

The girl tainted by me.

Those autumn eyes stared and blinked and tried to process.

"Eden...baby...Eden."

"You need anything else?" My words were a low grunt as I hovered at the doorway of the master bathroom.

Didn't want to step out. Like maybe if I remained rooted, I could hold onto her forever.

Wrapped in a huge towel, Eden shifted on her bare feet. Water pelted the floor of the massive shower, the air misting with vapor and heat.

That quiet intensity that was this girl banged against the walls and hammered against my heart.

That's what she'd been since the police had arrived on the scene.

Quiet.

Restrained.

Horrified.

Withdrawn.

Girl couldn't even look at me.

Didn't blame her a bit. I'd sucked her into this sordid world. Tainted her with who I was.

Bloodied this girl's pure hands.

"No, I don't think so. Thank you."

My face contorted as my hands fisted in shame. "Don't thank me, Eden."

"Trent—" That gorgeous face pinched in something I didn't recognize.

"I'm going to take a shower downstairs." I cut her off before she said things she likely felt obligated to say.

I knew she'd say I shouldn't feel bad. Claim she would be okay. Tell me not to worry about her when she went back to her safe life where I should have left her in the first place.

Or maybe she'd just give it to me straight. Tell me she was disgusted.

Violated.

Say she finally saw me for the monster that I was.

A savage who'd brought injustice to her door.

It'd only taken about thirty seconds after Cutter had crumbled to the ground for the police and paramedics to show. Apparently, Eden had called 911 as she'd raced to my house.

They'd wrapped her in a blanket and brought her in to sit on the couch while they'd gathered evidence.

While she'd shaken.

Cried silent tears.

Stared out into the space.

While they'd taken Cutter's body away.

He was dead.

No question this time.

We'd also gotten word that all three of Cutter's men had been arrested.

The threat was finally silenced all because I'd drawn this innocent, pure girl into the darkness. Into the corruption and degradation of this life.

Whole time, I'd itched to take that precious frame into my arms and mold her to my shape. Promise her we could fit.

"I'll get rid of these." My throat was thick as I glanced at the pile of bloodied clothes discarded on the floor.

She hugged the towel tighter to that body, still shivering from the shock.

From the strain.

From the thousand questions the investigators had asked, all while telling her she would need to come down to make an official statement tomorrow.

Warily, she nodded. "Okay."

She dropped the towel, peeked back at me once, before she stepped into the spray.

Had to fucking tear myself from the lure of it, this girl my demise, my hands shaking like mad as I gathered up the soiled fabric from the floor and stuffed it into a black garbage bag.

Swore, I could actually hear the shape of her body under the fall of the water. Way it drummed and danced across that lust-inducing flesh.

I backed out, hurried downstairs, and stripped myself down to my underwear, shoving my things into the bag before I tossed it out into the garage.

The garage probably just needed to be burned.

Whole fucking house.

Set to ash.

It wasn't like I could bring my kid back here. To the place where I'd been so close to losing everything.

I moved into the guest bathroom and turned on the showerhead, stepped under the heated spray. Closing my eyes, I tried not to picture her up there washing away the blood that stained her hands. Tried like fuck to just be thankful.

Gage was safe.

My brothers were safe.

Eden was safe.

But at what cost?

Juna.

Poor fucking Juna.

Wasn't sure how I felt the grief of it, but I did. In the end, she'd made the ultimate sacrifice, and right then, I knew Eden was currently upstairs mourning her sister.

My thoughts spiraled to the rest. My mother. Her sweet voice. Nathan. His belief.

Agony clutched all while gratefulness throbbed.

I scrubbed my skin until it was raw and red, then I stepped out, toweled off, and pulled on a fresh pair of jeans and a tee.

My ribs clamped down when I heard the shower turn off overhead.

This ache so great that I wasn't sure how I was going to make it through.

I wandered out into the main room. Not sure what to do. Where to go. Not when I wanted to go to the girl.

The girl who I felt pad up behind me.

Warmth spread like a flashfire.

Wrapping me like an embrace.

Like she could hold me the way I was dying to hold her.

Fuck. The only thing I wanted to do was curl into those arms, wrap her in mine, and never let go.

I could barely keep it together when I shifted a fraction to look at Eden standing on the other side of the island.

Dressed in a floral knee-length dress.

Hair soaked and skin damp and turmoil in those eyes.

Eyes the color of fallen leaves.

So fuckin' beautiful.

Her sweet spirit written on my soul.

"You feel better?" I forced out.

Awesome. Small talk and a fucking foot in my mouth.

Like she was just going to feel better?

Could just wash the day away?

This fuckin' nightmare?

Her throat tremored when she swallowed, the angles of her stunning face twisting in severity. "Trent—"

There she went again.

I turned my back, mumbled, "We should get you home. I need to go grab a few things. Going to stay at Logan's until I find a—"

The book that went whizzing by my head and slammed against the wall cut off my words, and I whirled around to Eden trembling and shaking.

That gorgeous mouth quivered at the edges. "Don't you dare, Trent Lawson."

My brow furrowed in a pained knot. "Eden—"

Energy lashed.

A shockwave.

Thunder.

She lifted that defiant chin.

"Don't you dare turn your back on me. Don't you dare act like this didn't happen to both of us. Don't you dare try to put a wall between us."

Agony clutched me by the throat. "And just what do you want me to do?"

Her head shook in disbelief as she clutched her chest. "Love me."

A tormented scoff ripped up my throat. "Love you? Loving you isn't the fucking problem, Eden."

I was.

Who I was.

Emotion blasted from her body. Scattering. Slamming the walls.

An earthquake.

"Then what's the problem, Trent? Tell me."

Anger ignited.

Old, old anger that I'd held onto my entire fucking life.

I stormed her way.

Greed lit in the air.

Possession.

"I dragged you into my mess. Like I knew I was going to do. Tainted you. Ruined it all."

Her head shook. "The only way you could ruin me is by walking away."

My head angled as I got close to her face.

My senses were pummeled by that sweet, honeyed scent.

It was all mixed with the smell of me—my soap and my body and my hands.

Like there'd be no washing me off her.

My guts clenched, the same as my hands. "You killed a man today."

Tears streamed from her eyes. Tears I knew had been falling straight for the last two days. Wanted to reach out and wipe them away.

Hold her.

Keep her.

Fuck.

I wanted to scream.

"I did, Trent. I did. And it was horrible. Horrible. But I don't regret it."

My face pinched, voice haggard. "That's on me."

Her mouth fell into a grim line. "No. It's on him. He came looking for death, and he found it. He was going to hurt you, and I refused to let that happen. Because that...that is what would destroy me."

Squeezing my eyes shut, I backed away. "Your sister..."

It was a confession. Disgust underscoring the words.

Whimpering, Eden pressed her arms tight over that sweet, sweet heart. "I'll miss her forever."

"On me."

"No, Trent, that was also on her. I know. I know what she did. She betrayed you. Hurt you. Destroyed so much of you. And I might hate her for that, but I love her for everything else. For the days we spent as children laughing. For the glimpses of joy. For her bringing me you and Gage."

Shame sliced right through the center of my being. "You can't honestly say you can look at me and not see your sister."

She sniffled, a heave of air rushing from her lungs. "Do you really want to know what I see when I look at you? You want me to see a monster, Trent. But I don't. The only thing I see is a man who is willing to sacrifice. I see goodness. I see an amazing father. I see a sweet, vicious warrior. Someone who's fought for me. For his son. For his family. And that's what you are to me, Trent. Family. My life."

She heaved a breath, still clutching her chest. "So you really want to know what I see when I look at you? I see the man I want to spend my life with, and that is the truth."

"Eden…"

"I know what you're thinking, Trent. I saw it the second you realized what I'd done. But I was only doing the same thing you've been doing for your entire life. Fighting for the ones I love. And I love you. You told me you love me. That you'll stay with me forever. Tell me you meant it. Tell me I'm a reason worth fighting for."

Chapter Forty-One

Eden

THAT MENACING, INTIMIDATING MAN PANTED IN FRONT of me.

A wicked temptation.

A beautiful wish.

Hungry eyes and trembling hands.

This gorgeous being. If only he could see what I saw.

"Eden." He rumbled the grunt.

"I love you, Trent. With all of me. With everything. You are my light. The fire that burns inside me."

His darkly beautiful brow curled.

I took a step his direction. I swore, I felt the Earth tremble beneath my feet. "There is nothing that could stand in the way of that. As long as you don't allow it to. I see your demons, Trent. I've felt them, and I've fought them. And I'll do it forever as long as you do it for me. You just have to make the choice to love me. Choose me, Trent. Because you and your son? You've become *my* reason."

Energy lashed.

Shockwaves of intensity.

Strikes of need.

But there was also something else in his expression.

Surrender.

Like maybe he finally understood.

"Kitten." A big palm cupped my face, and he exhaled. Heated and hard. "Tell me you mean it. Tell me you want this. Tell me I'm not dreaming. Tell me you're mine."

My hand covered his.

A quiver of chaos.

A perfect disorder.

My tongue darted out to wet my lips. "I think I've been yours since the first time I walked through Absolution's doors."

A lure and a trap.

The way I didn't belong but there'd been nowhere to run.

Sooty eyes flashed, and we began to sway. "It's not even a choice, Kitten. You stole my heart with a glance."

"And you owned me with the first whisper of your fingers."

His nose brushed against mine. "I want to be right."

"You're everything."

He exhaled. "You and me?"

"Forever," I answered.

His mouth captured mine.

It wasn't sweet.

It was rough.

Hard and raw.

Darkly beautiful like the man.

I felt it like a landslide.

He hiked me up, pressed me to the wall. By the chin, he forced me to look at him as his hips pressed against mine.

He gazed down at me like I was the sun. "Little Temptress."

But he was the hope of my eternity. "Sweet Warrior."

Because that's what he'd been all along. From day one.

He groaned as he ripped at the collar of my dress and exposed my breast. A moan clawed up from my spirit as he palmed it, as he devoured my neck, the man leaving a trail of sizzling kisses from my jaw down to my nipple.

He sucked and licked and whipped me into a bundle of white-hot nerves.

Desperate hands and a tangle of souls.

Greed and possession.

He tore free my underwear while I yanked at his fly.

Desperate.

"I need you…I need this," I confessed.

"Never thought I'd get this again." His was a lament. "Fuck, Eden, love you."

"Forever."

He stumbled with me in his arms, turning me until we were falling onto the couch.

Emotion swept.

Overwhelming.

Consuming.

All the pieces shifting to right, where they'd been meant to be all along.

This man had brought me back from the dead. Stoked to life a heart that had never truly beat. Now every beat would beat for him.

I fumbled to shove his jeans down his hips while he shoved up my skirt.

He thrust into me. So big and so incredibly deep.

The air raked from my lungs and a grunt tumbled from his mouth.

I struggled to adjust to the perfect feel of him while he frantically wrapped me in his arms.

"Gonna be right," he whispered, brushing back the wet hair matted to my face.

"You already are," I whispered back.

This beautiful, terrifying man.

The one I gave my heart.

My body.

My belief.

Because loving someone was worth the risk.

We didn't know our days and we couldn't control our histories.

But we had here. We had now. And every one of those minutes would belong to Trent Lawson and his son.

~·~

"Thank you." Massive arms squeezed me tight.

A crush of affection and gratitude crested from the burly, brute of a man as Jud hugged me against his giant frame.

His words came as a low, tight murmur at my ear. "Thank you for fightin' for him. For Gage. For saving him. Fuck…for saving all of us, really. You crazy, brave girl." The last was a tease. An admonition.

I'd gotten lectured for about an hour straight by Logan and Jud not to ever do something so reckless again. I told them I prayed we'd never be back in that position.

But the truth was, I didn't regret it. Would do it all over again. A hundred times over.

I squeezed him back just as fiercely as he hugged me. "We fight for the ones we love."

His nod was slow. "And you see him for who he really is."

I tightened my hold.

A promise.

I did.

I saw Trent for who he was, and I'd love him through it all, no matter what it meant.

Jud peeled himself back then strode over to where Trent waited by the door. The fortress of a man overcome. It was clear he was dealing with his own demons right then.

Jud squeezed Trent's shoulder.

Trent gave him a tight dip of his chin.

The two were immersed in a silent conversation. Silent understanding.

Like in the connection, every atrocity they witnessed, every fear they'd shared, every hope that had been shattered, passed between them.

Now Trent and I shared in some of that, too.

The trauma.

The tragedy.

A crater in the middle where the ones we loved would echo their presence forever.

My gaze met the ferocity of Trent's from across the space.

But I believed we had the ability to rise above it.

The suffering and the regrets. The questions and what-ifs.

Gage came bounding down Logan's stairs, that huge backpack bouncing all over his shoulders.

So sweet he nearly dropped me to my knees. "Miss Murphy, Miss Murphy. I'm all ready to go. I got all my things and my colors and I made you something super extra special while I was waiting on you guys forever. Sheesh. Dontcha know you shouldn't work so much?"

My heart lifted.

Expanded and danced.

I took him by the hand. "I'm sorry we took so long, but we're here now."

And we weren't going anywhere.

"Okay, good because you know we've gotta have all the special times because we love each other so much to the highest mountain and you gotta make time for the ones you love."

He gave one of those resolute nods.

Cheeks dimpling.

So sincere.

My smile was soft and slow as the fingers on my free hand fluttered through the strands of gold that framed his precious face.

This child—he had my life.

"You ready?" Trent asked.

"I am." It came on a whisper. A promise.

Yes. I was ready. Ready to move on.

To live.

To love.

To hope.

To believe.

It was time Trent got all of those, too, and I couldn't wait to share it with him.

I hugged Logan who stepped back and watched us with one of his cocky, playful smirks, though there was no hiding the affection that flooded out as he glanced at his brother then back at me. "Make sure he gets some."

Gage started jumping at my side. "What's he gonna get? Ice cream? Please, please, please say it's ice cream!"

Redness flushed.

"F-off dude." Trent widened his eyes at his brother.

Logan cracked up. "You know you love me."

Trent looked between his brothers. "Couldn't do this life without you."

Love pressed and rippled. Pushed against the walls.

Ricocheted and amplified.

So much of it, it made it hard to breathe.

For a moment, the three of them just stood silent, like they were giving themselves a moment to finally put their pasts in the past.

Realizing they had a future. That they no longer had to watch their backs or live in fear.

That owl bobbed on Trent's throat when he swallowed hard, then he shifted a fraction and took my hand.

Inviting me into it.

Then he reached over and took Gage's.

Joy bounded.

We all clamored out to my rental and climbed in.

We totally got ice cream. The three of us sat together in a little parlor while Gage rambled away.

Hope surrounded us.

Wrapped us in warmth.

Yes, there was sadness, too. A bone deep kind that would probably never heal. A piece in the shape of my sister carved in the middle of me.

Aaron.

My own mother.

Trent threaded his fingers in mine, glancing my way with understanding.

"Together," he whispered.

I gripped his hand tight. "Together."

Then all the somberness fled and he shot me one of those wicked smiles. The playful kind. The kind that would do me in.

He dabbed my nose with his ice cream cone.

"Ah, Kitten, you've got a little something right here." He teased it on a low voice before he leaned in and licked it off.

My mouth dropped open in surprise.

He laughed, this rumbly sound that vibrated all the way to my thighs.

I pushed him against the shoulder. "You jerk."

"What?" He was all feigned innocence.

Gage howled like it was the funniest thing his dad had ever done. "My turn!"

He climbed over the table and did the same to his dad. All except for the licking part. "Dad, you got something right here!"

Laughter filled our table.

Our hearts.

The room.

The softest smile played at my mouth as I gazed over at Trent. "You're a terrible influence."

It was so low I almost mouthed it, and then Trent was pressing that delicious mouth to my ear. "I'll show you terrible influence."

Butterflies scattered and danced.

Anticipation.

Yearning.

Intent.

"I can't wait."

We finished our ice cream and then drove back to my house, the trees shifting in the deepening night, the stars twinkling to life.

Trent grabbed their bags, and I unlocked the door, and we piled inside.

We planned to stay here temporarily.

Or maybe forever.

Because these walls no longer felt like loneliness.

They no longer echoed with the vacancy.

And I prayed, here in this little place, we'd find peace.

Gage went racing for *his room*, and I helped him put away his things and get ready for bed.

I knelt beside that bed, my heart pressing full against my ribs as I read him a story.

As the dreams I'd once had bloomed.

Blossomed in the most beautiful way.

He grinned that dimpled grin, kissed my nose before he reached out and touched the bracelet on my wrist. "I love you to the highest mountain in the world, Miss Murphy."

"And I love you all the way back."

Trent tucked him in, kissed his temple, and tickled him a little before he moved away and flicked off the light.

Then he took my hand, led me to my room, and over to my bed.

This menacing, intimidating man with the biggest heart.

He laid us down and curled the strength of those arms around me.

I propped myself on my elbow so I could look down at him.

At the fierce lines and unforgettable angles.

This man who'd changed everything.

Tongue darting out to lick across his plush lips, he tucked the lock of hair that fell against my face behind my ear. "Can't believe I'm here with you. After everything. You're amazing, Eden. Hope you know it's grace I see when I look at you."

My chest squeezed.

"I love you...more than you could know."

"If it's a fraction as much as I love you, then it's more than enough." He grinned a soft grin. One that twisted through my insides and sent need drumming in my veins.

"Hmm...good thing I love you to the highest mountain." A smile played around my lips as I let go of the tease.

Affection flooded Trent's face.

Adoration.

"We do this family thing together, yeah?"

I nodded, sucking my bottom lip between my teeth. Warmth flooding fast. "I'll never think of him as anything but my own."

The wings on the owl bobbed and danced as he swallowed deep. "Never could have imagined we'd get a gift like you. Good thing you're stubborn."

I feigned a gasp. "Stubborn? Me?"

"Refusing to leave without an interview. Fierce little kitten."

I let my fingertips play along his jaw. "I'm pretty sure had I left you would have come prowling after me."

"Probably so. Saw you sitting in that booth and knew you were nothing but trouble. Wanted you the second I saw you."

A hand spread across my bottom.

I suppressed a moan and a giggle, whispered, "Is that all you want me for, this body?"

"No, Eden. I want this kind heart and this quick mind. I want this sweet soul and your devoted spirit."

Love rushed.

Ran and overflowed.

The man a dark sea where I'd be glad to drown.

I yelped in surprise when he suddenly flipped me and pinned me to the bed, nothing but a wicked, lustful grin looking down on me.

"Of course, I'll take this tight, little body of yours, too."

"Good thing because it's yours."

His smile softened, and he pressed a tender kiss to my lips, whispered, "Oh, Kitten, we're gonna have so much fun."

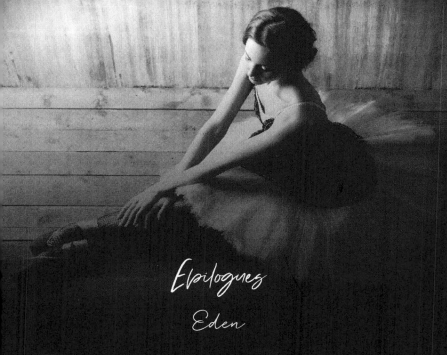

Epilogues

Eden

RAYS OF AFTERNOON LIGHT STREAKED FROM THE SUN-kissed sky, the heavens the bluest blue. It wrapped our mountain town in a warmth that chased away the cool breeze that blew through the towering pines and oaks.

Lifting my face to it, I inhaled and drew the crisp air into my lungs. Appreciating it all.

The love.

The joy.

The hope.

I couldn't believe an entire school year had passed since Gage had sat in the front row at his desk.

The little boy who'd stolen my heart with a glance.

I guessed that was about all it'd taken for his dad to steal mine, too.

The days and months had gone by in a blur that I cherished. So thankful for what we'd been given. For what we'd found.

Even though there'd been so much grief finding our way here.

Most of the money Harmony had taken had been recovered, and the school and my father's home were safe and secure.

There was a huge amount of peace in that, although my daddy was still struggling to find it.

I prayed that one day he would. That he would find his own happiness. A way for his heart to beat again. To spark to life the way mine had.

Squeals of joy rang out, and I returned my attention to the playground where my kindergarten class ran and played on the last day of school.

Gage was out there, playing with the other children, his hands moving almost as wildly as his mouth as he told some animated story.

I tried to hide my grin when Tessa came sauntering my way. She leaned close to my ear and whispered like it was a horrible secret. "Someone looks like she ate too much cake."

I choked out a laugh, though I smirked. "I found I like cake. A lot."

"Hooker."

I smacked at her arm. "Jerk."

"You know you love me. Mad, mad love."

A smile tugged at the corner of my mouth, and I lifted my fingers in a pinch. "Barely."

"That's because some obscenely hot guy came and stole all my BFF time...always baking you cake." She poked out her bottom lip in an exaggerated pout.

"Don't be jealous."

"Um...so jealous. Speaking of..." She angled her head in the direction of the white Porsche Panamera that pulled into the parent pick-up line on the other side of the wrought-iron fence.

Memories swarmed me from the first time it'd pulled into the drive. When I'd wondered if I were seeing things.

Hallucinating.

If it was some kind of cruel, sick joke or if I'd just done something really terrible in another life and it was my punishment.

Little had I known, it was the greatest gift. That in it, I'd find a love that I'd believed impossible.

From where he pulled to a stop at the curb, Trent smirked from behind the windshield. The man looked at me like he wanted to eat me alive.

I gave him a stern look back.

Later.

Only he smirked wider and climbed out of his car. Straightened to his full, menacing height.

What was he doing?

He knew better. He needed to wait in his car. Drive home. Meet me there. Because the man was far too much of a distraction.

But no. He climbed to the curb.

Shivers raced. This disordered, chaotic feeling that something was coming.

Something big and beautiful.

"There he is! There he is! Look it, Miss Murphy!" Gage came barreling over from where he'd been by the slide, arms thrown above his head and hands waving in the air. "Hi, Dad, hi! Over here! Are you ready?"

A frown took to my face. "You have two more minutes, Gage. You need to stay on the playground until it's time to go."

Yeah, it was hard to correct a child when he was that excited, when I knew firsthand how much he loved his dad.

His dad who was going to be in so much trouble later because he kept coming toward the gate.

Ignoring all those signs to wait in the car.

That seething intensity flashed through the air.

It didn't matter how much time passed. It still made my head spin and my knees weak.

Trent Lawson strode toward the gate, all dark swagger.

But those eyes were on me.

Warm and wicked.

Dressed in black jeans and a black v-neck tee and black boots that were unlaced. All that exposed, inked flesh that somehow appeared obscene.

He came all the way up to the gate, and I managed to make the words form on my tongue. "Sir, you need to wait in your car."

Trent smirked. "That so?"

Butterflies scattered when he lifted the latch.

Trent kept coming my way.

My heart hammered and my stomach fisted. It wasn't until then that I realized everyone was gathering around.

The teachers.

The students.

Jud and Logan came out of nowhere.

Leann and Sage.

Milo and Kult, too.

And my daddy. My daddy who looked at me with so much love and affection that my entire being swayed.

Moisture stung my eyes. I blinked furiously, my sight catching on the man who was watching me like he was seeing his joy break at the horizon.

"Trent, what are you doing?" It left me on a plea.

Pure adoration.

That feeling rising.

The air shifting.

This gorgeous, intimidating man smiling with the kind of love that went on for eternity.

Gage giggled and giggled as he took up his father's side.

I choked, and my heart raced at an erratic beat.

"What are you doing?" I whispered again.

Heart flying.

Spirit soaring.

"Eden, Kitten, look at me."

My eyes traced every inch.

Took in the beauty.

The chaos.

My perfection.

He lifted his arms in a show of surrender. Nothing to hide. "Never thought in all my days that I'd be standing in front of a woman like you. A woman who is a treasure. So kind strangers can't help but smile when she walks into a room, so gorgeous she still nearly drops me to my knees every time I see her. A woman who steals every single one of my breaths. The woman who stole my heart."

Energy crashed. A shockwave of it. So intense it was me who'd lost air.

Tears blurred my eyes as he continued, "I'm in love with you, Eden. Gone for you. When I first met you, I thought fighting it would be the right thing to do. But I don't want to fight it. Not ever again. And even if I did, I'm pretty sure I'd still end up standing right here in front of you."

Love struck with each emphatic word.

"Trent." I whispered his name.

He dropped to a knee and pulled out a ring. "So, I was hoping that maybe you'd put me out of my misery and marry me. Say you'll be mine forever because that's how long I'll be loving you."

Gage dropped to a knee, too, dug into his little pocket, and pulled out another blue string.

This one was tiny with a charm tied in the middle of it.

"And I'm gonna love you for all of forever, too, to the highest mountain, so I was hoping you'd be my mom. Will you, Miss Murphy, will you?"

A sob climbed to my throat.

But in it was no sadness.

No shame.

No question.

My men were each on a knee, so I dropped to both of mine. "Yes, yes, forever, yes."

Trent slid the ring onto my trembling finger, kissed me in a way that probably wasn't prudent for the audience.

But neither of us could mind right then.

It was passion and a promise.

Everything.

Everything.

The tears kept flooding when he pulled back.

"My turn," Gage shouted. He scooted forward and worked the ring made of string onto my index finger. "There you go! It's so the prettiest ring ever. Even prettier than the one my dad got you, right, Mom, right?"

Gage grinned in all that hope, looking up at me for approval.

For commitment.

For everything I'd give him for the rest of my days.

His father grinned at his side.

And I knew I'd never feel greater joy in all my life. And I was going to hold it forever.

Trent

I took Eden's hand in mine and helped her to stand.

People surrounding us cheered and shouted. Rushed in for hugs and congratulations.

Eden hugged them. Cried and laughed.

The sound of it filled me whole, same way as her spirit had done.

I'd never imagined it. Never thought I'd deserve it. But I'd fight for it, for her, for my son, for this family, for the rest of my life.

My purpose was finally clear.

One reason.

I just had finally figured out what that really meant.

I glanced around at the smiling faces of the people who loved us.

My brothers.

Eden's dad who'd become like a father to me.

And for a beat, I lifted my gaze to the endless sky, searching that eternity.

In it, I could almost hear my mother's voice. Singing that song she'd loved so quietly.

I shifted back when I felt the warmest gaze wash over me.

Eden.

Sweet, fucking Eden.

Autumn eyes and the purest soul.

My life.

My hope.

The most beautiful belief.

And I thought maybe...maybe there was forgiveness, after all, for a sinner like me.

the end

Thank you for reading **Give Me a Reason!**
Trent and Eden's story was such a whirlwind to write – I fell so in love with them and sweet Gage, and I hope you loved them every bit as much as I did! If you didn't get enough, head to my website, www.aljacksonauthor.com, for your free bonus scene!

Jud and Logan's stories are coming soon in *Say It's Forever* and *Never Look Back*.

Looking for more swoony words to hold you over until then?
I recommend hopping over to read my Bad Boys of Sunder, Bleeding Stars! Start with

A Stone in the Sea
https://geni.us/ASITSAmznOP

Or if you love another single-dad romance, I recommend hanging out with my small-town alphas!
Start with *Show Me the Way*
https://geni.us/SMTWAmzn

Text "aljackson" to 33222 to get your LIVE release mobile alert
(US Only)

Join the A.L. Jackson Book Club
(delivered via newsletter!)
https://geni.us/ALJacksonBookClub

About the Author

A.L. Jackson is the *New York Times* & *USA Today* Bestselling author of contemporary romance. She writes emotional, sexy, heart-filled stories about boys who usually like to be a little bit bad.

Her bestselling series include THE REGRET SERIES, CLOSER TO YOU, BLEEDING STARS, FIGHT FOR ME, CONFESSIONS OF THE HEART, and FALLING STARS.

If she's not writing, you can find her hanging out by the pool with her family, sipping cocktails with her friends, or of course with her nose buried in a book.

Be sure not to miss new releases and sales from A.L. Jackson - Sign up to receive her newsletter http://smarturl.it/NewsFromALJackson or text "aljackson" to 33222 to receive short but sweet updates on all the important news.

Connect with A.L. Jackson online:

FB Page https://geni.us/ALJacksonFB
A.L. Jackson Bookclub https://geni.us/ALJacksonBookClub
Angels https://geni.us/AmysAngels
Amazon https://geni.us/ALJacksonAmzn
Book Bub https://geni.us/ALJacksonBookbub

Text "aljackson" to 33222 to receive short but
sweet updates on all the important news.

Made in the USA
Columbia, SC
05 January 2023